A Season to Celebrate

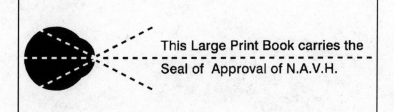

This Large Print Book carries the
Seal of Approval of N.A.V.H.

A SEASON TO CELEBRATE

FERN MICHAELS
KATE PEARCE
DONNA KAUFFMAN
PRISCILLA OLIVERAS

WHEELER PUBLISHING
A part of Gale, a Cengage Company

GALE
A Cengage Company

Farmington Hills, Mich • San Francisco • New York • Waterville, Maine
Meriden, Conn • Mason, Ohio • Chicago

Compilation Copyright © 2018 by Kensington Publishing Corporation.
A Christmas Homecoming © copyright 2018 by Fern Michaels
An Unexpected Gift © copyright 2018 by Kate Pearce
Christmas in Blue Hollow Falls © copyright 2018 by Donna Kauffman
Holiday Home Run © copyright 2018 by Priscilla Oliveras
Fern Michaels is a registered trademark of KAP 5, Inc.
Wheeler Publishing, a part of Gale, a Cengage Company.

LIBRARY OF CONGRESS CIP DATA ON FILE.
CATALOGUING IN PUBLICATION FOR THIS BOOK
IS AVAILABLE FROM THE LIBRARY OF CONGRESS

ISBN-13: 978-1-4328-5529-1 (hardcover)

Published in 2018 by arrangement with Zebra Books, an imprint of Kensington Publishing Corp.

Printed in Mexico
1 2 3 4 5 6 7 22 21 20 19 18

CONTENTS

■ ■ ■ ■

A Christmas
Homecoming

FERN MICHAELS

■ ■ ■ ■

CHAPTER ONE

Kevin Matthews watched from his window seat as the tarmac faded from view. He was finally heading home to Texas after three tours in the military. Home for the holidays. The first time in six years.

At thirty-two, he was going to start his life all over again. Yes, again . . . for the second time. Third if you were counting his birth. He had accumulated a lot of experience in the past several years, and his appreciation and vitality for living had been renewed.

Kevin was twenty-six when he joined the Air Force. A Special Forces group known as Pararescues — "PJs" for short. His proficiency at skydiving and scuba, hobbies from his high school days, had made him a much sought after airman. Throw in six years as an EMS volunteer, and he was the perfect candidate to join the group. And it was the perfect group for him to join.

He needed a serious change of scenery,

and the French Foreign Legion was no longer an option. Did people really do that years ago? Join the Foreign Legion? He wondered. But being a Texan, it was hard to imagine joining any international organization that wasn't homegrown American, even if Texas would make noise about seceding from the Union every couple of years. He thought the new term "Texit" was hilarious. Nope. He was going to serve his country, the USA, and the PJs' slogan, "Relief from Above," was something he could easily adopt, especially since he was in need of relief as well.

Running his fingers through his full, black, wavy hair — a habit he had had since he was a kid — he hoped he could endure the next ten hours on the plane to Dallas. Sitting in one position for any length of time could get uncomfortable.

He considered asking the fellow in the aisle seat to switch with him, but the guy had his head buried in what looked like an *Avengers* comic book and simply grunted when Kevin approached the row. He didn't even make a move to allow Kevin easy access. When Kevin squeezed past him, the guy gave another annoying grunt. It was obvious he wasn't going to be very cooperative. As Kevin folded his six-foot-two-inch, lean, muscular body into the seat, he resigned himself to discomfort until he absolutely needed to move around.

Two years back, during a precision air-drop exercise, some of the supplies had plunged from the cargo plane too soon, and he had to jump to retrieve them. His chute got caught in a bizarre tangle that sent him spinning perilously to the ground. Fortunately, he was able to come out of free fall and managed to land safely but not well. Two operations later and he had his mobility back, though he still had a slight limp. No, sir. Rigorous activities were no longer an option. If he ever took a bad fall, the titanium that held his femur together would stay intact, but it would also cause the shattering of what remained of his own bone structure. Nope. Horseback riding wasn't on the menu, and neither was skydiving anymore — maybe scuba diving if he ever got back to Lake Travis. Hiking, fishing, and riding a bike would be his limit. He'd have to avoid anything that would threaten his Humpty-Dumpty leg.

He sighed and smiled at the same time. *It was worth it,* he told himself. The faces on the refugees as they clamored for the lifesaving supplies were more than a "thank-you," and the rescues from the earthquake in

Japan that he participated in were experiences he could never have imagined. Knowing he actually made a difference in people's lives — total strangers, in fact — gave him a sense of satisfaction that nothing else on this earth could replicate.

The broken bones eventually healed. But the greatest recovery was his heart. It had been broken — devastated. Now he was whole, with the additional help of some titanium and screws, and an experience that gave new meaning to life and the little things in it.

Yes, he was thankful for it. He was still alive and heading home to his mom's skillet corn bread. During the flight attendant's safety speech, Kevin thought back to the circumstances that had brought him on this journey: the hobbies that would scare the bejesus out of his mother, and the breakup with Melissa. Funny thing about it — he was grateful. Grateful for the breakup, but at the time, he couldn't imagine what his future life would be like.

They had been high-school sweethearts. Getting married, having a family, and — one day — opening a sporting goods shop were the only things he envisioned. Yes, he was going to thank Melissa when he saw her, because running into her was inevitable.

Cedar Park was a small town: the very reason he started his life all over for the second time, counting his birth. Now here he was again, starting fresh. This time, though, he had a much better attitude.

Kevin squirmed in his seat as he imagined what his homecoming would be like. Mom would have the house decorated, as in everything. There was not one tabletop, chair, or dresser that didn't have some kind of Christmas ornament. Even the vanity in the bathroom had elves doling out toilet paper. When he was in his teens, he thought it was totally corny. Almost embarrassing. Now it would be a sight for sore eyes, and he'd be thrilled to assemble the hundreds of pieces that were transformed into a Christmas village, surrounded by the miniature trains that would run around the entire perimeter of the living room. As soon as Mrs. Matthews gave it the seal of approval, Kevin and his dad would start working on the exterior of the house, stringing the thousands of lights collected over the years on every tree, bush, and shrub that had a branch. The giant Santa and his entire entourage would sit proudly on the front lawn. Yes, the Matthews house would rival anyone else's attempt at decorating. "Eat your heart out, Macy's!" would be his dad's battle cry when he flipped the switch. The only other place that presented any challenge was the Cedar Park Christmas Tree Farm, with acres of cedars. Hence the name of the town, Cedar Park. His grandfather had started the farm just under a century ago, and his dad started managing it when Pops retired. As soon as Halloween arrived and the hayrides were over, Mrs. Matthews would be in charge of decorating everything in sight at the tree farm, and everyone would joke about being able to see Cedar Park from the International Space Station.

They had been airborne for over an hour, and Kevin's leg was beginning to stiffen. He softly nudged the guy sleeping next to him. "Excuse me, sir, sorry to disturb you." His Texas drawl let the words drop politely from his mouth.

Suddenly, he got the attention of a very attractive young woman in a blue suit, whose name tag on her navy blue uniform said ALLISON. "Oh, sir. You're with the military, correct? Thank you for your service!" She beamed her very best flight attendant smile.

"My pleasure, ma'am." Kevin was never fully aware of the effect he had on women. He had always been ruggedly handsome, with his deep blue eyes and his tanned skin from the outdoors. But he and Melissa started going steady at fifteen, so the thought of dating other girls had never been on his radar. Then, after enlisting, he had no time for anything resembling a relationship. Once in a while he would have friendly drinks with other military folks, but a love affair was by no means on the table.

He winced slightly as he climbed over his drowsy seat partner. His leg was aching a bit, and he needed to walk the aisle. Noticing his slight limp, and the cramped situation he was in, the flight attendant touched his forearm, and whispered, "Follow me." She guided him into first class, where there was an unoccupied, sumptuous seat. Being aware his flight was gratis due to his military status, he immediately began to protest. "Ma'am, I do very much appreciate the gesture, but I'm fine." The words poured easily from his lips.

"It's the least we can do for our brave soldiers. The seat is empty, and I am sure you have more than earned it." Again, the beaming, gleaming white teeth, as she flirted with him. "Can I get you something to drink? Headphones? A snack?"

"I do appreciate your kindness, but I should be just fine." Kevin was almost embarrassed by her doting.

"Surely, you could use something?" She looked at him with puppy-dog eyes.

"Well, if you insist. I don't suppose you could wrestle up a very cold beer?" Kevin was beginning to fall into his easy Texas style.

"I think I could find something to your liking." Allison stared into his dreamy pools of azure blue and hoped she would be to his liking. She reached into her pocket and pulled out a small plastic bag containing earbuds. "Here. There are a dozen music channels you can listen to, or you can watch one of the in-flight movies."

"Well, thank you very much, ma'am. I sure do appreciate your kindness. And this comfort is heavenly."

Allison headed toward the galley and re-appeared minutes later with an icy cold beer and a platter of sandwiches.

Kevin was by no means a virgin, but he was unaccustomed to this kind of attention — even with his strapping good looks, he was surprisingly shy and unassuming. Notic-ing her name tag, he addressed her by name: "Allison. Thank you for making my journey home enjoyable. A man could get used to this! Don't you go spoiling me, now!"

Thinking she could get used to a few more passengers like Kevin, she lightly touched his arm and lowered her voice. "If you need anything, just ring that bell." She winked and turned her attention to the other passengers, who were noticeably antsy waiting for their unlimited supply of cocktails.

Reminding himself that this was "starting over" number three, perhaps it was time to begin looking at women from a different perspective instead of as heartbreakers. Even though the split with Melissa gave him the second start-over of his life, his subconscious continued to protect him from any sort of emotional entanglement. Allison's kindness struck a chord. This was the next new beginning, and maybe, just maybe, there was someone out there for him. Someone. Obviously, not Allison. She was, after all, the first pretty woman he had encountered in a while, but he wasn't going all gaga. No, she was there to remind him that there was hope. He laughed, and wryly observed to himself, *Yes, old boy. You got a lot of catching up to do.*

He settled into the lush leather seat, stretched his leg to a comfortable position, inserted the earbuds, and searched for a country music station. Contentment was beginning to envelop him, and he easily let it wrap him in its arms.

His long-overdue nap was interrupted by the flight attendant's announcement: "Ladies and gentlemen, we are beginning our final approach into Dallas/Fort Worth International Airport. Please turn off all electronic devices, make sure your seat back is in an upright position and your seat belt is securely fastened. We should be on the ground shortly."

This had been the longest part of his journey home. Almost ten hours. He had made his way to London via Germany, and before that from Istanbul. Four flights in almost twenty-four hours. It would be good to be on terra firma again. And this time in his home state.

As the plane touched down, the captain's voice came over the intercom. "Ladies and gentlemen, welcome to Dallas, Texas — the United States of America." The cabin burst with applause as the captain continued: "And we would personally like to thank our military personnel for their service."

Kevin was surprised at his own reaction of getting a little teary eyed. It had been a long journey — emotionally and geographically. He could barely keep himself from salivating, just thinking about his mom's home cooking. When he had written to his family informing them he would be coming home, not just for the holidays, but for good, he jokingly said, "No parades, please."

Once the FASTEN SEAT BELT sign dimmed, he walked back to his original seat to fetch his duffel. His drowsy seatmate had commandeered both seats and was sloppily draped across the armrest, still snoring, and drooling on his Avengers T-shirt, which was about three sizes too small.

Now Kevin was grateful to Allison for two things: reminding him there was an entire gender with which he could become re-acquainted and for saving him from having some strange dude inadvertently snuggle with him.

As he stepped off the Jetway, he headed toward the baggage claim area, where his father had said he would meet him. Looking for the carousel that would be hurling his duffel bag, he heard shouts and cheers: "Kevin Matthews, you are great! Welcome home to the Lone Star State! Kevin Matthews, you are great! Welcome home to the Lone Star State!" There must have been over twenty people surrounding his mom and dad, both of whom were sporting handkerchiefs soaking up the tears of joy and relief. He hurried toward his mom, picked her up, and in good old-fashioned

Texas style, gave her a spin that almost knocked his father over!

His mother clung to him as if she would never let go, until his dad had to pry her off so he could give his son the bear hug he had been longing for.

As Kevin steadied himself, he noticed the banner with his name on it, KEVIN MATTHEWS, OUR HERO. He was trying hard not to be overwhelmed by this welcome, but the accolades mixed with holiday decorations were almost too much. He recalled his training, gained his composure, stood erect, smiled, and waved to the onlookers.

"Holy smoke! What a homecoming! Wow! I'm . . . I'm . . . blown away. Okay, maybe not the best choice of words." Shrieks of laughter came from the bunch. "Who knew I was this popular!"

When he was able to focus beyond his tear-filled eyes, he recognized friends of his parents and folks from the church. "Okay, Dad. Mom. Now that you have thoroughly humiliated me, can we please get home to some of that corn bread I've been dreaming about? Let me grab my bag, and let's get outta here!"

"Sure, son! The car is just outside. They let me leave it there because I told them I was picking up my son who had just served six years in the military." Kevin's dad beamed with pride as they exited the airport. A security guard standing next to the vehicle saluted, and remarked: "Thank you for your service." Kevin saluted back and wiped away the tears he had been trying to quell. Yes, this was a new, new beginning and his heart filled with joy and hope.

They piled into the car and jumped on the interstate, I-35, for the three-hour ride home. Kevin could have flown from Dallas to Austin, but his parents insisted on picking him up, and another plane ride would have been more than Kevin could tolerate. Even though it was a haul to Cedar Park, they could stop along the way and grab a bite to eat, stretch their legs, and catch up. "How did everyone else get here, Dad?"

"Well, it just so happened that there is a Christmas festival in Dallas tonight, and the pastor offered to bring people on the church bus."

"Remind me to put some extra coins in the basket next time I'm there." Kevin was still reeling from the welcome home he had just received.

"Coins? Maybe a few greenbacks would do! And by the way, speaking of green, we need to get the trees over to the church pronto. We're almost a week late."

"Home five minutes, and you're already putting me to work?" Kevin teased, but in reality he was thrilled to be working among the cedar trees again. Dust had become the only thing he had inhaled for a long time. The fresh green scent of the trees would be heavenly.

"How's that leg of yours? Will you be all right to cut, wrap, and carry the trees to people's cars?" Kevin's mom said with concern.

"I couldn't be better. Just a little stiff, but otherwise, I'm good to go!"

"Well, you better not be going anywhere anytime soon. The last time you were thinking about reevaluating your life, you ended up in the Air Force!"

"I learned a lot, Mom. A lot about discipline, a lot about loyalty, and a lot about family.

"When you're as far away from home as I was, and for as long as I was, the people you share life-and-death experiences with become part of a family. And it helped me appreciate my own family. Before I left, I was just going through the motions, living from one day to the next, not fully realizing what I had and what I could do with my life. Now I understand how important it is to be grounded. Be a part of something.

The loyalty. The love. The unwavering attention you give to each other. Everyone needs to learn to love just a little more and learn to accept it."

"Oh, Kevin, you sound so grown-up! And philosophical!" His mother began tearing up again.

"Okay. Let's focus on the tasks at hand," his father calmly interrupted. "We have a lot of holiday cheer to spread. So Mr. Philosophical, I hope you're up to it! We're going to have to get up very early tomorrow to bring the trees to the church before Sunday school starts. Otherwise, there will be too many people around for us to get anything done."

"Roger that!" Kevin replied with an enthusiastic laugh. "How much longer before I can sink my teeth into some home cooking?"

"I'm driving as fast as I can. I may have been able to talk my way into a parking spot, but not sure if I'd be able to talk my way out of a speeding ticket!" his dad said, peering into the rearview mirror.

Kevin mentally shifted gears, which he soon realized was something that would continue to happen for quite some time, something he was going to have to get used to. He had to remember where he was, not where he had been. He was back home now. He could relax. He might not have changed the world, but he could say that he had tried. And in the case of many of those he had helped rescue, he had succeeded.

Once they were out of the airport traffic confusion and on the highway, Mrs. Matthews leaned over and pulled something out of a tote bag. A plastic container. Turning around, she handed it to Kevin. "Is this what you're hankering for?"

Opening the Tupperware tub, he was surprised to see that the corn bread was still warm, and the savory smell was divine. And that was the moment Kevin fully realized that he really was home again.

CHAPTER TWO

Thirty-year-old Kate Stafford, recently divorced, and her five-year-old daughter Emma were finally moving into their own little cottage in a small town outside Austin. Kate had secured a job at the Cedar Park Medical Center, which was about twenty minutes from their new home — something Kate could afford on her salary and the modest child support she received. She and Roger Martin had dated for several years and gotten married right after Kate finished her internship at Baylor. Much to Roger's chagrin, she kept her maiden name since all of her education records were under Stafford. She had thought it was sweet that he had a little bit of the old-fashioned stuff in him and wanted her to be Mrs. Kate Martin. It had never occurred to her that he was competitive. But occasionally a little bit of a chauvinistic streak would emerge. She was too busy with her studies and adored

Roger, so even the thought of it would not have occurred to her. Sometimes a hint of jealousy would surface, especially when Kate would attract the attention of other men. Not only was she bright, but she was stunning, with her shoulder-length, rich chestnut hair and green eyes. Kate would explain about the transference syndrome — in which patients thought they were falling in love with their doctors — to quell Roger's annoyance. But much to her dismay, rather than allaying his jealousy, it often would fuel the argument. She didn't get it. At least not at first. But after several years, the resentment was becoming obvious. She was coming into her own, and Roger didn't like it.

Shortly after they were married, her pregnancy came as a big surprise. They had been extra careful, knowing it would be several years before Kate would be eligible for a full-time job, but she was among the two percent for whom birth control didn't work. Even though she was pro-choice, abortion was out of the question. She was going to keep the baby. She still had four years of residency to complete at Joseph Barnhart, and there would be a lot of juggling involved, but Kate was bright and determined to make all of it work: her marriage, her career, and her baby. She was adamant. She would be wife, mother, and doctor. After all, weren't women encouraged to "do it all"?

Things really started to go downhill when an argument arose about Emma's last name. Kate suggested hyphenating to Stafford-Martin, but Roger was vehemently opposed to any name but Martin. "My kid is going to have *my* name!"

That was the first time Kate really put some thought into what her husband's view of marriage was. The looming economic burdens and her husband's on-again, off-again employment began to take its toll, both financially and emotionally. Roger couldn't find enough work in Houston — at least that was his excuse — and being a stay-at-home dad wasn't going to cut it financially. When Kate would make suggestions about different employment opportunities, he would respond with bitter remarks. Could he be talking his way out of a job rather than into one?

It was becoming obvious that his ego was being bruised by his wife's success. There had been other early warning signs that she and Roger weren't compatible, but they were eighteen when they had met, and who knew anything about love and relationships? Didn't all teenagers think they knew everything, especially when it came to matters of the heart?

As the months dragged on, Roger's opportunities for obtaining and keeping a steady job seemed to dwindle. Then one day he announced that he had heard there were a lot of opportunities in Vancouver, British Columbia, for people in Roger's line of work. That would have definitely created a problem with Kate's progress toward a career in medicine. Not all of her credits and time spent would count, and she would lose an entire year repeating some of her residency. Furthermore, Canada wasn't eager to employ people from other countries, even if that other country was just across the border.

At that point, Kate had the horrible thought that maybe keeping her from a successful career in medicine was Roger's plan. If they moved to Canada and he got a good job, then Kate might have to give up her aspirations and let him wear the pants in the family. No. That was not the answer. She had put too much into her studies and her career. She couldn't remember a time when she didn't want to become a doctor. A pediatric orthopedist. Helping kids get their limbs working again. It was time she faced the ugly truth. The marriage was over.

Kate was thinking back to when she first told her mother the news of the divorce. "Teenage love is so naive. Why don't kids listen to their parents?" Kate smiled a wry grin.

"But Roger is a good egg, and he deserves to be happy. At least we're grown up enough to realize we're young enough to have a chance at happiness — even if it isn't with each other!"

"You both deserve to be happy, sweetie. I'm glad you didn't take the other road and walk away from your career. You put so much time into your education, and you still have a bit left on your student loans!" Kate's mom was very proud of her daughter's drive and success and bragged incessantly about her "daughter the doctor."

Fortunately, the divorce was amicable. Roger almost seemed relieved. As they parted ways, Roger agreed to send her two hundred dollars a month in child support. Not a lot to go on, but it was better than nothing. He promised to send more when things got better, but four years later, it looked as if things were never going to get better for Roger.

The year that followed the divorce, Kate had Emma's last name changed to Stafford. It was hard enough being a kid with only one parent; at the very least they should have the same name. Roger raised a bit of a fuss but backed down after the second argument over the phone. "I don't want Emma, or anyone else for that matter, to be confused as to who her mother is, particularly with an absent father. End of story — unless you want to pay a lawyer to try to stop me." He acquiesced, and Kate sent him the paperwork — with a prepaid return FedEx envelope.

Four years had passed since she had broken the news of the divorce, and the latest change — the big move to Cedar Park — was not about to sit well with her mother. When she met with her mother to break the news, her mom was very excited about the upcoming holidays. "Santa will be coming in a few weeks, and this year Emma should really get a kick out of it. She is such a joy."

Kate became quiet as she began to find the words to explain to her mother that she and Emma were moving to Cedar Park. Not too far, but not last-minute babysitting or dinner several times a week proximity. It would be at least a two-and-a-half-hour drive.

"Mom. I've been looking into permanent positions at hospitals that have orthopedic specialty clinics."

"Of course, dear. That's something you've always wanted."

"Well, there is a wonderful opportunity for me at Cedar Park, and —"

"Cedar Park? Near Austin?" Kate's mother sounded horrified. "You'll be so far away! And what about our Emma? We won't be able to watch her grow up!" She began to cry.

"Oh, Mom. Don't cry. It's only about two hours away. We'll visit on weekends. You can visit us. We'll spend all the holidays together. I promise! It won't be all that bad!"

"Kate, honey, your daddy and I live for the two of you. I don't know what we're going to do if you leave!" Mrs. Stafford was beside herself.

"Mom, it's not 'if,' it's 'when.' " Kate was determined. "It's a wonderful opportunity for me. They have day care, and after Emma starts school, they will work around my schedule. Besides, Houston is getting so expensive. My other option was Boston, and I'm sure you would agree that was totally out of the question."

"You're damn right!" Mrs. Stafford was regaining her self-control. "I don't know how I'm going to explain this to your father. He wasn't thrilled about the divorce, but losing you and Emma might be just too much for him."

It wasn't a pleasant exchange. Mrs. Stafford had always been easygoing, but this time she "showed her teeth," an expression Kate picked up from her internship when the chief of staff would be having a bad day. A few weeks later, her mom begrudgingly threw her a good-bye party, helped Kate and Emma pack, and sobbed as they pulled out of the driveway.

As Kate checked out her new surroundings, she thought her mom would approve — if she could only get her to drive the 160 or so miles to visit. Kate settled into the big wicker chair on the front porch of her new home, convinced this was the right choice for her and for Emma. It had to be. She would make plans for the holidays with her folks as soon as she knew what days she would be working at the Cedar Park Medical Center Department of Orthopedics.

Kate had graduated near the top of her class at the Baylor College of Medicine, had stellar reviews during her internship, and was very much sought after once she completed her residency at the Joseph Barnhart Department of Orthopedic Surgery, so negotiating a reasonable schedule was rather easy.

Yep. She was finally free and ready for a

new start. Making new friends might be a little challenging, but she had heard good things about the area, which was one reason why she had chosen it. She and Emma were on a new adventure, and Kate was pleased that Emma felt the same way about the move.

Emma rarely asked about her daddy. He had left when she was just over a year old. Occasionally, she would ask if she would ever have one, like everybody else. Kate was always patient and optimistic: "Yes, someday you will have a daddy. We just need to shop for one!" Emma would giggle at the thought of going to a store and picking out a daddy! But Kate knew that the start of a new job and caring for Emma would be more than she could handle. She didn't have the time or emotional wherewithal to seek out a partner. And you could forget about online dating. That was a fulltime job in itself and seemed to attract a lot of losers. She was resolute, with a tinge of faith. Meeting someone would have to happen on its own.

Kate enrolled Emma in Sunday school classes at the local church. It would give Emma an opportunity to meet kids her age and give Kate a chance to be involved in her new community. Another upside was that there would be plenty of holiday activities that would allow a lot of social interaction. Yes, they were excited. The coming weekend would be their coming-out party, so to speak.

When Sunday arrived they headed toward the church. "Mommy, I have googly-bumps!" Emma whispered.

"And I have goose bumps!" Kate tried to subtly correct her daughter.

As they approached the side door for the Sunday school class, Kate noticed a banner inside the hallway: KEVIN MATTHEWS, OUR HERO!

I wonder who Kevin Matthews is, she thought to herself. Must be a local big shot to have a banner in the hallway among what appeared to be a tsunami of decorating happening. There were people scattered about hanging stars and ornaments and stringing garland.

"Make way for the trees!" an older gentleman shouted. "Sorry we're late. C'mon, folks . . . scoot!"

It was a mild form of chaos, but Emma and Kate could feel it was a good kind of commotion.

"My son had a bit of a struggle getting used to the time change and the jet lag," the gentleman apologized breathlessly.

Kate and Emma moved to one side of the

hall trying to decide if they should stop and ask where they should go or wait until the tree hubbub was settled. Behind the older gentleman was a younger man — about Kate's age — also carrying a tree. They opted for staying put for the moment and being spectators in this parade of Christmas trees, as another young man dragged the third into the hallway.

"Kevin, get the big one and bring it into the chapel. Get your cousin Jake to give you a hand." The older man barked orders.

"Yes, sir!" was the response. "As soon as I get this one in place."

Suddenly, people started clamoring, "Yo, Kevin! Welcome home!" "You're back!" "You made it!" "How does it feel to be home?"

"Thanks!" was his humble response. "Glad to be home!" Once again, Kevin was feeling overwhelmed and a little embarrassed by the attention he was getting.

"That must be the Kevin Matthews on the banner," Kate whispered to Emma, as she pointed to the letters on the sign, spelling it out for her: K-E-V-I-N.

"Kevin!" Emma shouted. "That's *your* name up there?" She thought he might be someone famous, and her excitement was palpable.

Kevin propped the tree against the wall and knelt to address the little girl. "I think it is." He smiled a big, generous grin. "I don't know why everyone is making such a big fuss about me." Looking up at Kate, he gave her a friendly wink, and a shiver of excitement went up her spine. She could have sworn those deep blue pools twinkled. He held on to the tree with one hand and extended the other to Emma: "I am very happy to meet you. Now you know my name, what is yours?" He looked at Kate to assure her he was just being polite and not being a creep.

Emma looked up at her mother as if to ask if it was okay to answer him. Kate extended her hand instead. "Hi. I'm Kate Stafford. This is Emma. Emma, it's okay. He's the famous Kevin Matthews." Kate leaned closer to Kevin. "You *are* famous, right?"

Kevin laughed out loud. "No. Not really. Just got back from a tour of duty, and the town thinks it's cause for celebration."

"Well, if you served in the military, it *is* cause for celebration. Thank you for your service." Kate was beginning to blush.

"My pleasure to serve. And a pleasure to meet you both. Have you been members of the church for long? I've been away for six

36

years, so I'm a little out of the loop."

"Actually, we just moved here. This is Emma's first day of Sunday school."

"Well, welcome to Cedar Park. If you and your husband are in the market for a Christmas tree, stop by our farm. We still have lots of them!" Kevin was showing his big, warm smile.

"Oh, no! I mean, no husband, but yes, to the tree." Kate thought she sounded like an idiot and started to grow anxious.

"That's fine. I mean, not the no-husband part, but the tree part." Kevin also thought he was being too forward. "Sorry. That's not what I meant."

"That's okay. I mean . . . I will definitely stop by to get a tree. Where are you located?"

Her embarrassment was starting to unnerve her.

"Just a couple miles down the road. I guess everything in Texas is just a couple miles down the road, but we really are only a couple miles." He smiled that big grin again. "Let me unload these trees, and I'll write it down for you. That is, if you have the time."

"Yes. That's fine. I have to get Emma to her Sunday school class — if I can find it."

"This should take about ten more minutes. Meet you back here?"

"Shhh . . . sure." Kate wanted to disappear into the woodwork. Feeling like a fool, she hadn't been this excited around a man in a very long time, and she certainly didn't know his situation. *I guess I'll find out, though,* she thought to herself.

Kate and Emma finally found their way to the Sunday school class, and Kate was very happy to see a dozen children Emma's age. The teacher welcomed them warmly and introduced everyone to Emma. "Kids, this is Emma Stafford. She and her mom, Mrs. Stafford, just moved into town. Can we all say, 'Welcome, Emma'?" A wave of enthusiasm filled the room, and Kate knew that she had made the right decision — to move to Cedar Park. And thinking she was on a roll, she decided to go buy that Christmas tree.

Glancing at her watch, Kate realized it had been almost a half hour since her encounter with the "famous" Kevin Matthews and started to panic. She gave Emma a big hug, and said, "Mommy will be back in a little while. You have yourself some fun, okay?"

"Yes, Mommy!" Emma was very excited at the attention she was getting and the newness of everything. "You gonna meet 'the famous tree man'? K-E-V-I-N?" Emma

38

proudly spelled out his name. Kate was mortified. How on earth did her little girl remember that? "I am going to speak to him about shopping for a Christmas tree!" Kate recovered, kissed Emma on the cheek, and hurried back to the area where she had first met "the famous tree man."

The bustle had subsided, and "the famous tree man" was nowhere in sight. Heaving a big sigh of disappointment, she turned to see the pastor's wife standing nearby. "Oh, hello dear. You must be Kate Stafford. I'm Betty Palmer, Pastor Palmer's wife. But everyone calls him Pastor Teddy."

Kate regained her composure and extended her hand. "It's so nice to meet you. I just dropped Emma at Sunday school. Lots going on here today!"

"Oh, yes! We are so excited to be getting into the Christmas swing of things. It does get a little busy." Betty Palmer shook Kate's hand, and continued, "We have a lot of activities for the children and the parents. After all, Christmas is for everyone!"

"I'm looking forward to this holiday season. It's difficult when you don't have family locally, but everyone I've met so far has been lovely."

"Well, we're going to have our tree-lighting ceremony this Friday night if those boys ever finish bringing them in. Speaking of trees, Kevin Matthews asked me to give this to you. He said he had to get back to the farm to get another load." Betty handed Kate a piece of paper as Kate tried to keep her hand from trembling.

"Oh. Thank you. Yes, he said he would give me the address." Kate was both relieved and concerned that her embarrassment was showing again.

"The tree farm is just a couple miles down the road," the women spontaneously said in unison, and began to laugh.

"Seems like everything is!" Kate smiled, thinking about seeing "the famous tree man" again.

Still a little shaken by her encounter with Kevin Matthews and the note he left, Kate went outside to get some air before she had to fetch Emma from her class.

As she was walking around the grounds of the church, she spotted a truck pulling in with the sign CEDAR PARK CHRISTMAS TREE FARM. He was back! Not wanting to seem like she had been waiting for his return, Kate twisted to run back into the church, stumbled, and fell facedown into the dirt! Now she was certain she was making a spectacle of herself. Trying to recover from her clumsiness, she teetered a bit as she brushed the soil off her face, slacks, and gloves. She was adjusting her headband and glasses when she felt a hand at her elbow.

"Ma'am, you're gonna have to get yourself some Texas two-step lessons. That was abominable." She had already recognized the voice of "the famous tree man," who was clearly teasing her.

"Oh, I am such a clumsy thing!" Kate responded in her best damsel-in-distress tone as their eyes met. "Good thing I'm an orthopedic doctor! I may need some of my own medicine!"

"Good thing, indeed. I may be in need of one, too!" Kevin released her arm when he felt she was steady enough to stand. "You all right? I'm also a paramedic, so if you need some first aid . . . I mean, I'm not trained like you are, but in a pinch, I'm your man." Kevin realized he might have just insulted this pretty young woman — a pretty young doctor, no less!

I'm your man, sent a tingle up Kate's spine, followed by her next thought: *Let's not get ahead of ourselves. You need to buy a tree first. Or maybe get to know him. And his situation.*

"Kate? You did say your name was Kate, right?" Kevin looked deeper into her eyes. "Are you sure you're okay?"

"Oh . . . yes. I'm fine. Thank you so much. Talk about a first impression. Dr. Klutz. A fine name for a clumsy orthopedist!" She began to tremble and fidget with her Clark Kent–style glasses.

"Well, okay then, Dr. Klutz. I do hope to see you at the tree farm." Kevin's Lone Star accent had returned full force after only a few days.

Kate thought she would faint. "Yes. Yes, you will. When is a good time?" Darn it! Was she being too forward? It wasn't as if she were going on a date.

As she was starting to feel like she had put both feet in her mouth, Kevin replied, "I'm usually there from ten in the morning until nine at night, with a few breaks for some of my mama's good home cooking. But there's always someone who can help you."

Kate thought, *There is no one I want to help me but you, Mr. Famous Tree Man.* What she said was, "I'll come by after supper one night this week. Emma has to be in bed by seven, so it will probably be around six."

"Tonight? Tomorrow?" Kevin queried, trying not to seem too anxious.

"What works best for you? I mean, I don't want to disrupt your dinner or anything."

"Well, sure. Tomorrow would probably be

better. We'll be in and out of here all day today. Mama usually has dinner on the table around five this time of year since most folks come by in the evening. See you tomorrow then. Gotta get the rest of these trees inside, or Betty will have my hide!"

Kate took a deep breath before she took another step. Falling in front of him was bad enough; she didn't want to reprise her little tumble. Feeling steady, she held her head up high and went back to get Emma.

Chapter Three

Even though he was a little uncomfortable with all the attention his homecoming was generating, Kevin was secretly excited about meeting that new woman in town, Kate. Had it not been for the banner, she might not have spoken to him. And her little girl was a darling, asking if he was famous.

It had been very chaotic at the church, and Kate seemed a little overwhelmed, but Kevin sensed she would do just fine in their little community. She sure was pretty enough — even with those geeky-looking glasses. He laughed when he thought about her little tumble outside in the courtyard. She seemed to have become slightly un-glued, but he was thoroughly amused at her self-deprecating reference to herself as "Dr. Klutz." A doctor. Interesting. An orthopedic one at that. Kevin wondered if he should make his requisite appointment with her, ask her for a date, or do both? Was that allowed? He reeled himself in — he was getting too far ahead of himself. But she did say she wasn't married. That was a plus. Although she didn't say anything about a boyfriend, either. He guessed he would eventually find out what the situation was. He'd do a little of his own intel gathering when she came by for the tree. He'd offer to deliver it. Yes. Good solution.

When Monday evening rolled around, Mrs. Matthews had her well-known chicken potpie cooling on the stove top.

When Kevin opened the front door, he thought he would faint from the sheer pleasure of that welcoming aroma. The savory tang was wafting through the house.

"Is that what I think it is?" Kevin kissed his mom on the cheek. Grabbing a fork, he was about to dig into the pie before it cooled enough to eat.

Mrs. Matthews swatted his hand away. "You go wash up first, then you can eat like a person. At the table. Now shoo . . ."

"But, Mom! It's been years since I had some of that deliciousness! Give a guy a break!" He feigned desperation.

"You stop that now. You may be able to charm some of those girls at church, but you're not going to ruin my beautiful crust!"

Kevin stopped in his tracks. "What girls?"

"Oh, I heard you met the new member of the church yesterday. Kate, is it? Lovely doctor with a little girl?" Mrs. Matthews was fishing.

"Uh, yeah. I met that new woman when we were delivering the trees. So?" Kevin was still feigning indifference.

"And you helped her up after she took a tumble?" More fishing.

"Mother. What on earth? Who have you been talking to? Or are you stalking me?" Kevin was amused but found himself even more curious.

"Betty Palmer said you gave her a note to give to Kate."

"Yes. It was the address to the farm. She needs a tree."

"Huh. Well, of course she needs a tree. But she could have found her way there without a personal invitation, no?" Kevin couldn't tell if his mom was teasing now.

"She's new in town. I was just trying to be friendly and drum up some business." Kevin attempted to be convincing, but his fingers were raking his hair — another sign that he was either thinking or talking his way into or out of something.

"Oh, son. I think it's sweet of you to take an interest in a newcomer. Especially a pretty one. *And* a doctor." Mrs. Matthews wanted her son to feel as if he could discuss anything with her. They had always had a good, open relationship, but as boys became teenagers, then men, they didn't share their feelings very easily. Unless it involved rooting for a sports team, or a heated argument over something trivial, she knew men did not easily express themselves when it came to their feelings. That was a given.

"Yes. I think she said she was an orthopedist. I suppose that could come in handy." Kevin was still trying to maintain a facade of nonchalance.

"Aren't you supposed to make an appointment with an orthopedist to get your leg checked?" Mrs. Matthews was indeed prying while attempting to sound blasé.

"Well, Mother. If she's my doctor, I don't suppose I could ask her out on a date, now, could I?"

"A date?" Mrs. Matthews tried to sound incredulous, but it came off as more of a cheer.

"Yes, Mother, a date. Isn't that what you were getting at with all these questions?" Kevin looked her smack in the face, grinning from ear to ear.

"Kevin Matthews, I do declare you are being a bit direct."

"Yes, ma'am. Di-rect. She seems like a

very nice woman. But I don't know her relationship status, so before you get all 'dating game' on me, let's just take it slow. Is that all right with you, Mama?"

"Of course, dear. I was just making an observation. New, attractive woman comes into town. That's all." She picked up her glass of sweet tea, trying to mask her enthusiasm.

"I guess we'll find out soon enough. She's supposed to come by the farm to pick out a tree. Tomorrow, I think."

"And, of course, you will deliver it to her home?"

"Of course, Mother. You didn't raise no dummy!" Kevin gave her a peck on the cheek and turned to the chicken potpie again. "You don't suppose it's cool enough to eat now? I can't tell you how many times I dreamed of this!" Picking up the fork, he jammed it into the middle of the potpie, pulling out a big hunk of chicken.

"Kevin Matthews! What did I say about eating like a person?"

"But I *am* a person! And this person is hungry!" He got a big serving spoon and took what seemed like half the pie and plopped it into a dish. "Happy now?"

She threw her arms around her son. "I

am so happy. You cannot imagine how much."

CHAPTER FOUR

By the time Monday evening rolled around, Kate wasn't sure if she should take the ride to the Christmas tree farm. Would she seem desperate? *Don't be ridiculous,* she told herself. A Christmas tree farm was an appropriate place to visit this time of year.

She could not wrap her head around her anxiety. She had graduated from medical school, did a year of grueling internship, then four years of residency. She had seen and worked on some of the worst accident victims one could imagine. Why was this so daunting? It was *just* a tree.

But, she had to admit to herself, it was really more than that. For the first time since she had met Roger, she was actually attracted to a man. Why did he have to be so handsome? And charming? Why? Why? Why? Kate was beginning to think she was losing her cool. Maybe it was the move. That was a very big deal. All the hoopla with her mom and dad, begging her to stay until she could find a job in Houston. Stay with them? Uh, no. Kate had a great relationship with her folks, but that was due, in part, to the fact that she didn't live under the same roof. She was able to afford the special housing provided for residents, but now that her residency was over, she needed to find another place to live. Might as well start over somewhere — anywhere. As long as she could provide a good environment for Emma, Kate was up for anything. Luckily, the position opened up at Cedar Park, so she wouldn't be forced to move all the way across the country.

Yes, that was it. She was just anxious over the big move and the new job. Okay, and the new guy. Then it dawned on her that she did not know his situation. Maybe he was married. Engaged. Involved. "Dang. What is wrong with me? It's just a gosh-darn tree." And the new guy. The anxiety of not knowing his situation and her eagerness to find out was making her edgy.

"Mommy? Why are you walking around in a circle?"

Emma broke her mother's restless spell.

"Oh, sweetie. Sorry. I was lost in my thoughts."

"Whaddaya thinking about, Mama?"

Emma looked up at her mother with wide eyes.

"I'm thinking about getting us a Christmas tree, that's what!" Kate leaned over and scooped Emma into her arms.

"But you look worried. Are you worried about 'the famous tree man'? Do you want to see him again?" Emma was certainly more in tune than Kate had imagined.

"He seemed very nice. And we might see him again, but I don't know for sure."

"I liked him, Mommy. He's famous!" Emma wrapped her arms around her mother's neck. "Can we go today? I want to start dec'rating our own tree. The ones at the church are really big, and they only let us put orm-a-ments on the lower branches."

"It's orn-a-ments," Kate corrected her daughter's consonant switching.

"Orn-a-ments," Emma repeated, and continued with "K-E-V-I-N. See, I remembered!"

Kate laughed. "Yes, you did! Let's have a little bite to eat, then we'll take a ride, okay?"

"Yay! We're getting a Christmas tree. . . . We're getting a Christmas tree . . ." Emma repeated to herself with delight.

Kate took a deep breath and released it, hoping she would exhale some of her apprehension. "Grilled cheese?"

Emma squealed. "Yes! Mommy! Yes!"

"Go wash your hands, and I'll whip up a couple of sandwiches, then we're off to the tree farm!" Kate was feeling the beads of sweat form on her forehead. *Get a grip! It's just a dang tree.* Kate thought that if she kept repeating that mantra, she might actually come to believe it.

Kate fumbled around her desk, looking for the sheet of paper with the address. Where could she have put it? What if she couldn't find it? Panic was starting to creep in again.

It's the Cedar Park Tree Farm, you ninny! Lifting the pile of mail that had arrived earlier, she revealed the slightly crumpled piece of paper. With a sigh of relief, she plugged the address into her phone so she could find it via her GPS. When the directions came up, she saw that it was almost eighteen miles away. "Just down the road." Kate laughed to herself.

The two of them piled into their SUV, Kate making sure Emma's car seat was secure.

"What kind of music shall we listen to on the way?"

"Silly, Mommy! Christmas music!" Emma was elated they were going on a new adventure and began to sing along with "Rocking around the Christmas Tree" as Kate pumped up the volume on the radio.

The earlier anxiety had turned to excitement. Kate was thrilled that Emma was in such a good frame of mind. She had been concerned that Emma would be homesick for Grandmama and Pop-Pop, but she was totally occupied by the new surroundings and the kids she had met at Sunday school.

"Mommy. There's a girl at the school who I liked. Her name is Victoria. I think her pop-pop might be the pastor."

"Would you like to invite her to come and decorate our tree?"

"Yes! That would be So! Much! Fun!" Emma clapped her hands to each word.

"I'm going to have to get her phone number from Mrs. Palmer. I'll get in touch with her in the morning, okay?"

"Yes! Fun! Fun! Fun!" Emma was keeping with the beat of the music.

When they finally arrived at the tree farm, Kate wasn't sure where she should go. It was much larger than she had expected. As she pulled into the main entrance, she recognized Jake from the day before.

"Howdy, ma'am! Nice to see you and your little girl! Sorry we almost stampeded you yesterday!" Jake removed his hat and shook the pine needles off.

"Yes, it was a bit hectic! I can't wait to see all of them decorated. Exactly how many did you deliver?"

"Eighteen total!"

"Wow. That's a lot of tinsel!" Kate was surreptitiously looking past Jake to see if she could spot Kevin.

"Is 'Mr. Famous Tree Man' here?" Emma blurted out. "K-E-V-I-N?" she spelled inquisitively.

"No. 'Fraid not. Something came up, and he asked me to hold down the fort for him. What can I help you with?" Jake's disappointing news hit Kate like a brick.

"Oh — Oh . . ." Kate was stammering.

"A Christmas tree, Mommy!" Emma's excitement wasn't diluted by the absence of the tall, handsome, "famous tree man." Her interest was only in a tree at the moment.

"What size ya lookin' for?" It seemed like Jake was having to pry information from Kate.

"Gee. I'm not sure. We don't have a very big house." Kate was trying to mask her disappointment. "What do people normally get?"

"Somethin' a little over six feet. This way you can cut it down a bit if need be. Can't add it on!" Jake was amused at his attempt at humor.

Kate laughed nervously. "Well, I will leave it up to you."

"Come with me, and I'll show you some of my favorites." Jake was being very accommodating, but Kate felt as if the wind had been knocked right out of her. At that point, she was indifferent. *It's just a tree, for heaven's sake,* she reminded herself once again.

In contrast, Emma was giggling and squealing with delight over the magical atmosphere of the tree farm. "Mommy! Look! Angels!" Then a minute later, "Mommy! Look! Reindeer!" She was running among the trees with a freedom Kate had never before witnessed her daughter exhibit.

Kate took in another big inhale and reminded herself, *This is for Emma. You'll get your turn . . . one of these days.*

CHAPTER FIVE

Betty Palmer had been married to Theodore Palmer for thirty-five years. Their work in the church and community made them a very popular couple in Cedar Park. There probably wasn't anyone who didn't know them by name. Pastor Palmer had been the minister in Cedar Park for almost twenty years. Looking in the mirror, Betty thought, *Not bad for pushing sixty!* The big six-0 was looming in the New Year. Yes, her family had had its ups and downs however calm and reverent the townspeople thought their lives were, especially six years ago, when the *you-know-what* had hit the fan.

It had come as a big shock to everyone when their daughter, Melissa, and Kevin Matthews had broken up six years earlier. It was also a huge embarrassment. Having their daughter run off with a musician!

Kevin was well liked, and there was no reason for anyone to believe that he and

Melissa weren't the perfect couple. At first, Betty was excited when Melissa took the job at the bank, but the so-called travel and her emotional distance began to worry Betty. Her little girl had become aloof.

She and Teddy had several nasty disagreements as to who was to blame for Melissa's transgression. "We were too strict! We never let her find her own way!" Betty had thrown that in his face more than once.

"My dear woman. I am the pastor of the church. How would it look if I let my daughter traipse around with some of those girls?"

"Those girls came from fine families. Just because they experimented with a few tattoos and piercings didn't make them the Devil's children!"

Pastor Teddy just grunted. "Well, you saw what happened when Melissa started going to those clubs in Austin. She met up with some gee-tar player and almost ruined her life!"

"Stop exaggerating, Teddy. She was going through a stage — a stage we could have probably avoided if you had just given her a little room to grow." Betty would insist Teddy had been overreacting, but Teddy had his reputation to maintain. "And what about Kevin? He got the worst of it. He didn't hang around more than a couple of weeks before he left town."

Betty was very disappointed about her daughter's behavior and losing Kevin as a son-in-law, but Melissa was, after all, her daughter and she had to stand up for her. Thankfully, it had truly been a stage, and Melissa started dating someone from work a few months later. A clean-cut banking associate named Greg Sullivan. By that time, Kevin Matthews had enlisted in the Air Force and was thousands of miles away. That was enough distance to prevent any interference in Melissa's life.

Almost a year later, Melissa and Greg were married, and the following year they had a child, Victoria. The marriage and the baby helped people to forget the earlier scandal, and the newly married couple fit right in with the community, which helped to quell Betty and Teddy's embarrassment.

This year, with the holidays upon them, and Victoria turning five, it would be a pleasant and joyful season. Victoria would certainly be more engaged in the decorating and cookie baking. She was also more active in Sunday school, and she and the new girl, Emma, seemed to have taken a liking to each other. Most of the other children were a year or two older than Victoria, so

59

having someone her own age was a blessing. Kids could be mean sometimes. *What was that all about?* Betty would wonder. Surely they would learn lessons about being kind. She shrugged and continued powdering her nose, then ran the pink lipstick over her lips. Pulling back her hair in a chignon, she took another look and agreed with herself. "Not too bad."

Just as she was about to grab her coat, the home-office phone rang. "Good morning. This is Betty Palmer. How can I help you?"

"Hello, Mrs. Palmer. This is Kate Stafford. We met the other day when I brought Emma to Sunday school."

"Well, hello, Kate. How can I help you?"

"First, I wanted to say thank you for your warm welcome. Everyone has been so kind in making us feel at home."

"It's always a pleasure to meet new folks. What can I do for you?" Betty urged. She was starting to run late to set up the tables for the bake sale.

"I'm sorry to bother you, but Emma mentioned how much she enjoyed meeting Victoria, and I was wondering if you had her mother's phone number. I'd like to set up a play-date for them."

"I most certainly do have her number. Victoria is my granddaughter!" Betty responded with delight.

Kate laughed slightly, realizing how small the town was. "If you think it would be all right for me to call, or if you wanted to call Victoria's mom first, I would be most appreciative."

"Don't be silly. I am sure Melissa would be happy to have a new friend for Vic. The number is 512-555-1533. That's 512-555-1533. I have to run, but please get in touch if you need anything else. I know the holidays can be very stressful, especially when you're new in town! Hope to see you for the tree lighting. Bye-bye, now." Betty rested the phone back in the cradle and dashed out the door.

CHAPTER SIX

After gorging himself by eating almost the entire chicken potpie — which was supposed to have served all three of them — Kevin flung himself on the sofa and fell into a deep sleep. The jet lag and the excitement had finally caught up with him. He was supposed to go to the tree farm after dinner, but when he didn't spring up after his mom tried to rouse him, she let him sleep.

Suddenly, he jerked up out of his deep sleep. "What time is it? What day is it?" He almost seemed panicked.

"It's Monday evening, around eight o'clock. You okay? You were sound asleep. Obviously, you needed your rest." His mom was working on one of her dozen gingerbread houses.

"Darn! I was supposed to work the farm tonight!"

"It's okay, honey. I called your dad and let him know, and Jake was on hand to help."

Then it dawned on her that the new doctor in town was supposed to stop by to get her tree. "Oh dear. I was so busy with my baking I forgot tonight was *the* night. You know, when Dr. Kate was coming by. I'm so sorry!"

"Mom. It's okay," Kevin consoled his mother. He knew she meant well in everything she did, but the holidays were jampacked with things that needed to be done, and it was easy to get sidetracked. "I'm sure I will run in to her again. I do have to make that appointment!" He thought his reassurance would mask his frustration.

"And I was the one chiding you. I should have remembered!" Mrs. Matthews seemed genuinely distraught.

"It's really okay. I'll probably see her at the tree lighting, or at the very least, at church. Now get back to icing those rooftops! The bake sale is in three days!" Kevin was making light of the oversight and grabbed a paintbrush to give his mom a hand.

"Okay, but we still need to find out her situation." Mrs. Matthews seemed relieved and gave her son a wink.

"Mama, you are just too much sometimes!"

After a few hours of painting the shutters

for the gingerbread houses, Kevin yawned and stretched. "I think I need to get some more serious shut-eye, Mama. Sweet dreams."

"Same to you, son!" she said, as she blew him a kiss.

The next morning the phone rang. It was Betty Palmer on the other line. "Hey, Maggie, it's Betty. Is Kevin available?"

"Good morning! I bet you are just up to your ears with activities! Hang on one second, let me go get him." Maggie Matthews brought the phone into the kitchen and handed it to her son. "It's Betty Palmer," she whispered.

" 'Morning, Betty. What can I do for you? Need more trees?" Kevin was being playful. There wasn't an extra square inch that could accommodate another tree at the church.

"Hey, Kevin. Do you think you could stop by Melissa's today? She needs some help getting her decorations from the attic, and Greg is out of town until Saturday."

Kevin knew he would eventually run into Melissa very soon, but not this soon. He had figured it would most likely be at the tree lighting — not going to her house to help her out.

Hesitating, he responded, "Well. Sure. I

guess. When?"

"Could you stop by this morning? That'll give her a chance to sort everything out before the weekend."

"Yeah. Okay. I'll go over in an hour. What's the address?" Kevin gave his mom a horrified look. Meeting up with Melissa after six years was going to be uncomfortable even though he knew he was over her. Just plain awkward was more like it.

He looked around for a pen and paper and jotted the address down. "Got it. Will do. No. No problem, Betty. See you soon."

He hung up the phone and turned to his mother. "I have to help Melissa with some boxes. I didn't want to say no, but I certainly didn't want to say yes either."

"Well, I suppose it's like pulling off a Band-Aid. The quicker you do it, the less pain you'll feel."

"I know you're right. I just wasn't really prepared for it. Sure, I'd thought about it — our first encounter after six years — but now that it's an hour away, I'm really not sure how I am going to feel. Or what to say, for that matter."

"Start with, 'Hey, Mel. Good to see you. You look well.' Then let her do the talking." Kevin's mom understood how difficult this could be for him. After the breakup, he had

65

left town suddenly and never spoken to Melissa again. Today was going to be challenging, for sure.

"Good idea. You're right. I really don't have to say too much, do I?" Kevin smiled and took in a deep breath. "I guess it's like diving out of a plane. You're pretty sure the chute is going to open, and you hope for the best!"

"You'll be fine, son. Six years is long enough to mend a broken heart, don't you think?"

"Yes, and yes. But as I said, I've had a number of scenarios in my head about this moment." He tossed on his heavy denim shirt, his Air Force insignia baseball cap, and headed toward the door, stopping to give his mom a peck on the cheek. "Let's hope the chute opens!"

CHAPTER SEVEN

"Emma honey! Time to get up! I have a surprise for you!" Kate nuzzled her little girl and pulled the covers off.

"What, Mommy? Santa come already?" Emma rubbed her nose, her pink cheeks glowing with her smile.

"Not yet, sweetie. We still have a couple weeks. Santa has a *lot* of work to do! But guess what? I remember you said you liked that girl Victoria, so I called her mama, and we arranged for the two of you to spend the morning together. Would you like that?"

Emma threw her arms around her mother's neck. "Mommy! Mommy! Oh yay!"

Kate had an orientation meeting at the hospital and thought it would be a good opportunity for the two girls to get to know each other better. It would be less than two hours — what could go wrong? Hopefully, nothing, and they would become tight friends.

"Go brush your teeth and come have breakfast," Kate instructed Emma.

"But, Mommy, I am going to brush after breakfast. Why do I have to do it now?" Emma was being a little whiny.

"Because Mr. Slippery Slime sneaks into your mouth at night, and you have to chase him away so you don't get cavities!"

"But I *am* going to chase him away. Chase him with my pancakes!" Emma tried to negotiate with her mother.

"Very funny, missy, but you know the rules! Now skedaddle. Meet you in the kitchen."

Kate listened for Emma to pull up the step stool so she could reach the sink, followed by the water running, then Emma exaggerating spitting out the toothpaste.

Kate smiled to herself. *She's going to be just fine. We're starting a new life in our new home.* Then she grimaced as she considered her reaction to the famous Christmas tree man. *What was I thinking? Well, Dr. Kate, you will be just fine, too!*

Emma skipped into the kitchen, wearing a very mismatched outfit. "Honey, do you really want to wear those purple flower pants with the orange kitty top?"

Emma looked perplexed. "I like them!"

"Okay. I just thought you might want to

wear one of your new outfits to go visit Victoria."

"But these are my new outfits!" Emma protested, not realizing the top and bottom went with two different items.

"You are correct! But they are a *part* of two different outfits!" Kate was trying to be reassuring and instructive at the same time. "The kitty top goes with the furry striped bottoms, and the . . ."

"Purple pants go with the pink top. I know, Mommy . . . but I like these parts the best!"

Kate worried that the Sullivans would think she was a terrible mother, allowing her daughter to wear mismatched clothes, as if she hadn't been paying attention.

Attempting to bargain with her, Kate suggested Emma pretend she liked all of them so as not to hurt their feelings. Emma was still young enough to buy into the personification of almost anything, so maybe this would do the trick.

"Really, Mommy? Do you think purple pants would be upset if I wear kitty pants?" Now Emma was becoming concerned.

"Oh, I think if you explain to purple pants that furry striped needs to go out and play, and you promise to wear purple pants tomorrow, Mr. Purple Pants would be just fine with that!"

Breathing a sigh of resignation, Emma marched herself into her room and slipped off her purple pants and slipped on her kitty pants.

As she made her way back to the kitchen, Kate reminded her to brush her teeth again.

"Oh, Mommy. Sometimes you are bossy!"

Kate wasn't sure if she should laugh or not. It wasn't something she would have expected to hear from Emma, but she was being exposed to more people and a lot more television. More than Kate liked, but for now it acted as company for her only child.

"Bossy?" Kate teased. "I know you're just teasing me. But you do have to brush your teeth! Now make it quick-a-dee-quick! We have to be at Victoria's in a half hour!"

Emma rushed to scrub her teeth and pulled out a pink sweater from the closet.

Kate cringed but realized that one fashion victory was probably all she would be able to manage for the day.

As Kate was buckling Emma into the car seat, she reminded her, "Jake will be bringing our tree over later today, so we'll need to pick out a good spot for it. Once he sets it up, it's gonna have to stay put."

"Will 'the famous tree man' come, too?"

Kate thought Emma would have forgotten all about him by now and was a little stunned.

"I don't know, honey. But we *will* have a tree by dinner-time, no matter who brings it!"

Kate punched the address of Melissa Sullivan into her GPS and pulled out of the driveway.

As they made their way across town, Emma pointed out all the decorations, as in *all* the decorations. "Look! Mommy! Santa! Look! Mommy! Angels!" It was very similar to her excitement at the tree farm, when Kate remembered her disappointment in the missing "famous tree man."

They turned onto Miller Lane and looked for the numbers on the house. When they were approaching the Sullivan house, Kate noticed a familiar truck in the driveway. She saw the logo for Cedar Park Christmas Tree Farm on the side of the truck, and she thought her heart was going to stop beating.

Tiny beads of sweat began to form on her forehead. Then her palms. She could feel her face turning red.

"Mom! Mommy!" Emma broke Kate's angst for a moment.

"Huh. Yes, sweetie. We're here." Kate was

trying to regroup. It was Kevin Matthews's truck. In Melissa's driveway. At ten o'clock in the morning. She was crestfallen. Obviously, "Mr. Famous Tree Man" had someone in his life. She hesitated, not knowing if she should ring the doorbell. Surely, they were expecting them. And he had no idea Kate had fancied him in any way. Or did he? Kate's mind was racing.

"Mom?" Emma was starting to sound impatient. "Are we getting out of the car?"

"Of course! I was just trying to remember something, that's all. Hang on a sec."

Kate slowly unbuckled her seat belt, hoping for some miracle that would enable her to avoid seeing "the famous Christmas tree man" again. Especially in the company of another woman. Maybe if she waited long enough, he'd get in his truck and drive away.

"Mommy! I want to go see Victoria!"

"Okay. I'm coming." Kate was gulping back this odd emotional struggle.

"Yay!" Emma was finally free of the confinement of her seat. "Hurry, Mommy! Look! It's 'the famous tree man'!" Kate observed Kevin giving the woman at the door a slight hug while Victoria waved from the window.

Kate continued to busy herself with the straps of the seat, trying to avoid any eye contact as she held her breath, praying he wouldn't notice them before he got into his truck.

Slowly, Kate lifted her head and, to her relief, Kevin jumped into the cab and pulled away. She then realized he didn't know what kind of car she drove — hence another reprieve from embarrassment.

Kate grabbed Emma's hand as they crossed the street to Melissa's house, all the while wondering what kind of relationship she had just observed.

Melissa had spotted them walking up the sidewalk and greeted them warmly.

"Hi. You must be Kate and Emma. I'm Melissa. Victoria's mom. We didn't have a chance to meet on Sunday, but I am so glad you reached out." She leaned over to look directly into the little girl's eyes. "Victoria is looking forward to spending time with you, Emma."

"Hi. I'm Emma Stafford. It is nice to meet you." She held out her hand in such grown-up fashion, Kate was almost brought to tears. Or was it the encounter she had just witnessed?

"Well, it's certainly very nice to meet you, too!" Melissa shook Emma's hand, then extended her own to Kate. "You have a very polite daughter. It's refreshing!"

Both mothers burst into laughter. "Isn't that the truth?" Kate thought she might actually like this woman — this woman who was with the man she was so interested in getting to know. Kate wasn't sure if she should be blunt and come right out and ask, but then she thought better of it. What else would a man be doing at a woman's house at this hour of the morning? Although she did recall someone saying that Melissa was married, and her husband was out of town. That horrified Kate even more. The charming Kevin was having an affair with the pastor's daughter? She shook off that thought as best she could.

Melissa turned, and called into the house, "Vic, Emma is here! Come say hello to Mrs. Stafford."

Victoria was a pretty little girl with curly blond hair and a very light complexion. Kate thought she was a little too fair to be Kevin's child when she realized her imagination was running amuck.

"Emma, honey, Mommy has to go to a meeting and will be back around lunchtime. You have some fun with Victoria." Giving Emma a hug, she thanked Melissa and walked back to her car, still rattled from what she had witnessed a few minutes ago.

"Bye, Mommy! See you later, alligator!"

The two little girls scrambled into the house as Melissa waved to Kate.

"I'll be back around noon! Thanks very much!" Kate could barely eke out the words. What was happening? She had become unglued. Again . . . by that man.

Remembering what she had on her agenda, Kate began to pull herself together, started the motor, and drove off. She was still having trouble shaking her anxiety and forgot to program the GPS for the hospital and it took ten minutes for her to discover that she had been driving in a circle.

"Get a grip!" she admonished herself out loud. "What is wrong with you? I mean me? Oh, my goodness. Do I need therapy?" Once again she thought about the big move, the new job, and chalked off her neurotic behavior to all the changes occurring in her life.

Finally, when the hospital was in her sights, she brought her mind around to the tasks at hand. Meet with the new boss. Check out her new office. Meet the staff. Get a feel for the layout. She was beginning to feel more like herself. Dr. Kate Stafford, orthopedist.

She parked her car in a space that said RESERVED FOR DOCTORS. The action helped her to recover from her recent meltdown, reassuring her that she was, in fact, a doctor. Sitting for a moment, taking in the newness of everything, Kate checked her watch and her tote bag to be sure she was prepared for the orientation. The emotional roller-coaster ride was over, and now she was stepping into her world. Filled with a sense of excitement, she checked herself in the mirror — no gunk between the teeth, lipstick on the lips not smudged over, hair in place. She was ready.

She grabbed the handle of the big hospital door, flung it open, and marched in as if she owned the place. Yes, this was the Kate she knew. Not the silly, starstruck teenager she had been experiencing.

As she walked toward the orthopedic clinic, she observed an area that was dedicated to orthopediatrics. That was the area she wanted to pursue. Helping kids get back on their feet — literally. She remembered when she was twelve years old and had fallen from a friend's tree house, broke her arm, collarbone, and a few ribs, forcing her to spend the entire summer in an awkward cast and Ace bandages. It was excruciating, both physically and mentally. She had missed the whole season of playing, swimming, and riding her bike. Her friends would visit occasionally, bringing her teen

76

magazines, but they didn't want to be inside when the sun was shining and they didn't have to be in school. It was a very lonely time for her, and often it seemed like the only person who was paying attention to her was her doctor. He reminded Kate of her grandfather, and was very kind. He didn't speak to her as if she was a mere child of twelve years, but spent time explaining a lot of details, showing her the X-rays, and helping her to understand her injuries and why they would take a while to heal. Being a very bright girl, Kate took an interest in the information and began reading more about bones, cartilage, ligaments, and tendons. Having to spend so much time alone, she asked her mother to check out some books from the library about anatomy — not such an easy task to find material that a child could understand. But Kate dove into the pages and would shock her parents when she would recite some of the passages she had read, especially when she opened up the conversation one evening with "Did you know that some clavicle fractures can heal without surgery?" Kate's parents were impressed and surprised.

Kate had never shown interest in any of the sciences before. She was strictly an arts and music student up until that point. Having tried to paint watercolors with her left hand proved problematic, and she couldn't practice the piano, so reading was her only form of entertainment — and she immersed herself in books.

During her days in high school, she excelled in biology, anatomy, and chemistry. And it was then that she recognized that she wanted to become a doctor — just like the one who had patched up her bones. By the time she was sixteen, she was taking advanced classes and maintaining her straight A average. Kate had become a brainiac, which was a good thing because she would need some form of scholarship and loans to get through college and all the postgraduate work.

Her parents encouraged her but secretly doubted their daughter could manage to reach the level she imagined. But when she got a full scholarship to Baylor, they were relieved and stunned. Maybe, just maybe, Kate would become a doctor. Paying for med school was another issue, but they would cross that bridge when and if they came to it.

Kate continued to excel, graduated with honors, and attended medical school with the help of a small student loan. It was only small in comparison to the hundred-thousand-dollar loans many of her fellow students were saddled with. She seemed to breeze through her internship; then came the pregnancy. Her residency was a bit of a struggle. Maintaining her schedule and raising a baby was no easy task. But she managed, and managed it quite well, thank you very much.

Now here she was, a first-year, on-staff orthopedist. Yes, it had been a long haul, and now she could practice her craft as a full-fledged professional.

Kate slowly strolled down the hallway, taking in her new surroundings. She had seen some horribly mangled bodies during her studies and knew that would not be the end of it. The hard work was about to begin, and she was ready for the challenge.

Walking up to the office marked DR. SIMON REGAN, ORTHOPEDICS, she felt butterflies in her stomach. This was really happening. With her head held high, she firmly knocked on the open door. "Yes! Come in!" boomed the voice of a very large man. Large in stature, and large in his specialty. Dr. Regan was a fine orthopedic surgeon, and people would wait months for a consultation.

"Kate! How good to see you! Please come in, sit down. Can I get you something? Coffee? Water?" He was impeccably dressed. It was obvious he had his suits specially tailored to fit his large frame.

"Dr. Regan! I am so excited to be here!" Kate tried not to gush, but her new boss was an icon in the healing business. "Maybe a cup of coffee?"

"Sure thing. Let's take a walk to the lounge, and I can show you around a bit. Then we'll meet with the rest of the staff in about a half hour." He was genuinely kind — a big teddy bear of sorts.

As they passed by the glass walls of the rooms, Kate felt a pang of empathy. "I remember when I spent an entire summer in a cast. But at least I was able to be at home."

"Yeah, some of these kids are in bad shape, but most of them will be okay. There's one kid whose leg was crushed in an accident. We did some radical surgery to try to save the leg, but it will be a few days to see if we worked a miracle."

They came upon a space that was a large community room for those patients who were more mobile, and where families could spend time interacting with other families. Children and adults were busily making paper stars, while others were cutting strips of paper and turning them into a chain of garland. Soft holiday music was playing in the background.

"It's nice to see that the PC Police haven't stopped the holiday spirit here!" Kate was delighted to observe good fellowship and laughter in this kind of setting. "It's tough being in a hospital during the holidays. I guess it's tough being in a hospital, period!" She laughed at her own obvious remark.

"Indeed. And we are very happy you were able to start now, with everyone trying to get their schedules wrapped up. No pun intended!" Dr. Regan, too, laughed at his own comment.

"We're getting a tree later today and a menorah, and we'll have the Kwanza candles, too. I think, well, at least I hope, we've covered almost everyone. It's not about religion. It's about honoring each other as human beings, kindness, brotherly love, and all that — at least for a couple of weeks!"

Kate was struck by how genuine this man was. He was a healer on many levels.

"I am sure it will be very festive!"

"We're going to have to make some room for the tree," Dr. Regan addressed one of the orderlies. "Ryan, the Cedar Park Tree Farm folks are coming by this afternoon. Be sure they have a clear path and the corner is ready for them."

Kate's stomach went into her throat. Just when she thought she had forgotten about that man. It was as if he were following her.

"You okay?" Dr. Regan noticed that Kate had turned a little pale.

"Oh, yes. I'm fine. It's just a little overwhelming. The big move. The new job."

"Completely understandable. Come on. Follow me."

Dr. Regan walked Kate down another corridor, where they came upon the lounge.

"This is where you'll get your nanosecond breaks. There's a Keurig, a Nespresso, Magic Bullet if you want to make your own shakes, fridge, microwave, pantry. We try to stock it with some items like protein bars, canned soup — organic, of course — and occasionally donuts." He patted his girth. "We try to keep it healthy, but everyone needs something sweet once in a while."

"I usually pack a salad and some fruit," Kate replied. "But I am a sucker for a buttery croissant if they're ever on the menu!"

"Speaking of menu, the cafeteria is on the fifth floor. It's not too bad for hospital food, and it's reasonable."

"Good to know. But I've had so much hospital food over the past five years that the smell makes me want to gag!" Kate was trying to regroup from the Cedar Park tree comment, hoping she would be out of there before she ran into "the famous tree man" again.

As they were about to walk out of the lounge a familiar voice called out: "Kate? Kate Stafford? Holy smoke, is that really you?"

Turning abruptly, she recognized an old friend from medical school. "Brian! What on earth are you doing here?" She saw he was wearing nurse's scrubs.

"Had to get out of town!" Brian said teasingly. "Seriously. Been working here for about two years. The question is what are *you* doing here?"

"Kate is our new on-staff ortho. She starts this week. How do you two know each other?" Dr. Regan took the lead.

"We were in med school together, but I went on to get my RN instead." Brian had been one of Kate's buddies in school, but he didn't have the discipline for the rigorous program. "It's a job I can take with me." Brian was also a wanderer, thinking his medical career would lead him to the Peace Corps or some other organization, like Doctors without Borders. But he couldn't cut it and had left med school after the first year. "Yeah, I worked in Chicago for a while, but the weather was brutal, so I moved back here."

"It's so good to see you!" Kate gushed. A friend. Or at least someone she knew. "We must get together!"

"That would be great, but I'm going to have a hefty schedule starting next week. The holidays. Most people want to spend time with their family, and if you remember, mine wasn't the easiest. They invented the word 'dysfunctional.' " As Brian laughed, Kate remembered how difficult it had been for him.

"Well, how about tonight? We're getting our tree. You can help decorate!" Kate was effusive and excited about reconnecting with an old pal.

"Yeah. Sure. What time? I get off at four. What's the address?" Brian seemed genuinely pleased with the reunion as well.

"Sounds like old home week to me!" Dr. Regan continued. "Okay, you two. Figure out the details posthaste. Kate still has a few more people to meet."

Kate wrote down her address and phone number. "Great! Come over around six? I'll rustle up something for us to eat that doesn't resemble hospital food! And you'll get to meet my daughter, Emma."

"Wow! A kid, too? You must have been

some kind of busy woman!" Brian was slightly startled by the news. "I'll bring the wine! If I remember correctly, you fancied Malbec. Australian?"

"And you, sir, have an excellent memory." Kate threw her arms around Brian, giving him a big squeeze. "See you later!"

"So, Dr. Stafford, or do you prefer Dr. Kate? Some of the kids' doctors use their first names. Seems to put them — the kids — more at ease," Dr. Regan said.

" 'Dr. Kate' is fine with me. Unless you don't think it's professional enough?"

"I'll let you play it by ear. Some people like the official — professional way of addressing a doctor, but the kids seem to like the more casual approach. Heck, it's scary being in here, and the more relaxed the patient, the quicker the recovery; although we don't let them slack off on their PT!"

"Gotcha!" Kate was beginning to feel her way.

"Paging Dr. Regan. Dr. Regan," a voice came over the PA. He walked over to the nearest desk and picked up the phone. "Dr. Regan here. They are? A little early, but I guess we'll have to scramble a bit. Yes, let them know and show them the way. Thanks."

He turned to Kate. "The Christmas trees

have arrived. Better tell them to clear the corner, pronto!"

Kate tried not to worry. But how was she going to avoid him for the second time that day?

"Dr. Regan. Were there some other people you wanted me to see? Other people I need to meet today?"

"Well, you can watch the tree guys create havoc, or we can take this up again on Friday." He gave her a wide grin.

"I told Emma I would pick her up before lunch. She's visiting a new friend, and I don't want her to feel abandoned." Kate tried to make light of it, but was aware that her feet were pointing toward the door — hoping for a quick exit.

"All right then! Eight o'clock sharp on Friday morning. You know where the day-care center is, right? Second floor just outside that elevator. Have a good evening with Brian. Glad to have you on board!" He shook her hand, and Kate dashed to the nearest exit, trying to avoid any contact with the tree people.

Sweat was running down her back. This guy seemed to be everywhere. Even now! In *her* place! She was beginning to think moving to Cedar Park had not been such a brilliant idea, after all.

How long would it take to deliver a tree? Twenty minutes? Ten? Her mind was racing. As she came around to the physicians' entrance to the building she looked frantically for the truck. In her haste, she stumbled — again. This time landing in the boxwood. "Dr. Klutz, for sure. I have to stop wearing these chunky heels. I'm a fashion victim. God forbid I end up as a patient before I start my rounds!" Kate was muttering to herself. As she was about to climb out of the bush, she spotted the trees being carried into the building but couldn't see the faces of the people carrying them. *Just sit tight until they're gone,* she told herself.

As she was peering from behind the shrubbery, waiting for an opportunity to escape the humiliation, someone's Yorkshire terrier started yapping at her. "Oh crap! Shoo . . . Get lost, pooch. Where's your mama?"

"It's his brother. Dr. Klutz, I presume?" It was *him*! "The famous Christmas tree man." Again! "Do you have a thing for dirt and brush?" Kevin could hardly contain his laughter. If mortification had a face associated with it in the dictionary, it would be Kate's.

"First day on the job, sorta."

"Landscaping? I thought you were a doctor?" Kevin was confused and amused.

"Very funny. I was checking out my new place of employment, got a little disoriented, and tripped. So, yes. Dr. Klutz." Kate was actually on the offense, which suited her. She pointed to the little dog: "They have veterinary clinics for those."

Stifling a grin, Kevin retorted with, "I must have made a left at Albuquerque," mimicking Bugs Bunny, one of his favorite Warner Bros. cartoon characters.

Kate couldn't hold back the laugh. "You must think I'm Looney Tunes!"

"Well, no. Not exactly. But it does seem like the only time I see you is when you're covered in topsoil!" He held out one hand to help her out of the brush, while he scooped up Wylie with the other.

"Dr. Klutz, meet my mom's favorite son, Wylie. He doesn't normally travel with me, but the kids get a kick out of him."

"Come here often?" That sounded really stupid to Kate. "I mean, do you bring him here often?"

"No, but Mom does sometimes when she volunteers. They let her smuggle him in. There's one little guy who got his leg smashed up pretty bad, and she thought I should go talk to him. Being I had my leg smashed up a bit, too."

"So you were serious when you said you might need an orthopedist?"

"Yes, ma'am. Shattered my femur during a jump."

"From a plane?" Kate was incredulous.

"Certainly not from a building!" Kevin was starting to relax with this new woman in town. "I heard you stopped by the farm last night, and Jake helped you pick out a fine one."

"Yes, we did. Emma was enthralled with the winter wonderland. You folks certainly know how to decorate!"

"You should see our house. It's almost as bright."

Kate thought she would love to see his house. But who lived there with him? she wondered.

"I don't doubt it. I've got to get going. Nice to see you again." Kate tried to act nonchalant.

"Good to see you as well. Maybe next time it won't be in the dirt!" He tipped his hat and made his way into the hospital.

CHAPTER EIGHT

Kevin's reunion with Melissa had been surprisingly cordial. Almost anticlimactic.

All the angst and worry earlier that morning proved to be silly. Maybe not silly but not necessary. They had known each other for a long time, and six years had passed. Enough time to mature, and with maturity came acceptance. It wasn't that he hadn't accepted the breakup. It had been all the plans that would never materialize that caused so much pain at that time. He remembered something he had once read by Kierkegaard — "The most painful state of being is remembering the future, particularly the one you'll never have." Thankfully, he was over that, too. Yes. He was good with all of it. And happy for Melissa. She seemed content with her life. Although happiness wasn't always a product of contentment. He let out a big rush of air. He thought he must have been holding his breath for at least two hours.

He shook out the tension in his shoulders and relaxed into the seat of his truck as he headed toward the farm. Speaking into the Bluetooth smartphone, he instructed it to call home. He felt like E.T.

"Calling 'home,' " came the robo response.

"Hello?" Kevin heard his mother's voice.

"Mom. I survived. It wasn't as bad as I thought it would be."

Mrs. Matthews could feel the smile coming through the phone. "Oh. Thank Goodness. I was praying!"

"Me too!" Kevin joked. He was a spiritual guy, but not necessarily religious, so the thought of him praying made his mother laugh.

"Now, don't you go take the Lord for granted. He does do miraculous things for us!" Maggie Matthews was always reminding her son of God's work, even though it was hard to justify things like famine, war, and poverty. When questioned, she would turn the argument around by pointing out the many blessings, no matter how small.

"Oh, Mama. You know I respect Him and all the fine people who do His work. I am not taking anything for granted. Believe me!" Even Kevin was beginning to believe in miracles — regardless of size and circumstance. Thinking of the many times his squadron had dropped food and medical supplies to the desperate and the sick, he realized that it must have seemed like a miracle to them. Faith wasn't something he had given much thought to, but he was beginning to appreciate it more and more as he thought about the life he had led.

"Are you heading to the farm? You should find out if that pretty doctor stopped by last night. Maybe Jake has some information to share."

"I am way ahead of you. After Melissa's, I stopped by the hospital to deliver a tree and introduce Wylie to a kid who had had his leg crushed. Found her in a bush."

"You what? Found who in a bush? The doctor? What on earth was she doing in a bush?"

"She was leaving the hospital and tripped. This is the second time, by the way, so I'm beginning to wonder about her agility. Let's hope she's sitting down when she's in the OR!" Kevin was surely joking at that point. "Yep. She picked out a tree, and it's going to be delivered tonight. So can we just let things fall where they may? You know, the old *que sera, sera* philosophy?"

"Well, some things *will* be what they *will* be, and some things need a little encouragement. And I think this fits into the latter category."

"Roger that! I'm pulling into the yard now. By the way, what's for dinner?"

"Kevin, didn't you just finish lunch? And you're thinking about dinner already?"

"I need something to look forward to after a hard day on the farm." Kevin was only half serious. The really hard work was done by the farmhands. Kevin's big job was to make sure no potential customer left without a tree and several bags of ornaments.

"Maybe you can look forward to delivering a certain tree to a certain doctor tonight."

"Over and out, Mama!" Kevin was grinning from ear to ear. The first encounter with Melissa after six years had gone smoothly. It was just two old friends casually getting together. No animosity. No blame. Both realized they had moved on, and neither was bitter or distressed. At least, not anymore.

Kevin jumped out of the truck and headed to the main building, where he checked the sales slips from the night before, looking for Dr. Klutz's receipt. A six-footer. *That's a lot of tree for such a petite woman. Guess she's going to need a hand.* Kevin was feeling very sure of himself.

CHAPTER NINE

Struggling with her emotions and her embarrassment, Kate headed to Melissa's to pick up Emma, but continued to think about her latest escapade with the local scenery. How could she have been so foolish? Tripping because of a guy — not once but twice in just a few days? She tried to shake off her jitters from her encounter with "the famous tree man," imagining what kind of impression she must have made.

Turning her thoughts to something where she had a better grip, Kate mused about what to serve for dinner. She decided to ask Emma what would be to her liking. Kate hadn't thought about how Emma would react to having someone over for dinner this soon. Especially a man. Allowing Emma some input would probably help her feel more comfortable. It had already been a big day. A big day for both of them. Emma had made a new friend. Kate had started a new job. Kate had reunited with an old friend. Kate had seen "the famous tree man" leaving a woman's house. Kate had fallen into the bushes. Yep. A big day indeed. And tonight they would be getting their tree. Kate tried to imagine Jake delivering the tree. She didn't want to get herself in a tizzy thinking it could be Kevin.

Pulling onto Miller Lane, she parked in Melissa's driveway. This time it wasn't blocked by a truck. *His* truck.

She confidently strutted to the front door, where she was greeted by Emma and Victoria. "Mommy! Mommy! Look what we made!" Emma proudly presented her mother with a piece of kraft paper covered in doilies. "It's snowflakes! Lots of them!"

"That's just beautiful!" Kate gushed. Her little girl was doing just fine. Now if only she could say the same for herself. She was going to have to do a lot of self-analysis.

"Hey, Melissa! How did everything go today?"

"The girls got along really well. I gave them this little project while I sorted out the decorations. I want the house to be festive when Greg gets home."

Kate tried desperately to stay away from that dark place that was forming in her head.

Yeah. Festive and homey. Is your boyfriend going to be there too?

Kate shook her head as if she was trying to get a bug out of her ear.

"You okay?" Melissa looked concerned.

"Oh, yes. I think I got some water in my ear this morning. It's so annoying." Kate quickly recovered from her wandering mind.

"Don't you just hate when that happens?" Melissa's singsong voice was about to get on Kate's one last nerve.

Kate knew she was being secretly mean — even jealous. Wow. Feeling that way was something she was hard-pressed to remember. When *was* the last time she felt that way? Right. Earlier that morning.

"Okay, honey pie. You ready to get a move on?"

"Yes, Mommy, but can I come back again?" Emma looked a little distressed.

"If Mrs. Sullivan says it's okay. And you can also invite Victoria to our house! How about that?"

Emma's cheerful disposition immediately returned, and she gave her new friend a kiss on the cheek. "Thank you, Mrs. Sullivan! Bye-bye!"

The two little girls were adorable together. Face it. They were cute kids. Then again every parent thought their kid was cute and smart.

"Thanks again, Melissa. Maybe next week? I don't have my full schedule yet."

"No problem. No problem at all. You just let me know. Buh-bye now."

Kate revisited her feelings of annoyance. *Buh-bye? Okay. Stop it. She's very nice, and she was nice to Emma.*

Emma climbed into her seat, and Kate buckled her in. "Did you have a good time with Victoria?"

"Oh, yes, Mommy! We had lots of fun!"

"I am so happy to hear that. So, listen. I went to my new job today, and I ran into an old friend of mine from school! His name is Brian. He's a nurse at the hospital. I invited him to come to dinner tonight. Is that okay with you?"

"Sure, Mommy! Guess what? Victoria's Mommy had a friend come over today, too! Yep. Victoria told me that a man who wasn't her daddy came today. She didn't know who he was. But said he was nice."

"Oh, really?" Kate's interest went through the roof. "What else did she say about the man?"

"Nothing. Just that he was a friend of her mommy's."

Kate knew it would be like trying to pry

an oyster open with a noodle to get any other information out of Emma.

"Must be friendship day today! Right, sweetie? You, me, and Melissa all found friends!"

Kate thought she was going to scream. *Friends my behind.*

Switching the channels in her head, Kate asked Emma, "So what would you like to have for dinner tonight?"

"Pizza!" Emma exclaimed.

"Oh, honey, I promised Brian I would cook something."

"You can cook pizza!" Emma exuded enthusiasm with just about anything.

"Not really. We can heat it up, but I think we need to actually *cook* something. Chicken? Beef? Tacos? C'mon. I know you can come up with something special!"

Emma tapped her pointy finger on her chin. It was uncanny. That was something Roger would do from time to time. DNA. Scary.

"Can we have the not-so-crunchy kind?" Emma was referring to soft tacos.

"Excellent plan! Let's stop at the grocery store and pick up what we need." Kate put the car in gear and headed toward Costco.

Emma was a very well-adjusted child considering the crazy scheduling during

Kate's residency, and now the big move. Kate was very mindful and grateful for having such a good kid.

A few minutes into the trip to the grocery store, Emma asked, "Mommy, is 'the famous tree man' bringing our tree tonight?"

Just when she thought she was safe from thinking about *him,* her well-behaved little girl derailed her. *I know where she got the finger-on-chin gesture, but where did she get that steel-trap memory? Oh, yeah. Probably from me.*

"Sweetie, I don't know who is bringing the tree, but it will be so much fun! I think you will like Brian. He's fun *and* funny."

"Is he your boyfriend, Mommy?"

"What? No! He's a guy friend. Not daddy-type friend. You know what I mean, right, sweetie?"

"I think so. Daddy friends live with you and other friends don't. Right?"

"Yes! Correctomundo!" Kate thought she had just dodged a birds-and-the-bees bullet. Emma was too young to even notice these things — but it was a different world from when she had grown up.

"Are we ever going to go Daddy shopping, Mommy?"

Kate burst out laughing. "One of these days. Just not today!"

Kate pulled into the parking lot of the big warehouse store and looked around for an empty cart.

Just as she was about to grab one, she noticed Betty Palmer leaving. Her stomach started that butterfly thing again. Betty, Melissa, tree man. It was almost too much.

"Why, hello, Kate! Emma! Did you have fun with Victoria?" Betty addressed Emma directly.

"Sure did." Emma yawned as she was starting to wane from the day's activity.

"Just rushing through to pick up a few things." Then she lowered her voice. "And this one needs a bit of a nap." She winked at Betty and practically skipped away. "See you at the tree lighting! Have a good afternoon!"

Betty looked a little perplexed. "You too!"

Kate knew she had been a little rude. It was a "thing" to chat when you ran into somebody, but Kate rarely had time. "Chatting" wasn't in her bailiwick — at least not idle chatter.

Kate realized Emma was slightly bedraggled, so she lifted her into the main part of the shopping cart. The kid seat wasn't up to Emma's standards. She started making a fuss when she turned four. "It's for little kids!" she would protest. But riding in the big cart was okay, according to Emma.

Kate hurried to the back of the store, where the meat, vegetables, and bread were on gigantic display. The dairy section was just to the left.

Calculating in her head what items she needed, Kate headed to the register as Emma was about to doze off.

Managing the food and a thirty-seven-pound child was going to take some balancing.

Strapping her sleepy child into her seat, Kate put the groceries in the back as well.

She headed home. Their home. And a friend was coming over for dinner. Their first guest.

When they got to the house, Kate carried Emma inside and put her on her bed for a nap. She was out like a light. Kate decided a short nap would be okay since the evening ahead would be jam-packed, what with company coming over and the tree arriving.

Kate thought she should probably take a nap as well. She put the groceries away, headed for the sofa, lay down, and pulled a toss pillow over her face. She couldn't stop thinking about events of the morning. Seeing Kevin in Melissa's driveway. Falling into the bushes. She had to remind herself that she had also gone to the hospital — a place where she felt most in control. Yes, she would concentrate on that. Then her mind wandered to the little boy with the crushed leg. Then back to Kevin and the dog. She turned onto her stomach. Then onto her back again. No nap for her. It just wasn't going to happen.

Resigned to staying awake, Kate started moving some furniture to make room in the corner for the tree. They had considered several different sizes, and they were all so pretty. It was hard to decide, but Jake had been very helpful as she described her cottage to him.

Before she knew it, the clock showed it was almost five. "Emma! Honey! Get up, sleepyhead!"

Emma dragged herself from her room. "Mommy. I don't feel so good. My tummy hurts." Her face was flush, and Kate touched her forehead.

"What did you eat for lunch?"

"A sandwich." Emma went from rubbing her eyes to rubbing her stomach.

"What kind of sandwich?"

But before Emma could answer, a gush of vomit flew from Emma's mouth.

Kate ran toward Emma before she could redecorate the living room with the remaining contents of her stomach. "It's okay, honey. Let Mommy help you."

Kate carried Emma to the bathroom, where she proceeded to remove the puked-on clothes and set her in the tub. "Sweetie. What did you have for lunch?" Kate was trying to diagnose the root of the problem.

"We had bologna sandwiches."

"What else?"

"Don't be mad."

"I'm not mad, honey. Just tell Mommy what happened. What else did you eat?"

"Victoria had a box of chocolate mint cookies."

"And?"

"And we ate all of them!" Emma was about to cry.

"Just the cookies? Anything else?"

"No. But. But we were so thirsty."

Kate was trying to be patient and not panic. "What did you drink, Emma?"

"Pineapple juice." Tears were rolling down Emma's face at that point.

"Pineapple juice? And chocolate mint cookies? Was that all?" Kate wanted to be sure Emma didn't leave out any important detail.

"Yes. We drank a whole big can of it. I don't feel so good."

Kate's stomach almost turned over thinking about that combination. "It's okay, sweetie. We'll let Mr. Bubble wash away all the gunk." She turned on the faucet and let the warm water mix with the bubble bath. "Should we wash your hair, too? I think I see some cookie crumbles in it!" Kate was trying to lift Emma's wilting spirit.

"I'm sorry. I promise I will never, ever eat bologna and cookies and pineapple juice ever again." It came out more of a groan than a proclamation.

Kate laughed softly. "It's okay, honey." She wiped Emma's face and gave her hair a quick scrub. "Now dry off. I'll go get you a fresh pair of PJs."

"But what about the tree man? What about our Christmas tree?" Emma was definitely distressed.

"Don't worry. We'll have our tree, and we can decorate it tomorrow, when you feel better."

"What about your friend? Will he come back tomorrow?"

"I think he may have to work. But I'll be sure he helps put the lights on, so you and I won't have to work so hard when we decorate. Okay with you?"

"Yep!" Emma blew some bubbles from her nose.

"Okay. Let's get those jammies on and

back to bed. Feeling a little better?"

Kate was startled at the sound of the doorbell. "Geez, I didn't realize what time it was!" Then she yelled toward the door, "Be right there!"

She ushered Emma to her room, wiped the remaining bubbles from her hand, and headed to the front door. "Brian! So glad you could make it tonight. But we have a little issue happening."

"Everything all right?"

"Yes. Just a bad combination of bologna, cookies, and juice. Emma got sick. I just gave her a quick bath and put her back to bed. Come in!"

She showed him into the living room. "Take a seat. Pinot Grigio, if I remember correctly?"

"Great memory! No wonder you aced all your tests!" Brian had always been in awe of Kate's ability to recall what seemed to be every inch of the human anatomy.

"Make yourself comfortable."

"I will! My dogs are barking!" He kicked off his loafers.

Kate went into the kitchen and poured Brian a glass of wine and checked the cabinet for some children's Pepto-Bismol. Frowning, she returned with the wine and handed it to Brian.

"I need to run to the drugstore. Emma is in bed, and the Christmas tree is about to be delivered. Do you mind tree and kid sitting for about fifteen minutes?"

"No problem. But would you rather that I go?" Brian offered.

"It's okay. I'll only be a few minutes." She grabbed her keys and wallet and dashed out the door.

Chapter Ten

Kevin left the farm a little earlier than usual. He wanted to be sure he had time to grab some dinner and deliver the tree to "Dr. Klutz." He chuckled, thinking about her second bit of clumsiness.

When he walked into the kitchen, his mother couldn't help but notice that he was looking rather dapper for a delivery. With a twinkle in her eye, she checked him up and down. "My, don't you look rather handsome. Is that cologne I smell, too? A little fancy for a tree-farm delivery run, no?"

"Ha! You caught me!" Kevin knew it was obvious, so he didn't bother to protest. "I thought you'd be pleased to know that I intend to deliver the tree to the pretty new doctor in town. That is if you approve."

Maggie Matthews grabbed both of her son's broad shoulders and beamed. "I am tickled pink! I think it's wonderful that you are showing some interest! Do you want to bring over some date-nut bread? I made several loaves this morning for the bake sale. Or maybe a nice gingerbread house for her little girl?"

"Let's not get ahead of ourselves, Mama. This isn't a date. It's just a delivery." He ran his hands through his hair. "And a bit of a fact-finding mission, you could say."

"Well, okay, dear. But you could say it was courtesy of the tree farm. We give every new customer a loaf!"

"I wouldn't let that news out of the bag." He laughed. "There are a bunch of folks who would be mighty P-O'd thinking they should have gotten a date-nut bread years ago!"

"Hmmm . . . Maybe you're right. Okay, then. Just say it's from me. A little welcome token."

"I guess that would be okay. I just don't want to come off being foolish. Or too eager. We don't want to scare her! And she may become my doctor. That could turn into an embarrassing situation!"

"Oh, for heaven's sake, Kevin. It's just date-nut bread! Not an engagement ring." Maggie was surprised at her own casual attitude, considering she was the one who kept encouraging him to make a gesture. Something. Anything.

"If you insist. I will tell her it's compliments of Maggie Matthews, Baker Extraordinaire. And your goods will be on display for sale at the church this Thursday. I'll tell her it's a promotional item."

Both laughed at their sophomoric behavior. It was, after all, just a tree delivery, wasn't it?

"Tell her it's good with honey butter. Betty Palmer will be selling some of that at the bake sale as well!"

Kevin gave his mother a wry look. "Since when did you become a marketing maven?"

"Ha! About two years ago, I bungled one as I was trying to get it out of the pan. I didn't want to throw it away, so I cut it up into pieces, stuck some toothpicks in them, and brought the whole kit and caboodle to church the night we were setting up the tables. Within five minutes, the plate was empty. Crumbs and all! Apparently, word got out, and I sold all twelve within the first hour! Everyone thought I was a marketing genius after that! Funny thing, doncha think?" Kevin could see the pride in his mother's face.

"Funny, indeed. Well, your secret's safe with me." He gave her a peck on the cheek, pulled on his hat, and strutted out the door.

Since he had known that he was going to

make the delivery after dinner, he had brought Kate's tree home with him, so he wouldn't have to drive all the way back to the farm.

Checking the address on the receipt, he headed in her direction.

When he arrived at Kate's house, he noticed that there wasn't a car in the driveway, but there was one on the street. He didn't know what she drove so assumed she had left the driveway clear for him. As he backed in, he could hear some music playing softly in the background. It was *The Nutcracker Suite.*

Jumping from the cab, he grabbed the date-nut bread, then lowered the gate on the back of the truck. Getting his Texas swagger on, he moved toward the front porch, removed his hat, and rang the bell.

A man's voice came from inside the house. "Hang on!" And then heavy footsteps. For a moment, Kevin considered that he might have the wrong place, but then the door swung open, and there stood Brian. "Hey! You the tree guy?"

Kevin became instantly flustered. "Uh. Yes. I have a tree for Kate Stafford."

"Yeah. She had to run out for a minute. Emma has a little stomach thing going on."

Looking down, he noticed that the guy

wasn't wearing any shoes. *So the new doctor has a boyfriend.*

"Need a hand?" Brian offered. "Let me get my shoes."

"No problem. I can handle it." He turned and headed toward the truck. Realizing he had the bread in his hand, he tossed it casually to Brian. "It's courtesy of Cedar Park Tree Farm."

Surprised by the lob, Brian missed the catch and the bread hit the porch, which gave Kevin a huge sense of satisfaction. *What a doofus,* he thought to himself. *How can she be with a guy like him? Now, there was a klutz. What guy can't make an easy catch like that?* Then he thought of Emma. *That poor kid. She's going to be tripping through life.*

Kevin hauled the big tree from the truck and carried it onto the porch. "Where would you like me to put this?" Kevin's mind was going toward the gutter at this point, and he suppressed a sly grin.

"Kate made some room in the corner. Wow. That's one big tree."

"Most people say the same thing. They look a lot smaller outside. We try to tell them, but they never listen. Then they have to cut a foot off the bottom and can never get it to stand right. We get calls every day asking if we can come out and help."

Brian wasn't sure what to do. Clearly, the tree was going to invade a third of the living room. "Are you sure this is the tree Kate picked out?"

"Hey, I wasn't there. All I know is that *this* is the tree she paid for." Kevin was losing his patience. He couldn't wait to get out of that house.

"Well, okay. I guess." Brian was beginning to seem wimpier every minute. "Would you mind putting it in the stand?"

Irritation was setting in. "No problem. I cut the bottom branches earlier to make it easier." He slammed the tree into the stand. "Anything else?"

"I don't think so." Brian reached into his wallet and pulled out a twenty-dollar bill and proceeded to tip Kevin.

Kevin held up his hand. "Not necessary. Part of our service. Merry Christmas." Marching back to his truck, he couldn't remember the last time he had felt so exasperated.

CHAPTER ELEVEN

As Kevin was rounding the corner of Kate's street, she was coming from the other direction and didn't notice the Cedar Park Christmas Tree Farm truck.

She pulled into the driveway and bounded up the porch steps. When she opened the front door, all she could see was a tree. A very large one.

"Brian! You under there?" She didn't know what to make of it.

"Kinda big, doncha think?" Brian was standing in the doorway to the kitchen.

"I . . . I had no idea it would be *that* big once it was in the house." Kate was trying to wrap her mind around what had taken place in the few minutes she was gone.

"Yeah. That's what the guy said."

Kate gulped. "Which guy was it?"

"I dunno. He was tall, black hair. Oh, and he left this for you." Brian picked up the squashed remains of the date-nut bread.

Kate looked forlorn and confused as she stared at the mangled lump. "What else did he say?"

"Something like 'Compliments of Cedar Park Christmas Tree Farm.' He seemed a little pissy to me."

"Huh." Kate wadded the remains of the loaf into a ball and tossed it on the counter. "Now, what in the heck can we do so the living room doesn't look like a national forest?"

"Maybe that's where the term 'tree trimming' came from?" Brian was noticing Kate's agitation and tried to make light of the situation. "He did say people usually call for help."

"Well, that's not going to happen. We'll figure it out. I am a surgeon, after all!"

"Tree surgeon, Dr. Arboretum?" Brian teased, and walked over to the refrigerator.

"Well, I do work on limbs!" Kate called back, amused at her repartee.

Brian returned from the kitchen with a refill for himself and a fresh glass of wine for Kate. "Here. You look like you could use something medicinal."

Kate took the glass and chugged it down, almost choking from the acidity. "Cripes, that's awful! I should have known better than to buy something we used to drink when we were in med school!"

The daunting task of fitting the huge cedar into the living area was upon them, and Kate made her way to the basement to fetch a pair of shears. Returning, she donned a surgical mask to lighten the mood a little more. "Good thing I don't have a chain saw!"

It took several hours for them to cut back the branches so the tree didn't dwarf the room. When they were done, Kate stood back and gave it the once-over. "Tree surgeon, indeed! You up for stringing the lights?"

"Only if you go on a mission of mercy and get us a decent bottle of vino!" Brian had always been a good sport and easygoing about most things. Another reason why he never finished med school.

Kate gave him a big bear hug. "Emma will be thrilled to see the tree with lights! Be back in a flash! Oh, and if anyone comes to the door again, don't let them in! Especially if they're from the tree farm!" Laughing, she grabbed her keys and headed to the liquor store. As promised, she was back in ten minutes with two very nice bottles of Lucien Crochet Sancerre.

"Wow!" Brian eyed the wine. "So this is what you get if you finish medical school?"

"See what you're missing?" Kate teased. "But I'm not about to get used to it. I still have a modest loan to pay. But tonight is special, and you're such a pal to put up with all of this. Sorry about dinner. Emma did say pizza!"

It was just before midnight when they decided the tree was in acceptable shape. The piles of trimmings from the branches were almost as much as what was left of the mammoth cedar. "At least it doesn't look like Charlie Brown bought it!"

"Really, Kate. What the heck were you thinking?"

"Like I said, it didn't seem as large outside with all the other trees."

"Next year, you may want to take a chaperone." Brian was picking the needles out of his socks.

Kate thought to herself, *Maybe I'll just skip that farm and get a fake one.*

"Listen, it's really late, and we polished off two bottles of wine. I'm not counting the first one of swill. Maybe you should crash on the couch?"

"Thought you'd never ask! I am bushed. No pun intended!" Brian finally took off his socks, which were sticky with sap, and plucked the last few needles out of them. "I don't suppose you have a pair of these?" He held out the socks, indicating they were no longer fit to be worn.

"Let me see what I have that isn't too girly." Kate went into the bedroom and appeared with a pair of white tube socks, a blanket, and a pillow. "Not glamorous, but neither are your feet! Thanks again, Brian. This would have been a nightmare if I had to do it on my own. Sweet dreams, my friend!"

"Nighty night. By the way, I expect bacon and eggs in the morning. Rye toast, slightly buttered. Coffee. Black."

"No problem. Everything you need is in the fridge!" Kate gave him her biggest smile and waved good night.

CHAPTER TWELVE

Kevin was sullen when he walked into the house. It was almost midnight. Wylie greeted him at the door and did his funny gesture of lying on his back and covering his eyes with his front paws. "Yeah. You got that right, buddy. What the heck was I thinking?" He felt so foolish, showing up with the date-nut bread; and then there was the cologne. He'd just had to try that new Giorgio Armani Acqua de Gio. And who was that wimpy guy?

"Kevin?" his mom called out from the kitchen. "So?" She glided her words like an arpeggio.

"So nothin'. I delivered a tree. Period." Kevin tossed his hat onto the side table and threw himself on the sofa.

"What about the date-nut bread? What did she say?"

"She wasn't there. Some dude — no, change that to 'weakling,' answered the door. He couldn't even catch the bread!"

"What are you talking about?"

"She had to run an errand. Apparently Emma was sick. A guy — with no shoes on, by the way — answered the door. I figure he's her boyfriend. End of story."

"What about the bread?"

"I tossed it to him and he missed catching it and it got a little smashed up on the porch." Kevin then smiled a wry grin, getting some small amount of satisfaction from that part of what had happened.

"Oh my. Oh, Kevin. I'm so sorry. Maybe he's just a friend." Maggie Matthews was attempting consolation.

"Yeah. Whatever. I don't think she'd leave her kid with just a friend. And he reached into his wallet to try to tip me, but I refused."

"You know what I always say — unless there's a ring on the finger, anyone is game!"

"Mother! What *have* you been doing for the past six years?" Kevin was astonished at his mother's newly acquired bravado.

"Listen, I've been around long enough to know that relationships can come and go. You, of all people, should know that. I'm just sayin' that maybe he isn't her boyfriend. She doesn't wear an engagement ring, does she?"

"Not that I noticed."

"Well, okay then. Before you write her off, you might want to do a little more investigatin'."

"Ha. I'm done embarrassing myself."

"Oh, honey, you just got back. You'll get into the swing of things. And I don't think you embarrassed yourself."

"But I was wearing cologne!" He was an inch away from outright whining.

"For heaven's sake, Kevin. You sound like an adolescent. Lots of men wear cologne. Women happen to like it! In fact, we think it makes men sexy."

"Oh my God, Mother! This conversation has gone a little too far." Kevin was beyond mortified at this point. Now his mother was using the word "sexy" as if it were part of her normal conversational language.

"Son. You're a grown man. I am a grown woman. We can have grown-up conversations."

"Yeah, but not about 'sexy' stuff," Kevin said, using air quotes around the words.

"You *have* been away too long! Here, try these cookies. They're a spin-off from my gingerbread house. Actually, they were supposed to be shingles, but they didn't quite make it!"

"Is this another one of your promotional

ideas? Maybe do a YouTube video of you bungling the baking?" Kevin was finally starting to lighten up as he chomped away.

"I think you need some sleep. Go to bed. We have the bake sale in two days, then the tree lighting the following night. You're going to need all your energy!"

"Good idea. Sweet dreams, Mama. I think I'll take Wylie to bed with me. We can commiserate about females."

Two days later, there was a bustle of baked goods and gingerbread houses. With Kevin's help, Maggie had managed to build twelve of the culinary constructions. Then there were the dozen carrot cakes, two dozen date-nut breads, twenty-four tins of cookies, and three of her bûche de noël, her finest works of art. The meringue mushrooms were the most tedious to prepare, and she would make them weeks in advance. Counting the various items, she calculated over a thousand dollars' worth of baked goods for the sale. That would be her best yet. She had started purchasing the ingredients a few months ago. Spreading out the costs helped not to pinch her wallet too much. She wanted all the proceeds to go to the church fund that provided hot meals for the elderly at Christmas. It had been a very busy few weeks, and she was elated at the bounty she was able to produce. With her donation of goods, the handmade ornaments from Betty Palmer and Melissa, along with the other Christmas confections, the bake sale was sure to be a huge success.

"Now be careful with those houses, boys. I don't want any of them condemned because of poor structure!" She was almost giddy.

"Not to worry, Mama. We'll move them with kid gloves." Kevin winked as he pulled away and headed toward the church. They had been up for several hours setting up the tables and the signs. Now it was time for the scrumptious part of the day!

At four o'clock, the doors opened for business to the biggest cake and holiday sale Cedar Park had ever seen. The assembly room had been transformed into a smaller version of the winter wonderland at the tree farm.

Yes, Maggie Matthews could not be outdone when it came to the holidays. Her only worry right now was Kevin's state of mind. She was very much aware that being home was going to be a big adjustment for him, and she didn't want him to be depressed because one new pretty face wasn't available. If nothing else, she would find out if

Dr. Kate was, in fact, involved. That wouldn't take much detective work, and at least she would have some peace of mind that Kevin was not walking away from something just because his ego was a little bruised.

The assembly room was buzzing with shoppers, and volunteers were handing out pieces of Maggie's cakes to sample. They would all be gone in the first hour if last year was any indication as to their popularity.

She spotted Kate, strolling around the tables with Emma, picking at a few freebees.

She also witnessed Kevin talking to Melissa about her and Betty's handcrafted decorations.

It's nice to see them getting along, Maggie thought to herself. That is until she witnessed Kate watching them, then move Emma to the other side of the room. It appeared that Kate was trying to avoid him, and there was also a look in Kate's eyes that seemed to spell out the word "jealous." *Interesting. Very interesting.*

Maggie took a few steps in Kate's direction but was immediately sidetracked by someone asking if she would reveal her recipe for the date-nut bread. By the time she finished explaining — purposely giving

the woman some wrong measurements —
she had lost sight of Kate and Emma.

*Dang. I guess that's God punishing me for
substituting a tablespoon for a teaspoon. But
it's for a good cause, Lord. It's for the meals
for the elderly.* Maggie secretly prayed that
she would be forgiven for being slightly
dishonest.

Kevin and Melissa were still almost head
to head as Melissa showed him the various
angels and French horns. Maggie was starting to get annoyed. *Melissa had her chance
with Kevin, and she had dumped him. She
better not think about doing anything foolish.
And neither should he.*

Maggie made a beeline toward them, hoping she could break up their tête-à-tête in
time for Kate to get another look. But it
was too late. She couldn't see Kate anywhere in the crowd. But now Maggie was
really motivated. She had definitely seen
that look in Kate's eyes. There was definitely
a flash of something.

"Hey, Mom! Looks like you're selling out
already!" Kevin was almost animated.
"Melissa has been showing me her latest
hobby. She does some mighty fine work."

Maggie wasn't liking Kevin's tone. While
she was happy that he was in a good mood,
he was a tad too effusive for her taste. Too

much gush came out of his mouth.

"Melissa, you certainly outdid yourself this year! You and Betty! Kevin, can you help me with something in the back?" Maggie was desperately thinking about what exactly she needed him to do. Even if Kate had left, she did not want her son to be love-smacked by a woman who had broken his heart and happened to be married. Sometimes people do that. Go back to something familiar. Even if it isn't the right thing. Consistency and fear were two great motivators, but they very often led people to make some very bad decisions.

"What do you need, Mama?" Kevin was following Maggie, who was cutting a path through the crowd. She still wasn't sure what task she could request and was fervently hoping that someone would interrupt her trip out back to ask for recipe instructions. She finally spotted someone from the garden club and spun off course in her direction.

"Kevin, give me just a second. I need to talk to Mrs. Anderson for a minute."

Maggie continued to pursue the woman even though she really had nothing to say to her.

"Mama? Is there something you need?" Kevin stood where he was and stared blankly at his mother, wondering what the heck was going on.

"Oh, never mind, honey. It can wait." Maggie was satisfied that she had accomplished her mission to break up the duo as she kept scanning the room for Kate and Emma. They were nowhere in sight. Maggie's cheerful mood was starting to cloud over, but then she got a glimpse of them returning from the restroom. She quickly moved in their direction, hoping she could garner some information about Kate's status.

"Kate! Hi, I'm Maggie Matthews. We met briefly — actually it was more like a rush-by on Sunday." Maggie had forgotten she really hadn't been introduced to the new doctor and was trying to cover up her curiosity about the woman and her situation. "Kevin mentioned that you got a tree from our farm?"

"Oh, yes. Hello, Mrs. Matthews." The mere mention of his name gave Kate the willies. "The tree is beautiful and so *big*! It needed a little trimming." Making a futile attempt at being casual, she continued, "This is my daughter, Emma. Emma, this is Mrs. Matthews. They own the tree farm where we got our tree."

"Oh, it was so beautiful there! I loved all

the angels!" Emma gushed her approval. "Are you 'the famous tree man's' mother?"

Kate thought she was going to faint. Her daughter couldn't let that one go.

Maggie squatted as far as she could to look Emma in the eyes. "I'm so glad you loved the angels. They're my favorite! 'Famous tree man'?"

"Yes. K-E-V-I-N. Kevin!" Emma once again proudly spelled his name. "There was a sign at the church! And he was carrying a big tree!" She started giggling, which helped break some of the tension Kate was feeling.

"And I think he delivered the tree to your house the other night." Maggie was turning into a supersleuth.

"He did? I got sick that day, so I didn't see him."

"I hope you're feeling better and had a chance to try *my* famous date-nut bread." More prodding.

"Mommy? Did I taste the nut bread?"

"No, honey. I was waiting for your stomach to be all better." Kate was hiding the fact that she had tossed the ball of bakery into the trash. Now she had to buy one out of guilt.

"Well, I do hope you enjoy it. Will you be coming to the tree lighting tomorrow night?" Maggie was amused at her own

audacity and knew Kevin would be horrified, yet she went on. "With your husband?"

"Husband? No. I'm not married. I mean,
I *was* married but . . ."

"Mommy said we have to go Daddy shopping!" Emma interrupted with the best
news Maggie had heard since she was told
they had sold out of the gingerbread houses.

"Daddy shopping? Now that sounds like
quite a job!" Still fishing.

"Yep! I don't know when, but Mommy
said 'one of these days.' "

Bingo! Maggie had gotten the info she had
been longing for. Apparently, the guy who
was at Kate's house wasn't daddy material,
which meant he most likely wasn't boyfriend
material, either. She was ecstatic.

"It was so nice to meet the two of you.
We'll see you tomorrow night. Remember,
Santa will be there, so you may want to get
in line early! Ta-ta!" Maggie was almost
gliding across the room. Her next mission
was to make sure Kevin didn't decide to
fawn over Melissa again.

She purposely went to the table where
Betty and Melissa were selling their decorations.

"Have you seen Kevin?"

"He was here a few minutes ago. It seemed
like he recognized someone he knew, but

then he dashed out the door."

Maggie headed to the hallway and pulled out her cell phone and punched in the speed dial number for Kevin. It went straight to voice mail. "Kevin. It's your mom. Call me when you get a minute. I think I have some news for you." She paced the hall for several minutes, then decided the conversation with Kevin could wait. Thinking about it a little more, she decided she wouldn't tell him everything she had discovered. He would be mortified about her having obtained the info, so she had to come up with a different plan.

By the end of the afternoon, every crumb had been purchased, and there were no more ornaments to sell. The sale had been a huge success, raising over three thousand dollars for the meals for the elderly. Kids from the local grade school lent a hand in folding the tables and cleaning up the space. All that remained were the decorations and the big seat for Santa for the next evening.

"My work here is done," Maggie proudly whispered under her breath. "On to the next project!"

CHAPTER THIRTEEN

The following morning was another flurry of organizing the final details for the tree lighting. Maggie counted out fifty copies of the book of Christmas carols and placed them in boxes and added one small pack of cookies for the children to give to Santa. She liked the reversal of the trade. The parents did, too. Their kids were giving sugar to someone else for a change. Each child was handed a cookie just sitting on his lap. Volunteers would gently correct them if they showed any sign of biting into one. Occasionally, one of the kids would kick up a fuss, but the parents would intercede with "You don't want to be on Santa's list of naughty little boys and girls, do you?" That usually ended any kind of ruckus.

The afternoon slipped away, and the Matthewses were having an early dinner before they left for the tree-lighting ceremony. Maggie was having a hard time trying to keep quiet about what she had learned from her conversation with Kate.

"Kevin, what are you going to wear tonight?"

He gave his mother an odd look. "What? What am I wearing? Since when did you join the fashion police?"

"Just curious. I really like that cobalt-blue sweater you wore when we picked you up."

"It's not very Christmassy."

"You have the Christmas spirit. That's what matters." Maggie was thinking that Kevin would stand out in the crowd, and the sweater made his eyes appear even a deeper blue.

"Mom. Are you okay? You've always insisted on a holiday-themed sweater. I have several that I know will fit."

"I didn't have a chance to get them dry cleaned, and they've been sitting in the closet for six years. Wear the blue one. It looks so nice on you." Maggie tried to play down her out-of-the-ordinary stand on the holiday dress code.

"Fine. Whatever makes you happy, Mama."

Maggie had been pondering the nitty-gritty of the ceremony for almost twenty-four hours. It seemed obvious that Kate and Kevin were deliberately avoiding each other.

At the very least, there was some kind of tension between them. Getting them to speak to each other was going to take a bit of strategy.

"And I think that new cologne you were wearing the other night is very nice. Splash a little on. For me. I like it." She knew she was close to being over the top, but she wanted this to be a special, magical holiday.

"Mother, you're starting to sound like you've been dipping into the eggnog a little heavily." Kevin wasn't sure if he was close to being right. She was acting a little odd. Or maybe it was just the holiday spirit. He reminded himself that this was his first time home at Christmas in six years.

"Just a little sip." Maggie decided she'd rather have her son think she was tipsy instead of meddling in his love life, and she wasn't fibbing. She had tasted it with a tablespoon earlier.

"Well, that would explain a lot. Otherwise, I'd think you were trying out a new career as a personal stylist!"

"I read a lot of blogs." It was rather matter-of-fact. That small taste gave her a welcome sense of bravado.

"Holy smoke! Things really have changed around here. I wouldn't have thought you even knew what a blog was!"

"Never underestimate your mama! Now go get Wylie. Make sure he's wearing his holiday duds! Get a move on. We want to make sure we get a good spot." Maggie grabbed her purse and a shawl, chuckling to herself about the mischievous notions running through her mind.

"We always get a good spot." Kevin resigned himself to the fact that he would be carrying Wylie around, so he pulled out the doggie papoose. The first time his mother had insisted on this kind of holiday antic had met with a great deal of resistance. "The dog is the size of my head!" Kevin protested. "Oh, hush and make your mama happy," would be the response, so he could not object.

A few minutes later, they arrived in the parking lot of the church. Kevin glanced over to the area where he had helped the clumsy doctor the first day they met. At first he smiled, but then remembered Mr. Wimp-o in his stocking feet at Kate's. He felt a little prickle at the back of his neck and wondered if his thought about giving the female gender a second chance at love was still a good idea. He shook his head no. *Nope.*

"Kevin? You okay? You got a little red-faced for a second." Maggie was beginning to worry about whether he would be okay so that she could execute her plan.

"Yeah. I'm fine. Why do you ask?" Furrowing his brow, Kevin asked, "Are you sure *you're* okay? You've been acting a little strange."

"Don't be silly. I'm just excited that you're here, and it's Christmas, and we're at the tree lighting. Remember, dear, it's been six years! I'm over the moon!"

"I think it's that eggnog!" Kevin looped her arm through his and led the way to the courtyard.

It was an hour before the activities would start, and there were several dozen people milling about.

The festivities would proceed in layers of light. One of the parishioners had once worked as a lighting technician for Prince and knew how to program the lights to coincide with the music. And the tree had some very small twinkle lights just to give the area some atmosphere. The choir would assemble and begin its fifteen-minute recital before leading the entire group singing four or five familiar carols. With each song, another layer of lights would go on until they got to the finale, "Joy to the World," at which point the entire courtyard would explode like fireworks, with thousands of lights. It was a truly mystical experience regardless of one's religion. For a few moments in time, the atmosphere — and what seemed like the entire world — vibrated with good cheer, peace on earth, and goodwill toward all.

Maggie thought she caught sight of Kate and Emma. Kate looked particularly radiant. Her hair had a soft wave sans the headband, and she wasn't wearing those googly eyed glasses. Emma was adorable, with her soft white scarf, matching hat, mittens, and her pink cheeks surrounding a big smile. They were standing with a little boy about four years old, and two other adults who appeared to be his parents. Maggie recognized him as Jesse Myers, the little boy with the crushed leg. The stars were lining up in a way that even Maggie couldn't have orchestrated.

Earlier that morning, Kate had been given her patient duty roster and was assigned Jesse's case. His parents were visiting, and they were trying to explain to him that he wouldn't be able to go to the tree lighting. Jesse was deflated. All of them had hoped he would have been released by then.

She had scrutinized his chart, X-rays, recent MRI, and his progress with his physical therapy and the Trekker Gait Trainer.

She was cautiously optimistic that it might be possible to release him from the hospital.

"Hello, I'm Dr. Kate Stafford. I'm taking over Jesse's case. Do you have a moment?"

She had ushered them into her small office.

"I see he's made great progress, and I am wondering if you would be comfortable if we arranged for medical transport for him to attend the tree-lighting ceremony tonight? I will accompany him, and both of you, of course, but I need you to sign a waiver."

Both parents looked at each other with shock and curiosity. "We were told he needed to stay another two to three days," Mr. Myers offered.

"Yes, I know. It was primarily for physical therapy, but the weekend is coming up, and he wouldn't be doing much anyway. I think it would be a boost for his frame of mind. It's been shown that a patient who is happy and has a positive attitude heals faster than those who do not."

Tears started rolling down Mrs. Myers's face. "He's been here for almost two months. We made all the preparations in his room, installed a ramp, retrofitted the bathroom to accommodate his gait trainer. . . ."

Mr. Myers took his wife's hand and spoke

gently. "We are certainly ready to take him home if you think *he's* ready."

"Well, I do. I'll have his discharge papers drawn up and arrange for a medivan to take y'all to the tree lighting. The van will wait and take you home afterward. How does that sound?"

The couple hugged each other and practically tackled the petite doctor. "We don't know how to thank you! This will be the best homecoming ever!"

Kate ushered them out the door and busily filled out the forms and made the arrangements.

Kate smiled, thinking about her own family joining her and Emma for their first Christmas in the new house. She would have her personal homecoming, too.

Kate had brought a change of clothes, her contact lenses, and peeked in a small mirror to freshen up her makeup. She picked Emma up from day care and followed the medivan to the church courtyard, hoping her parents would have no difficulty finding the church.

When the entourage from the hospital arrived, the crowd parted like the Red Sea to allow Jesse in his gait trainer and his family a spot right in front. Brian was also there with his fiancée and Kate's family.

Kate's dad gave her the biggest bear hug he could manage without squeezing the air out of her. Her mom was beaming, kissing Emma all over her cherub-like face when Jesse yelled out, "Wylie! Wylie! We're over here!" Jesse was waving to Wylie in the papoose wrapped around Kevin.

Kate snapped back to reality. *No! Not him! Not here! Not now!* her brain was screaming silently.

Kevin was having a similar reaction until he saw Brian put his arm around a woman standing next to him and realized where he had first seen the man — before the debacle tree delivery. Brian was a nurse at the hospital. Approaching the brink of an awkward moment, Kevin stood tall and held out his hand. "Merry Christmas. I believe we met a few days ago when I was delivering a tree."

"Yes. Sorry I wasn't much help. This is Anita, my fiancée."

"*Very* pleased to meet you." Kevin was effusive as he turned to greet Kate.

She looked radiant. "Dr. Klutz, I presume?"

Kate broke out in a hoot. "Please. Not in front of my patient! And my family!"

"How do you do. I'm Kevin Matthews, and this here is Wylie. He thinks he's a therapy dog." A roar of laughter filled the air. "When did you stumble in?" Kevin could not hold back his teasing.

"Besides being a 'famous Christmas tree man,' are you also a comedian?" Kate volleyed back.

Kevin pulled out his biggest smile, exuding all the charm and warmth he could. "That's an occupation I hadn't considered, but perhaps we can discuss it over dinner some time?"

"I would like that very much. And I promise that I will try to stay vertical!"

Maggie was witnessing the camaraderie and pulled her husband over to the group.

"Hello, Maggie and Mr. Matthews!" Kate was beaming. "This is my mom, Eliza, and my dad, Henry."

As they exchanged greetings, Kate felt a hand on her elbow. "I don't want you to be falling down in front of your family," Kevin whispered in her ear.

His touch felt warm and secure, and she looked into his azure eyes. "I guess I'm going to need a therapy tree man to make sure I don't!"

Just before the music started, someone dressed in an elf costume made an announcement. "Before we begin, we want to dedicate this first song to those of you who have been away — Mr. Kevin Matthews; for those of you who are making your home here for the first time — Kate and Emma Stafford; and for those who are going home from the hospital, Jesse Myers!" After the cheers and applause died down, the choir began to sing "Home for the Holidays."

Kate and Kevin gazed into each other's eyes, as if to say, "best homecoming ever!" Emma tugged at her mother's coat and, pointing her finger at "the famous tree man," announced in a voice loud enough for everyone around them to hear, "Mommy? I don't think we need to go Daddy shopping after all."

■ ■ ■ ■

An Unexpected
Gift

KATE PEARCE

■ ■ ■ ■

CHAPTER ONE

Morgantown, Morgan Valley, California

After saying his good-byes, Billy Morgan came out of the feed store and checked that everything he'd loaded in the back of his truck was secure. It was one of the beautiful crisp, clear winter days he loved, with just enough bite in the air to catch at his breath and taste the incoming snow on his tongue. Even though the inclement weather would soon cut off Morgan Valley, winter had always been his favorite season.

He checked the list his mother Ruth had given him, and headed off to Main Street. The smell of coffee from Yvonne's French Café drifted across the road, and he inhaled appreciatively. When he'd completed his errands, he'd pop in and finish off his morning in style. The Morgantown shop owners had draped their old-fashioned storefronts and boardwalks in Christmas lights, which would come on at night, and make the old

145

gold rush town look enchanting.

The place hadn't changed much since he was a kid. He always remembered the day his grandfather had sat him down and told him how his great grandfather had come all the way from Wales during the California gold rush, and ended up owning a livery stable and saloon in the new settlement before buying himself a ranch on the profits. Having a whole town named after your family was something special, and Billy had sworn to his grandfather that he'd never let his family down.

He grimaced as he went into the post office. He'd sure messed that up. Twenty-three years ago the disappearance of his wife and baby daughter had almost destroyed him, and sent a tremor worthy of an earthquake through the lives of his four sons and his mother, Ruth. It had taken him twenty years to come home, and he was still working at being forgiven.

He sorted out the mail noticing none of it was actually for him, but that his mother had received a whole bunch of Christmas cards. A couple of letters had stuck together, and when he separated them out he discovered one was addressed to his old friend Bella Williams at the Red Dragon Bar.

Being close to the bar, which sat on the

corner of Main and Morgan, he walked around into the parking lot and approached the back entrance. The door was open, and Bella and some guy were standing on the threshold. Something about the young guy's stance set everything protective in Billy to attention. He altered his angle of approach and came up behind the man.

"Axel, I asked you to leave." Bella was speaking, her voice calm.

"And I told you to give me my wages or I'll take them myself."

"Jay will be back any second now." Bella raised her chin. She wasn't a tall woman, but after running a bar for twenty-five years she wasn't easily intimidated. "Do you really want to take on a retired Navy SEAL?"

"He's not coming, Bella," Axel said. "I saw him heading out on the county road toward Bridgeport." Axel took a step closer, invading Bella's personal space. "Give me my damned money, bitch!"

Billy gently cleared his throat. "Hey, you."

Axel swung around, his hands curling into fists. "What the hell do you want?"

"I want you to leave." Billy held up his cell. "I just sent a text to Nate Turner and he's coming right now, so maybe you'd better stop menacing women and take a hike."

"Like you'd be able to stop me," Axel

sneered.

Billy stepped closer and held the young fool's gaze. "Do you really want to find out if that's true?"

Something in Billy's eyes made Axel pause, which was just as well because Billy had survived a year in prison and was nobody's pushover.

A siren blared on Main Street, and with one last disgusted snarl, Axel ran off into the parking lot, got on his motorbike, and roared away.

Billy instantly went over to Bella. "Are you okay?"

She let out her breath and pressed her hand to her heart before reaching for him. "Thank goodness you came along, Billy. I was getting scared."

"You didn't look it." Billy wrapped an arm around his old school friend and she leaned into him, her whole body trembling. "You'll be okay. It's just the shock."

"I know." She took a deep, shaky breath. "There was something in his eyes that frightened me. Do you think he's on drugs or something?"

"Probably." Billy looked up as Nate Turner, the local sheriff, pulled into the parking lot. "Do you want to talk to Nate, or shall I do it?"

"Why don't you both come inside my kitchen and we can talk there?" Bella suggested. "It's cold out here."

Billy hadn't noticed the chill, but he was used to working outside in all weathers and had grown up on the ranch herding cattle and riding horses. After being incarcerated for a year, he'd yearned for open spaces, and never felt happier than when he was out in the fresh air.

"You go on in." Billy patted her shoulder. "I'll bring Nate."

He waited as Nate got out of his truck and put on his official hat before strolling over to greet him. Nate had been to school with his sons, and was another local boy.

"Hey, Mr. Morgan. What's up?" Nate asked.

"Some guy was threatening Bella Williams."

Nate frowned. "I assume Jay isn't around?"

"If he was, you'd probably be investigating a murder," Billy said dryly. "No one would be stupid enough to misbehave with the mother of a retired Navy SEAL if they knew he was on the premises."

"So it was probably a good thing you were around instead." Nate gestured at the open door. "Is Mrs. Williams in there? Is she okay?"

"Yeah, she's a bit shaken up, but no harm done. She said for us both to come in."

Billy went through the back door and into the large kitchen where Bella dealt with all the culinary needs of the Red Dragon Bar. She was sitting at the kitchen table with a cafetière of coffee and three mugs.

"Morning, Mrs. Williams." Nate touched his hat. "Is it okay if I come in?"

"Of course, take a seat, Nate." Bella smiled, but still looked a little upset. "Did Billy tell you what happened?"

Nate sat at the table and took out his notebook. "He gave me the basics, but I'd like to get your take on it. Did you know the guy who was harassing you?"

"Yes, he's been working here as my assistant for the past three months."

"Great. So you have his name and social security?"

"His name is Axel Jordan. He came with good references from a San Francisco hotel, but I did notice he'd moved around a lot." Bella sighed. "Everything was going okay until last Friday when he didn't turn up on time. It's our busiest day and we were really shorthanded. When he did arrive, he was sullen, uncooperative, and kept messing up the orders."

Bella sipped her coffee and cradled the mug in her hands, her brown gaze distant. "At first I thought he was sickening for something, but it was more than that. Eventually, Jay got mad and told him to go home and only come back when he was willing to put in a day's work for a day's wages."

"And he turned up today?" Nate asked.

"Yes, after three days of nothing and me having to do everything myself." Bella grimaced. "I tried texting him and calling, but he didn't bother to pick up. Today he came seeking his wages for last week. I told him that Jay was the only one who can authorize those payments. He didn't believe me."

"Which is where I came in," Billy said. "He was demanding his wages and threatening to take them if Bella didn't cooperate."

"Do you have his address here?" Nate asked. "I'll go and pay him a visit."

"He rents a room over Ted Baker's garage," Bella said.

Nate got to his feet. "Then if you don't mind, I'll go over there and see if I can head him off at the pass. I'll come back for your full statement later this afternoon."

"Go ahead. I'll be fine." Bella waved him

151

on. "Thanks for coming so quickly."

"Thank Billy," Nate said, smiling at her. "He's the one who texted me."

Billy waited until Nate shut the door behind him, and turned back to Bella. "Are you sure you're okay? Would you like me to call Jay?"

"No, I don't want to worry him. He's gone to an appointment at the VA and I would hate for him to miss it."

"You still look a bit shaken up," Billy said slowly.

"It's not the first time this has happened, but it's never pleasant." She let out a long breath. "Thank you for being there. I really appreciate it."

"You're welcome." He dug out the letter he'd found mixed in with his mail. "I was just coming to deliver this. It was in the wrong box."

She picked up the letter and laughed. "This must be the first time the IRS has ever done something right."

"Fancy that." He joined in her laughter and noticed that she was starting to look a lot better. He hated to bring her back on topic, but he had no choice.

"I'm worried that you're all alone here if Axel comes back."

Bella patted his hand. "I'm not entirely

helpless, Billy." Her smile was both charming and wicked. "I know how to shoot a gun. Jay taught me."

"I bet you do, but still . . ." Billy's gaze scanned the kitchen. "What time are you supposed to start serving lunch today?"

"In about two hours." Bella pointed at the walk-in refrigerator. "I prep a lot of stuff so it's ready to go when needed."

"I could stay," Billy said impulsively. "And help out."

"You?" Now she was definitely smiling at him. "Don't you have a huge dude ranch to run or something?"

"Not really," Billy confessed. "My boys seem to have that in hand. I suspect I'd be more useful right here. I'm a trained chef."

"You *are*?" Bella blinked at him. "Since when?"

"When I decided to stop drinking and get a job, the only place that would hire me on was as a dishwasher in a restaurant. I stuck it out for about two years, and somehow ended up moving on to more useful things like washing and prepping the fruit and veg. Eventually, I took classes at night school and earned my stripes."

Now Bella was looking at him as if she'd never seen him before. "That's amazing."

He literally squirmed in his seat. "Not

really. I'd already messed up so badly that there wasn't anywhere else to go but up."

"A lot of people never work that out." She sat back and studied him. "Can you man a grill?"

"With one hand tied behind my back." He held her gaze. "I'll check in with Mom, but I don't think anyone will miss me if I'm not up at the ranch."

She reached over and shook his hand. "Okay then, you're hired."

Bella snuck another glance at Billy Morgan as he put on an apron and went to wash his hands in the big industrial-sized, stainless steel sink. He wore the Morgantown uniform of jeans, a plaid shirt, cowboy boots, and a hat. Now he'd taken off his Stetson and looked quite different. His hair was streaked with silver, as was his short beard.

She'd known him since they were in kindergarten together, which was more than forty years ago. He'd gone on to marry a girl from out of town and had five kids whereas she'd married a local boy and only had Jay before her husband died in a car accident. Both of them were widowers now, and had resumed their friendship when Billy had sweet-talked her into using organic Morgan Ranch beef in her patties and other dishes she created for the bar.

"Okay," he said as he came toward her, his vivid blue gaze meeting hers. "Where do you want me to start?"

For a moment, she couldn't think what to say. After the shock of the morning, seeing him in her kitchen was so unexpected her brain wasn't functioning properly.

"How about I show you where everything is?" Bella suggested. "I know you won't remember it all, but some of it will stick."

He laughed, displaying his nice white teeth and the fine lines around his eyes. "I dunno, Bella. At my age remembering my name is a bit of a challenge."

"You're not that old," she scoffed.

"I was twenty-one when Chase was born, and he insists he's thirty-two now, so that makes me pretty damn old."

"You're a year older than me, and I'm not old," Bella told him firmly. "You've still got all your own hair, your teeth, and no beer belly, so you're doing good."

"You too." His blue eyes twinkled back at her. "Unless that's a wig."

Bella patted her dark hair, which was drawn into a bun on the top of her head. "It's all mine. I can promise you that."

"Yeah?" He smoothed a hand through his own hair. "Do I need one of those stupid

155

hairnets?"

"I think you'll be okay." His hair was still very thick, but he kept it quite short. "Unless you'd like one. I could do with a laugh."

In fact, just being with him was calming her down and making her feel better. He had a soothing effect on everyone, which, considering his history, was somewhat surprising. He definitely wasn't the boy she'd known, but unlike some of the townsfolk who whispered about his past, she wasn't afraid of him. She'd never believed he'd murdered his wife and baby in cold blood, and she'd been proven right.

"Let's start with the pantry." Bella led him into the walk-in storage cupboard. "I used to make all the buns and bread, but thank goodness Yvonne does it for me now." She pointed at the freezer space beyond. "The patties, steaks, and poultry start off in there, and depending on the health and safety requirements, either thaw in the refrigerators or come directly out of there."

"Got it." Billy was right at her shoulder.

Despite removing his cowboy gear, he still smelled of leather, horses, and the outdoors. A day in her hot, steamy kitchen dispatching orders would probably change that. . . . Sometimes she thought she'd never get the smell of fried food out of her pores.

"Where do you keep your eggs?" Billy asked.

"Some of the organic eggs are out on the counter and others, like the omelet mixes and egg-white-only ones, are in the refrigerator. I make them up earlier and put them in big plastic jugs so they are easier to pour."

"Good thinking." Billy leaned against the countertop and surveyed the huge metal grill plate and industrial-sized extractor fan over it. "I assume most of your food is grilled or fried?"

"Correct. What can I say? It's a bar." She shrugged. "We keep the menu quite simple because most people around here don't like change. Jay made me get a bit more adventurous, and I'm enjoying supplying organic and locally produced meals. Apart from the thinking up new and seasonal recipe ideas, it's kind of fun."

"I worked in a great organic restaurant in San Francisco," Billy said. "I'll have to see if I can remember any of their recipes for you."

"That would be awesome." She closed the door into the pantry. "Let me show you the rest of the kitchen and how the orders come up and are sent out."

"Mom?"

Jay Williams limped into the kitchen and pulled up short when he saw Billy washing pans in the sink. His sharp, wary gaze rapidly assessed the situation for any sign of a threat, reminding Billy of his son Blue, who was also retired military.

"Hi, Jay. Your mom was a bit shorthanded today, so I offered to help out."

"That was good of you, Mr. Morgan." Jay sat down at the table. "I didn't know you could cook."

"I get by." Billy shrugged. "It wasn't too busy so we managed just fine."

Bella backed into the kitchen from the bar side of the property and Billy went around to take the tray from her.

"I've got it, Bella. Jay's back, by the way."

Her smile as she turned and saw her son was so glorious it made Billy blink. She loved Jay the same way he loved his boys, but without the complications. It was a pleasure to see.

"Jay! How did it go?"

He shrugged his wide shoulders. "Okay, I think. They don't want to see me for six months, so that's progress."

He'd been invalided out of the Navy SEALS after being blown up by an incendiary device. From what Billy had been told, he'd endured a long and arduous return to fitness.

"That's great!" Bella said. "Did you tell Erin?"

"Yeah, I called her on the way back. She'll be here tomorrow. She had to go back and tell her parents the news." Jay got to his feet. "If you're okay with it, I'm going to take a nap before we open up for the evening."

Bella nodded. "I was just clearing the last of the tables, so we're almost good to go." She paused and tucked a strand of her dark hair behind her ear. "Billy offered to help out today, and he's been awesome."

"That's great." Jay turned to Billy. "Thanks. Let me know if you'd like to make the job permanent, okay?"

Bella laughed. "As if Billy doesn't have enough to do, what with running that huge ranch up there."

"No harm in asking." Jay grinned at his mother and kissed her cheek. "I'll be down as soon as I wake up. Nancy knows how to set up, so don't go and do it all yourself."

Jay left and Bella's smile faded.

"Are you okay?" Billy asked.

She picked up a dish towel and started drying one of the bowls he'd washed. "I try not to be *that mother,* you know? But I wish he were a bit more forthcoming about how

159

he's doing. I hope he tells Erin these things."

"It's hard when your kids start confiding in other people, isn't it?" Billy washed another plate.

"Yes," Bella sighed. "You get so used to soothing their hurts and telling them that everything is going to be all right that when they no longer need that from you, it feels weird."

"I think they still need to hear it occasionally," Billy said. "Even when they think they don't."

"The first year after Jay got injured and came out of the rehab hospital, he was so down, and in so much pain, that I really used to worry he wasn't going to make it," Bella confessed. "Every morning I'd go into his bedroom and just be grateful that he was still alive, and talking — even if he *was* telling me to get out and leave him alone."

"It's hard to see our kids suffer like that." Billy rinsed another plate.

"I think that's why I try not to be too intrusive now." Bella looked over at him. "I'm scared to push him away again even though he's feeling so much better."

"I know just how you feel," Billy said. "I walked out on my boys when they were kids and left them with their grandmother. I got lost in a bottle because I blamed myself for losing Annie and baby Rachel. I lost *myself*. And now I'm back, I worry about giving them advice sometimes because what the heck do I know? Why should they listen to a guy who wasn't there for them?"

Bella patted his cheek. "But at least you came back. That was a brave thing to do."

"I don't know about that." He smiled down at her. "It just seemed to happen."

Bella snorted. "With Ruth Morgan involved, I doubt that. Your mother is a magician. She got all her family back to the ranch and saved it from being sold off."

"Yeah, she is incredible." Billy grinned. "Scary sometimes, but still remarkable. And we were talking about you and Jay, so how come I ended up monopolizing the conversation?"

Bella shrugged. "Because I'd said everything I needed to say, and was interested in what you had to say? You know, one of those conversation things that people have?"

"Oh yeah, one of those give and take things, right?" He let out the water in the sink and quickly rinsed off the rest of the silverware and plates so that he could stack them in the industrial-sized dishwasher. "In my family it comes down to who shouts the loudest, and Blue usually wins that game."

"Jay talks to Blue."

"Which is probably good for both of them." Billy closed the dishwasher and wiped his hands on his apron. "None of us can really understand what it must be like to be in a war." He checked his watch. "Are you going to tell Jay about what happened with Axel?"

Bella made a face. "I suppose I'll have to."

"I think it would be wise," Billy agreed. "Aren't he and Erin moving into a new house up the street after they get married?"

"What's that got to do with it?"

"Won't you be here on your own?" Billy held her gaze. "What if Axel decides to come back and try and break in?"

She shrugged. "Jay's got this place wired up like a bank vault. Nothing can get in."

"Bella . . ." Billy put his hand on her shoulder and she covered it with her own.

"It's okay, *really.* I'll tell him what happened when he comes down, and if he wants to go all Navy SEAL on the guy, it's on you."

"Nate won't let him do that." Billy grinned. "Well, I hope he won't. Do you need help tonight?"

"I think I'm good, but thanks for offering." She went on tiptoe and planted a kiss on his lips. "Thanks so much for everything you've done today. I can't tell you how

162

much I appreciate it."

"You're welcome." He kept his hand on her shoulder. "If you can't get anyone to help out, please call me."

"Like you have time to help me everyday," she gently mocked him.

"I meant what I said earlier. The boys are running the ranch really well, Mom cooks for the family, and there's a chef for the guest dining room. I struggle to find enough to do everyday."

"I think you underestimate yourself." She eased away from him and he immediately missed her presence. "Thanks again, and I promise I'll tell Jay what happened before Nate gets around to it."

Aware that he was being dismissed, and still not quite happy about it, Billy gathered up his belongings and left the bar. As he walked back toward his truck, he rubbed his finger against his lips where Bella's kiss lingered. He couldn't remember the last time a simple kiss had given him such pleasure or made him feel so special.

He'd loved Annie and had never looked at another woman while she'd been with him. After her disappearance, when the guilt and the drink had drowned him, he'd had the odd hookup, but nothing measured up to the sweetness of that first kiss. Billy fished out his truck keys and stared blindly at the parking lot. Until now. He'd wanted to slip his arm around Bella's waist and kiss her back. . . .

With a snort, Billy got into his truck. The sweetness and nostalgia of Christmas were obviously getting to him. Bella was his friend. She'd meant nothing more than a thank-you, and he was a fool to think anything else.

CHAPTER TWO

"I'm not happy about this," Jay muttered as he stared at Bella, arms crossed over his muscled chest.

The evening rush had ended and Bella finally had time to tell him what had happened with Axel. To no one's surprise, Jay wasn't happy.

"What would you have done if Billy Morgan hadn't turned up?" Jay asked.

Bella raised an eyebrow. "I'm not a fool, or a damsel in distress, young man. I *can* take care of myself."

"I *know* that." Jay leaned over to pat her shoulder. "I've seen you knock out a drunk with one of your cast iron pans. But this guy was threatening you in broad daylight. That sucks."

"Nate knows all about it, and he'll swing by every so often to make sure I'm okay," Bella reminded him.

"And that's another thing. Why didn't

Nate find this bastard and lock him up already?" Jay demanded.

"Because Axel wasn't at his apartment," Bella explained again. "Nate will keep checking there as well."

"I don't like it," Jay said stubbornly. "This is even more reason why you should move down the street to our new house. Erin wouldn't mind at all."

"Erin is a saint to put up with you. The last thing she needs is your mother moving in as well."

"Hey, she loves you," Jay protested.

"I know she does, and I love her right back, but you two need some privacy right now. You just got married." She mock frowned at him. "In Vegas, without your mother."

Jay groaned. "Don't bring that up right now. I know, we *suck,* okay? I only agreed to it because Erin's parents were behaving like giant assholes about having this massive society wedding, and neither of us wanted that."

"It's okay, I know why you did it." Bella had a plan of her own to execute over Christmas to make sure the family got to celebrate the wedding, but she wasn't giving away anything yet. "I still don't want to live in your new house."

166

"Mom . . ."

"Look, I'll make sure I lock the doors when I'm alone here — which doesn't happen very often anyway, and I'll keep my phone with me. If I see Axel or his Harley anywhere near here, I'll call Nate."

"Call me," Jay stated.

"No, because I don't want you arrested for murder," Bella countered.

Jay gave a reluctant grin. "You know me too well."

Bella rose and kissed his forehead. "Now, how about you go on home? Erin will be wondering what's happened to you."

"Erin's fast asleep." Jay winked. "She's still dealing with jet lag, but I might think of a few ways to wake her up."

Bella stuck her fingers in her ears. "I can't hear you. La la la!"

Jay was still laughing as she practically pushed him out the door and locked it securely behind him. The fact that her son was enjoying his sex life was great, but not something she *really* needed to hear about.

Bella walked through the silent bar checking and setting the alarms, and then went up the stairs to the large apartment above the bar. What would it be like to have sex with someone again? As she brushed her teeth, she paused to consider the unexpected question that had popped into her head.

She looked okay for her age; she was definitely plump and bosomy, but that never seemed to worry most men. After Ron had died, she'd had the occasional boyfriend, but only rarely had such a relationship led to sex. She missed it. She'd been good at it.

Chuckling at her own boast, Bella made her way into her bedroom. Tomorrow she was going to call Billy Morgan and ask his advice about something. . . .

Not about sex — although when she'd kissed him, she'd got an unexpected kick out of his reaction — but about hosting an event up at the ranch. That the thought of seeing him again made her heart race was odd, but still thrilling. She lay down on her bed and stared up at the ceiling. How would his beard feel under her hand? How would it feel against her *skin*?

With a groan, Bella turned on her side and clicked off the light. She had enough to worry about without involving her old friend Billy Morgan in her romantic fantasies. Just because he'd helped out, didn't mean he was her white knight. Although he did look fantastic on a horse . . .

Billy finished mucking out the stall and

wiped his brow. It was weird how his four sons were so good at organizing things on the dude ranch, but often forgot to do the basics. . . . Not that he minded much. He enjoyed spending time with the horses, and was at peace just being around them. He sometimes felt as if he no longer had a stake in the old place, but it was in his blood, and he wasn't planning on walking away any time soon.

He'd offered to take on the cooking for the dude ranch guests, but no one had wanted him to do that. He'd told Ruth to let him know if she needed his help in her kitchen, but she hardly ever let him assist her. He liked to cook, and had enjoyed working in Bella's kitchen more than he had anticipated. But that might have been the company. . . .

"Billy?"

As if he'd conjured her from his thoughts, Bella Williams stood in the middle of his yard smiling at him. Her car was parked close to the ranch house. Today she wore jeans, red cowboy boots, and a thick pink fleece that made her skin glow. He could hardly believe she'd turned fifty. She looked just like the girl he'd known at school.

"Hey!" He walked over to her and held up his hands. "I've been mucking out the

169

stalls so I won't shake your hand just yet. Would you like to come up to the house?"

"I'd love to." She pushed her sunglasses back on top of her head where her long hair was piled up in a messy bun.

He had no idea why she'd appeared or wanted to speak to him, but he wasn't complaining. He led the way into the house through the screen door and heel and toed his boots off in the mudroom.

"Does this visit require you sit in the parlor or the kitchen?" Billy asked Bella, who was unzipping her fleece.

"Kitchen's fine with me. It's my natural habitat."

He walked her through to the kitchen and pulled out a chair for her. "I'll be back in a minute; make yourself at home. Ruth's out looking at the pigs with Roy. I've never met a ranch foreman who loves his pigs more than his horses before."

When he returned, Bella was sitting at the kitchen table rummaging in her large purse. She looked up as he entered and took out her phone.

He smiled at her. "I'm all clean now so we can shake hands."

"No kisses today?" she joked.

"I'm good either way." He went over to the ancient refrigerator. "Would you like iced tea or something warmer?"

"Coffee if you have it." She mock shivered. "It's getting cold out there."

"Yeah, the Sierra passes are closing up and won't be open until late spring."

He poured them both a mug of coffee from the pot, gathered up some cream, and brought everything over to the table.

"So what can I do for you today?" Billy asked as she stirred cream into her coffee. "Do you need my help in the bar?"

She made a face. "I'm still shorthanded if that's what you mean, but I'm not here to offer you a job." She hesitated. "I didn't want to say anything the other day until I cleared it with Jay, but he and Erin got married last month."

Billy blinked at her. "Really? That's great, isn't it?"

"Well, yes and no, seeing as they did it in Vegas without anyone being present."

He registered the hurt behind her smile and instinctively reached over to take her hand. "That's kind of sucky."

She sighed. "I know why they did it like that, and Jay did FaceTime me just before the ceremony so I could kind of be there with them while they said their vows, but it wasn't the same."

"I wouldn't be very happy if any of my

kids did that to me either," Billy confessed. "I'd be happy for *them,* and I'd never say a word, but inside? I'd probably feel hurt as well."

She squeezed his fingers. "Thanks for understanding. Jay knows I'm hurt, and he's trying to make it up to me, and I'm trying to tell him it doesn't matter, because it really doesn't. . . ."

"But it does." Billy nodded. "It's okay. I get it."

"So I thought maybe the best way to get it out in the open was to have a party for them," Bella continued. "I'd invite Erin's parents and family, and everyone here, and then we could all enjoy *that* and move on."

Billy stared at her for a long moment. "I think that's a great idea."

"You do?" Her brilliant smile made him catch his breath. "Then that's what I need to talk to you about. I don't want to hold it in the bar because Erin's parents aren't that kind of people, but I thought they'd love it up here."

"When were you thinking about doing this?" Billy asked.

"In the next couple of weeks?" She stared at him hopefully. "Or do you shut everything down between Christmas and New Year?"

"We'll be here, but we're no longer taking

guests over the holidays because it's too much work."

"Oh, then never mind." She bit her lip. "Maybe I can find another venue."

"Don't do that yet," Billy suggested. "I'll talk to Ruth and Chase and see what we can do. How many guests are you planning on inviting?"

"To stay over? Only Erin's family. Everyone else is local. I doubt it will be above fifty in total."

"So it won't be that much work," Billy mused almost to himself. "Gustav, the guest chef, is off to Switzerland for a month, which means I'd have to do the cooking."

"We could do that together." She raised their joined hands, kissed his knuckles, and laughed. "Now I'm getting ahead of myself."

"Be my guest," Billy said. "I'll talk to Chase and Ruth, and get back to you."

Confident that Billy would work something out, Bella gave him her cell phone. "Can you put your number in there for me, please?"

"Sure. Maria taught me how to text last year, and now there's no stopping me." He winked at her. "Who knew teenagers could be so useful?"

She stood up, and he walked her back to the mudroom so she could collect her boots and fleece.

"Is it weird having a granddaughter already?" Bella asked impulsively.

"It was something of a surprise to all of us," Billy acknowledged. "Blue most of all. He had no idea he'd become a father at such a young age, but once he found out, he did the right thing and stuck by his responsibilities. We all love Maria very much."

Bella gazed up at him. In the confines of the mudroom they were very close, and his eyes were very blue. "That's because you brought him up right."

His smile disappeared. "Not me. I wandered off in a drunken haze of grief, remember? Everything Blue became is down to Ruth."

She cupped his jaw, amazed at how soft his beard was under her hand. "I think you're undervaluing yourself here."

"Nope, I'm really not."

"Yeah, you are." Her thumb drifted to the corner of his mouth. There was a small scar on his lip. She couldn't look away from his eyes. . . .

Behind her someone cleared their throat, and they jumped apart like guilty teenagers.

"Hey, Dad, I just wanted to run some stock numbers by you, but I can come back later if you're busy." Chase Morgan stood there, his interested gaze on his father. "Is everything okay?"

Bella grabbed her fleece. She wasn't usually the kind of person who got flustered, but she was definitely blushing. "I was just going. Thanks for the coffee, Billy, and let me know about that other matter. There's no need to come out with me."

"Bella . . ."

Ignoring Billy's outstretched hand, she bolted out the back door, ran down the steps, and got into her car. She pressed one hand to her hot cheek as she started the engine, and carefully backed out. She'd wanted to kiss him again. *Would* have kissed him if Chase Morgan hadn't interrupted them.

After checking the time, Bella drove back to town and parked up close to the village store. Her best friend, Maureen, who owned and operated the shop, looked up as she came through the door.

"Hey! I wasn't expecting to see you until tomorrow at knitting club."

Bella glanced around the store, noting there was someone working at the checkout, and turned back to Maureen. "Have you got a minute?"

"Sure! What's up?" Maureen walked her through into the private part of the store. "You look kind of flustered."

Bella dumped her purse on the table and rushed over to check herself out in the mirror. She scrubbed at both her cheeks.

"Maybe it's hormonal? Yes! That's got to be it! Maybe I'm just all confused right now."

"You're not the only one who's confused." Maureen regarded her warily. "What's going on?"

Bella collapsed beside her old friend on the couch. "I wanted to kiss Billy Morgan."

"So?"

"That's all you've got?" Bella asked.

"Well, he's a good-looking guy, he's a widower, and his son is a multimillionaire. What's not to like?"

"But *I'm* not looking for a man!" Bella said. "I've never wanted to kiss someone like that before."

"Not even your husband?" Maureen looked mildly curious now.

"Of course I wanted to kiss *him,* but this is different!"

"Why?" Maureen shrugged. "He's a man, you're a woman. It's only natural."

"Not for me," Bella said fervently. "What am I going to do?"

Maureen just looked at her as if she was nuts, but maybe she was nuts. "It seems you have two choices here."

"Okay."

"You can kiss Billy Morgan, or you can not kiss him."

"That's not really helping, Maureen," Bella growled. "He's my friend, he lives here, and I can't spend the rest of my life avoiding him if everything goes wrong."

Maureen shrugged. "Then don't avoid him."

"But what if I want to kiss him *again*?"

"You think you'll want to do that?"

"Yes." Bella nodded.

"Then maybe you should listen to your gut and kiss him until you no longer want to kiss him, and have fun with it."

"Fun?" Bella practically levitated off the couch. Sometimes she could see where Nancy, Maureen's daughter, got her outspokenness from. "I don't do fun, and you know it. I was always the sensible one while you and Beth Miller were being crazy. I drove you home, let you crash at my house, mopped up your tears."

Maureen grinned at her. "So maybe this is your time to cut loose and be the wild and crazy one?"

"I'm over fifty!" Bella protested.

"And so is Billy, which means it's all quite legal," Maureen pointed out.

Bella sank back on the couch. "He might not want to be kissed either."

"Oh, come off it. You know when a man wants to kiss you. Did he run away screaming?"

"No, he seemed quite interested in the idea."

Maureen patted her shoulder. "Look, I have to get back, but how about you talk it through with Billy? You know that thing we always tell our kids to do when they're having issues with a relationship?"

"Won't he think that's terribly presumptuous?" Bella asked.

"Honey, you're over fifty. Half your life has already been lived, and time is rapidly running out. How about you forget about your manners, and just have an honest conversation with the guy?"

Bella rose from the couch and collected her purse. "I suppose you've got a point, but reminding me of my mortality seems a bit heavy handed."

"Maybe it's the only way to get through to you." Maureen poked her in the ribs. "Now, get along with you, and make sure you call and tell me all the filthy details if you do get it on with that fine figure of a man."

"Glad you're okay with what I'm suggesting." Chase closed his laptop and smiled at
Billy. "I'm great with company stocks, but
not so good with the bovine version."

Billy shrugged. "You could've asked Roy
or Ruth. They are way more knowledgeable
than I am."

"But it's your ranch," Chase pointed out.

"You know how I feel about that, son.
Sure, it's legally in my name, but Ruth is
the heart of this place, and then it'll be
handed down to you guys."

Chase frowned. "You underestimate yourself. You grew up here, you're a Morgan,
and the land is in your blood."

"And I betrayed and almost destroyed that
legacy," Billy reminded his son. "I left Ruth
bringing up my kids, and walked away."

"But you came back. That took some
guts."

"Yeah." Billy smiled at Chase. "It did. I
wasn't sure if you'd let me stay."

He remembered those first few weeks
when his two oldest sons had viewed him
with suspicion in Chase's case, and outright
hostility in Blue's. He'd deserved it, but it
had still been hard. The moment he'd
stepped foot back on the ranch, he'd found

his purpose, and his family again. The fact that they'd let him stay meant the world to him.

"It's your ranch," Chase stated again. He wasn't one to beat around the bush. "Ruth likes to threaten us all with changing her will, but now that you are back, the place, *and* its future, are in your hands."

"And you're all doing a fantastic job of making sure the ranch survives well into the twenty-first century," Billy replied, keen to change the subject. "Now, is there anything else you need to talk to me about, or can I ask *you* something?"

"I'm done." Chase checked his cell phone. "What's up?"

Billy explained what Bella had suggested, and Chase listened intently.

"I don't have a problem with it. Jay's practically family, but run it by Ruth as well."

"I intend to." Billy nodded and went to rise.

"So what's going on with you and Bella?" Chase asked, his gaze still on his cell.

"Nothing at all, why?" Billy was glad he had a beard because he was fairly certain he was blushing.

"Didn't look like nothing," Chase said, a hint of amusement in his voice. "Neither of

180

you even noticed I was there until I practically tapped you on the shoulder."

"That's because I'm old and deaf," Billy countered.

"Who's old and deaf?" Ruth came into the kitchen and stared at Billy and her grandson, one eyebrow raised. "I hope you're not talking about me."

"Never." Chase traced a cross over his heart. "I was talking about Dad getting up close and personal with Bella Williams in our mudroom." He stood up, tucked his laptop under his arm, and winked at Billy. "Have a great day!"

Billy turned to Ruth, who was watching him in some surprise, and tried to look unconcerned.

"I have no idea what he's talking about. The mudroom is pretty small, and we were just standing close together."

"If Chase noticed something was up, then there must have been something going on," Ruth observed. "He's usually oblivious."

"We were just talking." Billy realized he sounded as lame as a teenager now. "She came up here to ask whether we'd be able to host a party to celebrate Jay and Erin getting married."

Ruth got herself some coffee and put on her apron. "When is the wedding?"

"It's already happened. They got married in Vegas last month. Bella wants to host a celebration party here at our ranch in the next couple of weeks. I explained that we were shut down for guests over Christmas, but I thought I'd sound you and Chase out about the possibility of doing it anyway."

"What did Chase say?" Ruth sat down at the table, her blue gaze fixed on Billy's face.

Billy shrugged. "He was fine about the idea."

"How big is this party going to be?"

"Just Erin and Jay's family, and a few locals. You'd only need to offer accommodation if the Hayes family can't put guests up at the hotel."

"Gustav's on vacation."

"So I'll take over the kitchen." Billy held Ruth's gaze. "You won't have to do a thing."

Ruth snorted. "Like I'd ever sit back and let that happen."

"You could, you know," Billy encouraged her.

"Sit back?" Ruth smiled at him. "And then what? Stay on the couch and watch TV all day? I'll rest when I'm dead." She sipped her coffee. "I have no objection to Bella hosting a party for her only son and his bride at our ranch."

"Great. I'll give her a call, and then we

can hash out the details." Billy smiled at his mother. "Thanks so much."

"Bella didn't mention she had been to Vegas for the wedding when I saw her at church last week," Ruth murmured.

"That's because she didn't know there was going to be a wedding until it was just about to happen," Billy said. "And then she only got to watch it on a screen."

"If anyone in my immediate family did that to me, I wouldn't be very happy at all," Ruth observed.

"Bella was quite upset, but she doesn't want Jay to know that. It wasn't about her. From what she said, it had something to do with Erin's family being overprotective, and wanting to take charge of the arrangements."

"So you *have* been exchanging confidences with Bella Williams after all." Ruth chuckled. "Chase was right." She waved a hand at Billy. "Don't worry. I'm not going to say anything; you're a grown man who can take care of himself."

"Exactly." Billy blew his mother a kiss. "Not that there is anything for you to worry about anyway."

"Get along with you. I'm not worried." Ruth winked at him. "I'm enjoying the show."

CHAPTER THREE

Bella wiped a hand across her brow and studied the mountain of plates, pots, pans, and silverware she'd left to pile up while she made sure every diner got fed. She'd originally had one of her servers to help out in the kitchen, but they'd had an unexpected rush of tourists, and she'd had to send him back out front. To make sure she got the food out, she'd decided not to clean up as she went, which was her normal practice.

The thought of doing it all over again in the evening was almost making her weep.

A knock at the back door had her spinning around to see Billy Morgan peering through the glass. She let him in and walked back into the kitchen proper as he took in the chaos.

"Are you okay, Bella?" Billy asked.

She let out her breath as he came toward her. "Barely."

"So I can see." He took off his thick denim

jacket and hung it on the back of the door. "I'll start loading the dishwasher."

With a calm efficiency that startled her, he managed to help her bring order to her kitchen in a remarkably short period. By the time the dishwasher was humming and the pots were put back in their places, she'd regained her composure and they were working happily alongside each other.

"What do you need to prep for tonight?" Billy asked as he cleaned down her work surfaces.

She waved a hand at the refrigerator. "Just fruit and veg mainly. The bread's here, the patties are made, and everything else comes out of the freezer."

"So the same as we did the other day?"

"Yes, exactly," she said, smiling at him. "But I'm good now, *really.* Jay will be in soon. He just had to take Erin to pick up her new car in Bridgeport."

Billy put his hands on her shoulders. "How about we do this? You go upstairs, get yourself some lunch, and I'll come find you when Jay gets here?"

"I'm fine," Bella immediately protested.

"Have you eaten anything substantial today?" His blue gaze captured her attention.

"Not really," she admitted.

"Then go and fix yourself something." He gently rocked her back and forth. "Take half an hour. I promise I won't ruin your business in that time."

Despite her tiredness, he'd made her smile, and she really was feeling a bit wobbly.

"Okay, half an hour, and then I'll be down again."

"Great." He turned her to face the exit. "Off you go."

At the door she looked over her shoulder. "Are you sure you know where — ?"

"Whatever it is, I'll find it." He pointed his finger at her. "Go."

Bella climbed the stairs to her apartment and let out a relieved sigh as she closed the door. That was possibly the nicest thing any man had done for her in decades — if ever. And all without a lecture or any mansplaining . . .

Okay, so she'd wanted to kiss him again, but this time he deserved it.

Her smile faded. She couldn't go on without a full staff. She'd have to talk to Jay.

Billy set about dealing with the fruit and vegetables until he'd filled the stacks of boxes, and replaced everything in the refrigerator. Noticing there was very little soup left, he set a huge pan of vegetable and lentil soup on the stove to slowly cook through. He glanced at the kitchen clock, noting that an hour had gone past, and that Bella hadn't reappeared. He could only hope she'd fallen asleep.

She was a strong woman who'd prioritized the needs of her customers over the state of her kitchen, and he could only admire her for that. The problem was, one person couldn't do everything. She was wearing herself out.

The back door banged, and Jay came into the kitchen. Billy nodded to him.

"Hey, Bella's just upstairs getting herself some lunch. I volunteered to finish up in here for her. She had quite a day."

Jay glanced at the door that led into the bar. "Is everything okay? I asked two of my waitstaff to help out so Mom wouldn't be alone in the kitchen."

"I think it got busy out there, so Bella sent them back out." Billy wiped his hands on the towel. "I know it isn't any of my business, but I don't think she should be trying to do everything out here."

"It's okay. You're preaching to the choir." Jay sat down at the table with a *thump*. "She's always been reluctant to accept any help out here. I even offered to get a full-time chef and staff so that she could retire, but she was horrified at the idea."

"She sounds just like my mother," Billy said. "Are you okay if I talk to Avery our event coordinator about getting someone to help out more permanently? She usually has really good leads, and great ideas."

"Be my guest." Jay sighed. "I feel like I'm failing her all around right now." He struggled to his feet. "I should go up and make sure she's okay."

"I think she might be taking a nap," Billy said. "She looked worn out."

"Then I'll leave her to it." Jay nodded. "Thanks for helping out again. Are you sure you don't want a job?"

"I'm happy to help out when I can." Billy shrugged. "And I'm cheap."

"A win-win for Mom then." Jay grinned at him. "I'll be back in two hours to check the bar stock and get set up for the evening rush. There are fewer orders for food, so hopefully we'll cope. I'm sure Erin will lend a hand, too."

With a brisk nod, Jay left and Billy made himself a cup of coffee. He'd given up alcohol after ending up in prison, and still attended the regular AA meetings held in the church hall in Morgantown. He'd never

188

really liked the taste of alcohol, and had just used it to drown his own guilt. Fifteen years ago he'd vowed never to touch another drop, and he hadn't.

Even being this close to the bar wasn't making him regret that decision, which gave him a great deal of satisfaction. But he knew himself now — knew how easily a good man could turn to crutches to help himself deal with grief. He finished his coffee and remembered his original reason for turning up at the bar. In the immediate emergency of helping Bella out, he'd completely forgotten to mention the wedding party.

At least he hadn't blabbed anything to Jay, who did seem genuinely concerned about his mother and was definitely trying to help her. Billy glanced up at the ceiling. Should he go up there and see if Bella was awake, or come back later when she was working the evening shift?

The floorboards creaked, and he made up his mind. If she was already up and about, he'd go and speak to her.

Bella yawned so hard she almost dislocated her jaw as she brushed her teeth in the bathroom. The apartment felt more like hers again since Jay had moved up the street, and secretly she quite liked it. After being widowed so young, and Jay being away in the military, she was comfortable in her own space and almost never felt lonely. She'd lived in Morgantown her whole life, knew everyone, and never felt like she had to be alone if she didn't want to be.

She came out of the bathroom and glanced at the clock in the kitchen. She hadn't meant to fall asleep, but her chair had proved too comfortable, and after finishing her sandwich she'd drifted off. . . .

There was a knock at the door, and she went to peer through the peephole, not wholly surprised to see Billy Morgan standing there.

"Hey." He smiled at her when she opened the door. "Just wanted to see that you were okay."

She held the door open. "Come on in."

He hesitated, his Stetson in his hand. "I don't want to be a bother."

"You are not bothering me in the slightest." She turned away. "Come in and at least let me make you a cup of coffee or something for all your hard work."

He followed her inside, wiping his boots on the mat, and shut the door behind him. He took his time walking through to the eat-in kitchen, quietly assessing the place, which amused her greatly.

"When was the last time you came up here?" she asked him as she set the coffee-maker working.

He perched himself on one of the stools set against the countertop. "About thirty-five years ago, I think. I came to pick up Ron for a football game." He smiled at her. "It looks a lot nicer than it did back then."

"Ron's parents weren't much into decorating." Bella smiled. "And there were five of them crammed into two rooms."

"Yeah, it certainly felt quite small to me, having grown up an only child in a big old Victorian ranch house."

"I'm surprised Ruth didn't have a big family."

Billy made a face. "She was young when she had me, and there were . . . complications. We both almost died, and my parents decided one kid was enough to carry on the family name."

"That was a sensible decision, and Ruth sure made up for it with grandkids."

To her surprise Billy didn't look any happier. "Maybe we should've stopped at one as well."

Bella stared at him. "You don't really mean that? I've seen the pride you take in your family. You love them all."

"Sure I do, but Annie . . ." He sighed.

"She didn't do so well."

Bella held his gaze. "I knew Annie quite well, and I can tell you that we all asked her why you wouldn't get the snip. She insisted she didn't want you to do that or get her tubes tied."

"I did offer several times," Billy said. "I should've just gone ahead and done it anyway."

"Hindsight is a marvelous thing," Bella said softly. "We've all done things that we just wish we could go back and erase from our timelines."

"Even you?" He studied her carefully. "I think you and Ron were the happiest couple I knew, apart from the Millers."

"We were happy, but we still had our differences." It was her turn to sigh. "I'll never forgive myself for letting him drive off the night he died. He'd had a few beers after the football game and decided he'd go pick Jay up from practice. I told him I'd go, and then I got busy, and just let him do it anyway." She looked down at the countertop. "He crashed into a wall on black ice and never got there."

"That was hardly your fault," Billy said gently.

"But it doesn't matter, does it?" She pressed her fist to her heart. "In *here* I feel responsible, and I always will."

He met her gaze. "Yeah."

She tried to smile, aware that she was actually closer to tears. "Thanks for understanding."

His answering smile was wry. "Remember you're talking to the king of regrets here. I let my wife down, walked out on my kids, *and* left my mother to run the ranch for me."

"That's certainly a long list," Bella agreed. "But you're forgetting that Annie made some bad choices as well. Ruth told me Annie tried to stab you with a kitchen knife."

"She was ill." Billy glanced down at his scarred hands. "She didn't know what she was doing."

Bella raised an eyebrow. "She knew enough to run off with another guy, and take your daughter with her without stopping to see if you were bleeding to death."

"That's true, but —"

"And she never came back. In fact she changed her name and went on with her life without you." Bella held his gaze. "You weren't the only one who walked out on their children, Billy."

"Okay, I get that, but —"

"If she *had* stayed, what would you have done?" Bella asked.

"I would've got her the treatment she needed."

"And you would have remained on the ranch looking after your kids, and none of the rest of it would have happened." Bella nodded. "Annie chose to leave, and her actions caused a lot of yours."

"I thought Annie was your friend."

"She was." Bella got two mugs down from the cupboard. "That doesn't mean I didn't see her faults. She wasn't suited to ranch life. She hated it out here, and she wasn't very happy."

Billy took the mug of coffee she poured him. "Seems as if everyone in town knew that except me. I was too busy running the ranch and trying to help out with the boys to have much time to ask the right questions."

"Just like me letting Ron drive when he was drunk because I was too busy doing other things."

"Bella, I appreciate the support," Billy interrupted her. "But stop trying to equate one stupid mistake with a whole catalogue of misdemeanors. I went to *prison,* for God's sake."

"I'm not." She met his gaze head-on. "I'm just saying that we all do things we regret. How we deal with that regret and move forward is more important than wanting to do the impossible, and go back in time to fix it."

"I think we can agree on that." He sipped his coffee. "I'm definitely trying to make it up to my family."

Bella added cream to her coffee and slowly stirred it in. She'd never imagined herself sitting in her kitchen exchanging heartfelt confidences with Billy Morgan of all people. But she'd noticed since his return that he was always making other people feel good about themselves, and had wanted to repay that instinct in kind.

"I forgot to tell you earlier that Chase and Ruth are happy for you to hold your wedding party up at the ranch," Billy said.

Billy had obviously decided the serious conversation was over, and she hastened to reply.

"That's wonderful."

"Maybe you could come up to the ranch one day this week, take a look at the kitchens, and create a menu?" Billy pointed at his chest. "I'm cooking, so don't make it too fancy."

"I don't think I want to do a sit-down dinner or anything," Bella said. "Just a buffet where everyone can serve themselves, and then maybe free-for-all speeches?"

"If you think that's a good idea."

Bella grinned at him. "Don't worry, I'm not going to get drunk and air my grievances at not being at the actual ceremony or anything."

"*You* might not, but what about Erin's parents? Weren't they the whole reason the couple eloped in the first place?"

"You're right." Bella frowned and tapped her spoon on the countertop. "Maybe we should have preapproved speeches instead — although those sometimes go off the rails as well."

"Feed them lots of carbs and limit the alcohol. They'll be too full and too sleepy to cause any problems," Billy advised. "That's what Avery says, and she should know seeing as she's organized hundreds of weddings and celebrations over the years."

"That's a great idea," Bella agreed. "I'm thinking it will only be about fifty people. It's short notice as well."

"Are you going to tell Jay or is it supposed to be a surprise?" Billy asked.

"I was thinking of surprising him. He certainly deserves it."

"Then I'll remind everyone at the ranch to keep quiet about the details." Billy finished his coffee and slid off his stool. "I'd better be getting home. They'll be wondering where I've gotten to."

Bella put down her mug and came around to his side of the counter. "I'm disrupting your life again, aren't I?"

"Trust me, this is much more fun than inoculating cows." He looked down at her, mischief dancing in his blue eyes, and she couldn't look away.

"I'm glad to hear that." She licked her lips and he stared at her mouth. "May I kiss you good-bye?" she asked.

He leaned in offering her his bearded cheek. She put her hand under his chin until their mouths lined up and kissed him full on the lips. It felt so good that she did it again, and with a groan, his lips parted, and she dove inside. He tasted like coffee, leather, and the great outdoors.

His arm came around her hips, locking her against him, and he took control of the kiss, pressing her against the countertop as she settled her hand on the back of his neck. He kissed with the same tender care he showed her in other ways, which made her feel so cherished.

Eventually he drew back and looked down at her for so long, she had to say something.

"Was I that bad? I am out of practice."

"Not at all, I just . . ." He continued to study her. "I just don't know what to do with this."

"With me kissing you?" Bella asked.

"No, with me kissing you back."

Bella smiled at him. "Well, if we both liked it, then maybe we should try it again sometime?" She held her breath.

He nodded. "I need to think about it. Is that okay?"

She shrugged, even though she was feeling pretty stupid now. So much for following her instincts like Maureen had suggested. She wasn't a kid anymore, and actions had consequences.

"Nothing to think about." She dismissed him with an airy wave of her hand. "Thanks so much for helping out today, Billy. I don't know how I would've coped if you hadn't turned up." She walked toward the hallway to the front door and opened it wide.

He came after her and was still putting his Stetson on when she literally shoved him out the door, saying, "Bye! I'll be in touch about the party."

She shut the door and leaned against it. He'd definitely kissed her back, and if she hadn't been mistaken, other areas of his anatomy had definitely been interested, too. What had she wanted him to do anyway? Toss her over his shoulder and head for the bedroom? A delicious shiver went through her as she contemplated that little fantasy.

Okay, so she wanted more, but she wasn't going to pursue him. Maureen wasn't always right. One thing being an adult had taught her was that patience and perseverance mattered far more than impulse. If Billy Morgan wanted more, then he'd have to work out how to ask for it without any further encouragement from her.

Billy almost fell down the stairs as he exited the top floor of the bar. Not that he wanted to get away from Bella. It was more a case of self-preservation — if he didn't get away he might do something really stupid like bang on her door and demand more. He let out a frustrated breath as he continued out into the parking lot. She'd tasted so good. . . . He missed that kind of physical intimacy so much. He'd tried to be honest though. He really didn't know what he wanted. The thought that Bella Williams liked him that way was still hard for him to get his head around.

Thinking about hard . . . Billy glanced down at his worn jeans. He was way too old to be worrying about embarrassing himself in public. He hadn't expected to react to Bella's kiss so fast, or so physically. With a groan, he checked his cell, and noticed he'd missed several messages from various family members. He'd been away half the day helping Bella, so he wasn't surprised they were all worried.

"Hey, Mr. Morgan."

He looked up to see Nate Turner hanging out the window of his official car in the street alongside him.

"Hey, Nate." Billy tried to look responsible. "Have you caught Axel yet?"

"Nope. He's disappeared. Hopefully back to wherever he came from, but I'm still keeping an eye out."

"Good. If he didn't get his wages, he might need the money."

"Bella has first-rate security at the bar," Nate said. "I went over the place with her and Jay to make sure."

"Yeah, but the bar is a public space, so anyone can get in there," Billy said. "It's never one-hundred percent secure."

"I know that, but I also reckon most people who know Jay wouldn't risk trying to get past him to his mother." Nate nodded. "I'll keep in touch. Have a great day, Mr. Morgan."

"Thanks." Billy found his truck and got inside. The temperature had dropped considerably since he'd arrived around lunchtime to find Bella in a fix. He used the time waiting for the condensation to clear from his windscreen to text his nearest and dearest that he was on his way home.

Quite what he was going to say to them when he got there, he wasn't so sure.

CHAPTER FOUR

To Billy's relief when he arrived home he met Avery coming out of the guest center and flagged her down. He really wasn't ready yet to face all the questions his disappearance would have generated. She still worked occasionally for her parents at the only hotel in town, but focused most of her efforts on the ever-increasing list of functions being held at the dude ranch. She was also his son Ry's fiancée, and the nicest, sweetest woman you could ever wish for a son to marry.

"Hey, Mr. Morgan!" She waved enthusiastically at him. He'd asked her to call him Billy, but she usually forgot. "Ry was wondering where you were. Apparently you were supposed to be hanging out with the cattle this afternoon."

Billy grimaced. "Yeah, I got stuck in town helping Bella Williams in the Red Dragon kitchen. I wanted to talk to you about her staffing situation."

"Sure! Come back into my office so we can chat. It's way too cold to be standing out here."

Glad to avoid his mother's kitchen and her questions for a few more minutes, Billy followed Avery into the newest part of the ranch, which housed the guest dining room, state of the art kitchen, and the company offices. She was using her stick today, which meant she was moving more slowly.

"What can I help with?" She perched on the corner of her desk. "Ruth said that Bella had been having some problems keeping staff."

"That's right." Billy sat down in the nearest chair. "I told her I'd ask you if you had anyone in mind who could help out — even temporarily."

"Well, there is someone." Avery reached over and picked up a piece of paper from her desk. "Do you remember Dev Patel, the architect who designed the guest center and the new barn?"

"Yeah, he's great, but why would he want to work in Bella's kitchen?"

"Not him — his sister Sonali," Avery said. "She's been staying in his apartment in town since she finished up her catering degree. She was working up here with

Gustav for a while, but now our kitchen is shut down for a month. I'm sure she'd be more than willing to work at Bella's."

"Have you asked her?"

"Not yet, but I know she's been looking for work because she told me Dev's been nagging her to pay her share of the apartment bills." Avery grinned. "Do you want me to give her a call and ask her formally? She's not far from Bella's place, so she could pop over for an interview anytime, and she'd be nice and local."

"That would be great." Billy smiled at Avery. "Bella's going to need someone long term eventually, but if Sonali can help out for a few weeks, that will certainly make things easier for her."

Billy stood up, came over to the desk, and kissed Avery on the cheek. "Thank you."

"You're very welcome." She blushed and tucked a curl of hair behind her ear. "Bella's a really nice person."

"She definitely is," Billy agreed. "We were in kindergarten together."

"Back when dinosaurs roamed the earth?"

"About then." He tried to smile. "We've certainly known each other a long time."

"Is there something wrong?" Avery asked shyly. "I mean, not that there should be, but you just look so sad."

"Nothing for you to worry about, Avery," Billy said. "I'm just trying to come to terms with how relationships can change and surprise you."

"You mean like between you and Bella?"

Billy grimaced. "You've been talking to Ruth and Chase, haven't you?"

"I *have* heard them discussing certain things about you — you know what they are like."

"And what are they saying?"

"Just that you seem to like her — a lot." Avery paused. "Not that they think that's bad, just that they're surprised."

"Not half as surprised as I am," Billy muttered. "I don't know what to do."

"About what?"

"About liking Bella," Billy confessed. "And I do like her."

"Then why don't you ask her out?" Avery looked at him expectantly.

"On a date?"

Avery grinned at him. "Isn't that what you old folks call it?"

"We're hardly likely to be hooking up, being friends with benefits, tindertweeting, or all the other stuff you guys use to knock boots these days," Billy pointed out.

"Good to know." Avery was obviously trying not to laugh. "Take her out to dinner, or bring her up here and cook her dinner." She studied him seriously. "What have you got to lose?"

"Her friendship?" Billy was long past thinking it was weird to be having a heart-to-heart about his current romantic predicament with his son's fiancée. "Neither of us are planning on leaving this town, so if things go wrong, we've got to live with the consequences."

"You're both reasonable people," Avery pointed out. "I don't see either of you making everything into a big drama if things don't work out. You'd both carry on being the nice, sweet people you are."

When Avery said it, it all sounded so reasonable.

"You think she'd like it if I cooked for her?" Billy said slowly.

"What woman wouldn't?" Avery asked. "Especially seeing as Bella spends her whole life cooking for other people."

"It might work. . . ." Billy nodded his head. "I have to get her up here to pick a menu for the wedding party. I could cook her a proper dinner after that."

"And I'd make sure the rest of the family stayed over in the ranch house," Avery promised. "Because otherwise they'd all be over here sticking their noses in your business." She hesitated. "I think you should go for it."

Billy nodded slowly. "Thanks, Avery. Then maybe I will."

Bella got out of Billy's truck and took in the silence and immediate sense of space around her. Spending her days in a busy kitchen made her happy, but coming out here where the skies rolled endlessly above your head and you could hear a pin drop was a whole 'nother world of peace. . . . She'd left Jay in charge of the bar and her newest team member, Sonali Patel, in charge of the evening shift.

Sonali had impressed Bella with her quick ability to understand the menu and serve up the food in a fast and furious manner. It was also midweek, so the volume of customers was lower and more centered on the local fries and burger clientele than the more fussy tourists.

Bella checked her phone, but there were no texts either from Jay or Sonali, so she could proceed with her meeting with Billy without a care in the world. Well — apart from the whole wanting to jump his bones thing, and him wanting to think about it. Bella retrieved her purse from the backseat and waited for Billy to come around the truck.

Maybe he had an answer for her tonight, and the meeting wouldn't all be about choosing cake. . . . Bella smiled at her own absurdity. If Billy didn't want to commit to a more complex relationship, then she was fine about it. She liked him just the way he was.

"Hey."

She turned as he came toward her, his smile so full of delight that all she could do was grin foolishly back at him. He hadn't gotten out of the truck when he'd picked her up seeing as he wasn't stopping and they'd spent the journey back exchanging local gossip and family news. He wore a blue checked shirt that matched his eyes, and his usual jeans and cowboy boots.

"Thanks for picking me up," Bella said. "My car needed gas and Jay said he'd get it for me after his shift."

"No problem." He leaned in to give her a quick hug. "I'm just glad you could get away."

She elbowed him in the side. "You knew I could. You're the one who sent that treasure of culinary goodness, Sonali Patel, my way."

"That was all Avery's doing." Billy took Bella's hand and walked her away from the house, toward the guest center. "She said Sonali was looking for something to do."

"Yes, Sonali told me that after she gets some practical experience, she's planning on becoming a personal chef to some Silicon Valley millionaire." Bella chuckled. "I told her she should be talking to Chase."

"She definitely should, but maybe not until you no longer need her." He opened the door into the quiet guest center. "You've been in here before, right?"

"Yes. It's a lovely space." Bella admired the dining room with its huge fireplace and the large windows looking out toward the impressive Sierras. "Perfect for a party."

"Sonali's brother Dev designed it."

"That's right. So she was telling me." Bella followed Billy through into the state of the art kitchen, and sighed with pleasure. "Sometimes I wish my place looked like this."

"Yeah, it's pretty awesome." Billy nodded. "Chase wanted it to be the best, and he's good at getting what he wants."

"He and Jay have a lot in common," Bella murmured as she noticed two places laid at the kitchen countertop. "They just exercised their talents in different ways."

Billy lit the candles and moved the bud vase containing a single rose out of the way.

"I know you said you wanted a buffet, but I thought we could work our way through the courses, sampling potential beverages and food as we go."

"Sounds good to me." Bella put her purse on the work top, and hitched herself up to sit in one of the chairs. She'd chosen a long skirt over her cowboy boots with a silky embroidered top with long sleeves. "Is there anything I can do to help?"

Billy returned from hanging up his hat and her coat. "Nope, not a thing. I want you to just sit there and enjoy."

Bella laughed. "It feels odd to be sitting in a kitchen and not working."

For the first time Billy hesitated. "Would you rather sit in the dining room? I can bring everything out there."

"No this is fine. I was just kidding." She wasn't sure why, but he seemed a little nervous. "It's all good."

"Okay." She fought a smile as he tied a flowery apron that she suspected must have belonged to Ruth around his lean waist. "We'll start with six cold appetizers, and take it from there."

Billy watched Bella's face as she sampled each plate, and tried to work out whether she was enjoying the food he'd so carefully chosen and cooked for her. She wore a red knitted skirt and a black flowery top, and her hair was down around her shoulders. He wanted to plunge his hands into her hair, and hold her still as he kissed her lips. . . .

"Mmm . . ." She licked her lips, and everything male in him stood to attention. "This is all so good! Did you make *everything*?"

"Yeah," he admitted. "I did." He wouldn't tell her that it had taken him all day and several trips to the nearest big town to get all the ingredients he required. "I like to cook."

"You've been holding out on me." She pointed her spoon at him, her brown eyes dancing. "You're capable of manning *way* more than a grill."

He shrugged. "I'm just glad you're enjoying yourself."

"If you have desserts, then I'll probably lose it completely."

Billy shot to his feet. "I have desserts." He hurried into the refrigerated section of the kitchen hoping a cold blast of air might restore his equilibrium. But the sight of Bella Williams licking her spoon and moaning over his food was now seared in his brain. He stuck his whole head in the industrial-sized refrigerator and dragged in a few lungfuls of super-cold air. Nope, nothing was going to help.

"I wasn't sure whether you'd want hot desserts because they're more labor intensive, so I made these seven cold ones. I have mini Pavlovas, banana pudding, baklava, Eton mess, all kinds of sorbets, ice-cream, and fancy ice pops." He set the plate down carefully in front of her. "I'm sure Ruth will insist on adding pie regardless, so we'll definitely have something hot."

Not as hot as he currently was . . . He hadn't felt like this since he'd been a horny teenager ogling his high school gym teacher.

"Oh, I *love* Pavlova," Bella breathed. "I never have time to make it at the bar." She picked up the small piped circle and popped it into her mouth, crunching down on the stiff sugar base, the cream, and berries.

A trickle of raspberry juice touched her lip, and Billy instinctively wiped it clean with his fingertip.

Bella grinned at him. "Am I making a mess? I don't care. This is to *die* for. . . ."

He offered her the second one, and she raised an eyebrow. "You like seeing me all messy?"

He could only nod as he presented the treat. She eased it into her mouth, leaving his fingertips pressed against her lips.

"Bella . . ." He might have groaned before he bent his head and kissed the sweet stickiness of her mouth and the lingering sharpness of the berries within.

With a soft sound, she wrapped one hand around the back of his neck and kissed him back.

He forgot everything except the fullness of her body now pressed against his and the tantalizing taste and scent of her. She fitted perfectly against him, and he never wanted to let her go again.

Sitting on the high stool meant Bella was at just the right height for them to be eye to eye. He eased his second hand around her waist and drew her closer to the edge of the chair.

"Is this okay?" he murmured.

"Oh *yes.*" She wiggled even closer until the bulging fly of his jeans pressed against the woolen fabric of her skirt. He wanted to take the skirt off her so badly. . . .

Before he lost all sense of decorum, he forced himself to remember that they were in a public place, and even if Avery barred the door of the ranch house and lay down across the threshold of the guest center, a determined Morgan would find a way to get around her.

"Come with me?" Billy asked.

For an answer, Bella slid off the stool right down his front, almost giving him a heart attack it felt so good. He took her hand, and led her deeper into the building. His only thoughts were he needed a horizontal surface, and a room with a door that locked.

He stumbled into his office, snapped on the lamp, and locked the door behind Bella. There was a couch against the wall, and he drew her down onto it, his mouth glued to hers, his hands now roaming over her body.

"Where are we?" Bella asked between kisses.

"My office." Billy kissed down her throat.

"I didn't know you had an office."

Billy wasn't really into making small talk, but he made the effort, straightening up, and looking right into her eyes. She looked gloriously rumpled and not at all worried.

"We don't have to do anything," Billy said. "We can just sit together and chat."

"Okay." Bella nodded, and then reached out to run her hand down his muscled upper arm. "I don't want to chat."

He smiled at her. "What do you want to do then?"

"Kiss you? Touch you?" She bit her lip. "But only if you are okay about that."

"I can't say I have any objections." Billy

tried to keep a straight face. "Seeing as it's a long time since either of us have been in this position, how about we start with a little making out on the couch session?"

Bella couldn't help noticing that Billy Morgan was definitely very happy to be with her, and that he'd obviously gotten over any doubts about kissing her. She liked the idea of taking it slow, though. Leaning in, she kissed him very carefully until he shuddered under her hands. He tasted of good food, and hot, excited man, a combination that was far more addictive than she had realized.

She toyed with the top button of his shirt. "May I?"

"Sure." He grimaced. "Not much to see except a few scars." He held his breath as she undid each button, sucking his stomach in to make her task easier as she yanked the ends of the shirt out of his jeans.

"When did you get this?" She touched the faded outline of a heart tattooed on his tanned skin. "It's the names of all your kids."

"Yeah." He let out a breath that stirred the top of her bent head. "I had it done when I was in prison to remind me not to give up on them again."

She kissed the ragged blue outline, and he shivered, his hand coming to rest in her hair.

"As soon as I got my head on straight, I missed the kids so much," Billy confessed. "After I got out of jail, I sent money home to Mom whenever I had any, and made sure she had some idea where I was. It was the least I could do after causing her all that pain."

"She never gave up on you." Bella raised her gaze to his face. "I'd see her in town and at church, and she always prayed that you would come home."

"Like the prodigal son?" Billy's smile was so wistful it made Bella's heart hurt. "Ruth is amazingly strong."

"She is, but I don't really want to be talking about your mother right now," Bella said. "I thought we were making out."

"We are." He picked her up and settled her on his lap. "Now it's my turn to kiss you."

She didn't argue, and didn't speak for quite a while as he took a leisurely tour of her mouth, his strong hands finding their way up inside her top to tease and cup her breasts. She might have moaned into his mouth as his fingertip grazed her nipple.

She tore her mouth away from his. "What base are we at now?" she gasped.

"It's so long since I even played the game, I can't remember." He paused. "Are you still okay with this?"

She opened her eyes wide. "Did you hear me complaining?"

"Just making sure." His hand settled over her hip. "Can I persuade you out of that top?"

She bit her lip. "I'm not as skinny as I used to be."

"In kindergarten?" He raised an eyebrow. "The last time I accidentally looked up your skirt was when we were climbing the monkey bars at recess."

"Billy Morgan, you didn't!" Bella exclaimed.

"Couldn't help myself." He winked at her. "I went home and told Mom you had dinosaurs on your panties, and that I wanted some just like yours." He chuckled. "She had a few things to say about that."

"I bet."

"And now I'm back to talking about my mom again." Billy sighed. "I'm beginning to feel like a real teenager."

Bella lifted her arms, took off her silky top, and watched his eyes glaze over as her still glorious bosom was revealed.

"Wow . . ." He leaned in and kissed the spot between her breasts. "Beautiful."

"Thank you." As she'd recently remarked to Maureen, her boobs were her best feature, and she wasn't afraid of showing a bit of cleavage occasionally.

Within moments, her bra had gone as well, and then she just leaned back and enjoyed the sensations Billy aroused in her as she squirmed on his lap. By the time she opened her eyes again, she was half lying on the couch with Billy almost on top of her. She grabbed his hand, and guided it between her legs, and he went still.

"You sure about this?"

"Only if you are," Bella said. "No pressure."

His half laugh, half groan did nothing to stop her arousal as he palmed her panties, his thumb zeroing in just where she wanted it. Her whole body tightened and she shuddered through a climax.

"Oh, dear Lord!" She stared up at Billy, who was looking as startled as she felt. "I've never done that before."

"Yeah?" His smile was full of wickedness. "Then maybe I'll have to investigate further, and make sure you can do it again."

He dropped to his knees and kissed his way up past her thighs, and . . .

Bella reached down and grabbed a fistful of his hair as his mouth and fingers descended on her most sensitive parts and took her straight to heaven and another climax. Tears sprang to her eyes because it was just so *good* to be touched after *so long. . . .*

Billy winced and eased Bella's fingers out of his hair. He knelt up and looked at her, and his heart stuttered. She looked so beautiful lying there, flushed with the emotions he'd aroused in her. He wanted more; he wanted it all.

She sniffed and wiped at something on her cheek, which had him getting off the floor and sitting back on the couch.

"Are you okay, Bella? Did I hurt you?" Billy had to ask.

She scrambled to sit up, drawing her skirt down over her legs, and grabbed for her bra.

"No, it was lovely. It's just that I didn't expect to have all these *feelings. . . .*" She waved a helpless hand in his direction as she struggled into her bra and put her top back on.

"It's okay," Billy said gently. "I get it."

"I feel so *stupid.*"

"There's no reason to feel like that." He wanted to give her a hug and tell her that everything would be okay, but he didn't want to touch her and upset her again.

"I've had some relationships since Ron died, and even the occasional bit of sex, but this felt different."

Billy wasn't sure whether to be proud or worried about what she was going to say next.

"It's okay," he repeated. "How about we do this? You go through to the bathroom, and I'll meet you back in the kitchen when you've freshened up. We can have coffee before I drive you home."

Billy opened the door that led into the shared bathroom with the office next door and switched on the light. He currently needed a really cold shower, but that could wait until Bella was feeling okay.

He went through to the kitchen, buttoned up his shirt, and washed himself thoroughly in the sink. He didn't dare tuck his shirt into his jeans again. Bella wasn't the only one who was confused. He'd felt things he hadn't experienced with any other woman other than his late wife. If Bella hadn't said anything, he wondered whether he would've been the one to pull back.

He studied his face in the small mirror above the sink. Did he regret what he'd done? No, he couldn't say that. He'd enjoyed every toe-curling minute. Was he simply too used up to open himself to the possibilities of a real relationship? This didn't feel casual. It felt like a commitment, and as everyone who knew him was aware; Billy Morgan had the ability to betray everyone. Did Bella deserve that? Would she be a fool to take that chance even if he had the nerve to ask her?

Better maybe to be grateful that she had second thoughts, and leave things as they were. . . .

Bella gasped as she looked at her flushed face and disheveled hair in the bathroom mirror. She looked like a very satisfied woman. Her whole body was humming with the sexual energy Billy had released in her, and yet she still felt like crying.

She washed her face and hands several times, and used her fingers to flatten down her hair, as she'd left her purse in the kitchen. Did she have the nerve to walk out there, smile at Billy, and pretend that nothing was wrong — that he hadn't just given her one of the best sexual experiences of her life without even trying?

She touched her reddened cheeks. If she hadn't cried, would he have carried on? How would it have felt to have Billy Morgan inside her? She was the one who'd encouraged him to kiss her and develop their relationship, and she was the one who'd lost her nerve. She had a sense that if she ever got naked and horizontal with Billy, she would no longer have the ability to deny that she cared for him very deeply.

"So much for a casual fling," Bella sighed. "I'm obviously not cut out for that."

She reluctantly left the bathroom and made her way back to the bright lights of the kitchen where Billy was busy cleaning away their meal. He glanced up as she entered and pointed at the coffeemaker.

"Help yourself. I'll join you when I've finished up."

Bella swallowed hard. "I could help if you like?"

"No, I'm good." The smile he offered her was no different than usual, which kind of hurt. "I'm just stacking the dishwasher. How about you fix me some coffee while you're getting yours? Cream's in the refrigerator."

Desperate for something to do with her hands, Bella complied, then sat at the countertop sipping her coffee while Billy worked. He didn't look upset. Maybe he was fine about everything, and she was the only one who'd gotten things out of proportion.

He washed his hands and dried them before coming to pick up his mug of coffee.

He didn't sit beside her, but stood on the other side of the countertop, keeping the barrier between them.

Bella waited to see what he was going to say, but he focused on his coffee. Maybe he was waiting for her to speak first, but what the heck was she supposed to say? Sorry? Thank you? Nothing seemed right.

After chugging his coffee with some speed, Billy went into the back of the kitchen, and returned with a pile of paper that he set on the countertop beside Bella.

"Here's a list of everything we tasted, and an approximate cost estimate depending on the quantities. When you get time, look through it, and get it back to me, okay?"

Bella nodded, took the printouts, and stuffed them in her purse. "Thank you."

"You're welcome. Would you like more coffee, or shall I see you home?"

Bella sat beside Billy in his truck as he navigated the ice-covered roads into Morgantown. He talked about the ranch, his kids, and the upcoming wedding celebration in an easy, conversational way that helped ease Bella's excruciating nerves.

When they reached the parking lot behind the bar, he pulled up and cut off the engine.

Bella rushed to open her door. "It's okay.

You don't have to get out. I'm fine from here."

"Jay would kill me if I didn't see you right to your door." Billy was already stepping down from his side of the truck. He walked beside Bella to the kitchen door and waited as she fumbled in her purse for her keys. The bar was still open, and the cheerful hum of the jukebox and conversation floated out from the open windows.

Bella found her keys, unlocked the door, and made herself look up into Billy's face.

"I'm sorry."

"Nothing to be sorry about." He smiled. "Let me know about the menu, okay?"

She touched his arm. "I didn't know I was going to feel like that — I . . ."

"Hey, it's all right." He held her gaze, his blue eyes steady, his tone soothing. "As long as you're okay, we're good."

"You're not mad that you didn't get any?" she blurted out, and then winced.

"I'll survive." This time his smile was crooked and way more genuine. "Night, Bella. Thanks for coming up to the ranch."

He tipped his hat to her, turned, and walked away, leaving her standing there feeling somewhere between foolish and very, very blessed.

CHAPTER FIVE

"Everything okay, Mom?" Jay's head came around the door of her office.

"Oh, hi! You scared me!"

Bella scrambled to hide the tab open on her laptop that held details of the wedding party. She'd received confirmation from Erin's family that they would attend, had sorted out accommodation at Hayes Hotel, and just needed to go over the final catering arrangements with Billy.

For some reason she was dragging her heels on that last matter. . . .

"You look kind of guilty to me," Jay joked. "Are you buying shoes again?"

She laughed. "You know me so well."

He leaned against the door frame and continued to regard her. "How's Sonali working out for you?"

Bella swiveled her chair around to face him. "She's amazing."

"Good." He nodded. "I'm just off to the

suppliers. Do you have a list for the kitchen?"

"Yup." She found it on her desk and handed it over to him. "Same old stuff."

"I haven't heard anyone complaining." Jay obviously wasn't finished. "Are you okay yourself?"

"What's that supposed to mean?" Bella asked.

"You seem a bit down."

"I've just been busy. Even though Sonali's a quick learner, I've still had to go through everything with her."

"You sure that's it?" Jay persisted.

Bella fixed him with her best Mom stare. "If you have something to say, Jay Ronald Williams, why don't you just spit it out?"

He came in and sat down on the only other chair. "I saw you with Billy Morgan at church last Sunday."

Bella raised her chin. "Doing what?"

"Nothing in particular." He hesitated. "It was just the way he was looking down at you — like you were really special to him."

She shrugged. Having a son who'd been a Navy SEAL meant he noticed every tiny detail. "We've known each other since we were kids. We're good friends."

"I know that, but this was something new." He looked at her. "If you want to have a relationship with him, I wouldn't mind."

She raised an eyebrow. "Like I'd be consulting you?"

He smiled. "You'd think I'd be worried you'd forgotten Dad. I wouldn't. I want you to be happy."

"That's very nice of you, but maybe I can't get over your father. Maybe it's *me* who's the problem," Bella said.

"There's no shame in moving forward, Mom," Jay said gently. "I had to learn to let go of the past, and trust Erin."

"I know you did." She smiled at him. "I'm very proud of you both."

"I just want you to know that I love you, and that I'll always have your back whatever you choose to do." He came over to drop a kiss on the top of her head. "Thanks for everything you did for me when I came home from the hospital. You were my rock. I don't tell you that enough."

"Oh, get along with you." She gave him an affectionate smack on the rear. "I've got to get back to the kitchen. Avery found me a great dishwasher as well, so I hardly have to do a thing anymore."

He laughed, and went out leaving her sitting there feeling like crying again. His words had hit home, but she still wasn't sure what she wanted to do with them. She glanced down at her desk, her gaze coming to rest on the menu options Billy had given her.

Whatever she did next, she owed Billy an explanation. They'd been friends for too long to not seek closure. She'd give him a call later and ask him to come round to discuss the details when he was next in town.

"Did you hear back from Bella?" Ruth asked Billy as he sat down to eat his dinner at the crowded family table.

"Yeah. I had a text from her today, actually. I'm going to sort out the details with her this evening after my AA meeting."

Billy was glad he had something to report. After three days of silence he had started to wonder whether Bella would ever speak to him again. And he already missed her company in so many ways. . . .

"Good, because if we are going to pull this party off, we really need to get the supplies in just in case it starts snowing and the roads become impassable." Ruth passed him the jug of iced tea.

"Good point."

"I hear you're going to do all the cooking, Dad." Chase spoke up from the other side of the table.

"Yeah, seeing as Gustav isn't here, I thought I'd pitch in."

"I keep forgetting you can cook," Chase said.

"That's because no one up here seems to require my help." Billy met his eldest son's gaze, aware that everyone else around the table was now focused on their conversation. Maybe it was because he was heart sore over Bella, or maybe it was just time for some plain speaking. "I offered to run the guest kitchen, but you all shouted me down."

Chase frowned. "Because that's not who you are."

"What exactly am I, then?" Billy asked. "You're the financial wizard, BB takes care of the horses, Ry and HW manage the special programs, and Roy runs the whole goddamn ranch with Ruth."

"That's not fair." Blue Boy, his bluntest son, was quick to get into the conversation. "You gave up those things. You said you didn't want the responsibility."

"I *said* I didn't want to rock the boat," Billy responded. "You know why."

BB glanced around the table at his siblings. "Because you don't deserve any of this, right? Because you walked out on us."

"*Yes.*"

BB shook his head. "You still tiptoe around here like you're a paying guest — like you can't comment on anything in case you offend someone."

Billy just stared at him. "Go on."

Chase stirred. "BB — maybe this isn't the time."

"No." Billy held up his hand. He was just glad his granddaughter Maria wasn't present to hear her father BB's speech because she wouldn't appreciate them arguing. "Let him speak."

BB sighed. "Look, all I'm trying to say is that you don't have to do that. It doesn't matter what you say, we all know this is your place — that you coming back to Morgan Ranch returned its soul. *Tell* us we're crap. Tell us where we're going wrong. We accepted you back a long time ago. We *want* you here."

Billy looked around the table where everyone was nodding along with BB's words. He gripped the table hard to remind himself that he wasn't dreaming as his son's blunt words sunk in.

"It's still your ranch, Dad," BB said quietly. "You're the one who taught us how to love it when we were kids, just like you did. *You're* the reason we all came home."

Billy managed a nod and then turned on

his heel and escaped the kitchen before he did something stupid like bawl his eyes out. How had his children managed to grow up so smart despite their parents' bad choices? He got into his truck and drove to town. The need to sit quietly in his AA meeting and process what had just happened consumed him. Perhaps listening to how others had overcome their demons, and still struggled, would reset and restore him.

Bella glanced at the clock as someone knocked on the back door and then checked her cell. There was a text from Billy suggesting he meet with her after she'd finished her shift. It was getting close to that time now. She usually stopped taking orders an hour before the bar closed, and it was almost ten now.

Sonali closed the refrigerator and came over. "I'm done — unless you can think of anything else that needs attending to?"

Bella smiled as she went to open the back door. "No, you've been great. I can't believe you agreed to work for me."

"It's fun! I love learning new things," Sonali said as she took off her apron. "I don't think I'll stay here forever, but I'd rather be cooking than sitting around the apartment feeling sorry for myself with Dev

231

moaning about me not paying rent."

Bella checked it was indeed Billy outside, and opened the door.

"Come on in. I'm just finishing up." She stepped aside as Sonali came back with her hat and coat. "Have you met Sonali, Billy?"

"Yes, we met at the ranch during her interview with Gustav." Billy shook Sonali's hand. "How are you doing? Is Bella treating you okay?"

Sonali grinned. "She's awesome and I'm having a great time." She glanced back at Bella. "I'll see you tomorrow, okay?"

"Are you good walking home, Sonali?" Billy asked.

"Thanks, Mr. Morgan, but it's literally across the street. Dev's probably already standing at the window twitching the drapes to make sure I cross the road properly." Sonali winked. "He takes his big brother duties very seriously."

She crammed her woolen hat on her head, put on her coat, and set off whistling, her hands in her pockets.

Suddenly all too aware that she was now alone with Billy Morgan, Bella went into the kitchen. There was very little left to do, but completing the regular tasks helped her calm down and get used to being around Billy again.

Without asking, he helped out, putting things away and cleaning surfaces. The bar was still packed, and the noise drifted through the kitchen as they completed their tasks.

"I'll just go and tell Jay I'm done and I'll be right with you," Bella said.

"Not a problem."

For some reason Billy looked more solemn than usual, his warm smile absent. Was he expecting her to deliver bad news, or was something else going on?

After saying good night to Jay, she returned to the kitchen and led the way upstairs to her apartment, where she'd left a single light burning in the window. Billy came in behind her and shut the door.

"What a great view of Main Street and the Christmas lights." He went into the kitchen and stared out over the street.

"It's great until the drunks get out," Bella said.

He swung around to look at her. "My AA meeting got out about an hour ago. Hopefully none of them showed up here."

Bella winced. "Sorry that came out wrong —"

"It's okay. It was my lame attempt at a joke." He drew a sheaf of papers out of his coat pocket. "I brought a copy of the menu suggestions in case you'd lost yours."

"I have them right here." Bella put on the coffeemaker. "I marked my choices, and I've written you a check for ten percent as a deposit."

"I think I trust you." His smile this time was sweet. "I even know where you live."

"Don't they say you should never mix business with pleasure?" Bella asked.

"Or attempt to seduce your old friends?" Billy countered.

Bella sighed. "I'm sorry about that."

"Hey, I wasn't talking about you." Billy frowned. "I was talking about *me.*"

Bella carefully lined up two mugs and then straightened them again. "Are you by any chance trying to take the blame for what happened between us?"

"Well, seeing as I'm the one who obviously pushed you too far, then, yeah."

She slowly raised her head to look him right in the eye. "You made me climax. Twice. And then when I panicked, you took me home. How in the world are you taking the blame for *that*?" She pointed her spoon at him. "I wanted you to touch me. I *loved* it!"

"Okay," Billy said, holding her gaze. "That's good to know." He held up the papers. "So do you want this copy?"

"Are you *listening* to me?" Bella asked. "What is up with you wanting to be Saint Billy the Perfect of Morgantown all the time?"

He went still. "You sound just like BB."

"What?"

"He just tore me off a strip at dinner for being too scared to accept any ownership of the ranch, or to rock anyone's boat."

"Maybe he has a point." Bella glared at him.

"Maybe he does," Billy sighed. "So here goes. I want to make things right with you. If that means I accept the blame for what happened the other night and we can move forward and still be friends, then I'm good with that."

"Well, at least that's honest."

"I'm trying here." His smile was crooked. "I never want you to feel frightened with me, or worried that I won't stop trying to get in your pants again."

Bella took a deep, steadying breath. "I wasn't frightened of what we did together. I was frightened of how it made me *feel* — emotionally, not physically, if that makes any sense."

He still looked puzzled, so Bella kept talking.

"When you touched me, it was so wonderful, and so special, that I couldn't handle it. It reminded me of how I'd felt with Ron, and that was such a shock that I didn't know how to deal with it. I felt *guilty.* Like I was betraying *him.* Can you understand that?"

He was nodding now. "Yeah, I think I can. I felt like that after Annie left. I was still technically married, but for a long time I had no idea whether she was dead or alive, and I was in no fit state to be as discriminating as I should've been. Knowing I'd been stupid just added to my guilt, made me drink even more and do even more stupid things."

"Maybe they both ruined us in different ways." Bella tried to smile.

"Not ruined," Billy objected. "Love is never wasted. The trick is moving on from the guilt, and finding new ways to give and receive that love." He hesitated. "It's fine if you're not ready to move on from your relationship with Ron yet."

"Now you're going back to being all reasonable again." Bella sniffed as she poured them both some coffee.

"I can't seem to help myself." Billy chuckled. "I just want the people I care about to be happy. I came so close to losing everyone and everything I loved that I value every precious second in case it's snatched away from me again." He grimaced. "If that makes me a pushover or too nice, I suppose that's how it is."

"You're definitely not a pushover."

"Thanks." He smiled as she handed over his coffee. "But am I too nice?"

"You're a good, strong man." She pressed her hand over her heart. "In here."

"I try to be. That's all I can do." He sipped his coffee. "So can we be friends again?"

Bella considered him for a long moment. "I can't do casual sex."

He blinked at her. "I beg your pardon?"

"That's what I've realized over the years since Ron died." Bella took a deep breath. "The thing is, I don't feel casual about you."

"Sexually or generally?" Billy asked.

"Either," Bella said, then took her courage in both hands. "It feels to me that if I did sleep with you, then we'd have to be a couple."

"Okay." Billy nodded.

"Doesn't that scare you?"

He sat back and regarded her. "Should it?"

"Well, because of your kids, and the ranch, and your mother — God, your mother — and Annie . . ." She ran out of breath. "What about them?"

"What would they have to do with us be-ing a couple?"

"Because they'd all *know,* and —"

"That would bother you?" He raised an eyebrow. "You'd prefer to keep everything secret?" His eyes were full of sympathy. "I don't think that's possible in a town this size, and if it does bother you, then maybe, as I said, you aren't yet ready to move on."

"I'm trying to be," Bella whispered.

He reached for her hand. "Look, I'm not going anywhere. If you get to a point where we can be a real couple, then come and tell me." He squeezed her fingers. "I mean it. I'll wait. You're worth it."

"Really?" Bella looked into his eyes and saw nothing but understanding and genuine concern in them. "I feel like I'm letting you down somehow."

"You're not. We're not kids anymore. We're old enough to speak our minds, take things slow, and get them *right.* I don't have a problem with that." Billy did his best to try and get through to her. "I just want you to be okay."

He wanted a lot more for her, but a year in jail had taught him all about patience — about how to pace himself, how to shed his past, and look forward to a better future. He'd even learned to forgive himself, which

238

had been the hardest thing of all. Some things in life were worth waiting for, and Bella Williams was definitely one of them.

She was still worrying at her lip, which made him want to kiss her real bad, but he also sensed she was relaxing a little.

A loud crash reverberated through the floor, and Billy stiffened. "Did you leave anything out in the kitchen?"

"No. But Jay might have gone in there for something, although it's unlikely that he'd make a mess." Bella slid off her stool in double-quick time.

"Could it be a raccoon or some kind of animal?" Billy asked.

"It's possible. It wouldn't be the first time that's happened." Bella was already heading toward the door. Billy caught her elbow.

"Where are you going?"

"To see what's happening. This is my home, and I'm not letting any raccoon or skunk run wild in my kitchen!"

"Don't you think Jay can handle it?"

"He might not have heard a thing. It gets really noisy out front on Friday nights."

Having rarely been in the bar since his return, Billy could only assume she was correct.

"Shall I call Nate?" Billy offered.

"Not yet. I don't want to look stupid or

waste his time. Let's see what we're dealing with first."

Bella went into her office, opened the closet, and started punching numbers in the safe. When the door swung open she grabbed a box and started loading bullets into the chamber of a gun.

"You're going to *kill it*?" Billy asked. "I was thinking about opening the back door and simply shooing it out."

"It depends how big it is," Bella said. "We had a wild pig in here once, and it was as big as a calf and caused so much damage you wouldn't believe it."

Just as they reached the front door leading to the stairs, there was a crash of breaking glass and the creaking sound of wood as the downstairs door was kicked in. Bella started forward, and Billy held her back.

"Wait," he whispered close to her ear. "I'm betting that's not a pig. How about we set up a trap?"

Bella nodded. He reached over her shoulder and unlatched the front door, leaving it slightly ajar. Taking her hand, he set off back toward her office where the safe was still open and on display in the moonlight.

"Let's leave it like that. Now, where can we hide, and make sure this particular pig can't get away?"

CHAPTER SIX

Bella directed Billy behind her desk and they crouched down together. She could clearly hear someone coming up the stairs, and it definitely wasn't Jay. Her teeth were chattering so hard she wondered why Billy didn't say something. He was busy texting while she laid the gun on the floor, making sure the safety was still on.

The stumbling footsteps grew louder and were accompanied by a litany of grunts and curses that Bella remembered only too well. She tensed as her former employee, Axel Jordan, swayed against the door frame, the smell of alcohol coming off him in waves.

"Stupid bitch," he muttered. "Can't even shut the safe properly. Thinks she's so safe with that disabled vet protecting her?"

Beside Bella, Billy's arm was rigid, his whole attention on Axel, and his normal expression obscured by an icy calmness that reminded her of Jay.

Axel stumbled against the desk, knocking piles of paper to the floor, and then leaned down to look into the safe, where the strongbox was clearly visible.

"I'll just take it all." Axel chuckled. "Bastards."

It took Bella a terrified second to notice Billy was on the move. He crawled around the other side of the desk, gathered himself, and leapt on Axel's back, bringing the younger man crashing to the ground.

Bella shot to her feet as Axel attempted to break free, his flailing fist connecting with the side of Billy's head making him jerk backward. With a *whoop,* Axel attempted to shake Billy off, but Bella wasn't going to let that happen.

"Stay right where you are," she yelled as she pointed the gun at Axel, and took up a two-handed shooting stance.

"Like you know how to fire that." Axel gasped as Billy recaptured one of his hands and wrenched it up against his spine.

"You don't think Jay taught me to defend myself?" Bella asked. "Try me."

Billy shoved Axel's head down to the floor again with some force, and he went quiet.

"Do you have any rope?" Billy asked.

"I have panty hose!" Bella laid the gun down on the desk and ran to her bedroom.

Her hands were shaking so hard, it was almost impossible to get the darn panty hose out of the packet. Not that she needed to worry about accidentally snagging them . . .

When she got back, Axel was still out of it and Billy had grabbed hold of his other wrist.

"Thanks." He took the black, silky hose. "What a waste."

Bella's knees gave way, and she sank down beside him. "I hardly wear them anymore. I prefer stay-up stockings or Spanx."

Billy chuckled. "Good to know."

"How can you be so cheerful?" Bella demanded.

"Because we won." Billy turned to look at her properly. "Are you okay?"

She reached out and cupped his cheek, her voice trembling. "I thought he was going to kill you, and then I thought that would be the second man I've loved taken away from me too quickly."

Billy placed his hand over hers. "You've had a terrible shock —"

"Yes, I have, and maybe I'm speaking the truth because there isn't anything left to hide behind when this kind of thing happens," Bella said. "I'd hate to be the kind of person who ignores a wake-up call."

Billy's cell buzzed, making them both jump. He took it out of his pocket and held Bella's gaze.

"It's Nate. I'm going to call him, okay?"

He pressed the screen and put the sheriff on speaker. "Hey, can you come on over to the Red Dragon? I've got Axel Jordan drunk and tied up in Bella's apartment."

"I'm already in the kitchen." Nate sounded his usual laidback self. "The back door was wide open."

Bella winced. "I guess I forgot to check if it was locked when Sonali went out, and I didn't put the alarm system on because Jay was still in the building."

Billy patted her shoulder. "It's okay." He could hear Nate coming up the stairs and kept talking to him. "Axel smashed through both doors, so you should be able to walk right in."

"So I see," Nate replied. "I'm coming in now."

Billy made sure that Bella's gun was in full view on the desk, and slowly stood up, offering Bella his hand to help her rise as well.

"You're bleeding," Bella gasped.

"Yeah, I think his ring caught me when he walloped me on the side of the head," Billy hastened to reassure her. "Nothing to worry about."

Nate stood in the doorway and slowly put his weapon away. "Nice job, guys."

"You're welcome," Billy said. "He's drunk and he's still breathing, and that's all you need to know."

"Got it." Nate went down on one knee and shook Axel's shoulder until he groaned. "You're under arrest . . ."

Billy moved over to where Bella was standing, one hand over her mouth, and put his arm around her. "How about we go into the kitchen and make some strong coffee?"

She nodded, and carefully stepped over Nate, who was busy calling for an ambulance and some backup.

Billy hugged her as they walked down the hallway. "You did good."

She shuddered. "I'm not sure about that."

"Yeah, you did. I believed you'd shoot him and more importantly, so did Axel. Your intervention gave me the moment I needed to knock him out once and for all." He led her to the couch. "I'll get the coffee. Do you want to text Jay?"

"I'm surprised he isn't already up here demanding to know what's going on," Bella said.

As if she'd conjured him up with her

words, Jay appeared in the doorway, his frantic gaze fastened on Bella, and he rushed over to her side.

"Are you okay? Nate just told me what happened. How the *hell* didn't I notice what was going down." He took Bella's hand in both of his. "Did he hurt you? How did he get in the kitchen? Did you let him in?"

Billy stepped into Jay's line of sight. "Maybe you could ease up on the questions, Jay. Your mom's pretty shaken up right now."

Jay briefly glanced at Billy and then returned his attention to his mother. "That's it. You're coming to live with Erin and me. I can't let you stay here another night."

Bella sat up straight. "No, I'm not going to do that."

"I'm sorry, but I'm not giving you a choice, okay?" Jay stated. "Just pack a few things and come with me right now."

Bella looked over Jay's head right at Billy, and he cleared his throat.

"Bella doesn't want to live with you."

Jay slowly stood and turned to Billy. "Look, I'm grateful that you were here, and Nate says you were the one who tackled Axel, but this isn't really your business, is it?"

"It is if Bella wants it to be." Billy held Jay's gaze. "Your mother is a grown woman.

If she wants to stay here maybe you should respect her decision or at least give her the time to come to one herself."

Silence fell as the retired Navy SEAL contemplated Billy long enough to set all the hairs on the back of Billy's neck on edge.

"Mom can't stay here tonight. The locks need fixing."

"Then she can choose what she wants to do." Billy looked at Bella. "Do you want to stay the night with Jay, or come back to the ranch with me?"

Bella rose from her seat and came to stand beside him. "Thanks for the offer, but I think I'll have to stay nearby so I can be here early in the morning when the locksmith arrives."

"Jay could do that," Billy said firmly. "Come home with me."

"Yeah." Jay cleared his throat. "I'll take care of everything. You do what you want, Mom."

Bella's smile was glorious as she placed her hand in Billy's. "Then I'll come with you."

Bella glanced over at Billy as they drove back to the ranch. She'd taken care of his bloodied head, talked to Nate, and made sure that Jay went home to Erin. The thought that Axel Jordan was now in custody made her feel so much safer.

"You okay?" Billy asked as they drew up in front of the silent ranch house.

"I'm getting there." She smiled at him, and in the darkness he leaned over and gently kissed her mouth. "Won't Ruth mind another guest?"

"I texted them all to let them know we were coming, so hopefully they've all gotten the message and gone to bed." The gentle humor in his voice was balm for her soul. "They're a nosy bunch."

She climbed down from the truck and looked up as a flurry of snow descended through the blackness of the night. "The ranch house looks like a Christmas card with all the lights and the snow."

"So I've been told." Billy took her hand. "Come on in."

The house smelled of Christmas spices and pine, and was lovely and warm. After shedding their coats and boots in the mudroom, they tiptoed up the stairs to the second floor. Billy opened a door and led her into a room with an angled roof that looked out over the barn.

"Chase converted these attic spaces into separate suites. He and January are across the hall."

"It's lovely." Bella gazed out over the snow-covered roofs and fields. "It smells so new and piney."

"It didn't exist when Annie lived here, so it was a good place for me to start afresh."

Bella pointed at the big wooden framed bed. "That's one of Ruth's quilts."

"Yeah, and BB made the headboard." Billy's smile was wry. "You can't get away from them even in here."

"And you wouldn't want to." She walked straight into his arms, and it felt like coming home. "Come on, admit it."

"It's my home," he said simply. "It's who I am."

Bella went to reply and yawned instead, giving him an up-close and personal view of her tonsils that made Billy smile.

"Let's go to bed."

"I don't think I'm going to be good for much more than just sleeping," Bella confessed.

"Then sleep." He kissed the top of her head. "No pressure, remember?"

She used the bathroom and then climbed into the big bed and lay on her back listening as the extraordinary, all-encompassing silence closed around her like a silken glove. She yawned again as Billy joined her wearing a Morgan Ranch T-shirt and pj pants with horses on them.

"Nice." She pointed at the pants.

"Last year's Christmas present from Maria. I have to wear them, or else she'll be upset." He laid his arm along the top of her pillow, inviting her to snuggle in against him, which she did. "Hmmm. That's nice."

She rubbed her cheek against the softness of his T-shirt. The fact that they were both here, and uninjured, suddenly hit her again. She slid her fingers under his shirt, needing to touch his skin.

"It's okay." He stroked her hair. "We're all good."

She lay there and breathed him in, enjoyed the rise and fall of his chest, and the way he held her as if she was made of spun sugar. She must have dozed off because she came to plastered all over his front, her inner thigh pressed against the heat and hardness of his need.

His hand was planted firmly on her butt, his fingers flexing.

"Billy?" she whispered into the darkness.

"Yeah?"

"I'm awake now."

His low chuckle reverberated against her skin. "I can see that."

"Will you kiss me?"

He slid a hand into her hair. "Always."

And then it all became so simple. Skin uncovered, kisses everywhere until he rolled her onto her back and entered her in one slow thrust that almost made her cry again. She held on to him, her hands everywhere as he brought her to a new peak of pleasure in his own sweet time.

"Bella . . ." He groaned her name as he came, and collapsed onto the pillow beside her. She stroked the back of his head, and let him stay there until he finally found the energy to roll away.

He reached for her hand, interlocking her fingers with his, and searched her face in the moonlight.

"I should've asked you about contraception."

"I'm past all that nonsense," she reassured him. "I would've mentioned it otherwise."

"And I can confirm that I got a clean bill of health from Dr. Tio last year."

They grinned at each other.

Bella kissed his nose. "So we can just have fun."

"Amen to that." He kissed her back. "Do you think you can sleep now?"

"Yes." She eased onto her side. "Just to let you know, I snore."

"So do I."

"Perfect." She spooned against him, and

he wrapped his arm around her waist. "Good night, Billy, and thanks for everything."

Within two minutes she was fast asleep.

"Dad, did you hear about what happened at the Red Dragon last night? I —"

Billy opened one eye to see Chase coming in through the door, laptop in hand. He pulled up short, a look of horror on his face as he took in the clothes strewn around the floor, and the two naked people in the bed.

"Dear God, I'm so sorry, I didn't realize —"

"What's going on?" BB put his head around the door and did a double take. "Jeez, Dad, gross. Lock the door next time, okay? You've traumatized Chase."

Chase backed out with all the care of a hostage situation. "So I'll assume you know what happened, and I'll see you at breakfast." He cleared his throat. "You too, Mrs. Williams."

When the door finally shut, Billy looked down at Bella, who had pulled the sheet almost over her head.

"I did tell you they were nosy, didn't I?"

He suddenly realized she was shaking with laughter, and felt much better.

"It could've been worse. It could've been

Jay," she spluttered.

"And now I'd be a dead man," Billy murmured. He glanced at the time. "You okay to get up and face the family over breakfast? I've got chores to do, and I bet you'll be wanting to get home."

Bella grabbed his hand. "Thank you."

"For what?"

"All of this." She waved a hand around, and the sheet fell to her waist. Billy made himself focus on her face, although it was almost impossible. "I'm okay with *everything.*"

"Like with us being a couple?"

"Yes." She met his gaze, her brown eyes so warm and full of shyness that he wanted to kiss her. "Especially that." She bit her lip. "I think I'm falling in love with you."

Billy nodded, too choked up right at that moment to do anything else. The fact that he was home, with his family, and now had this unimaginable, unexpected gift of love from a woman he liked, respected, and lusted after was almost too much to comprehend.

"Are you okay?" Bella asked softly.

"Yeah." He swallowed hard. "I'm just counting my blessings."

Everything he'd had and lost, everything he'd ever wanted to achieve with the blessing of this second chance now made sense. Bella made sense of it. Coming home to his old friend completed a circle he hadn't even been aware he was traveling.

He gave in to the temptation to kiss her, and then she touched him, and . . .

"Wait a sec." He eased himself away and went to lock the door before climbing back into bed. "Maybe just for once, the chores can wait."

CHAPTER SEVEN

"So what's so important that you had to drag me and Erin out here, Mom?" Jay inquired as Bella maneuvered him into the darkened guest center at the ranch.

"The lights aren't working."

"There are a load of Morgans up here to deal with that kind of thing," Jay protested. "Why —"

"SURPRISE!!"

Billy snapped the lights on to reveal the fifty or so guests Bella had invited to celebrate her son and new daughter-in-law's Vegas wedding. Following Bella's instructions, he immediately shut the door just in case Jay decided to bolt.

"Mom?" That was Erin's delighted voice. "You and Dad are *here*?"

Whatever Jay might have been going to say was lost as his wife ran over to her parents and started hugging them. Jay stared down at Bella, who gave him her best wide-eyed, innocent look.

"You did this?"

She shrugged. "With a little help from my friends." She touched his sleeve. "I wanted to do something special for you both."

He let out his breath and looked around the crowded room. She knew he wasn't at his happiest in crowds, but hopefully, seeing as he knew everyone who was present, he'd soon relax and enjoy himself.

"It's all good, Mom. Thank you."

"You're welcome, Jay." She gave him a little push in the right direction. "Now go and say hello to Erin's parents while I see how everything's going in the kitchen."

Bella rushed through the swing doors, her hand to her heart. She leaned against the wall and slowly exhaled. "I thought he was going to bolt."

Billy and Sonali looked up from whatever they were doing and stared at her.

"Yeah, there was a moment when I wondered the same thing," Billy said. "Probably not a good idea to spring too many surprises on a retired Navy SEAL."

"Tell me about it." Bella looked around the kitchen. "Now, what can I do to help?"

"Nothing. You're the mother of the groom, and you're the one throwing the party. Go out and be sociable." Billy came over and pointed at the exit.

"I'd much rather be helping in here."

"We're good." Billy held the door open. "Off you go and charm the pants off Erin's parents."

She raised an eyebrow and whispered, "The only pants I want to charm off are yours."

"Good to know." Billy's blue eyes glinted with warm amusement. "But you still need to get out there."

"Will you come and join me?" She stroked the collar of his shirt.

"When the buffet is all set up I'll come and sit with you, okay?"

"I suppose it's the best I can hope for." She sighed. "Maybe I'll go and talk to Chase. He still won't look me in the eye."

Billy grinned. "Not our fault that he's a prude."

"And then there's BB, who keeps winking and grinning at me like he thinks the idea of his father having sex is a big joke."

"BB does think that, but you can ignore him as well." He hesitated. "You might want to talk to Maria. She and I are very close, and I'd love it if you two could be friends."

"I'll do my best." She went on tiptoe and kissed him. "Don't be too long."

Bella made her way out to the dining

room and was immediately engulfed in a crowd of friends and family. By the time she'd talked to everyone, Billy and Sonali had already put out trays of appetizers, and Nancy, Jay's second in command, was doing brisk business at the bar.

Bella spotted Billy's granddaughter curled up on one of the big couches in front of the roaring log fire and went over to join her. Maria wore jeans, a black T-shirt with some kind of cartoon character on it, and a black hoodie.

"Are you having a good time?" Bella asked as she sat beside her.

Maria made a face. "Not really. It's all adults here, and Grandpa's busy in the kitchen, so I have no one to really talk to."

"You know, that's my fault," Bella confessed. "I didn't think to include any other kids your age when I was making up the guest lists."

"There aren't any kids out here," Maria pointed out. "That's why I have to go on the bus to Bridgeport for high school."

"That sucks." Bella nodded. "You should taste the food though. Your grandpa is a really good cook."

"I know. He's made me taste every single thing about fifty times, so I'm good." Maria grinned. "He really wanted to make things right for you."

"That's because he's a really nice man."

"And he really, *really* likes you," Maria said. "You know that, right?"

Bella glanced at the teen. "You think so?"

"Dude, he like can't stop talking about you, and his face goes all funny and goofy." Maria shook her head. "It's hilarious."

"Really?" Now Bella sounded like a teenager herself. "I like him, too."

Maria's smile disappeared. "I hope you mean it. Grandpa's life hasn't been easy, and I don't want anyone to hurt him again."

"I wouldn't do that," Bella reassured Maria. "Did he tell you that I've known him since kindergarten? That's a long time to know someone and still like them."

"That's true." Maria nodded. "Ruth said that you always stuck up for him even when some of the people around here were saying he was a murderer."

"As I said, I knew he couldn't have done that. He loved Annie, he really did. It's a real shame she died before he could make things right with her," Bella said. "So are you okay with me and your grandpa being a couple?"

Maria shrugged. "You make him happy. He smiles a lot more, and that makes me happy because now that I live with Dad and

Jenna I can't take care of him myself all the time."

"He's wonderful." Bella hesitated. "I never thought I'd find someone I could love again."

"That's awesome." Maria offered Bella a high five. "You should tell him."

"Tell me what?"

Bella looked up to see Billy smiling down at them, a tray of canapés in his hand.

Maria groaned. "Jeez, Grandpa, I ate about two million of those things last week! Take them away!"

"I thought you liked them," Billy protested.

"I liked the first couple of hundred." Maria stood up and stretched. "Is there any of that shrimp thing left?"

"Plenty," Billy said as Maria wandered off. "Poor kid got stuck being my number one taster for everything. She was really helpful, but I think I put her off eating for life."

"I think she'll pull through." Bella also rose and directed her gaze over to the buffet table where Maria was piling her plate with food and chatting to her father, Blue. "Are we almost ready to set out the main course?"

"Sonali and I decided we'd do it in about ten minutes. Do you want to make an announcement or something, or have a few speeches?"

"I'd rather not," Bella said. "It all seems to be going really well at the moment. Even Erin's parents are being gracious about the whole wedding fiasco — in fact, I bonded with Erin's Mom over our shared wish to have seen Erin in a beautiful wedding dress."

"Good for you." Billy gestured at the tray. "I'm going to put this down on the table. Is there anything I can get for you?"

"I'm good," Bella replied. "I just need to speak to Yvonne about the cake."

"She's in the kitchen right now setting it up." Billy looked down at her. "Is everything okay?"

"It's wonderful." She smiled into his eyes. "Jay's happy and Erin's parents have finally accepted the fact that their daughter hasn't married a potential member of Congress."

She went through to the kitchen and spoke to Yvonne, who had designed, baked, and decorated the most beautiful cake Bella could ever have imagined. They would set it out after the buffet along with champagne and hope that by then, everyone would be too full of good food and benevolent thoughts to do anything but toast the happy couple.

Billy came into the kitchen and caught

hold of her hand.

"Come and see this."

"Aren't you supposed to be managing a kitchen or something?" Bella asked.

"Sonali, Avery, and Yvonne are in charge. We can goof off for a few minutes."

He took her to put on her coat and they walked out into the crackling stillness of ice and the gentle fall of snow.

"Look up there," Billy said.

"At what?" Bella stopped and raised her face to the inky night sky. Billy stood behind with his arms wrapped around her waist. "Wow, that's a big moon, and the stars are so clear!"

"Now come and look at this." He led her toward the old barn that housed a mixed collection of farm animals and the family horses.

He paused by one of the stalls and unlocked the top half of the stable door. Bella stood on tiptoe and looked inside to see a newborn foal and her mother.

"Oh, my goodness," she whispered. "What a beautiful sight."

"Roy just came in to tell me the mare had foaled before he went off to take a shower." Billy's chuckle warmed the back of her neck. "Luckily for us we also have a vet in the family, and Jenna was right here on the spot. She's probably taking a shower, too."

Bella turned in Billy's arms to face him as he secured the top door again.

"Thank you for showing me such beautiful things."

He angled his head and looked down at her. "You're welcome."

"All of them give me hope," Bella said. "Jay finding himself again and falling in love, Erin, you . . ."

His smile was beautiful. "I give you hope?"

"Yes, that it's possible to find *two* wonderful men in one lifetime, and fall in love with them."

He kissed her very slowly and carefully. "I can't argue with that." He hesitated and looked down at her. "I'd like to ask you something."

"Okay."

He grimaced. "But I'm finding it hard to come up with the right words because I don't want to offend you, or presume too much, or —"

She pressed a finger to his lips. "How about you just ask?"

"You know that I love you, and —"

"I do?" Bella blinked up at him. "I don't think you've actually said it out loud to me before, although I'd kind of *assumed* that was where we were at —"

It was Billy's turn to stop her talking by kissing her. When he finally drew back they were both breathless.

"Will you marry me?" Billy asked. "I know we have some issues here, like where we would live, and whether we'd both be able to keep working if we wanted to, and all that other stuff. Not even to mention Jay's reaction, and Maria's, and the rest of my incredibly supportive, but nosy as hell family."

He ran out of breath and just stared down at her shocked face.

"Did you hear what I said?"

Bella nodded and bit her lip. "I'm just trying to process the first part."

"My proposal of marriage?" Billy asked.

"Yes, that."

"Am I being stupid here?" Billy asked. "Would we be better off staying as we are? I'm happy, you're happy, and we're old enough not to worry about what anyone else thinks about us being together and not actually married."

Bella was still staring at him as if he'd grown another head, and he felt like a complete idiot. "Okay, then maybe we should shelve this discussion until after the holidays when things have calmed down a bit, and we know where we stand."

"Billy."

"Yeah?"

"Could you stop talking for a minute?" Bella asked.

He pressed his lips together and just looked pleadingly down at her. Around them the horses and cattle slumbered in their stalls and the snow continued to fall.

"Yes."

Billy cleared his throat. "Yes, you'd like to marry me?"

She nodded.

A wave of happiness so profound that it consumed his whole body swept over him, and he framed her face in his hands. "Thank God."

Her smile was so beautiful, and so full of trust that he fought back the urge to cry.

"You'll never regret that decision, Bella." His voice trembled with emotion. "I swear that I will do my best to *never* let you down, and I'll always be there for you."

"I know you will." She used her thumb to gently wipe at the corner of his eye. "It's okay. We can work out the details later, or stay engaged until one of us decides to retire. We'll work it out. I *know* we will."

Billy kissed her again and she wrapped her arms around his neck and kissed him back.

"Oh, jeez, not *again.*"

That was Chase's horrified voice. Billy buried his face in Bella's shoulder and shook with laughter.

"Grandpa . . ."

And that was Maria. Bella pushed on his chest and he turned around to see his oldest son and granddaughter staring at him with matching expressions of horror on their faces.

"We came out to see the new foal," Maria explained.

"She's right in here." Billy pointed at the stall and stepped back. "Don't go in yet, okay?"

"I know that." Maria rolled her eyes as if she'd lived on the ranch forever. "Why don't you two go in? Chase can keep an eye on me, and Jay *was* looking for Mrs. Williams."

"Then we'd better go," Bella said.

Maria had one last thing to say. "You know, Grandpa, if you keep behaving like this you should do what I suggested and ask Mrs. Williams to marry you."

Billy nodded. "I just did and she said yes."

Chase grinned and slapped Billy on the back. "That's *awesome*! Congratulations. I can't wait to see Jay's face when he finds out about this."

"Then maybe we'd better mention it to

him before Chase starts spreading rumors," Billy murmured as Chase and Maria walked away hand in hand. "Are you okay with that?"

"Yes, better to be safe than sorry," Bella agreed, and squeezed his fingers as they retraced their steps through the snow to the guest center.

They paused outside the kitchen door to remove their boots before returning to the warmth of the dining room beyond. Leaving Bella in the kitchen, Billy went and found Jay and persuaded him to step away from the noise, and into the quieter part of the building.

Knowing Jay was a plain speaker, Billy didn't bother with a long, flowery speech.

"I wanted you to know that I asked your mother to marry me, and she said yes."

Jay stared at him, a muscle moving in his cheek. "Okay."

"That's all you've got?" Billy asked.

"She loves you. That's all I need to know." Jay took a step closer to Billy. "And all you need to remember is that if you hurt her I'll come after you, and no one will ever find your body."

"Understood." Billy nodded.

"Then we're good." Jay stuck out his hand. "Welcome to the family."

■ ■ ■ ■

Bella helped clear away the food and then
returned to the dining room to watch Jay
and Erin cut the cake. She'd barely had a
moment to speak to Billy, but seeing as both
he and Jay were still alive and smiling, she
assumed everything had gone as well as it
could've.

Billy wanted her to marry him . . . and
the funny thing was that she wanted it, too.
She hadn't expected him to propose so
quickly, but as Maureen would probably
remind her, they weren't spring chickens so
they might as well enjoy their time together.
The thought of that — the thought of being
with him every day made her so happy she
still couldn't quite get her head around it.

She watched him now, as he passed Erin
the knife to cut the cake, his blue eyes
gleaming, and the harsher lines on his face
disappearing beneath his smile. A man who
had disappointed others, had paid dearly
for his mistakes, and yet had come home to
face his demons, and repay his debts. . . .
That took courage and humility, qualities
she could appreciate and strive to improve
in herself.

And what about her? She pictured Ron

and imagined him smiling down at her. She truly had been blessed in her life.

"Mom?"

She looked up, startled as Jay called her out to stand beside him and Erin.

"I'd like to thank my mom, Bella, for organizing this amazing party for me and Erin. I'd also like to thank Erin's parents for coming all the way from the East Coast to celebrate with us."

Everyone clapped, cheered, and drank champagne.

"And I'd like to thank Billy and Sonali for providing all the amazing food and Morgan Ranch and their staff for their hospitality," Jay added. "I had *completely* the wrong idea about why Mom was making me come up here to the ranch this evening."

"What did you think she wanted then?" BB called out.

Jay's smile was crooked. "I knew she was up to something, but I thought it had to do with her and Billy Morgan."

"Well, we all know about *that,*" BB joked. "It's hardly a secret that they've got the hots for each other."

Jay raised an eyebrow. "As it happens, there is something to announce about that as well, isn't there, Mom?"

Bella tried to frown him down, but Billy

stepped forward.

"Bella Williams has agreed to become my wife." He held out his hand to her. "And she's made me the happiest man on this planet."

Bella walked toward him, aware that she was blushing. None of the Morgans looked particularly surprised by the announcement, and they all looked thrilled. Ruth was dabbing at her eyes and Maria was doing some kind of victory dance.

Billy took her hand in his and faced the guests. "Thank you very much, but tonight is about Erin and Jay, so let's get back to cutting the cake, toasting their good health, and wishing them the very best of everything for the rest of their days."

While everyone got on with that, Billy and Bella ended up in the kitchen, which felt right somehow. Billy grinned as she rolled up her sleeves, pinned up her hair, and set to work.

"I don't think I'm going to persuade you to leave this time, am I?"

"Not a chance. If anyone wants to come and say good-bye they'll know where to find me."

He threw a dishcloth in her direction and she threw it back and they ended up wrestling over it and giggling like two kids.

"This is going to be fun," Billy said.

"What is — us?"

"Yeah, us." He kissed her nose. "I love you, Bella."

"And I love you."

"Will you stay over?"

"At the speed we're cleaning up I'll probably be here all night anyway," Bella joked.

"We'll work things out." Billy looked down at her. "We'll *make* this work."

"Yes, we will." She nodded. "Despite my son and all the Morgans offering us advice."

"They mean well."

"Yes, but sometimes I wish they'd all butt out."

"We could build our own house halfway between your place and mine," Billy suggested.

"Or we could share our time between both places."

They smiled at each other. Whatever happened next, Bella was quite certain that Billy was right and that they would have fun. Maureen would be so proud of her. . . .

BILLY'S MINI FRUIT PAVLOVAS

For Pavlova
6 egg whites at room temperature
1 1/2 cups white sugar
2 tsp cornstarch
1 Tbsp lemon juice
1/2 Tbsp vanilla extract

For Cream
1 1/2 cups cold heavy whipping cream

For Topping/Decor
4 to 5 cups fresh fruits (berries are my favorite)

Instructions
1. Using stand mixer, beat 6 egg whites on high speed for 1 minute until soft peaks form. With mixer on, gradually add 1 1/2 cups of sugar and beat 10 minutes on high speed or until stiff peaks form. (Should be smooth and glossy.)

2. Use a spatula to quickly fold in lemon juice and vanilla extract, and then fold in cornstarch until blended.
3. Pipe meringue onto parchment paper and indent the center with a spoon. Bake at 225 degrees F for 1 hour and 15 minutes, then turn oven off. Without opening the door, leave for 30 minutes more. Outside of meringue should be dry and crisp to the tap.
4. Allow to cool. Can be stored for 3 to 5 days in airtight container. Or topped with whipped cream (follow instructions on carton) and fruit and eaten immediately!

For more recipes,
check out my Web site at
www.themorgansranch.com.

■ ■ ■ ■

CHRISTMAS IN BLUE HOLLOW FALLS

DONNA KAUFFMAN

■ ■ ■ ■

CHAPTER ONE

"Weddings on Christmas? There should be a law."

"For or against?"

Moira Brogan drained the last of the Coke from her glass until the straw made a slurping sound, jiggled the ice a bit, then found one last sip. *Because you need more sugar. And more caffeine.* Ignoring her little voice, as she had been all day — *week, month, year* — she glanced up at the bartender, pondering the question with all the gravity of the attorney she was. "Against, your honor. I mean, who wants to share their anniversary with Santa's big day? It should be all about him."

"Unless you don't believe in Santa," replied the bartender.

The bartender — Sally, according to her hotel name badge — looked about five or six years older than Moira's own twenty-seven, and eons wiser.

"Even if you don't, it should be recognized that many people do," Moira countered, warming to the debate. Debate she understood. Debate she knew how to win. Life outside the courtroom? Not so much with the winning there. Case in point? Sitting in a rural hotel bar drowning her sorrows in a gallon of carbonated sugar and caffeine instead of dancing the night away at her brother's lovely and beautiful wedding reception up in Blue Hollow Falls.

"Those people, the believers," Moira went on, perhaps more doggedly than required given the judge and jury was bartender Sally, "might, and quite probably would, construe a person marrying on such a day as being . . . well, sacreligious. Or, at the very least, unimaginative. Like, said person could only improve on the most celebrated day of the year by getting married on it. Somewhat self-aggrandizing, don't you think?"

"Point taken," Sally said judiciously.

Gaining momentum, Moira said, "I mean, I suppose we might include a clause for people like my wonderful and completely besotted brother, who are just so madly in love they think what could be more festive than getting married on Christmas? Because, really, what could be?"

"Getting married in Disney World?"

"Ha," Moira said with a grin, raising her empty glass in toast. "Point to the prosecution." Then she caught the look on Sally's face and set her glass down. "Oh my God. You didn't. Did you? Was Mickey Mouse the justice of the peace?" A splutter of laughter threatened and Moira tried to frown it into submission. Firstly, because it would be rude to her new friend Sally, and secondly, because she knew she was one-too-many-insomnia-riddled-nights away from the kind of laughter that would quickly devolve into a run of convulsive, bordering-on-hysterical giggles. And she doubted Sally would join in, given it was her nuptials that had triggered them.

"Not me, your honor." Sally smiled and lifted a hand, as if she was being sworn in. "Maid of honor."

"Me too!" Moira replied, perhaps a little too loudly. In addition to far too little sleep, she was definitely way too hopped up on wedding cake. "Well, co-maid of honor, anyway, with the bride's sister."

"Yeah," Sally replied, with a smile and a nod toward Moira's outfit. "I gathered."

Moira looked down to the strapless, silk and organza, emerald green formal she was wearing. She probably should have changed when she'd first gotten back to the hotel. She'd left the reception right after Seth and Pippa had taken off for their honeymoon in Ireland. She'd done her due diligence, smiled and laughed her way through all of her sworn duties. But once her brother and brand-new sister-in-law were gone, Moira had wanted nothing more than to be alone with her stupid, self-pitying misery. She was not proud of herself, of her apparent inability to get over her latest life disaster. Either of them. But the romantic disaster had been last spring, for God's sake.

Only when she'd gotten back to the hotel in Turtle Springs, itself a tiny town tucked into a curve of the Hawksbill River, in the shadow of the Blue Ridge Mountains, she'd realized the very last thing she wanted was to be alone.

She just hadn't wanted to be with people who knew her. People who would expect her to be overcome with joy and happiness for her brother, Seth, and his new bride, whom Moira adored almost as much as she adored her older brother. And she was quite sincerely thrilled for them. She was. It was just the host of painful memories watching them say their I do's had roused up, coupled with the recent collapse of all her future career plans, that had her escaping the family-clogged reception like Cinderella from the ball.

She didn't know which had made her more miserable, the tough love "oh, come now, Mouse, get on over yourself, lass," looks from her oldest brother and sister, Aiden and Kathleen, the "you poor, wee thing" pats on the shoulder from her dear Aunt Margery, or the endless variations of "don't you worry, you'll get married, too . . . someday," comments from what felt like every last one of the rest of her relatives and family friends. And given she was the youngest of six, as were both of her parents, their collective clan was a small army. And that was just the Brogan side.

Pippa's family, straight over from Ireland, was just as prolific when it came to propagating the family tree. *And they brought those lovely, awful accents with them.* Lovely because that beautiful lilt was still music to her ears, and her heart. Awful because she still missed that particular lilt and the man it had belonged to, and hearing it all around her, in conjunction with a wedding no less, had doomed any chance she might have had to avoid reliving every moment of their whirlwind love affair. All the good parts, which had been every moment of it, and the very, very sad parts . . . which had only been right at the end of it. Because it had been the end of it.

And no one in her family even knew that her big, bold career plans of being a trial attorney in Silicon Valley had suffered an equally swift and demoralizing demise when she'd learned she'd flunked the bar exam. *Yeah, won't that be a fun reveal.*

So, she'd fled back to the small hotel she'd booked herself into down in the valley, claiming she'd be fine there as all the lodgings in Blue Hollow Falls were fully taken by her family and the equally extensive MacMillan clan. In truth, she'd been relieved for the excuse. She'd liked knowing she had an escape route, a bolt hole, somewhere to hide, if needed.

Upon her return, the small hotel lounge had been packed to the gills with reporters from all over the globe, along with a fair number of the less-than-savory paparazzi, who'd all rushed to the rural mountain region — in most cases, judging by the bevy of accents in the room, from far, far away — in hopes of getting photos or footage of Moira's new sister-in-law, Pippa Mac-Millan. Well, Pippa Brogan now, she presumed. It just so happened, Pippa was a very famous Irish folk singer. The reporters hadn't been successful, though. Blue Hollow Falls had well and truly adopted Pippa, and they protected their own. The ranks had been locked up tight, and not so much as a single long-range lens had intruded upon the happy couple's special day.

From the raucous noise level inside the hotel bar, Moira presumed the collective journalist horde had apparently decided to drown their defeat as well, only in something far stronger than her Coke.

Moira took another long sip of her soda, the fizzy bubbles tickling her nose, absently realizing that while she'd slipped back into her melancholy, Sally had refreshed her drink. Moira continued to sip while she watched Sally deftly handle the gaggle pressed up against the bar. Moira shifted away, into the shadows where she had tucked herself at the very end of the bar.

The only reason she had a stool at all was because Sally had spied Moira edging her way around the periphery of the dimly lit place and had slid one under the exit gap at the end of the bar. Sally probably kept one on her side of the bar specifically for forlorn-looking creatures such as herself. Sally had even taken Moira's long, winter coat and tucked it back in the office, making Moira initially wonder if perhaps the bartender was angling for some kind of wedding scoop herself. But, even sleep-deprived and on a cake-frosting high, Moira was pretty good at reading people. Bartender Sally was a good egg. She'd bet her one and still only law license on it.

Moira really didn't want to think about that second law license, the one she didn't have. The lack of which had crushed all her future plans. Instead, she tilted up her glass, intent on crunching a few pieces of ice, only the full cluster slid down and splashed her in the face. Sally appeared like the magical genie Moira was beginning to suspect she was, and proffered a clean napkin to Moira while quickly mopping up the spill. "Thanks," Moira said, checking the front of her gown, relieved to see she hadn't stained the fabric.

She caught Sally checking out the dress, and held her arms out slightly. "I thought the bride did a pretty good job picking these out," Moira said. "I mean, they're tasteful, and they don't make me look like I'm playing dress-up as a Grecian goddess or anything." She looked back at Sally and sighed. "It still has bridesmaid written all over it, though, doesn't it?" Lifting a hand to her short mop of auburn curls, she said, "At least I don't have the teased and lacquered beehive up-do to go with it. It could be so much worse."

"Actually, you look great. Amazing even," Sally said, appearing quite sincere. "The green dress, with your red hair and fair skin? And don't get me started on the green eyes, which I'm just going to pretend are colored contacts, because, honestly, so not fair."

Moira blushed and laughed at the same time. "If you're angling for a bigger tip, done. I'll just be emptying my wallet on the bar right now."

Sally laughed, waved her hand. "Just being honest. But I'd have known it was a bridesmaid dress no matter what it looked like. This is Turtle Springs, Virginia," Sally added dryly. "Out here, we don't have much call for formal anything." She pulled another two beers from the tap, put them on a tray, and handed them to one of the waitresses, while taking three more orders from the other waitress, which she'd already started filling with her free hand. People jammed up against the bar shouted their orders nonstop and somehow Sally managed to pull their drinks, smile and joke with them, all while continuing the conversation with Moira as if they were seated at a café table alone together, dishing over wedding gossip.

"You're very good at your job," Moira told her, vaguely wondering what kind of money

285

a bartender made. Maybe she needed to completely rethink her life. *And maybe you need to steer clear of the caffeine and sugar and get more than a catnap at night.* She prudently pushed her once again empty glass away.

"Besides, it's not like your brother's wedding was flying under the radar," Sally continued, taking the compliment in stride. "It's been front-page news pretty much everywhere since the moment they got engaged." She nodded to the throng. "Hence this insanity."

"Well, they did initially try and keep the wedding date under wraps," Moira said. "In truth, I think Seth thought that having it today would kind of throw everybody off. Like, who would get married on Christmas? Because he'd never want to compete with Santa, either."

"Who would?" Sally offered.

"Right? But there was no way to keep it from getting out. I mean, you know all about it, everyone knows all about it." She waved at the crowded lounge. "The whole world knows about it, because, you know —"

"Pippa MacMillan," Sally finished for her, nodding, as if nothing else needed to be said. And it didn't.

"It's such a happily-ever-after story, too." Sally, who had seemed so pragmatic and seen-it-all, clearly wasn't immune to the Christmas fairy-tale wedding, either. "I mean, Pippa finally returns to the music scene just when speculation reached the point that everyone was convinced she'd never come back from her injury, and then she's getting engaged after a whirlwind romance during her secret hideaway trip to the States? And they're getting married on Christmas? Even Mickey Mouse has to bow to that." Sally let out a self-deprecating chuckle. "Listen to me, getting all sappy." She wiped down the bar and went to refill Moira's glass but Moira waved her away. "But, you know what, a gorgeous holiday wedding up in the mountains here? What could be more romantic than that?"

Falling in love while you're on a whirlwind trip to Ireland, was Moira's immediate thought. *Finally allowing yourself to consider having a personal life after years of studying, and studying, and more studying. Maybe even picturing your own wedding day for the first time.*

Only her whirlwind romance hadn't ended with the fairy-tale wedding, holiday or no. Nope. Hers had just . . . ended.

"I mean, they seem perfect for each

other," Sally went on. "I bet it was a really beautiful ceremony, too, up at your brother's winery. What with the recent snowfall and that view. I went to a tasting up there last fall. It's gorgeous." She filled another set of orders and began drying a few freshly washed glasses that someone had just brought out from the back. "I know you probably can't talk about it."

Moira had promised Pippa and Seth not to talk about the ceremony to anyone outside the family and invited guests. And she wouldn't. She just wished she didn't have to picture it in her own mind. Because it had been stunning and beautiful and perfect. Sally was also right that Seth and Pippa were perfect for each other. So much so, it made Moira's newly mended heart ache all over again, reliving their sweetly intimate ceremony in her mind.

She'd felt selfish and ridiculous, thinking about her own heartbreak while they said their I do's. But how was she supposed to watch them — their love shining so brightly as they shared both laughter and tears while speaking their personally written vows to each other — and not wonder what might have been for her? Maybe it wasn't selfish — she was sincere in celebrating their happiness after all — so much as simply human.

"If they'd really wanted to keep it secret, I guess they could have eloped," Sally said, then handed two more trays of beers over the bar.

Moira laughed at that. "Maybe, but it would have been a toss-up over which clan would have disowned them first. Turns out the only family more traditional and excited about all family events than the Brogans is the MacMillans."

Sally laughed along with her, then nodded toward two swarthy, good-looking men who'd pushed their way to the bar, laughing and jostling each other, while a third man, a bit older and quieter, moved in behind them. He was also good-looking, but of the tall, blond, and chiseled variety. He wore a beautifully tailored suit that didn't fit in with the relaxed throng.

"What'll you fellas have?" Sally asked. "That you haven't had already, that is?"

The two younger guys started flirting outrageously with Sally, despite being easily a decade her junior, their accents pegging them as French, maybe Belgian. Sally handled them with easy aplomb, and appeared just a little flattered by the attention. *Beware the accent,* Moira wanted to warn her. *That's how they get you to lower all your defenses and act like an idiot.* Never again, she vowed. No more pretty men from distant lands with beautiful accents.

Mr. Tall, Blond, and Chiseled decided to turn his attention toward Moira. He appeared something of the brooding hero type, big and broad shouldered, with darker eyebrows, sharp cheekbones, and a sensuously shaped mouth. His hair was painfully perfect, and his eyes were a deep, dark brown, but there was nothing warm in them.

Moira shifted away from him on instinct.

His smile was slow and did nothing to warm his gaze. "Member of the wedding party, I see?" he said, his accent thick as well, but decidedly American. By way of the South. Texas, she guessed, noting the expensive Stetson he carried in one hand.

Ha-ha, Karma, Moira thought. *Touché.*

Her lack of immediate response was all the invitation Texas needed to insert himself way too deep into her personal space.

Moira hadn't been genetically gifted in the stature department, topping out in the eighth grade at a few inches over five feet. However, as the youngest and shortest of six children, she'd long ago learned how to hold her own. She managed to slide her elbow onto the bar as she turned only her

290

head to look directly at her would-be lothario, creating both a barrier to his intrusion while simultaneously making it clear she was not welcoming his attention. Unfortunately, not enough of a barrier to keep from smelling the alcohol on his breath. "Observant," she said, not unkindly, but not kindly, either, then pointedly turned back to her soda. Which she belatedly remembered pushing away earlier. It now sat right in front of Texas.

"Looking for this?" He picked up her empty glass. "Why don't I buy you another and we'll get to know each other a little better." His smile deepened, but his eyes remained cold. She caught a flash of what looked like irritation at her lack of a positive reaction to his overture. When she saw his smile change to something darker, as if she'd just issued him a challenge he intended to meet, the first tinkling of alarm prickled at the hairs on her neck. Moira was suddenly glad she was sitting in a public place, filled with people. A lot of people.

"Who knows, darlin'," he added, picking up the glass and jiggling the ice, his gaze directly on hers now. "If you're real lucky, maybe we'll hit it off and someday you can upgrade that bridesmaid dress to the real deal."

Moira knew the best response was no response of any kind, but he'd caught her so off guard with that decidedly misogynistic bon mot, her mouth dropped open before she could stop herself. "How do you know I'm not married with three kids?"

"No ring."

"I'm liberated."

"I'm Max," he said, his gaze dropping to the front of her strapless dress, then back up to her eyes. "Nice to meet you, Libby."

The predatory look, along with the smell of stale alcohol that he seemed to wear like some men wore cologne, made her shudder involuntarily. Moira turned to look for Sally, but she'd joined her fellow barkeep at the far end of the long, scarred, oak bar to help him break up an argument. Which Sally managed to do rather handily, Moira noted. "I want to be her when I grow up," she murmured under her breath.

"I have something that wants to grow up," Texas said, his hot breath now right next to her ear. "And you're just the one to help me with that."

Moira had to lean way back when she turned to look at him so as not to actually come into contact with his body. So far back she almost fell off her stool. She could have simply slid to her feet and put more space between them, but for one, she wasn't letting this guy back her up. And secondly, she stayed seated because the high bar stool put her closer to even height with him. Standing, even in the heels she was still wearing, she'd have been at a sore disadvantage. "Max," she said, quite sympathetically, "I know this will come as a big disappointment to you, so I'm apologizing up front, but I'm afraid I'm already spoken for."

He made a big show of looking around. "Funny, I don't see anyone."

"I know," she said, helpfully. "And that's okay. I just didn't want to take up any more of your time."

He looked confused, which had been her goal.

"Now you're free to go dazzle someone else. Or maybe get a cab and call it a night?" Moira wasn't sure if Turtle Springs even had cabs. "Or an Uber." They were everywhere, right?

Texas surprised her again by neatly sliding his arm through hers and tugging her off the stool. Caught off balance, and now from a standpoint decidedly lower than his six-foot-plus height, she staggered a step or two. He took that as an excuse to put his other hand on her hip to help steady her. His fingertips were hard and dug into her flesh.

"Let's go outside and you can help me with that, too," he said, the cold light of what looked like victory gleaming in his dark eyes.

Moira felt a brief wave of nausea, and knew it was only partly due to her instinctive reaction to him and the sudden, untenable situation she'd somehow gotten herself into. She hadn't had a full night sleep in longer than she could remember, and the catnaps she'd convinced herself were enough had just been proven woefully inadequate.

"Your other gentleman caller will have to wait his turn," Texas told her. He let his gaze dip to the front of her dress again, and that light in his eyes, when he looked back up, had gone from victorious to predatory. The kind of predator who looked like he'd take great pleasure in claiming his prey, and not necessarily in a way the prey was going to enjoy. "First come, first get, right, darlin'?"

"First — get?" Moira repeated, trying not to splutter. Okay, now she was done being nice. Actually, she'd been done the moment he'd put his hands on her. She tried to tug her arm free. "What on earth gave you the idea that I would ever —"

"You're a bridesmaid, sitting in a bar, drinking alone." This time he raked his gaze up and down the full length of her body. "What other idea would I get?"

Fair point, Moira conceded, and yet, that still didn't give anyone license to put their hands on her. "I've said I'm not interested. Please respect that, and remove your hands," she said in her best courtroom voice.

He merely stepped in closer, forcing her to look up at him to maintain eye contact. "When I said first come," he began as he leaned down closer, making her almost gag with the stench of his breath, "I didn't mean me. I'm a generous man, Libby. You'll get yours, too."

Moira's long dress made kneeing the guy impossible. Even if her knee would reach up that high. She wasn't averse to the idea of using a balled fist to get the same point across. Being short did have its advantages, and due to her size, her brothers had taught her how to fight, and not always fairly. However, Max still had her arm in one hand and his other hand tightly gripped her hip, blocking her from getting in a good left hook.

Moira preferred to fight — and win — her own battles, but, given the day she'd had, on top of the week she'd had, and the month, and the year, well, right now, she'd settle for expediency. She glanced down the bar, knowing Sally would set Max here straight in two seconds flat. Only now there was some other argument going on, this one not so easily controlled. Moira's eyes widened as she saw Sally pull a silver whistle out from under the neck of her shirt, while the other bartender reached under the bar and came up with a thick, wooden baseball bat. *Uh oh.*

Moira supposed it shouldn't have surprised her that things would get out of hand. She suspected the hotel lounge had seen its share of bar fights, but she'd bet they'd never once been overrun by this many people all at the same time. And most certainly not from such a global community of travelers. Not to mention it was also Christmas Day.

Voices were being raised in multiple languages now, and the mood had begun to shift from overly festive to something far less jovial. Then Sally put the whistle in her mouth and the resulting series of shrill blasts instantly silenced the room. For about two seconds.

Max also noted the disturbance and tightened his hold on her arm to the point she was sure he'd leave marks. "I believe that's our cue to go find somewhere a little quieter, and a lot more private." Without warn-ing, Max tugged her into the crowd, head-ing in the general direction of the door that led to the side parking lot of the small hotel. Her car was parked out front. Dressed as she was, and given their height and strength differences, she didn't like her chances for making a clean getaway once outside.

So, there was only one thing to do. The moment he'd let go of her hip to pull her into the crowd, she'd snagged her clutch from the bar. She slid her hand to one end of the long, tubular shaped bag, then clutched it in her fist like her own little satin-and-pearl encrusted bat. *It might not be thick and made of wood, but then my target is probably a lot smaller.*

When he turned to move them sideways between two clusters of shouting patrons, she swung her bag right at the zippered front of his trousers. Any other impact site might result in an immediate retaliatory response. Her brothers had taught her that there was one particular spot guaranteed to make a man drop whatever he was holding and immediately cover the injured area with his hands. Do it well enough, he'd be on his knees while cupping himself.

Moira only needed Max to let go of her. She could lose herself in the crowd in an instant, and they'd never lay eyes on each other again. The only question would be whether it was better to head upstairs to her room, or to run to her car, so she could drive back to the Hollow and the security of her family.

An instant before impact, however, she was spared from having to make that split-second decision when a large, warm hand blocked her shot. His palm was broad enough to encompass her hand and her bag, which he proved by gently, but firmly wrapping long fingers around them both. "There you are, sweetheart," he said, swinging their joined fists neatly downward, appearing for all the world like they were simply a couple holding hands. "I looked at the bar for you."

Pinned as she was between her errant Good Samaritan and Max, with the crowd pressing in all around them, Moira couldn't turn her head enough to see much more than a flash of what looked like . . . a white lab coat? She could feel his large frame behind her like a big, sturdy wall of support, however, and unlike Max's egotistical slithering, this guy's somewhat Neanderthal approach didn't make her feel threatened at all. Quite the opposite.

"Sorry I'm late," he added, then shocked her by leaning down and pressing what felt like a kiss to the top of her head. She quickly realized it was an excuse to put his mouth closer to her ear when she heard him whisper, "Go with me on this and I'll have you out of here in a jiff."

Moira had gone from fight-or-flight to instant-pretend-girlfriend so quickly it took a second for her to switch gears. The fact that Mr. Good Samaritan had a deep voice and a killer Aussie accent only served to cap the surreal scene. *What is it with the accents? I get it, Karma, okay?*

Her lack of immediate response to her supposed boyfriend allowed Max to turn fully back around and reassert himself. He still had Moira's other arm in his grasp, painfully so now, but it didn't appear he'd seen her attempt to clock him in the crotch. Which meant he'd likely bought Mr. Sexy Aussie's ploy. All she had to do was play along and hopefully a few minutes from now she'd be in her room, putting this very long day in her rearview mirror. Mr. Aussie and all.

"You must be the errant suitor," Max said. His smile was now as cold as his eyes. "Didn't your mama raise you to know it's impolite to leave a pretty woman sitting alone? Especially in an establishment such as this?"

"If I'd had a mama, perhaps," her Sexy Aussie replied good-naturedly. "But even if I'd been raised by a pack of dingoes, I'd have sense enough to know if I have to drag a lady out of an establishment, then perhaps I need to rethink my choice of companions for the evening."

Moira saw the gleam in Max's eyes turn to a hard glint and finally found her voice. "I was handling it," Moira said, pasting on a teeth-gritting smile as she tried to glance back at her pretend boyfriend. "Sweetie."

Sexy Aussie leaned down again and murmured, "Aye, but I didn't think it would be a great idea if the lawyer sister-of-the-groom found herself up on charges of assault and battery."

His breath was also warm against her neck, but it affected her in an entirely different way. *Seriously, I get it, Universe. I promise, no more men with accents. We all get it.*

"No jury would convict me," she whispered back.

She heard him chuckle and that, too, did delicious things to her equilibrium. "Point to the lawyer," he said. "And yet, maybe we should just avoid the whole courtroom drama, this go, yes?"

"Unfortunately, second place doesn't go

home with the trophy this evening," Max said, interrupting their whispered byplay. His tightened hold made her gasp.

Moira turned and pinned Max with an annoyed look. "Well, this might come as a shock to both of you, but this 'trophy' isn't some inanimate object, ripe for the claiming. I not only get a say, I get the only say, and I'll be going home now. Alone." Moira might have raised her voice a bit and saw heads starting to turn their way. She tried to tug both her hands free. "I won't swing," she said out of the side of her mouth.

Aussie just chuckled. And kept his hold on her hand and her clutch. *Smart man.* She tried not to smile. And failed.

Max caught their back-and-forth but instead of narrowing his gaze in anger, his eyes widened briefly; then his smile returned. "Reptilian" was the word that came to Moira's mind. "Feisty," he said. "Point in your favor, Red. That'll just make this even more fun." Before Moira could reply to that, Max shifted his gaze to the man standing behind her. He gave Mr. Aussie a dismissive once-over, and when he spoke, his voice was silky smooth and twice as deadly. "Listen, Crocodile Dundee, I could buy and sell you five times over before breakfast. Now, be a good little chef and go put some shrimp on the barbie, or whatever it is you do Down Under."

Chef, Moira thought. That explained the white lab coat. Then she put it together. How Sexy Aussie knew who she was. He was the caterer. Or, more specifically, the chef at the best man's gastropub up in Blue Hollow Falls, who'd been overseeing the amazing reception spread. She hadn't caught his name, or had the chance to meet him, didn't even know he was Australian. But the glimpses she'd caught of the towering Aussie reminded her that his looks were every bit as sexy as the accent. *Yet another reason to get yourself out of this predicament.*

"The lady and I will be leaving now." Max turned to her and threatening dark eyes made Moira's blood run cold. "I promise you she'll be in very, very capable hands." He squeezed her arm tightly enough to make her wince. "I think she'll be delighted to learn that paying proper deference comes with great rewards." The gleam in his eyes told her he was going to take great delight in teaching her that particular lesson.

Moira wasn't about to go anywhere, with Max or anyone else. That he thought he'd actually get away with that plan was further testament to his enormous ego. *Probably his only enormous attribute,* she thought, less than charitably, but given the bruises she'd have to remember him by, she didn't feel too bad about that. He had to know she'd scream the building down if necessary before she'd let him get her a single step closer to the door. Her main concern at the moment was keeping Mr. Sexy Aussie Chef from getting himself caught up any further in the situation. *What is he doing down in Turtle Springs, anyway?*

Moira knew it was in everyone's best interest to find a way to deescalate things, not ramp them up further, but before she could figure out exactly how to go about doing that, Max settled his Stetson on his head, then made the critical mistake of reaching out and covering Aussie's hand, which was still wrapped around Moira's clutch and fist.

"You'll get your turn when I'm done," Max said, with a cold grin. "Now, hurry off before I decide to destroy whatever little life you've put together for yourself out in this godforsaken place. Trust me, your girlfriend here won't be interested in what's left of you when I get done."

Aussie only chuckled at that. "Well, you've just threatened the wrong fella there, mate." Moira's eyes widened when he broke Max's hold simply by flexing his fingers, which had the fortunate additional bonus of freeing her hand and clutch. Unfortunately, before she could take aim and swing again, Max swung at Aussie.

"Duck," Aussie calmly told her, pushing her head down right before blocking Max's swing with his forearm and delivering a perfectly aimed gut punch in return.

Max staggered back, his Stetson toppling off as he banged into several unsuspecting bar patrons behind him. Unfortunately, his hold on her arm had her stumbling with him. She tried to use the momentum to tug it free, even if it meant she fell to the floor, but the men he'd staggered into pushed Max right back toward Aussie, sending her reeling in the other direction, her long dress making it impossible to keep her balance.

"For goodness' sake," she said, jerking at her arm, which Max was now using as leverage to keep his balance. "Just stop it. Let go of me before we both go down."

Grunting, Max righted himself, looking a sickly shade of green now from the gut punch. That didn't stop him from turning on her. "The only one going that direction tonight will be you." He jerked her right up against him so that her toes all but left the ground, his grip an iron fist now, making her cry out in pain. "And you're gonna have to be real nice to me, darlin', to make up for startin' this ruckus. I'll be more than happy to teach you some manners."

"Okay," Aussie said from right behind her. "Playtime is over."

Max actually pulled her in front of him to use as a shield in case Aussie was going to punch him again. An instant later her now throbbing arm was mercifully freed when Aussie clamped his hand on Max's arm and squeezed until the weasel of a man let go. Moira stumbled to the side, banging into several patrons who, along with about a dozen others, had turned to see what the commotion was about. She distantly realized that the argument at the bar apparently hadn't abated either. The charged tension in the air wasn't only due to Max and Aussie taking swings. The same moment Max went flying backward, booted feet pointing upward as he landed on a table on his back, a fistfight erupted at the bar. In an instant, the entire atmosphere in the crowded lounge took an instantaneous shift for the worse.

"Merry Christmas to all," she murmured as she careened into someone else and the mob surged forward. Someone helped her regain her balance just in time for her to see the two young guys Max had ap-

proached the bar with an earlier push through the crowd. From the looks on their faces, she assumed they were coming to Max's defense. They launched themselves at Aussie, making her gasp, then two men standing right beside her jumped into the fray, and she could only hope they were on Aussie's side. She heard more glass break behind her as the other fight escalated into a full-on brawl as well.

And then, as they say, all hell broke loose.

Sally's whistle did no good and Moira decided she didn't want to know what, if anything, was being done with the other bartender's bat. Bodies moved around her too fast to anticipate their actions, much less their reactions. It was like watching some kind of macabre ballet of violence.

"The door, Moira," she heard Aussie shout from somewhere over her crouched position. "Stay low," he ordered. Then she heard a grunt, and flinched, pretty sure it was his.

She didn't run from a fight. No Brogan worth his or her salt did. Her parents ran an Irish pub in Seattle, and she'd witnessed a brawl or three in her time, though admittedly none on this scale, with this many people, this out of control.

"Now!" Aussie shouted from somewhere

306

in the melee, and in that moment, Moira saw a hole open up in front of her between heaving bodies. One that gave her a straight shot, right to the front door.

Given her size and mode of dress, she had no way to help extricate Aussie from the brawl, but as an officer of the court, there was one thing she could do. Get herself out of there and get the police involved before anyone got really hurt.

From the sounds erupting inside the bar as she was all but ejected through the front door by the heaving mob within, it was probably too late for that.

All of which turned into the story of how Moira Brogan, licensed attorney still only in the state of Washington, co-maid of honor to the biggest wedding in Blue Hollow Falls history, and demoralized dumpee of Finn O'Doherty, of Donegal, Ireland, found herself in the Turtle Springs police station at one in the morning, paying bail for the person who'd ended up being the one charged with assault and battery. Mr. Sexy Aussie Chef, Hudson Walker.

He was tall, with long dark hair pulled into a small knot, samurai style, on the crown of his head. He had a gash on his forehead, a knot on one cheek, a cut on his chin, and the white chef's coat he wore looked like it had been through, well, exactly what it had been through, a bar brawl. And yet he still managed to be quite possibly the sexiest man she'd ever seen. And that was before his face split into a wide, devastatingly handsome grin.

"Well, it looks like I'll be the one needing a lawyer," Hudson said cheerfully, as the deputy let him out of the cell and into her custody. "Know any?"

Weddings on Christmas. There really should be a law.

Chapter Two

Hudson flipped the perfectly folded omelet over in the pan and slid it onto a waiting plate, then grinned when he heard a sudden commotion coming from the other room.

"What's going on? Where am I? What happened?"

"Breakfast is going on. You're in my guest room. And nothing happened," he called out cheerfully. "Well, other than that whole bar brawl, mass arrest, and you springing me from the big house in the wee hours of the morning thing, then driving me home," he added. "Well, I drove me home in your car, and by the time we got here you were dead to the world, so I carried you in and thought I'd let you sleep. Seemed like the least I could do, seeing as you posted my bail."

There was no response to that. Instead, a moment later a sleepy-eyed Moira shuffled into his kitchen in her stocking feet, pulling up the front of her strapless, now hopelessly crumpled bridesmaid gown. Her short red curls stuck out in all directions like there had been an electric socket mishap in her not so distant past, the bulk of her mascara was no longer in its original location, and she had wrinkle marks on her cheek from sleeping for nine hours straight in the exact same position. How she could be all of that and still look utterly adorable was a mystery, but there it was, all the same.

She squinted in reaction to the sunshine streaming in through the long row of windows that ran along the opposite wall, then looked down at herself and frowned. "I'm still wearing my bridesmaid gown," she remarked, as if puzzled by the discovery.

"Aye, well, I considered getting you out of it so you'd sleep more comfortably. A task I've performed countless times for my sisters in years past." He arranged sliced melon and several strawberries on the plate next to the omelet, then glanced up and smiled. "Only you're not my sister, and I figured you'd had enough manhandling for one night."

She just stared at him and blinked. "I've had a really bad time with insomnia," she said, as if that explained everything.

"Not anymore," he told her, his smile

widening to a grin. "Coffee?"

"If there is a God."

"I don't know that He had anything to do with it, but there's a fresh pot on the counter there."

"Bless you." She shuffled over to the counter where the fancy coffeemaker was stationed. He'd laid out a fresh mug, small pitcher of cream, and a pot of sugar.

"If you'd rather some tea or hot chocolate, the pot on the left is hot water. Tea and cocoa mix are in the two containers there. Tea bag is on the tray. I can heat up some milk if you prefer your hot chocolate —"

"Coffee," she said, and poured herself a mug, took a deep, appreciative whiff of the rich, freshly brewed aroma, then took a sip. Her shoulders relaxed instantly and her eyes closed. She made a soft moaning sound as she swallowed. "I'm pretty sure you're wrong. Some higher power was definitely involved in making that." She took another sip, then another, her eyes remaining closed, palms wrapped around the warm mug.

Hudson chuckled, shook his head, and carried their plates to the small table that was bolted to the wall across from the galley style kitchen. He'd liked her from the moment they'd met, but he liked her even more now. She was a sensualist. Someone who appreciated and used all her senses to enjoy what life had to offer. Taste, touch, sight, scent, sound.

Truthfully, he'd liked her even before their less-than-conventional meeting. He'd come into the lounge specifically to find her and had observed her handling the man Hudson now knew was media mogul Maxwell Taggert like he was nothing more than your standard, run-of-the-mill barfly nuisance.

The request to track her down, make sure she was doing okay, had come from her big brother, the groom, before he'd taken off with his lovely new wife on their honeymoon. Without going into specifics, Seth had explained to Hudson that his sister had had something of a challenging year and he wanted to make sure she didn't close herself off from the rest of the family while they were all in the Hollow. Hudson knew that of the six Brogan kids, all grown adults now, Moira and Seth were the closest. Age didn't matter when it came to a big brother looking out for his kid sister. Hudson knew more than a little something about that and had respected Seth all the more for it.

Seth's good friend, Sawyer Hartwell, was Hudson's boss. Seth owned and operated a winery higher up in the hills. Sawyer owned part of a century-old, long defunct silk mill in Blue Hollow Falls that he, Seth, a few other close friends, and a good part of the town had rehabilitated and renovated. They'd turned the old place into an artists' enclave, complete with workshops, and a beehive of shops and stalls run by a wide variety of crafters, artists, musicians, and other makers. The mill had been open for business for a little over a year now, and Sawyer operated a gastropub microbrewery built into the rear of the old place.

Actually, it had been a microbrewery with a limited food truck menu when Hudson had come on board just after the place opened. He'd been the creative mind behind the menu expansion that had turned micro-brewery to gastropub. Live music happened spontaneously on the small stage built into the back of the pub, more so now that Pippa was in residence, and it had become some-thing of a central meeting spot for the locals and the tourists who came to visit the mill, to shop, and to take classes.

Hudson loved everything about the pub, the mill, and the small mountain town it now supported. He had complete control over the kitchen, the menu, and the staff. All without the hassle of ownership, which suited him just fine, as it meant he got to do what he loved to do most. Cook. It was the dream job he'd never known he wanted, and now he couldn't imagine doing anything else.

"That smells heavenly," Moira said.

He turned to find her still clutching the coffee mug, filled once again to the brim. "Have a seat then, and tuck in." Hudson adjusted the blinds on the window positioned directly above the small dining table to filter out the direct sunlight.

She hiked up the hem of the long dress and slid into the bench seat that was bolted to both floor and wall. "Interesting place," she said, as he moved onto the bench opposite hers. "Looks like something you'd see on board a train in an old movie, with the booth table, the slider windows."

Hudson swallowed a bite of omelet, wiped his mouth with a napkin, and grinned again. "It looks exactly like something you'd see on board a train, because it is."

Moira paused with a strawberry halfway to her mouth, then put it back down and looked around. The other booths from that side of the train had been removed. The floor had been redone in hardwood, and the opposite side of the train car had been gutted and rebuilt into his galley kitchen. There were no visible windows on that side of the train car, but all the original windows on the table side were still in use. Behind her, the rest of the car had been turned into a tiny bedroom. That had been his bedroom once upon a time, but was used for guests now. Not that he'd ever had any.

A push through the swinging door behind him led to a short, enclosed passageway that had been constructed around the connector between the car they sat in and the one immediately behind it. That car was his personal living space now. Half lounge area, half bedroom.

Marveling, she turned to look at the entire car. "It seems a lot more spacious, with more headroom than I remember from the few trains I've been on."

"It was a sleeper car originally, one of the taller models." He nodded at her plate, silently encouraging her to eat while the food was warm. "Being as I'm also one of the taller models, it seemed like a sign when I found it."

She was still holding the strawberry. "So, you live in a converted train car." She'd made it a statement, not a question, but he nodded anyway.

"Cars. There are two of them, actually." He lifted a shoulder. "I work in a gastropub inside a converted silk mill. Seeing what they've done with that place inspired me."

Moira put her strawberry down altogether then and peered out through the slats in the window blinds. She immediately framed her eyes due to the glare of the sun off the landscape of sparkling white snow that dominated the scenic view. "All I see is a big open field, mountains, and a whole lot of pine trees. No other trains, and no train tracks for that matter."

"I live in two train cars, yes, but not at a train station."

She let the blinds clatter back together and turned to face him again, the corner of her mouth curving upward in a dry smile. "Of course. Silly me for thinking otherwise."

"A rail did run through Blue Hollow Falls many decades ago when there were plans to start a lumber company up here. I think there was a possibility for mining as well. None of that panned out in the long run, so the railway was never finished. What stretch of track remains is buried in an overgrown forest now. I happened upon some of the track while hiking with some friends, and they mentioned there was a stretch down in the valley below with old cars still sitting on the rails."

"And you thought, hey, my housing problems are all solved now."

He forked up a chunk of omelet and

grinned again. "Exactly." He popped the bite of creamy eggs, mushrooms, peppers, and cheese into his mouth. When he finished, he said, "I'll tell you the whole story if you promise to go ahead and eat."

She gave him a rather considering look. "I thought we weren't manhandling me any longer."

"That's not manhandling. Bossing around maybe," he added with a wink, as he loaded his fork once more. "I'm a chef, food is important to me, and I want it to be enjoyed to its fullest. All my work making you the perfect gastronomical delight will be ruined if you take a bite of it gone cold."

"Quite sure of yourself," she said, teasing him, but cutting herself a piece of omelet, all the same.

"You have tried my coffee," he reminded her.

"Truth to that," she said, pointing the tip of her knife in his direction, while sliding the loaded fork into her mouth. She immediately closed her eyes and groaned again. "Oh my God," she said, the words muffled as she was still chewing and swallowing. "That's not an omelet," she pronounced after she'd finished the mouthful. "That's like a bunch of eggs and vegetables got together and had a wild and crazy orgy,

317

and everybody was left wanting a cigarette afterward."

Hudson barked out a laugh. "I've never had my food compared to an orgy, but I have to admit, I rather like it." Yeah, he rather liked her, that he did. Hudson found himself wondering if Seth had had any ulterior motives in sending his wedding caterer and good friend down to Turtle Springs to look after his single sister. *I sure hope so.* "I'd love to hear one of your closing arguments," he said, still grinning. "I bet they're inspired."

Moira smiled, but there was a flicker of something else entirely that passed through her eyes. She turned her attention back to her food before he could figure out whether it was disappointment or resignation.

"What made you decide to become a chef?" she asked, somewhat obviously changing the topic. "Other than your ridiculous, God-given talent for making everything taste out of this world, I mean," she said, smiling as she popped another bite into her mouth.

"Oh, that was pretty much it," he said, wondering if she'd always make him grin like a madman, hoping he got the chance to find out.

She laughed at that, then took a moment

to enjoy another bite. Then another. She finally put her fork down, dabbed her mouth with her napkin, and let out a contented sigh. "Well, I think I can speak on behalf of the entire planet when I say thank goodness you figured that out and went with it."

He dipped his chin in a nod at the compliment. "What got you into law? I know from Seth that you're the only lawyer in the family." He smiled. "Did you discover you have a God-given talent for adjudicating?"

Despite the earlier flicker, she smiled good-naturedly. "With five older siblings, it's a handy skill to have."

"So, it *is* your superpower then. Good, that will come in handy at my hearing."

She frowned then. "What hearing?"

"The one happening the morning after tomorrow, down at the courthouse in Turtle Springs." He nodded at the plate again. "Go on and finish. We can talk about it later."

She laid her napkin on the table, all vestiges of sleep-of-the-dead hangover gone. Her gorgeous green eyes were clear, sharp, and focused now. On his legal predicament, anyway. He wondered what it would take to get her to be interested in the rest of him like that. "Assault and battery. Right. Sorry. Who charged you? The county?"

He shook his head. "Maxwell Taggert's attorney."

"Maxwell —" She broke off as her eyes went wide. "That sleazy pervert who hit on me? That Max was — is — Maxwell Taggert? The king of the tabloid? What was he doing in Turtle —" She broke off with a wave of her hand. "Never mind. Silly question. I guess given his ego, he thought he might directly crash the wedding. So, his interest in me wasn't just because he's a creepster. He probably was looking for any way to get a story for his paper."

Hudson saw her visibly shudder. She rubbed her arms and winced, then looked down and noted the purple marks on her bicep and forearm.

He slid from his side of the table and crouched next to her. "Here, let me take a look."

"It's okay," she said, but he gently took her arm and she shifted so he could turn it and see the bruising. "We should probably take pictures of those."

"The bruises?" he asked her, surprised.

"Evidence for your case."

"Ah, right. Let me get you a pain reliever, and some ice. You've a bit of swelling there."

His fingers were gently stroking the soft skin near but not on the bruised area when her gaze met his, and held. They were mere inches apart, and he got all caught up in the emerald green of her eyes.

"I'm not feeling any pain," she said, somewhat faintly, as they continued to look at one another.

"Good," he said, but their gazes held for another long moment.

Had it been any other time or situation, he'd have leaned in for a kiss. He was dying to taste her, to connect with her in a far more direct way. But there was that whole manhandling thing and he knew she'd likely had more than enough direct contact with the opposite sex in the past twenty-four hours to last her a good long while.

So, he eased back and stood. "I'll make a cool compress then," he said. Anything to keep his hands busy, and off her. "With or without the photos, I'm thinking we can make a pretty good case that he was asking for it," Hudson said.

"I think he'll have a team of very, and I mean *very* high-priced attorneys here by tomorrow morning, if he doesn't already." She looked at him straight on, her expression as serious as he'd seen it yet. "You need to get an attorney. A very, very good one."

He flashed her a smile as he folded up a dish towel and ran it under cold water, then

321

wrung out the excess. "Lucky I already have one of those."

"Oh, good," she said, relieved. Then she looked at his smile and her eyebrows lifted. "You mean me? No. First of all, I don't have a license to practice law in Virginia. Secondly, even if I got the judge to allow it in this instance, you need someone a whole lot more experienced than me on this. Not to mention someone familiar with the laws in this state. I could make some calls, get a few names. If you can't afford —"

"It's not about what I can afford," Hudson told her. "It's about that I'm not in the wrong here. Maxwell Taggert can file all the lawsuits against me he wants, but he won't win them."

Moira shook her head. "He doesn't need to win them. In fact, he never even has to go to trial to get what he wants."

"What, some sort of plea deal? Moira, he has no case. I'm sure if we explain to his attorneys the things he said to you, they'll be begging me not to file my own lawsuit. Or you not to file one." He walked over and carefully wrapped the towel around her bruised bicep.

She placed her hand on it to keep it in place, then met his gaze. "Thank you," she told him. "That does feel better."

He nodded. "Good. Let me know if you change your mind about the pain reliever." Seeing the marks on her arm filled him with the same uncustomary anger he'd experienced last night when he'd watched it happening right in front of him. Growing up as he had, he wasn't a stranger to using his fists to solve things when it was demanded of him, but those times were well in his past. It was his nature to resolve issues with words, not fists. He was pretty easygoing, all told. But seeing those bruises made him feel anything but pacifistic. *Probably not a good mind-set to have when you're standing accused of assault,* he thought, no matter how much provoked.

Moira waited for him to sit down across from her again before continuing. "Taggert's not looking to make a deal, or even to send you to jail. That's not what men like Taggert do. Don't you remember what he said to you? He said he'd ruin your life. Unless you have a fortune stashed away somewhere — and it better be a really, really big one — he can do that without ever setting foot in court. Or back in the state of Virginia for that matter. He'll simply have his attorneys tie this thing up six ways to Sunday for months on end until he bankrupts you by drowning you in your own legal fees trying to keep up with them."

Hudson hadn't thought of it like that. "I didn't do anything wrong. He started it. I know that sounds like a grade school response, but it's the truth. I merely finished it to protect you. And it's neither of our faults that the rest of the bar got involved. I'm not responsible for that."

"And, again, none of that matters. He's not trying to beat you in court. He's going to beat you by draining your bank account dry."

"Well, then, he'll be disappointed. I've worked from nothing and for nothing, more often in my life than not. I mean, I do quite well for myself, but I don't measure success in dollars. He can take what I have. I'll just go on and earn it back. It's just money."

Hudson would like to think Taggert would have better things to do than target some unknown chef in a little mountain town. But he'd looked the man in the eye. Guys like Taggert did not like to lose. Most especially to someone they felt was beneath them. He suspected Moira was right. Sighing, he added, "So, if that is his strategy, can we simply refuse to play? I mean, let him file whatever he wants to file. What if we simply don't respond? Worst case is our lack of response will force it into a courtroom, where he will lose, or get it thrown out, right? We're not the ones trying to win anything."

"It doesn't always work that way. Your attorney can be compelled to respond. Listen, Hudson, there are a million ways this guy can get you. A frivolous lawsuit is merely one of them. Certainly, the easiest one for him, as it doesn't require him to do anything."

Hudson leaned back in his chair, all thoughts of enjoying a late morning breakfast with an adorably disheveled maid of honor forcibly replaced by the dawning of a new reality he had no desire to embrace. "So, what's the worst case then? What if I refuse to hire an attorney, represent myself. Just saying," he added when she immediately began to shake her head. "My point being, if he's trying to bankrupt me and I represent myself, then I'm out nothing. Except sound legal advice, I know. What I'm asking is, if I remove that outcome from the table, then what does he do to counter me? They can't penalize me without some kind of trial, and if we get into a courtroom, it's over — he loses."

"I'll be honest and say I don't know what other options he might be willing to exercise. I don't know the laws in this state.

Even if this was happening in my own home state where I am licensed to practice law, I'd be recommending you find someone who carries much bigger guns than I do." She smiled at that. "And given I've only been practicing a little over a year, that would be pretty much everybody."

"But you are a trial attorney," he said.

She lifted her eyebrows. "Does Seth really talk about me that much?"

Hudson lifted a shoulder, and his smile returned. "He's proud of you. With good reason." He saw that flicker again, and this time he didn't let it pass. "Is there something else going on?"

"Why do you ask that?"

Her expression had become immediately guarded, which told him he'd hit the nail right on the head.

"The few times I've said something flattering about you in regard to your occupation, let's just say you've looked a little . . . conflicted? Maybe that's not the right word. Is it that now you're in the job, you've come to realize it's not for you? Because now that I've met and fed every person in your immediate family, I think I can safely say they'd support you no matter what."

She shook her head. "It's not that. I love my job. Is it possible to know you want to be a lawyer right from childhood? That would describe me." She found a smile then. "Other kids were outside playing and I was watching *Law & Order* marathons, imagining how I'd do my closing statement."

Hudson laughed. "I completely understand that remark, only with me it was *The French Chef* with Julia Child." Moira let out a short laugh at that, and he said, "She was like the crazy aunt I always wanted and never had."

Moira studied him for a moment, as if wanting to say something, but judiciously holding her tongue.

"What?" he asked easily, liking that she wanted to know more about him. He wanted to know everything about her.

"In the bar last night, you told Max you didn't have a mom." She lifted her hand. "It's none of my business, and if you don't want to talk about it, please don't. It's just, you said something about helping your sisters earlier and so I was curious." Her smile came naturally this time, and made her green eyes dance. "Being an inveterate snoop is also a key attribute of a born defense attorney."

"I thought that was reserved for journalists and detectives."

"Them too. But we all need to get at the truth." Her smile turned a shade dry. "Just for different reasons."

He smiled in response. "I don't mind. It's not a sensitive subject, or I wouldn't have offered it up to the likes of Taggert. I'm not embarrassed or proud of the fact. I didn't have any say in the matter. It's simply my story."

"That's a good way to look at it."

He shrugged. "The only way, as I see it. Wanting it to be different won't change it. Best to just own it."

She plucked another strawberry from her plate. "So, what is the story of Hudson Walker?" She bit into the strawberry and his pulse leapt. Not because she'd done so in any particularly vampish manner. Far from. She looked a fair fright and she ate like a woman starved. Both of those things were insanely attractive to him. A woman who wasn't freaked out by looking less than her best and didn't enter every calorie she consumed into some dieting phone app? Where did he sign up?

He relaxed back in his seat now, but not before picking up the strawberries from his own plate and popping one, then the other in his mouth. She made him hungry. Starved, in fact. But given the events that had led them to this morning breakfast together, the last thing he could do right now was come on to her, no matter how sincerely and respectfully. So, instead, he gave her the part of him he could, and perhaps that was the more important part to share first, anyway. "I'm just a poor orphan boy," he told her, smiling as he said it. "I was raised in a convent orphanage in Queensland by a group of nuns."

Moira burst out laughing, then immediately clapped her hand over her mouth. "Oh my gosh, that was so rude," she said. "I'm so sorry. I just . . . You said earlier about having experience helping your sisters with their clothes —"

Hudson busted out a laugh at that. "Ah, no, I wasn't referring to the nuns."

Their gazes caught, and Moira giggled, which turned into a snicker, that might have included a short snort, which sent Hudson off laughing again, and the two of them ended up laughing until they were left gasping for breath.

"I really . . . am . . . sorry," Moira said, still struggling to breathe evenly. "So wrong of me." She sipped her now cool coffee, trying to get her voice back, and he drank the rest of his orange juice, trying to do the same. "So," she said at length, attempting a sober tone, "how many sisters did you have?"

"Twenty-four," he replied, every bit as soberly, then smiled at her stunned reaction. "That's how many girls were in the mission with me. I was the oldest, and the only boy. The orphanage was for girls. I was left on their doorstep when I was two. There was no place for me to go, so I stayed on with them until they could find me a place, either in another mission or with a foster family."

"And they never did?" Her expression softened.

"It's okay," he told her. "I was like their big brother and, well . . . I liked it. I mean, I went to school, I had plenty of mates, some of whom I still consider to be good friends. But at the end of each day, I went home to a place where I was looked up to, I was needed, I was important. And I was good with that."

"How old were you when you left? Or did you stay on? Is that where you learned to cook? When did you come to the States?"

Hudson laughed. She was so serious, so concerned, so wanting to get to the bottom of it, of him. And he was very okay with that. "I was seventeen when the mission closed. I had graduated school and it was ruled that I be considered emancipated. My first job at age fourteen was flipping burgers in a take-out place owned by a retired couple."

"Fourteen?"

"Minimum age for employment was thirteen. And granted, I shouldn't have been anywhere near a hot griddle, but I looked older than I was, and I could be a bit of a charmer when I put my mind to it."

She laughed. "I'm not having a hard time at all believing that."

"Why, thank you," he said, with a wink. "I'll keep that in mind." She didn't blush, but neither did she say anything to negate his first openly flirtatious comment, and he tucked that information away, too, and went on. "I started experimenting with their very limited menu on my own time." He grinned. "Eventually the owners caught on and put a stop to that, but I'd done a little experimenting in the kitchens at the mission, too. Mostly it was out of desperation for better tasting food." He smiled. "Or food that had any taste at all. They didn't have any cookbooks, so I really was flying blind. That's when I discovered my patron saint, Julia Child."

Moira grinned at that. "And then you went on to take over that burger joint, right?" she said, only half teasingly.

He shook his head. "I decided that my life had been untraditional enough, so when I finished my senior secondary years — your junior and senior high school years here, I believe — I went off and applied to a cooking school. Not the best of the best, but one I could afford, or at least work my way through. Which I did." He smiled. "There I learned that I wasn't so much drawn to fancy French cooking, or fancy anything. I just wanted to make food we all enjoy taste better."

"And you thought we Americans would be the best test subjects?"

He laughed, shook his head. "I became something of a vagabond. Traveled the world, worked long enough in one place to learn what I could about the cuisine, or the parts that interested me, anyway, then took off for another place. Wherever I could afford to get to on whatever I'd saved up. I'd been to the States a few times before this go."

"This . . . go? So, you're just temporary here?" She looked around the renovated train car. "A lot of trouble to go to for a short-term stay, isn't it? I mean, you can't be much older than me. A few years maybe? So I'm assuming you don't stay all that long in one place." She looked back at him.

"How long have you been here?"

"Christmas Eve was my one-year anniversary, actually." His smile widened at her surprise. "I was first hired on as a chef at the little inn in town. Fought my way through a pretty gnarly snowstorm to start that job, in fact. Ended up swapping spots with a man who'd applied to work for Sawyer — your brother's friend who —"

"Owns the microbrewery and part of the mill," she finished for him with a smile. "Yes, I know who Sawyer Hartwell is. He and my brother served in the military together before Seth came here." She contemplated the berries on her plate, but kept her hand on the cool compress and looked back at him. "So, you swapped spots with the cook Sawyer hired?"

Hudson nodded. "Turned out he was well suited to the more intimate details of running the inn's kitchen."

"And the gastropub at the mill was born," she finished for him.

"Something like that," he said, wondering if he was imagining the bit of distance that had entered her tone. Or maybe it was the way she was now sitting a little straighter. More temporary guest than relaxed friend-in-the-making.

"So . . . what will you do with this place

when you move on?"

Ah, he thought. She thought he was temporary here. Of course, she was a mere visitor as well, but the fact that knowing he might move on had changed her perception of him made him wonder why it mattered to her at all. He was interested in Moira Brogan. And that interest was rapidly growing the more they talked. Perhaps he wasn't alone in that growing attraction, which was a happy discovery indeed. And yet, maybe she had it right, and it was best to put a bit of distance between them and keep that attraction at bay, given they'd go their separate ways sooner than later.

Except "maybe" had never been in his vocabulary. And he was a firm believer that things worked out as they were supposed to, but only if you went after what you wanted in the first place. So, she lived in Seattle. He'd lived in a lot of places. Geography was the last thing he'd ever let get in his way before, so he wasn't about to look at it as an obstacle now.

"If and when that time comes, I'll worry about it then," he said, which was the honest truth.

"If?" she asked. "Are you looking to put down roots?" She smiled politely. "Or more railroad tracks as the case may be?"

"I've never not been looking, if that's what you mean. I traveled, explored, roamed, because I could. It's not like a life mandate or anything."

"Never been tempted to stick in one place?"

"Until I landed in Blue Hollow Falls? No." He held her gaze, wanting her to know that while he might like to live in the moment, he wasn't frivolous or irresponsible, either.

"No one ever tempted you to stick around?"

He grinned then. "Are you asking if I'm unattached?"

She didn't blush or appear embarrassed, and her stock with him continued to rise. He liked a woman who was direct and met life head on. "No," she said, just as bluntly, and apparently as honestly as he had.

Careful what you wish for there, mate.

"I'm just curious about your outlook, that's all. I've . . . made a few impulsive decisions in my life recently, and they didn't turn out so well." She said it simply, owning her failures without appearing to be asking for sympathy, or worse, pity. "So, I guess I'm just kind of fascinated that you've made such a success of a life spent following your heart, or your gut, or both, most likely." She let out a dry laugh then, and the self-deprecation was charming. Somehow even more so, considering her outfit, the bedhead, and day-old mascara. "I'm a pretty goal-oriented person. I like to make plans, and stick to those plans. But, I guess I came to a turning point, and for the first time ever, I finally made a few bold, completely unplanned choices. The end result of which was a complete train wreck." Her smile widened. "You, on the other hand, wander the globe on a whim, and end up making the wrecked train into an amazing home." She batted her eyelashes, and said, "So, you can understand my curiosity."

He laughed and shook his head at the same time. "Maybe we define success differently. Or have different expectations. I live simply; my wants are few. I want to feed people and make them happy. I want them to know just how good food can taste, how comforting a nice warm meal can be." He grinned. "I guess you can take the orphan out of the mission, but you can't take the mission out of the boy."

"A caretaker," she said musingly. "It does all make sense when you put it like that."

He leaned forward and propped his elbows on the table. "And you want to right wrongs, seek justice, or at the least, fairness. Does that come from playing mediator at home, in a house full of people?"

"If you mean in any sort of disturbing way, no. My family is close —"

"No, I didn't mean it that way. I know Seth, and have heard many, many stories about the Brogan clan. I know you come from a home filled with love." He smiled. "But it's also a very filled home. Or was when you were growing up. That's all I meant. Some folks are born leaders, meaning bossy. Some are born mediators, some born people pleasers. And some just want things to go right for a person." His smile widened. "Or wrong, if they so deserve."

Moira laughed then. "I don't know that I ever saw it that way, but you might be on to something there. I definitely wanted life to be fair, even when that wasn't possible."

He caught her gaze and held it again. "So, what were those big, bold decisions?" he asked easily, but quietly, inviting her confidence, rather than demanding it. "Are things really a train wreck? Or more of an unexpected fender bender?"

"A little of both, I suppose," she said thoughtfully, but with a brief smile as well. Then she broke his gaze to look down at the napkin she was twisting around her fingers. "Nothing I can't overcome," she added, "if that's what you're asking." She looked up again. "But big enough that I have to rethink pretty much my whole life. Or at least what I'm willing to do to get what I want." She smiled ruefully. "Just as soon as I figure out what that is now."

"Irrevocable loss then?"

"One of them yes. The other, no. Although it might as well be. I could go and try again, I just . . . don't know if I want to."

"Failure does put a hurting on confidence," he said. "It can feel like rejection, when it might be a host of other things in reality, and you just the unfortunate victim."

"That's just it," she said. "It used to be that failure, or the threat of it, made me work harder. To prove the people who doubted me wrong, or even to prove to myself that my own doubts were wrong. Failure challenges your confidence, sure, but sometimes you can use that same threat to your confidence as a whole new kind of challenge. Like . . . how can I get back to where I was? Sometimes that feels impossible. When you lose a court case, someone's life is affected, sometimes — maybe most of the time — permanently. Usually not in a good way. And there is no going back and doing it over. It's done. And you have to live with that irrevocable outcome and yet somehow regain your confidence to take on someone else's big, potentially life-altering case. It's a crushing blow on so many levels when it doesn't go as you hope, but I knew the first time it happened that if I wanted to be a lawyer, and more importantly, a good one, then I had to find a way to deal with the losses and not let them gut me. You can't just quit and walk away. And no lawyer wins every trial."

"But this isn't about a lost case."

She looked surprised by the insight, but shook her head.

"And you can't apply whatever methods you've come up with to deal with the court losses, to help in this situation?"

She didn't immediately shake her head. She took the compress off her arm and laid it, folded neatly, on the edge of her plate as she seemed to consider the question. "Well, for the job-related issue, I suppose I should." She looked up from the napkin she'd now twisted into a tiny spiral. "I'm still asking myself if I want to, I suppose."

Hudson nodded in understanding, while simultaneously working to swallow his own regret. *The job-related issue.* That meant the other train wreck in her life was personal. She'd asked if he was unattached, but he hadn't asked the same of her. Seth had made a point of mentioning she was, but that didn't mean she'd been single for any length of time.

"I suppose no amount of coping mechanisms work when it comes to matters of the heart," he said, not sorry that he'd probed that possible wound. His attraction wasn't showing any signs of slowing down, so best he knew what he was dealing with sooner than later.

Her gaze jerked to his, surprise in her clear green eyes.

He smiled briefly. "You said one was work related, so I assumed."

A rueful smile curved her lips. "You wouldn't be wrong."

"I'm sorry," he said, and he meant it. She was sharp, funny, beautiful, determined. She should have it all. The career, the love of her life, whatever she wanted. She certainly didn't seem like a personal train wreck, the type of person who found it impossible to get out of his or her own way.

"Thanks," she said. "That's kind of you to say."

"I wouldn't wish a broken heart on anyone."

"Do you have experience with that?" She smiled then, and it was a clear attempt at diverting the topic away from herself. "Globe-trotter that you are, have you left a string of them in your wake?"

She was clearly teasing, so he took no offense. "I've always been honest and upfront about my vagabond ways, as you called them. But hearts can get involved despite the best of intentions."

She studied him. "But not yours."

Now it was his turn to look surprised. "No," he admitted. "Not in the way you mean. But it's painful no matter which one is hurting, the one who falls, or the one who doesn't. It's not something I'd wish on anyone, either."

"I suppose you're right," she said quietly. "It's foolish really, in my case anyway. It was a holiday romance that was supposed to be a fun, light, flirty diversion while I enjoyed my time in Ireland. We'd both agreed on that. Only, like you said, I couldn't seem to keep my heart out of it. But neither could he. Or, at least, I thought that was how it was going. It was just so good, you know?" She met his gaze again and he saw the pain in her eyes now. "Who wouldn't want to do whatever was necessary to make that last forever?"

"An idiot," he said, the words out before he could think better of them.

She let out a little laugh at that, mercifully — for his sake — missing the meaning behind his response. "It would be lovely if that were true, and certainly easier to move on if he'd been some kind of player. It's funny, because as much as I miss him, that's not the issue at hand. It's trusting my own judgment. I mean, he was a great guy. Honest, sincere. He could have taken gross advantage of me had he wanted to, truly broken my heart. I was certainly foolish enough to give him that power. But he was, well, perfect in that way, too. The moment he realized that I was falling and he wasn't, he broke it off, and in the gentlest, kindest way possible." She let out a sad laugh. "It almost made it worse, because I couldn't even hate him for it. But that's just it. In truth, I have moved on. It was ages ago. What I'm struggling with is . . . move on to what?"

He frowned. "What do you mean?"

"I didn't pick a loser. I didn't fall for someone who treated me poorly. My judgment was fabulous, right? And therein lies the train wreck."

"Because poor judgment can be adjusted," he said. "But when you've done all the right things . . . ?"

"Exactly. Then it's you, personally, who didn't measure up," she said. "What can you take from that? Except you're somehow not enough and you don't have the first clue what to work on, how to fix it, what to do to ensure it doesn't happen again. Because he seemed to really like me. We had a grand time. So why did only one of us fall? What do I do about that?"

She seemed taken aback by his immediate grin, so he said, "You don't do anything," he said. "And that's good news."

She rolled her eyes, but paired it with a wry smile. "Seriously?"

"Quite seriously." Impulsively he reached across the small table and took her hands in his. Her gaze flew up, but she didn't slide her hands free. "Yes, it's true, you fell, he didn't. Let me ask you this, though. If he'd fallen and you hadn't, would you have counseled him to somehow change himself so he'd have a better shot at it next time?"

"No, of course not, I —" She broke off, and the light dawned. "Oh," she said, somewhat faintly, looking away, looking inward. "Oh," she repeated, as the truth of it sank in. She looked back at him. "You're right. I fell. And he didn't. Maybe it really is as simple, and as awful, as that." She looked at him. "I wanted something tangible I could work on, could fix. Goal oriented, remember?" she added, her smile faint, but sincere. "So, you're saying it's just a great

343

big crapshoot and there's no way to safe-guard against getting your heart smashed to smithereens."

Hudson smiled. "More or less." They both shared a brief laugh, but he tugged on her hands when she'd have looked away again. "Moira, there are so many reasons why someone doesn't commit. At the end of it all, though, would you want a man who wasn't as head over heels for you as you were for him?"

"Of course not." She studied his eyes, as if hoping she'd find the answer she was looking for. "The thing is, though, what if I don't ever find him?"

"You can't find what you're not looking for."

"What if it's just heartbreak and train wrecks? Because I don't know how long I could do that. I'm not sure I can give end-less pieces of my heart away, only to have them handed back to me."

"Falling in love is never something to be sorry for. It's not a failure to love someone, any more than it is to be a failure if they don't love you in return. Letting yourself be vulnerable, taking that risk, that's what makes us human."

"Says the man who doesn't stay in one place long enough to really risk anything," she said, though not unkindly.

"You gave your heart while on holiday," he countered, catching her gaze when she lifted it to his. "Time is the least accurate and reliable measure for how long it takes to fall in love. For some people, it can take months, years." He realized he was running his fingertips over the back of her hand, and slowly lifted them away. "For others, it can happen in the blink of an eye."

CHAPTER THREE

"What makes you think he wasn't talking about the two of you?"

"Because he wasn't. Why would he? We just met."

"Why tell me all about it then, if not because you're wondering, too? I know you."

Moira didn't say anything to that, mostly because Katie was right. She pulled in and parked her car in the lot outside the converted silk mill. The huge waterwheel wasn't running now as it was wintertime, and the falls tumbling over the boulder-strewn ledge next to the mill appeared to have frozen in motion. Water still trickled through and under the ice, keeping a marginal flow running through Big Stone Creek as it rolled on down the mountainside. With snow-laden banks, and more of the white stuff piled on top of the tumble of rocks and boulders strewn along the creek bed, it was a breathtaking sight. Backed by towering pine trees with their snow-covered branches, it looked like a majestic winter tapestry. Moira could only wonder what Blue Hollow Falls looked like in the spring, with the waterfall cascading over the rocks and the waterwheel churning along.

"And when you said he lives on a train, you don't really mean a train, train, because . . . tall, sexy, and an amazing chef, it would just be too much if he lived in a converted train car. But he does, doesn't he?" Katie MacMillan, Moira's college chum and Pippa's sister — the other co-maid of honor — propped her hands under her chin and batted her long eyelashes. "Can I have him if you don't want him then, can I? That Aussie accent is utterly swoon worthy."

"Says the woman with the beautiful Irish accent," Moira said, rolling her eyes, though affectionately.

"It's as sexy to me as it is to you."

"I'm not the one calling it that."

Katie waved her silent, not buying it. She knew all about Finn and had listened to Moira wax rhapsodic about his beautiful voice. "Hudson Walker looks like a dream and sounds even dreamier. Add to that, when was the last time you met a man who's actually spent time thinking about life, and love, and could so beautifully sum it all up?" Katie sighed. "You're a fool if you don't let him finish seducing you."

"Finish? He cooked me breakfast and wrapped my arm in a towel. While, I remind you, I looked like the creature from the wedding-reception-walk-of-shame lagoon, only without the fun part. He was being kind to the kid sister of a good friend, nothing more."

Katie just gave her a look that said she knew what she knew, and Moira wasn't going to change her mind. "So, him inviting you to the gastropub for lunch today, is that still him being kind?"

"That's him wanting my legal advice for his hearing. It was moved back a day, and he wanted to ask me a few more questions." Moira put her rental car in park and turned off the engine. "Given it's basically my fault he's in that predicament, because he was trying to help me get away from that creep Taggert, it's the least I can do. Seriously, not only was he not flirting with me, much less trying to seduce me, I all but cried all over him about my stupid breakup with Finn. I not only looked like a train wreck, I literally told him I *was* a train wreck." She gathered her bag and the small satchel that held her laptop and notepads. "Trust me when I say, he believed me."

"He took your hands in his and said time is a — what was it again? I really need to write it down."

" 'Time is the least accurate or reliable measure of how long it takes to fall in love,' " Moira quoted.

Katie batted her lashes again. "You recall every word. I bet he was looking deep into your eyes when he said it, too."

Moira shook her head. "You're incorrigible. I never should have told you." She opened the door and sucked in a breath as the frigid December air hit her square in the face.

"You tell me everything, just as I do you." Katie laid a hand across her brow with dramatic flair, and said, "Our freshman-year bond can never be broken."

Moira just shook her head, but she was smiling as they both pulled the hoods of their coats up and hurried from the car to the mill. Katie and Moira had agreed before the wedding to stay in Blue Hollow Falls for a few days after, just to catch up and spend some much-needed girl time together before Katie flew back to Ireland. Moira had seen her best friend the past spring during her trip to Donegal, but it had been three long years prior to that since they'd last seen each other in person, and neither knew when the opportunity would present itself again.

They stepped inside the mill's big, sliding, barn-sized door, moving it closed again behind them once they were safely out of the cold. They stood right there, though, and took in the veritable explosion of color, scent, and sound before them. It might be cold and snowy outside, and only two days past Christmas, but the mill was alive with both crafters and shoppers alike. It was toasty warm, so they both slid out of their coats and hung them on the fanciful rows of knobs and painted hangers that were arranged like a giant peg-board on the wall just inside the door.

"Go talk to Hudson while he's on break, and I'm going to go lose myself in all the pretty," Katie said. "I'll wind my way back to the pub in a few hours and we'll have lunch."

"Oh, I don't know if that's a good idea. I was thinking we could —"

"You spent a good thirty minutes raving about the man's breakfast, and that was after you all but wrote a sonnet about his coffee. I'm not leaving here without a taste of his cooking."

"You have tasted his cooking — he catered the wedding," Moira reminded her, but Katie merely stared her down. "Fine, fine, but if you even give the slightest indication you're going to try and play matchmaker, lunchtime is over." She turned to head down the passageway that Hudson had told her to take.

"Hudson Walker," Katie said, and Moira immediately turned back around, thinking he'd walked up behind them. But there was no one there. She turned to Katie, a questioning look on her face.

Katie merely looked smug as she smiled and said, "Judging by the look on your face at the mere mention of the man's name, I won't need to be playin' matchmaker, lass." Her brogue got deeper the more she teased.

Moira waved her away. "Go play with pretty things. The very last thing I'd ever do is let myself fall in love while I'm away on holiday. Again." In the face of Katie's beaming certainty, Moira finally capitulated and confided in her best friend. "And most definitely not with someone who makes me think, makes me laugh, makes me breakfast, and, okay, okay, sounds like an ad for the perfect Down Under getaway." She fanned her face and wiggled her eyebrows, then laughed and said, "Happy now?"

Katie's eyes gleamed even more brightly at that and Moira knew her admission would just egg her friend on, but once Katie MacMillan set her mind to something, she wasn't likely to be dissuaded anyway.

"Hudson Walker," Katie said again.

"Ha, ha," Moira replied dryly. "You've had your fun and I've admitted all."

"No," Katie whispered, and dipped her chin while nodding toward something past Moira's shoulder.

Heat flushed Moira's cheeks, along with a goodly part of the rest of her as she turned to find Hudson standing right behind her. How much had he heard?

From the twinkle in his leonine gold eyes as he met her gaze, she suspected the answer was all of it. *Seriously, Karma?*

"G'day, Moira," he said, then glanced at her friend. "And Katie, right? Pippa's sister?"

"Aye, that I am." Katie stepped toward him with her hand extended. "I'm glad we had the chance to meet." She glanced at Moira, then back to Hudson, a broad smile on her pretty face. "I've heard so much about you."

Hudson glanced at Moira, his smile spreading to a grin. "Have you then?" he asked, his gaze lingering on Moira a mo-

352

ment longer, before he looked back at Katie. "Would you care to join us? Boring legal stuff, I'm afraid, but —"

She shook her head. "Thanks, but I'm off on a shopping spree. I've folks at home who still need Christmas presents and with so much wedding furor, I didn't really have time to take care of it all before leaving for the States." She looked around. "I'm sort of glad now. I think this will be the perfect way to bring my friends back home a little bit of Blue Hollow Falls."

"You've definitely come to the right place."

"Will you be cooking later? I was hoping for lunch when you and Moira are done."

"Katie —" Moira began, but Hudson responded before she could say more.

"I'd be insulted if you didn't."

"Perfect," Katie replied, beaming.

"I'll text you when we're done," Moira told her.

"Take your time," she said, grinning at Hudson, then winking at Moira before literally skipping off toward the stalls and small shop spaces.

Moira laughed despite her mortification and shook her head.

"You have good taste in friends, too," Hudson said.

Moira turned back to him. "Thank you," she said, knowing he was referencing their conversation of the day before.

"And you clean up quite nicely," he said, taking in her black slacks and teal blue sweater. That twinkle was back in his eyes when he added, "Though I'll always have a soft spot for emerald-green silk from now on."

Moira sent him a too-bright smile and batted her lashes. "I'll be happy to loan you mine anytime you like." They both chuckled. "In fact," she added, more drolly now, "after all but living in it for a day and a half, I'm fairly certain I'd be fine if I never saw it again."

"Today's tired recollection could be to-morrow's cherished memory," he told her, still smiling.

Before she could decide what he might have meant by that, much less how to respond, he turned and headed down the side corridor she'd started toward earlier.

"Sawyer said we could use his office," he told her. "He's off for the week with his family."

Moira followed him toward the back of the big building.

He opened Sawyer's office door for her and they both stepped inside. She turned back as he closed the door, surprised to see his expression had grown serious.

"What's wrong?" she asked. "Did something else happen with the case?"

"It's not that. There's something I should have told you yesterday."

Moira's heart sank, and she couldn't even say why. She and Hudson weren't a "thing" no matter how much Katie might wish they were. So, there was really nothing he could possibly say that could disappoint her, much less hurt her. *Then why are you braced like you're about to get a body blow?* "What is it?" she asked.

"When I went to the hotel bar Christmas night, I didn't run into you by accident." At her look of surprise, he added, "I was telling the truth when I said I looked for you at the bar. Actually, to be fully forthcoming, I watched you with Taggert and only intervened when I thought you might need an assist."

"Thank you?" Moira said, feeling as confused as she sounded.

"Seth asked me to go check on you, before he and Pippa left for the airport. He thought you might need cheering up."

Moira's cheeks warmed and she ducked her chin, trying not to feel mortified. "You already knew then. About Finn," she said,

355

staring at her feet, the floor, anywhere but up at Hudson Walker.

"No. Nothing like that. He wouldn't share anything you wanted kept private. He just mentioned you'd had a tough go over the past few months and might not feel much like celebrating. I was at the reception and thought you looked like you were having a fine time. I only came down to Turtle Springs because your brother and I have become mates over the past year, and he'd asked, so I honored the request. When I saw you at the bar, still in your dress, I decided to stay on a bit. Things were pretty ramped up in there." He smiled then. "You were holding your own, though. Even with Taggert."

Feeling like she was destined to be perpetually embarrassed in front of this man, Moira listened politely to everything he said, then nodded. "Thank you. And if I haven't properly thanked you for stepping in when you did, then please accept my sincere gratitude. I can typically hold my own, but I admit things were not looking good." She looked up at him directly then. "I'm sorry about your cuts and bruises, too. That was way above and beyond the call of duty, what you did for me, and I'm truly grateful for your help." She let a brief smile curve her lips. "I bet the next time my brother asks for a favor, you'll think twice."

"I'd do it again without hesitation," he said, his expression still as serious as it had been since he'd begun his confession. "Moira —"

"Hudson, listen . . ."

"Don't tell me to find another lawyer."

"I'm not your lawyer," she reminded him, as she had when he'd asked her to meet him at the mill. "I'm just here to help explain the options you have, so you can make an informed decision. Once you hire someone, they can give you more specific guidance. Like I said —"

"Moira," he said, cutting her off. He hadn't said it impatiently or urgently. He'd said it plainly, quietly, which had a far more unsettling effect on her.

She was afraid to meet his gaze then, afraid of what she'd see there. Katie had been right about him being attracted to her. Moira just hadn't wanted to admit it, much less trust it, or even consider acting on it. The relief she'd felt when his big revelation was simply that her brother had put him in her path . . . yeah, that was a big ol' sign that it wasn't just Hudson who was interested in more than legal advice.

She wanted to tell him she was flattered.

Because she was. She wanted to tell him that she was interested, too. Because, deny it all she might, she was that, too. No matter how hard she'd tried not to be.

The truth was, Hudson Walker made her feel all the same fluttering attraction that Finn had, but if she were being honest with herself, Hudson had already touched parts of her that ran so very much deeper than anything she'd experienced with Finn, or anyone else for that matter. Other men had made her laugh, had even charmed her. Hudson also made her think. He challenged her to push her boundaries, to look beyond the obvious. He made her feel like maybe being untethered wasn't so much terrifying as it was exciting.

And yet, how could she possibly consider starting anything with him? Not with the rest of her life in limbo, and definitely not with someone who lived on the opposite side of the country from her. What she needed in her life right now was stability, and focus. She needed to find her footing, then stick to it. If she were to look up into Hudson's beautiful face and oh-so-serious golden brown eyes, she knew she'd feel the opposite of all of those things.

And don't forget, you're going back home on New Year's Day.

"Moira," he said again, softer this time, and from a spot much closer than he'd been inhabiting moments ago.

To his credit, he didn't touch her, didn't do anything other than wait. When she finally looked up at him, it was all there. The desire, the hope, the fear. It was that last part that was a bit of a kick to the gut. Finn had been sad that he'd hurt her, but sad wasn't the same as hurt, much less heartbroken. His heart had never been in play. From the look on Hudson's face, visible despite the scrapes and bruises, the ball was in her court this time. He was throwing his hat in the ring. And maybe his heart along with it.

You're so much braver than me, she wanted to tell him, but what came out was, "I don't know if I can." Her voice was not much more than a whisper.

She saw his pupils go wide at that admission from her, and it made her heart squeeze inside her chest.

"Do you want to?" he asked, his voice raspier than she'd ever heard it.

She took a steadying breath. It would be kinder to them both if she lied and said no. End it before it even began. But that would be an insult to him. She'd only known him for a day, and she already understood him well enough to know he'd want her to be honest, no matter the fallout. "You listened to everything I confessed to you yesterday," she said, by way of response. "Even if I said yes, I'm clearly not ready to try again. I mean . . . you'd worry it was just a rebound and, heck, I'd worry it was just a rebound and —"

He did touch her then. He cupped her cheek and gently tipped her face up to his. "So, that's a yes, then?" He'd said the words seriously, but the amusement and affection in his eyes were what undid her.

She couldn't help it — she smiled. He really was good at cutting right to the core of things. "And a no," she said. "Weren't you listening?"

He shook his head. "I'm afraid it was all buzzing inside my head after you said yes."

"I said *if* I said yes."

"Come here, lawyer lady," he murmured, and started to lower his head to hers. He paused before his lips touched hers, though. He wasn't going to do anything she didn't want him to do.

Oh, but I want him to do, all right. So many things. That he wanted to make sure of her consent only added to that to-do list.

When she didn't close the distance between his lips and hers, he said, "My philosophy has always been you can't know if you don't try." He pulled back just enough to meet her gaze. "There's just one question — is it worth failing to find out?"

"I've got two strikes against me in the failure column at the moment, Hudson. Maybe I shouldn't risk a third," she said, even as her gaze dropped to his mouth.

She thought she heard him groan a little then, and his fingertips slid into her hair, stroking her scalp, causing a little moan of her own to slip past her lips. His hand was broad and warm, his touch surprisingly gentle for all the strength she felt in his fingertips. She supposed that came with his job, the dexterity it must require, and had sudden visions of just what it would feel like to have those hands, those fingertips, exploring other parts of her body. "Katie said I should let you finish seducing me," she murmured, her resolve wavering badly. "I told her that wasn't what you were doing." She opened her eyes, unaware she'd closed them. "I told her you were being my friend."

"Which is more seductive to you," he asked, "a man solely intent on being your lover . . . or a man intent on being your friend who is also your lover?"

No one had ever said anything like that to

her before. No one made her think about life, about what she wanted, whom she wanted in it, quite like Hudson did.

"I think of life as one grand seduction," he said when she didn't respond. "A taste of a perfectly prepared feast, the feel of snowflakes landing on your skin, the scent of wood smoke in the air." He waited until their gazes met again. "The sound of that moan you made when I touched you."

He didn't just make her knees weak; he made her heart pound. Her recently mended heart. Was it the height of foolhardiness to even dare try again? She was ready, oh so very ready, to be happy again, to be optimistic about the future. To fall in love. But could she handle being hurt again? Could she handle failing again?

"You didn't fail," he whispered in her ear. "Like I said, loving someone is never failing. It's living."

"How did you —"

"Someone not loving you is not your failure, Moira. Sadness happens, heartbreak happens, disappointment happens. We don't always get what we want. But, Moira . . . if you don't keep trying, if you shield yourself from wanting, then you might avoid heartbreak, but what you end up with is nothing."

She heard everything he was saying. He made so much sense. It all seemed so clear from his vantage point. *Of course, he's also trying to seduce you.* No, she thought, it wasn't just empty platitudes designed to get her into his bed. He was right about that much. Her gut instinct was good. Beyond even that, she seriously doubted he'd pursue the sister of one of his closest friends if his intentions weren't sincere.

"Be honest with me," she told him, looking him directly in the eyes. Her experience in the courtroom might be limited at this stage in her career, but she'd looked enough people in the eye to develop a pretty good sense of whether or not they were lying to her. "You've traveled the world over but kept your heart unscathed. Is this how you sweet talk someone into giving you a tumble?"

He looked surprised, but he immediately grinned, clearly not insulted. "Why, Miss Brogan, I was merely hoping for a kiss. Whatever are you suggesting?"

She laughed even as she shook her head. "You're as incorrigible as Katie."

"Yet another point in her favor," he said. His grin softened to a smile, but his words, when he continued, were spoken soberly and directly. "And the honest answer might not cast me in a very good light, but here it is. Given my somewhat vagabond ways, up until landing here in Blue Hollow Falls, I never set out to pursue anyone. Rather, I . . . well, I let them pursue me. I was always up front, never led anyone on, and while I'd like to think I never hurt anyone, I know that's not true. As I said before, feelings get in the way despite our best intentions to keep things light and carefree. I suspect I share that knowledge with your handsome Irish poet."

She giggled at that, which was a surprise in and of itself. Thoughts of Finn rarely made her laugh. "I never said he was a poet."

Hudson shrugged. "How could he not be?"

Moira just shook her head and laughed again. Oddly enough, it was Hudson's easy mention of Finn that made her realize how utterly opposite the two men were. That Hudson would speak of another man at all, and at such a potentially delicate time, told her better than anything that the trust she'd given him was well placed. That her ex was an easy subject between them, and not some taboo from her past to be danced around, also spoke volumes about how different her relationship with Hudson had begun, and would continue to be. If she were to let it.

There was one similarity, though, between this relationship and her last one, and it was hard to ignore.

Moira's life had been at a huge crossroads when she'd taken that trip to Ireland. She'd been practicing law in Seattle for close to a year, but realized it wasn't where she wanted to be. She'd thought practicing in her hometown was where she was meant to be, that it would feel comforting and familiar. Instead it had felt a little . . . claustrophobic and her large family a bit overwhelming with everyone's well-meaning interference. She'd gotten her undergrad degree in California, and it had been an exciting time, full of promise and much needed independence. So she'd thought maybe that's where she should have stayed, and ultimately had decided to try for the California bar, one of the hardest bar exams in the country.

Then she'd taken a holiday in Ireland before settling in to her new path in life . . . and she'd immediately found someone there who made her laugh, made life seem fun and exciting again. Had she fallen for that sense of excitement as much as she'd fallen for the man himself? Had she just been looking for a new place to land?

She looked up at Hudson, knowing her

life was once again at a crossroads. *And are you doing the same thing all over again, right now?*

CHAPTER FOUR

"I appreciate that, mate," Hudson said into the phone. "More than you know. Thanks so much. And tell your friends I appreciate their help, too. Next time you're in the Falls, your meals are all on me." Hudson shifted the phone to his other ear as he made more notes on the pad of paper lying on his prep table. "But it'll be a three-beer limit this time, mate," he added with a chuckle, and the man on the other end laughed as well. Hudson said his good-byes and hung up the phone, then turned to look at Moira. "You're a genius."

Moira shrugged, as if it were all in a day's work, but she was beaming as well. "So they're willing to send you all their footage from that night?"

Hudson nodded, then finished plating two of his specialty burgers and carried them to the café table he'd set up in his kitchen at the pub. Two days had passed since their conversation in Sawyer's office. Moira had stepped back from their intimate conversation, which had not ended in the kiss Hudson had hoped for. He respected that, respected her. That didn't mean he wasn't disappointed, though. Or that he'd given up hope.

"A room full of journalists and photographers — of course someone was filming the whole melee," Hudson said as he took the seat across from her. His hearing had been delayed yet again, and he suspected Moira might be right about Taggert playing games with the court system, hoping to bait him into spending more consultation time and money with his attorney. As yet, he hadn't even retained one. And with this latest development, he might never have to.

"And they said they got both me and Taggert on video?"

Hudson nodded. "They had two other mates who could likewise provide some footage, too."

"And they didn't angle for some kind of access to Seth or Pippa?"

Hudson shook his head. "No, that's last week's news now, apparently. Two of these guys were print journalists, not paparazzi. There's no money in it for them now. They're four assignments down the road at this point. Not sure if any of the conversation on their clips will be distinguishable though, given the level of noise in there that night."

Moira shook her head. "That won't matter. All we need is proof that Taggert took the first swing and you were defending yourself and me."

"So, what happens next?"

"We look at everything they forward to you, and if it shows what we need it to show, you can hire a lawyer who will take it to the judge. Then in all likelihood, the case will be dismissed."

Hudson nodded and urged her to try the burger. It was dry-aged, with Guinness butter, caramelized onions, and garlic aioli. He was thinking about adding it to the winter menu. He didn't bother arguing over the need to hire local counsel. He knew she couldn't represent him because she wasn't licensed in the state. She'd refused any compensation for her legal advice as well. So he was paying her in lunches and dinners instead. Well, one lunch, at any rate. Thus far.

"This is amazing," she said as she finished her first bite.

He picked up his napkin, and smiling, reached across the table to dab away the trickle of aioli that ran down her chin. "It's a big burger."

She nodded and laughed even as she tucked in to another bite. "There's no way I'll be able to finish this, but trust me, it's not a reflection on the chef." She put the burger down. "Even the bun is delicious."

Hudson nodded. "I think the bun is one of the most highly overlooked ingredients in a good burger. That's a potato bread bun, lightly buttered, with a few sesame seeds on top."

"All I know is it's hamburger bun perfection." Moira picked up a fry and popped it in her mouth. "Sweet potato fries," she said on a groan as soon as she swallowed. "My favorite."

"Try dipping them in this," he said, and slid a small silver pot of his own personal dressing across the table.

She did, and simply closed her eyes and nodded as she finished the fry, then another one, then another.

Hudson laughed. He also had to shift a little on his stool. Watching Moira Brogan eat might be as close to a sexual experience as he'd ever have with her, and his body was reacting like it was foreplay. He cooked to make people happy, and he'd been very successful in that endeavor, all over the world. So why was watching this woman enjoy his food so different? *Because this is your woman,* his little voice replied.

Yes, well, if wishes were horses, this beggar would ride, he thought.

She dabbed at her lips with her napkin and laid it by her plate, then picked up one more fry and grinned as she bit into it. "Seriously, these are addicting." She finished, then debated on another, before finally pushing her plate away. "If I let you keep feeding me, you're going to have to roll me all the way to the airport in a few days."

Hudson shifted his gaze to his plate, not wanting her to see his disappointment regarding that bit of reality. "What's in store for you back home?" he asked. "Have you given up California dreamin' altogether then?"

They'd had their legal consultation in Sawyer's office two days ago; then he'd cooked lunch for Moira and Katie, while Katie regaled them with her mill purchases and the impromptu class on loom weaving she'd taken. And he handled his disappointment in Moira's opting not to explore the undeniable attraction between them and the relationship they'd already begun with each other. He needed to put her in what the

Yanks called the "friend zone," but it wasn't working so well.

He'd watched the two of them leave after lunch, wondering if that was the last time he'd see Moira Brogan. So he'd made sure it wasn't, by calling and inviting her and Katie to meet up with him and the rest of the town on the big hill the following afternoon for a round of sledding. It hadn't been a date, per se, or if it had, they'd had about a hundred chaperones, ranging from six years old to sixty. But it had given them a chance to spend more time together, enjoy a little hot cocoa, and a lot more laughter.

It had been Katie who'd spilled the beans yesterday about the other train wreck in Moira's life. She'd assumed Moira had told Hudson and had mentioned it while they were enjoying their cocoa and cinnamon cookies around the bonfire at the bottom of the sledding hill. Either that or Moira's friend had intentionally put the information out there. Hudson couldn't be too sure. Despite the sledding being a group date at best, Katie had made no secret out of the fact that she was trying to play matchmaker between the two. Hudson was happy to let her try, given he'd been an epic failure at it himself thus far, but he didn't have much hope at this point. In lieu of that, he supposed he'd just torture himself with the chance to spend as much time with her as possible before she boarded the flight back to the West Coast.

But every moment they spent together just cemented in his mind how meant-to-be they were. He wondered if this was how Moira had felt with Finn, confused by why he wouldn't want to continue what was so obviously a good thing. If so, he wasn't all that thrilled to know he'd be having to take his own advice on how to handle heartbreak. *It all sounds so easy when it's someone else needin' the advice.*

Then Moira had surprised him by contacting him that morning. She'd done some searching online the night before, wading through all the postings and YouTube clips about Pippa and Seth's wedding. There hadn't been any leaks from the ceremony itself, or the reception, but among the loads of speculation on what it might have been like, quoting fictional "sources close to the couple," had been some tabloid-style coverage of the bar brawl in Turtle Springs that had happened after the wedding. Many of the posts had made it sound like the brawl had happened at the wedding, which had advanced the story far beyond any kind of coverage it would otherwise have gotten.

Moira had gotten a few names from the various postings and he'd taken it from there and made direct contact, asking for any footage showing Taggert in the bar that night. He'd hit pay dirt on the third contact on the list. The pub was closed on Sunday, so Hudson had invited Moira to a private lunch as a thank-you.

"Katie mentioned you could try for the bar again in February. Will you do that? If it's as hard as you say, it can't be all that unusual to have to take it more than once."

Moira lifted a shoulder. "I've given it a lot of thought while I've been here. Well, I've been giving it a lot of thought since I found out I didn't pass it the first time," she added dryly. "I could try again in February, yes, keep working as a paralegal until then. I suppose in retrospect, I shouldn't have put all my eggs in that basket before taking the exam. I should have stayed in Seattle until after I knew if I'd passed or not. But after coming home from Ireland . . . I just wanted to go ahead and make the change."

"Understandable," he said. "But?"

She smiled, as she always did when he seemed to read her mind. "After all of this, I'm not sure if California is what I want. If I don't pass again, I really don't want to stay on as a paralegal. I miss being a trial lawyer. I think I'm realizing now that I sort of had a knee jerk reaction to practicing law in Seattle. I grew up there, most of my extended family still lives there, and even though it's a big city, with plenty of room to be completely on my own and not feel like relatives are watching my every move . . ." She trailed off, lifted a shoulder. "It did feel a little like I'd gone back to being little Moira Brogan, baby of the family. I think that's why I loved my time at Stanford doing my undergrad. Loved being in California. I'd worked really, really hard to get there, put everything I had into earning my scholarship. When I got my acceptance, it was like the culmination of all my dreams. And being there, well, it was even better than I thought it would be. I realize now that's because it was the first time I was truly, truly on my own, completely independent. I loved it."

"Scholarship to Stanford?" Hudson made a pretend bowing motion with his arms. "Impressive."

Embarrassed, she waved at him to stop. "Oh, I'm such an overachieving, compulsive nerd, you have no idea," she said with a laugh. "I never missed a day of school, never missed a single class. Didn't date, didn't party. I was focused on the end goal from pretty early on."

"But your license is in Washington State?"

She nodded. "The decision to move back home was partly financial, but also, for all I loved California, by the time I graduated, I really missed my family, my home. And as much as I loved my time away, I thought the smart, responsible thing to do was pass the bar in my home state, get a good job, and start my life as an adult. Which I did. I had my own place, liked the defense firm I was working with. I had good prospects there for growth."

"But?" he asked, grinning as he did.

She laughed. "But . . . it wasn't what I wanted, either. I loved the job, but being back home again wasn't fulfilling me like I thought it would. I love my family, so very much, but they can be a little suffocating." She laughed. "Okay, a lot suffocating. As it turns out, no matter the size and population of the city, they can find a way to look over my shoulder. And the matchmaking . . . don't get me started."

"So, suddenly, California looked like the better choice after all," he said, smiling with her.

"Well, it was the only other place I knew, and I had loved it there. I thought about it for a few months, then took the big gamble and told my parents I wanted to move back, pass the bar there. And they were amazing and supportive, because my family really is wonderful like that. Ma and Dad encouraged me to move back in with them to study for the bar, save my money for moving to California. My lease was up, and I didn't want to sign on for another year, so I took them up on that. It was . . . challenging, living at home again, but cemented my decision to truly strike out on my own." Her smile became a little wistful. "Then Katie and I cooked up this grand scheme for me to do a house swap with her sister, Pippa. My last big fling before settling down and tackling adult life, and my very adult law school tuition bill. Only in reality I sort of traded Seth's place, so Pippa came here to Blue Hollow Falls and fell in love with my brother, and I went to Donegal —"

"And fell in love, too," Hudson said, smiling despite feeling as if he'd been socked in the gut. It was funny; he was both sad for her, angry at the idiot who'd dumped her, jealous of the guy at the same time, and relieved that she hadn't ended up married to the bloke. All for a woman who wasn't planning to stay. *Love isn't for the weak of will, mate,* his little voice said. *No kidding.*

Moira nodded. "I came home heartbroken

and just wanting a fresh start, a clean slate. So I packed myself up and moved to California right then and there, found the job as a paralegal, studied my brains out for the bar, looking forward not back. Only then I didn't pass the bar. I threw my whole lot into that gamble, and it didn't pay off. All of which is so unlike me. I don't do gambles. I don't take wild leaps. I'm a planner, a plotter, a goal setter and achiever."

"So not passing sent you into a tailspin, which isn't all that hard to understand. And you could take the exam again, so all is not lost."

"That's not it, though. I mean, yes, it was a crushing blow to work that hard and not pass. I've never flunked anything in my entire life. So, that was mortifying. But not passing the bar on my first try wasn't really the train wreck I was referring to."

Confused, he said, "What was?"

"Realizing that beyond feeling humiliated for not passing, and a bit panicked about how that would affect my income, the truth of the matter is . . . I was kind of relieved."

"Relieved?" She'd surprised him with that.

She nodded. "California was wonderful when I was there in school. I loved my time at Stanford. But the honest truth is . . . I discovered early on I wasn't all that keen about living there, working there. I convinced myself it was just the job, and as soon as I passed the bar, could go back to being a practicing attorney, it would be so much better. But deep down, I knew that wasn't true. My relief when I opened that envelope was hard to ignore." She looked at him. "But how in the world was I going to admit that to anyone? Most specifically myself? I've always had my life so carefully planned out, and I'd ticked off each box along the way, really happy to be reaching each milestone, so sure I knew what my future held in store for me. And yet I pass the Washington bar, enter the real world, and somehow inside the next eighteen months, end up in a state I don't really want to live in, studying for a bar exam I really didn't need to take, but the alternative is going back to Seattle, where I've already learned I don't really want to be. . . . This on top of my epic failure at attempting to have a love life." She lifted her hands and smiled a bit plaintively. "And meet Moira Brogan. Official train wreck."

"Moira, you know that just because you don't have your whole life figured out up front doesn't mean you're a wreck, much less a failure. You're smart, very well educated, with the support of an amazing family who only wants you to be happy, at least if what I know of how they've supported your brother Seth is any indication. So who cares if Seattle isn't your landing spot, or California? What if you go off and try a half dozen other things, and you still haven't found just the right thing? What harm is there in that? Who's keeping score?"

"I am, I guess," she said, but her tone was more one of wonder, with no trace of self-pity. "Maybe it's that I don't know how to handle this . . . the lack of having a clear path. I've never felt untethered and I don't do footloose and fancy-free. I need clear, direct goals to focus on."

"Okay, so what if your goal is discovering what fulfills you, what makes you happy? What if you allow yourself all the latitude in the world to figure out what that might be? Is there a deadline?"

She thought about that, then lifted a shoulder. "I never thought about it like that. I guess if I had, I'd have said that I always equated success with happiness, and success to me would be a good job, doing legal work I like, having a home of my own. Becoming a productive member of society, in a place I want to put down roots and grow." She smiled. "And somewhere in all of that, find the time to date, meet the man of my dreams, and get that white picket fence thing going. You know, otherwise, no pressure." She groaned and rested her forehead on the palm of her hand. "When did I become such a control freak?" She let out a laugh and looked at him. "Who am I kidding? When have I *not* been a control freak?"

"Everybody figures out their own path to success or happiness or both their own way. You do it with charts and plans, I do it by listening to my gut and jumping off the nearest cliff and hoping things turn out okay. There is no right or wrong way. The important thing to connect to in all of this is . . . you're aware of all that. You had a path figured out, but you admit it's not working for you. You could have just put your head down and gone the predetermined route because that's what you thought you had to do, only to wake up twenty years from now wondering why you're so miserable. What if you just give yourself permission to explore life, see where it takes you? You're only accountable to yourself."

Moira surprised him with a wry grin. "Did my brother put you up to saying all that, too?"

Hudson lifted his hand, palm forward.

"No, your honor. That was all me." He slid from his stool and held out his hand. She took it and he helped her slide from her stool until she stood just in front of him. "But I bet if you asked him, he'd agree with me one hundred percent."

She smiled up at him, and he was very aware she hadn't let go of his hand. "My brother who moved across the country to help his best friend renovate a silk mill and, oh, why not start up a winery while he's at it?" She laughed. "What else could he say?"

"Jump in, the water's fine?" Hudson suggested. He took her other hand. "Moira, you know —"

"Hey, Hud. Oh, Moira, good, you're still here." Drake Clarkson pushed through the swinging doors and walked into the pub kitchen. He was a few years older than Hudson and taught music classes at the mill in addition to being a regular on the little stage at the pub. "I heard you were helping Hud out here with his bar fight thing. I've got a legal question I was hoping you might help me with." He lifted his hand. "Just guidance, I promise." He smiled at Hud. "Hope I'm not interrupting anything."

Hudson swallowed a sigh, smiled, and shook his head. "Not at all. We were just finishing up lunch. But Moira's here on a bit of a vacation, so —"

"It's all right, Hudson," Moira said, then turned to Drake. "I don't know if I can be of any help though. What's the issue?"

Drake launched into a story about a visitor who'd come to the mill and signed up for fiddle classes. Drake had offered to let him borrow one of his fiddles for the class; then the man had taken off, never to return. "I've got all his contact information, but he doesn't respond. It's been more than two months now. Do I contact the police in his town? He lives about an hour from here. Or has too much time gone by? I don't want to cause trouble — I just want my fiddle back."

"You can certainly contact the police here and in his county or city. That'd be the first step to take in retrieving stolen property. Which is what this is, if you don't have some kind of signed agreement giving him use of the fiddle for longer than the two months it's been since you've seen him."

Drake shook his head. "We don't worry so much about contracts and such. He wanted classes, I signed him up, offered him use of the fiddle to practice on between classes. I figured if he took to it, I'd offer him a deal on one from my shop. It was a handshake deal. He took a class that day, left with the fiddle, and never came back."

"Well, if you wanted to file suit — and I'm not saying you should — it would be a matter for small claims court." She smiled. "But I'd see what the local police could do before incurring any legal fees."

"Thanks," Drake said, looking relieved. "I'd really like not to incur legal fees, either. I appreciate your advice." He looked at Hudson. "She's handy to have around." He looked back to her. "Used to be Judge Parsons would be the one we'd go to. He was a justice of the peace down in Turtle Springs and had a fishing cabin up here he'd come to pretty much every weekend. Lived up here full time after he retired." Drake smiled. "Couldn't catch fish worth nothing, but that didn't seem to bother him. Said he just liked dropping a line in now and again. Used to regale us with some of the craziest stories about cases he'd presided over, always willing to offer advice if we had a problem."

"Sounds like you both got something from the arrangement."

Drake nodded. "He passed on last spring. It's funny — I don't think we all realized just how much we relied on his advice until he was gone." He grinned. "Kind of like finding a great car mechanic or a good barber. Don't know how good you've got it

384

till they're gone." He laughed. "Only there's a lot more mechanics around than retired judges."

Moira smiled. "I would imagine so."

"So, I truly appreciate the advice. Hope I haven't imposed."

"Not at all," she said.

Drake waved and was back through the swinging door, leaving them alone in the kitchen.

Moira glanced up at Hudson consideringly. "I don't suppose you —"

"Put him up to that?" Hudson finished for her. "Hoping it might make you consider how you'd fit right here in Blue Hollow Falls?" He grinned broadly. "No. That was completely serendipitous. I would have if I'd thought of it, though."

She laughed. "At least you're honest."

"Always," he said, then looked down at their still joined hands. When he lifted his gaze back to hers, his expression had grown serious. "Let me ask you this. If Seattle is out, and California isn't where you want to be . . . maybe Blue Hollow Falls is worth considering. Not because of me," he added; then a smile curved his lips. "Though, naturally, I'd be a champion of the idea."

"Hudson," she began, and started to pull her hand away.

He held on a moment longer. "I mention it because your brother lives here, and your new sister-in-law. Katie would probably be a somewhat regular visitor. It's just, if you're looking for a place to start, of all the places in the world, you have some connection here. I know you and Seth are close. He'd be thrilled at the very idea, and your family would probably be on board. So, a little family, but not too much family," he added with a smile. "Not that you need any of those things to decide where to go next, but . . . it's something to consider, right?"

"Oh, I wouldn't be so sure about Seth being thrilled," she said with a smile. "He's my go-to guy for getting me out of jams, so I might be the last person he'd want living just down the mountain."

Hudson laughed and squeezed her hands gently, then let them go. She looked momentarily surprised by that, and a little disappointed. It was a small thing, but he better than anyone knew that sometimes the littlest things were what, in the end, made the most splendid of dishes. "All I'm saying is, it's worth considering. And what I started to say earlier was that I don't want to influence your decision. Not that I could, but —"

"You could," she said quietly.

Surprised by that admission — shocked, actually — he was momentarily speechless.

He must have looked it, because she let out a little laugh, and along with the amusement, what he saw in those green eyes was affection. For him.

"I listen, too," she said. "And I've heard everything you've been saying. You've given me a lot to think about, on all fronts. We have such a different way of looking at life." She smiled. "I'm a little envious of your way."

"It's up for adoption," he said, and they both laughed.

Their laughter abated and she simply held his gaze, as if searching, but for what he didn't know.

At length, she took a breath, and said, "Well, here's my stab at taking a Hudson Walker leap." She deliberately took his hands back in her own, and he thought his heart simply up and stopped right then and there. *Hold on, mate, until you know what she's about to say.* It was too late though; his hopes were already beginning to climb, and no amount of resolve was going to stop them.

"Since we've always been honest with each other, it's only fair for me to tell you that what you're saying, your viewpoint, not only intrigues me, it attracts me, too." Moira's expression turned more serious then. "I've been pulling back, hard, from that attraction." She smiled. "You don't make it easy."

"I'm sorry?" he offered gamely, and they both flashed a grin.

Her smile remained, but her words were serious when she said, "I think . . . my concern is, am I doing the same thing I did last time? Telling myself this is what I want because then I don't have to actually go back and figure out what that really is?"

"Is that what you think you did in Ireland?"

She nodded. "To some degree. I mean, he was worth loving; I didn't fabricate that. But I may have swooned over the larger picture, of which he was just a part."

"Meaning if you'd met him apart from all that, you might have felt different?"

She nodded. "I'm pretty sure of that. We weren't the love match of the century, we were just . . . right place, right time. For him, right place and time for something fun. For me, a nice, decent guy, in a lovely place, that looked like it could possibly be a whole new solution to my I-need-to-get-out-of-Seattle problems." She smiled again. "Not to encourage you or anything, but meeting you put a lot of that in very clear perspective."

His heart kicked up a notch or three, right along with his hopes. He tried to keep it all in check, because while she was giving him far more than he'd ever anticipated, he heard the caveat coming from a mile away. "Because . . . ?"

"Because I'm pretty sure I'd have been attracted to you no matter where you turned up, or at what point in my life. I'm attracted to you, yes. And you make me laugh, yes. I've experienced that before, though I'd say not nearly on the level that we connect. What's completely new, though, is how you make me think. How we both like to think, to ponder, to have a sense of what we're doing, and why. We're both goal oriented." At his look of surprise, she said, "We are. You just approach your goals differently, and they aren't as rigidly set as mine were. Your goal was to not be bored by life. And you set out to make sure that never happened. When it started to feel that way, you moved on. Forward thinking, forward looking." She smiled. "Dare I say, focused."

He grinned. "Well, to all of the above, counselor, can I say in much more simple terms . . . ditto. You care about things that matter, you're focused on helping others."

His grin spread even wider. "You sat at my table with day-old makeup on, in a gown that had gone through a wedding, a reception, a bar brawl, and a night's sleep, and you never once seemed perturbed." He tugged her a little closer. She let him. "You swooned over my food," he said, more quietly now, as she stared up at him with that green-eyed gaze of hers. His smile was intimate now. "You could have had me right then and there. And despite what you may think of me, I'm not that easy."

Her pupils slowly expanded as he lowered his head to hers. "I'm not trying to persuade you," he said, his voice so quiet it just reached her ears. "But if I don't find out how you taste, I think I truly will go mad."

She held his gaze for the longest moment, then whispered, "Then I think you should."

CHAPTER FIVE

His lips were warm and firm, and fit her mouth perfectly. He let go of her hands and slid his to her waist, lifting her effortlessly so she could sit on the edge of the café table, pushing their plates of food back when she pulled him in closer and returned his kiss.

She knew three things immediately. This definitely wasn't Ireland redux. Hudson wasn't remotely like Finn. *Finn, who?* And this absolutely wasn't going to be the only time she kissed this man.

He took his time, didn't hurry, didn't crush her mouth thinking that was the way to show his ardor. No, he took the slow, savory route. *Of course he would.* And she savored it right along with him.

Why had she balked at this? Why hadn't she trusted herself? Why had she wasted so much time wondering "what if" when they could have been doing this? *If you don't keep trying, if you shield yourself from wanting, then you might avoid heartbreak, but what you end up with is nothing.* This was not nothing.

"Moira," he said when he finally lifted his mouth from hers. His voice was husky now, and the sound of it sent a thrill of anticipation racing down her spine.

"Hudson," she replied, hearing the hoarseness in her own voice as well. With their noses pressed together, they both smiled.

"I said I'd always be honest with you," he said.

She tensed.

He felt it and immediately dropped a kiss on her mouth, then kissed her temple before lowering his mouth next to her ear. "Just so we're clear, I might be trying to persuade you now."

She burst out in giggles, then turned her head so her mouth was next to his ear. "I don't think the burden of persuasion lies solely with the defense counselor."

He lifted his head and smiled down at her. "Oh, I don't need any persuading. I knew you were it the moment you took a swing at Taggert's —"

"Bad manners?" she offered not so innocently.

"Those too," he said, chuckling.

They held each other's gaze, and he lifted

his hand, brushed her curls from her forehead, traced the blunt tips of his fingers down the side of her cheek. "In all seriousness, you need to do what is right and best for you. If you want to give Blue Hollow Falls a spin, then do it because it's all the things you think might suit you, both personally and professionally."

"I wish I could say I was certain this is the right fit, but . . . I guess I'll be smarter this time and say I can't be sure without trying."

He lifted a shoulder. "It might not be. It might be the first of many places you try."

"Then maybe we shouldn't —"

He tugged her close again. "I'm a big boy. No one is leading anyone down a garden path here. But if you're going to give the place a go, then give it all a go, aye? You can't figure things out in pieces. Life tends to come at you full on. My experience is embrace it for what it is, get out of it what you can. Discard what doesn't work, consider it a learning opportunity, and build on what does."

She wasn't sure how she felt about that. It was a lot to take in, a lot to consider. "I can't imagine bouncing from place to place," she said instead. "Not much of a way to build a career." Her tone was dry when she added, "And I'm really not looking to rack up frequent flyer miles by taking one state bar exam after the other, either. I do know I want to practice law."

"Big city law?"

She shrugged. "I could, and I did. The firm in Seattle and the one I worked for as a paralegal in California handled some huge corporate accounts, as well as defending some rather high profile individual clients."

"Trial attorneys, you mean, for the defense."

She nodded. "I like criminal law, it's where I specialized. But being honest, I can't say I got all that personally motivated by helping to get some big corporation off the hook on paying out a claim or doing the right thing by one of their vendors, or worse, their employees. I'm not saying I want to represent hardened criminals, either. That's why I shied away from the public defender's office. I guess I figured out while I was in California that I wanted to do something to help individual people. Make the law work for them, instead of the system working against them."

"Someone like Drake, who wants his fiddle back?"

She laughed. "A bit more complex and challenging than that would be nice, but in general, yes." She looked at him. "I'd have relished taking your case, if it went to trial. Taggert is exactly the kind of person I'd like to prosecute for taking gross advantage of others. That's personal, I know, but it's the kind of case I'm talking about. He could have crushed you financially, and you wouldn't have had the resources to fight back."

"There's not much of mine to have. I've had something and I've had nothing. The former didn't make me and the latter didn't break me. Taggert is barking into a hollow well."

"Interesting metaphor," she teased, "and that may be true, but don't underestimate the toll it would have taken on you emotionally, monopolizing your life for endless months, perhaps years. And I meant to add this before, but if the court drops the case, that isn't to say he won't try and come after you some other way. Recommend to your attorney that he or she ask the judge to block Taggert from filing frivolous lawsuits against you. Having evidence of his threatening to crush you however he can in those videos would help that request enormously."

Hudson's smile brightened. "If you did decide to move here, hypothetically speaking of course, and Taggert became a nuisance, then you could take him on, right? Assuming you did whatever it is you'd have to do to practice law here."

"Ah," Moira said with a laugh. "So that's what this is all about? You're just after me for my legal skills; then you'll cast me aside once I've vanquished the enemy?"

"You could start another bar brawl and I could defend your honor if that would help. I'd take a few lumps to keep you on retainer."

"First, I didn't start that bar brawl. Second, it's very kind of you to offer yourself up as a punching bag on the altar of my career growth." She tilted her head. "Third, should I be concerned about your apparent propensity for enjoying physical altercations?"

He lifted a shoulder. "I'm an Aussie, love. We don't back down. And if that means things get tricky, well, we might as well enjoy ourselves, then."

"I'm glad you were on my side."

He leaned down and kissed her. "I'm always on your side."

She sighed just a little, leaned into him just a little. *Can it really be so simple as this? Am I fooling myself again? Looking for the easy answer to all life's problems?*

"You won't know until you try," he said

quietly, his lips pressed against her curls.

She gave him a playful poke in the shoulder. "Will you stop reading my mind?"

"Why, when I'm so good at it?" he said with a chuckle. "It saves a lot of time spent mentally wrangling over every little thing if we just talk it out."

"You really do just live your life and take things as they come, don't you?"

"Life is going to do what it's going to do and there's only so much you can control. But that's not to say I don't care about things. I do. I've come to love this place very much. I've taken quite a liking to my unusual living quarters. In fact, I'm thinking about adding a third car. Believe it or not, I've found a caboose in West Virginia, and I already know we can unearth more of the rail." He grinned when she just shook her head in amazement. "What I mean is I'm not impervious to disappointment, or to being hurt. If I lost that place, lost my work here, it'd set me back on my heels. I'd have to really think about what to do next. I'm confident that I'd go on to be just fine. I'll always be able to support myself. But I'm not bulletproof. Nobody is. The point is, I want to be just fine here. The Falls have come to matter to me. More than any other place I've landed. I wasn't planning on it, but it turned out that way. Which is how the best things do."

Sort of like being saved from a bar snake by a handsome Australian chef, she thought. She hadn't planned on meeting Hudson Walker, hadn't planned on getting to know him, or starting to fall in love with him. *But I think it's turning out that way.*

"I wish I could be as confident as you," she said, and meant it. "I've been in the work force for just a short time and have already bounced around more than I wanted to. I want to be settled. I want to work on building something that will last, I want to do work that helps people, I want to have pride in myself and in what I'm doing with my life. And for me, that means stability and continuity. I don't know how else to be. You've made so much sense in suggesting that I don't put as much pressure on myself to get it right on the first try. I can try to do that." She smiled dryly. "Key word being 'try.' But I don't think I can be like you, either."

"You have to start somewhere, though, right?"

"I suppose you're right."

"Well, maybe Blue Hollow Falls has just the right amount of family," he said, and she laughed. "And there's the added benefit

398

of being close to Turtle Springs, which I imagine sees a fair share of cases in its courthouse. Valley View isn't that much farther out, which isn't big-city, big-city, but a city, nonetheless." He smiled. "Or you could hang out your own shingle, pick up where Judge Parsons left off. Of course, you'd have to start charging for your advice."

"Would I have to learn to fish?" she asked, wrinkling her nose and laughing at the same time. He made it all seem so easy, so doable. And maybe it was.

"I don't think having your own rod and reel is a prerequisite," he said with a laugh. "But in lieu of crazy case stories, you have the added advantage of being able to tell embarrassing childhood stories about your brother to all of his friends."

She laughed outright at that. "Yeah, that would backfire in a spectacular fashion. He has far more ammunition, trust me. No one would ever want to hire me when he got through."

Hudson's face took on a considering expression. "Does he now? Hmm."

She nudged his shoulder. "New rule. What's said in your kitchen, stays in your kitchen."

He chuckled. "I can live with that." He

surprised her by pulling her close and tipping her face up to his. "I'm not so sure I can live without you, though."

"Hudson," she whispered, her breath caught in her throat. She shouldn't be so shocked that he'd just put it on out there. It was just like him. *Jump off the nearest cliff, and hope things turn out okay.*

"Just being honest with you. I can adjust to anything, but I'd rather not have to learn to adjust to a daily routine that doesn't include you sitting at my breakfast table, swooning over breakfast — formal attire optional." He grinned, but she was still trying to get her equilibrium back. His voice quieter, his gaze steady on hers, he said, "Or racing me down a snow-covered hill." He pulled her closer. "Or kissing me in my kitchen." He leaned his head down and took her mouth, this time with more intent, and far more devastating results. At least where that already dangerously wobbly equilibrium of hers was concerned.

"This is . . . a lot," she managed, when he lifted his head.

"Good," he said. "Because I think it could be everything."

She stared into his eyes. "And if it turns out it's not? If Blue Hollow Falls isn't right for me, either?"

"If it's the Falls that doesn't fit, then we go find a place that does."

"We?"

"I love it here, but I can love it somewhere else, too."

She nodded, slammed by the very idea that he'd consider picking up and taking off if that's what she needed to do. In a quieter voice, she asked, "And if it turns out that it's you who isn't right for me? Or me not for you? What then?"

"Well, since I doubt either of us is the sort to out-and-out do wrong to each other, I suppose we'd hurt, we'd heal, then we'd respect each other enough to live and let live." He smiled gently. "Or I'd pack up my shattered heart and take my train cars and head out."

"You'd take your train cars?"

"I'd have to have something good to remember this place by. If you go and stomp my heart flat to the point I can't bear to stay, I don't think keeping my trains is too much to ask."

"No," she said, matching his mock seriousness, "of course not."

"Good," he said. "Now that we've got all that settled, we can just get started." He lifted her off the table and held her hips until she was steady on her feet.

"Started on what?"

"Finding out if we get to live happily ever after."

He was a nonstop whirlwind. Would she ever be able to keep up? *Could you bear not to try?* "Hudson —"

But he'd already taken her hand and turned toward the swinging doors.

"Wait, where are we going?"

"Do you have any pressing engagements for the rest of the day?"

She shook her head. "No, but —"

"I thought we could drive down to Turtle Springs and drop off the information we got about Taggert at the courthouse. Then I need to see a man about a caboose. I'd love to get your opinion on it."

Moira hurried to keep up with his long-legged stride. "Uh, well, sure. Why not?"

Grinning like, well, like a kid at Christmas, he turned back and spun her neatly into his arms. "Why not indeed?" They were standing out in the mill now, and he leaned down and kissed her in front of God and everybody, until she quite literally swooned.

Applause, several hoots and hollers, and one long whistle pierced the air when he finally lifted his mouth from hers. "In fact, that should be our new motto."

She blinked, still reeling from the kiss.

"We have a motto?"

"Every great endeavor should have a motto."

A giggle escaped her. "And ours is 'why not?' Seems a bit . . . wishy-washy, doesn't it?"

"Well, that's just our first-stage motto."

"Oh, we have mottos in stages now. I see."

He took her hand as they walked through the mill, and it was the most natural thing in the world. Being with Hudson Walker. She rather liked it. *Who are you kidding? You love it.* It was true. Try as she might to schedule falling in love like she scheduled college courses, or client appointments, that's not how this was going to go at all. Maybe she'd be okay with being a little more footloose and fancy free. *Seeing as that's happening anyway.*

Moira knew she should be concerned with all the happy faces of the artists and crafters they passed, who were giving them the thumbs-up and generally looking pleased as punch about this brand-new change in Hudson's life. If things didn't work out, that would make it all the more awkward. But she didn't want this to be a secret, either.

So . . . *why not?* She had to stifle another giggle.

They slipped their coats on and stepped

outside into a swirl of snowflakes and a world covered in white. She shivered and he took her hand in his, warming her slender fingers in his big, broad palm.

"So, if stage-one is 'why not,' what's the next stage motto?" she asked.

He pulled her hand up to his mouth and kissed the back of it. "I have a lot of pent-up kisses I need to get out. I hope you don't mind."

"Why not?" she said, and made him laugh.

"Stage-two motto," he said, musing, then turned and lifted her up on her toes and kissed her soundly. Snowflakes had gathered on his eyelashes when she opened her eyes. "How about 'we've got this,' " he said, and she liked his intimate smile. A lot.

They broke apart and hurried more quickly to his old Range Rover, both of them shivering now. She raced ahead, wanting to get out of the cold, and called back, "And I suppose the final stage will be 'we did it'?"

He grinned at her and trotted to catch up, palming his keys and hitting the unlock button on the remote. "Works for me," he said as he caught up to her and opened the passenger side door.

She turned in his arms. "Even better!" At his questioning look, she said, " 'Works for me.' Stage-three motto."

He laughed. "Done."

They drove down to Turtle Springs and met with the local assistant district attorney to pass along the files that had come in via e-mail to Hudson's phone while they'd been eating their burgers and talking. They didn't take the time to review them first, but the ADA promised she would and then she'd get back to them. There had been multiple lawsuits stemming from that night, as it turned out, not the least of which was the hotel seeking compensation for the damage done to the place by the brawl begun by the group of photographers and journalists who'd started things up back when Sally had blown her whistle.

Hudson had already sent the hotel a check for the cost of the table and glassware that had broken when Taggert had gone flying, and had offered himself as free labor doing other repair work, which hotel management had accepted. The ADA thought the tapes might help the hotel as well. Moira knew the lounge was still closed for repairs, which meant Sally was out of a job until it re-opened. So she was pleased by Hudson's forward thinking in helping more people than just himself with the video tape information they'd managed to dig up.

The drive to West Virginia took close to two hours, including a stop for frozen custard at a little mom-and-pop trailer stand that proudly served "the best custard in Hawksbill County" all year round.

"I'd never have thought of eating ice cream in December," Moira had told him before diving into the frozen concoction.

"That's what the hot fudge is for," Hudson had told her.

The snow had stopped, so they'd laughed and enjoyed the sundae, sitting bundled up in front of the huge fire pit the couple kept stoked and burning bright all winter long. Hudson had walked her to her side of the car, opening the door for her, as he'd done when they'd left the mill and the courthouse. She'd liked the gentleman he was. She'd also liked it when he'd turned her to face him before she'd slid into her seat, so he could steal the dab of hot fudge on her chin.

They'd spent the rest of the ride telling each other about their childhoods. His was so dramatically different from hers, but he thought her stories of growing up with five siblings and a huge extended family were equally unusual and fascinating. He told her about Australia and she told him about the Pacific Northwest, one of the few places he hadn't been to. As yet.

They even joked about how she should go about breaking the news to her family that she'd met a guy while on holiday, and how he had this amazing, killer accent. And, oh, by the way, she was packing up and heading to the Blue Ridge Mountains to see if that worked out for her. Because, oh, right, she'd forgotten to mention, she'd flunked the California bar, but that was okay, because it turned out California wasn't really for her anyway. And neither was Seattle.

Yeah, that'd totally work. They wouldn't worry at all about her now.

Hudson had said he thought her parents would ultimately just want their children to be happy and Moira was thinking about that as they passed the sign welcoming them to WILD AND WONDERFUL WEST VIRGINIA.

"You know, it's funny," she said, "but I'd forgotten the whole story about how my parents met. I mean, not forgotten it. But in the context of my current life predicament, I hadn't really thought about it."

He glanced over at her and smiled. "Good story?"

She smiled. "The best." Moira told him about how her mother won a college scholarship for volleyball — she was the first in her family to even go to college. Only she really didn't want to play collegiate level ball. She'd enjoyed it as a high school sport, but didn't think sport was going to be her future. The problem was, she didn't know what *was* going to be her future, and in the end, she hadn't wanted to disappoint her parents, so she'd taken the scholarship.

However, rather than become a physical education teacher, as everyone assumed she'd be, she'd gotten her bachelor's degree in business. She'd met Moira's father her freshman year at the Irish pub where she and her friends hung out and studied. His family owned the pub and he was working to help support his parents and grandparents, who all lived together, along with his five other siblings, in the rooms above the pub. No college for him, or any of his five other siblings, but he loved what he was doing, was a natural when it came to running the place, and as the oldest son, had long since planned on taking over the pub full time when his parents retired.

"Mom finished school, gave every last stitch of her volleyball gear away, and put her educated business acumen — which turned out to be her superpower and her passion — to work for her boyfriend's family-run pub." Moira grinned. "Thirty-nine years later, Stella and Mick Brogan still run that place."

"And they said it wouldn't last," Hudson said with a grin. "You're right. Very good story."

"My mom's mom and pop didn't decide to like my dad until he and my mom started having babies. Mom told them that they either loved all of her family, or they'd just let the Brogan clan spoil those babies rotten." Moira grinned. "Things changed pretty rapidly after that."

"A woman who knows how to get things done." Hudson looked over to her and smiled. "Why am I not surprised?" He slowed the vehicle and took a turn on what swiftly became a dirt and gravel road. "Did her family truly come to love and respect your dad?"

"You saw them all at the wedding — what do you think?"

Hudson chuckled. "Right, I forgot. You come from a small village of people, and that's just your immediate family."

"They can be a lot," she said with a laugh. "But you're right in that we — meaning my brothers and sisters and I — have never once doubted that we are loved. And supported. Our parents do want us to be happy, and they want us to succeed in life like they have, and sometimes that means they put their own hopes and dreams on us, because they don't know what else to do. Until we tell them what we want. Then we have the biggest cheering section west of the Mississippi." She leaned back in her seat, shook her head slowly, still smiling.

"What?" he asked, glancing at her, then back to the road.

"I should have given them more credit. I've been so far up inside my head about all of this, I haven't really stopped to think about who they are. Who they really are, I mean, outside of being my folks." She looked at Hudson then, and wondered if she'd still feel flushed and a little giddy when she looked at him ten years from now, twenty years from now. Her pop loved to say that her mom still "made his heart rev like a brand-new Chevy." She'd thought that was so corny and silly when she was a kid. She'd lost count of the number of times he'd embarrassed the daylights out of her by kissing her mom in front of his youngest daughter and her friends. "It's funny, but I forget they're people, too. I mean, with their own hopes and dreams, past failures and triumphs. I guess I just wanted to live up to that, to make them proud. We all do."

"That's a measure of the respect they've

earned, and a measure of how well they raised all of you."

She nodded. "You're right. I should also give them more credit for loving us first and foremost, and not measuring us against some ruler of success."

Hudson laughed and Moira sent him a questioning look. "It's a sign of how adorably nerdy you really are, that you'd think the parents of a woman who'd earned a scholarship to Stanford, and is now a practicing attorney, could ever be disappointed in her with regards to her success."

"Well," Moira said, "when you put it like that."

Hudson chuckled, then reached over and took her hand in his.

That felt nice, too, she thought. Solid, strong, dependable. She loved that they talked and shared their thoughts, and it didn't matter if they agreed or saw things the same way. She respected his process as he did hers. And oh, did he make her laugh. She loved that she made him laugh, too.

"I think your past successes would indicate that you can do anything you set your mind to," he told her. "Your folks won't worry over-much if you take a little time to figure out what, exactly, that's going to be, right?"

He glanced at her again, squeezed her

hand, but continued to hold it as they slowly bumped down the gravel road.

"Thank you," she said a few moments later. When he sent her a questioning look, she said, "For putting things in the kind of rational, bare bones perspective that speaks to me. I've been on what feels like a constantly spinning hamster wheel of confusion since those bar exam results came back. Who knows how long I'd have gone on spinning round and round, and you just cut right through it, put it all in perfect, rational, sensible order."

He wiggled his eyebrows. "It's all part of my master seduction plan."

She giggled. "And how, exactly, do you envision that working?"

"Simple. I plan to make myself so indispensable to you that you won't be able to live without me."

She grinned at that. "And what do you get out of the bargain? Besides free legal advice whenever you decide to toss an entire bar to save my skin?"

"Don't downplay that element. I brought you along today partly because I'm assuming you'll be a much better negotiator than I will on the caboose."

"Ah, now the truth comes out," she said drolly.

"It's true," he said. "I'll get one look at it and the guy will know he's got a sucker for the taking." He looked at her, a baleful, puppy dog look on his face. "You'll save me, right?"

She burst out laughing, then covered the hand that still held hers with her free one and patted it reassuringly. "I'll see what I can do."

"See?" He grinned. "Perfect match."

He slowed further and turned up a long, narrow drive that was even more deeply rutted than the one they'd just been on.

The snow had melted on the road, turning the ruts into muddy tracks, making her thankful they had four-wheel drive if needed. "Are you sure this is the right place?"

"Aye," he said, ducking so he could peer below the sun visor. "Pretty sure at any rate."

"It's a good thing my parents don't know about you yet," she joked. "They'd for sure think I'd run off with an ax murderer, and this is the proof right here."

Hudson chuckled. "I've met your parents. I've fed your parents. I think when it comes to getting them to accept me, we have them right where we want them."

She giggled at that. "You may have a point

there. Oh!" She said that last part on a gasp as they drove beyond the thick stand of trees into a little clearing. And right there in front of them was an old — a very, very old — badly faded, red caboose. "Would you look at that."

She heard Hudson sigh and his grip on her hand tightened. "Crikey," he said. "You big, red beauty, you," he breathed. "You might want me to just stay in the truck altogether, love."

Moira looked from the beaten down, falling apart train car to a starry-eyed Hudson, then back at the caboose. "You might have a point," she said on a laugh.

"If you can get him to lower his price by a few thousand —"

"Thousand?" Moira's eyebrows climbed upward. "Oh, honey, I can do better than that." She opened her door and carefully slid out of the car, stepping over the mud and into the snow, which only came a few inches up the side of her winter boots. She glanced back into the Range Rover. "When do you want to take delivery?"

Hudson tore his gaze away from the caboose and looked at her. "Can we hitch her to the back of the truck?"

"Oh, boy," Moira said under her breath, but winked at him and said, "Now who's the adorable nerd?" She motioned to the older man in a pair of oil-stained overalls who was standing beside the caboose, a very happy look on his face. Clearly, he'd seen Hudson's reaction. "Is that who I talk to?"

"Otto Trent," Hudson said. "He owns the place."

"The place" was a junkyard, for all intents and purposes. Heaps and piles of old junkers, farm equipment, and what even looked like part of an old carnival ride were stacked up all around the open lot. A small, white clapboard building with a sign that said OT-TO'S JUNKERS AND PARTS appeared to be the office, but the older man lifted his hand in a wave, so Moira turned his way. He frowned a bit when he realized he'd be talking to her and not Hudson. Moira smiled and looked back at Hudson and said, "Yes, definitely stay in the truck."

"Why not," he said. He grinned, she laughed, and as she walked across the lot, pulling out her phone to take photos of the caboose before saying a word to Otto, she could have sworn she heard Hudson say, "You are my volleyball player, Moira Brogan. I sure hope like hell you decide I'm your pub owner."

Hearing that didn't scare her, or make her nervous. It made her grin and want to do a little dance, right there in the mud and the snow. She realized it was because, after months of self-doubt and worry, of sleepless nights, and no idea how to plan what came next . . . she was happy. Well and truly happy. She had no idea if her future plans would work out. What she did know was that she was happy with who she was, where she was, and whom she was with. And that was a pretty good place to start. "My God, he's already rubbing off on me," she said under her breath, and her smile grew bigger still. *Why not?*

With a little extra oomph in her step, she proceeded to negotiate a deal for the caboose that would make Hudson the happiest man east of the Mississippi, while still putting a little bit more money in Otto's pocket than the thing was worth.

She walked back to the Range Rover twenty minutes later, beaming with triumph. The moment Hudson could see her face, he grinned and blew her an extravagant kiss, laughing as she pretended to stagger back under its impact. Then he was out of the Range Rover and covering the distance between them, a determined grin on his face. She had no idea what he was about now, but she couldn't wait to find out what was in store for them next.

"Dear Ma and Dad," she whispered under her breath. "The funniest thing happened to me after you left. I think I met your future son-in-law."

EPILOGUE

Five months, three weeks, and two days later, Hudson opened the passenger door of his Range Rover and carefully helped a blindfolded Moira down from her seat. "Almost there," he said.

Moira was grinning, then laughed as she almost ran into him when he stopped a few feet away from the truck. "As a seeing eye dog, you need a little work," she said.

"Oh, but the blind shall see again in a moment." He took her by the shoulders and turned her so she was facing a spot a little to her left. Then he moved behind her, and slowly slipped off the blindfold. He leaned down and whispered, "Happy new life to you, Moira Brogan."

She opened her eyes and gasped. "Oh, Hud! Would you look at her now."

New life had been breathed into the old caboose. Completely restored, freshly painted, she sat on her personal piece of recovered track like a happy little spot of sunshine in the warm, spring mountain air.

Moira turned into Hudson's arms. "You did it! She's perfect. Now can you explain the secrecy? Are you not going to bring her up and connect her to our two cars?"

"I've got another idea for that," he said, surprising her.

It had ended up taking several months for Moira to make the final move to Blue Hollow Falls. She'd taken the California bar exam again in February, just to prove to herself that she could do it. And she'd passed. Then she'd started work on getting accepted to the bar in Virginia. There'd been another exam to take, but not as involved, nor nearly as challenging, as the one out west.

It was true that her parents had met Hudson at the wedding, but he'd flown to Seattle to meet and charm and feed every last aunt, uncle, and cousin, assuring them he'd be taking very good care of their lass. That Moira's big brother was Hudson's good friend, and would also be keeping an eye on things by virtue of being their neighbor, had helped to sway the few remaining relatives who'd been holding out in hopes of her returning to Seattle for good.

Seth and Pippa had returned from their

Irish honeymoon, thrilled at the news that Moira was moving to the mountains. Seth might have been a teensy-tinesy bit smug, seeing as how he'd been the one to put Hudson directly in her path. And maybe that hadn't been by accident.

While Moira was busy working out the details of being able to practice law in her new mountain home, she'd also figured out just what kind of law she wanted to practice. She'd decided to hang out her own shingle, work for the folks of Blue Hollow Falls and Turtle Springs, and whoever else needed her help. She'd make sure folks who didn't have a lot were well represented, and folks who could afford to keep her on retainer, well, they were welcome, too. It wouldn't earn her a high dollar income, but the very first time she went before the judge in Turtle Springs and got Drake his fiddle back, she knew she'd been right that the rewards weren't all about financial compensation.

Of course, that was a might bit easier to say given that during the many months of transition time, she'd had the wonderful benefit of living on board Hudson's train car home, being fed the most wondrous meals, and best of all, without having a regular day job to keep her occupied, they'd had all the time they needed to finish falling deeply, irrevocably, and quite madly in love.

And now she was standing in the tiny town proper of Blue Hollow Falls, on a small plot of land across from the local library, and just down the street from the county courthouse, waiting to see what was about to happen next. On the plot of land was a single length of recovered and restored train track and the red caboose she'd negotiated into their lives so many months ago, just a few days after Christmas.

"What is it doing down here?"

Hudson took her hand. "Come with me and I'll show you."

They crossed the neatly manicured grassy lot, and she noted that someone had planted a row of shrubs and a few blooming azaleas around the steps leading up to what had been the rear of the caboose. It was a lot bigger up close than one would think, and somehow looked bigger still, all dolled up and polished to a bright gleam.

"After you," he said, gesturing for her to enter first.

She opened the door, and stopped dead right in the open doorway. "Oh, Hudson." The interior had been transformed into what looked like a little office. There was a tiny reception area to the left, with a few restored chairs and a short bench seat. To the right was a desk built out in an L-shape from the wall, with a small set of file drawers propping up the other end. The windows on both sides let in plenty of sunshine, making the space feel bigger than it was. Beyond the front area was a door leading to the back of the caboose.

"Go on," Hudson urged, and she could hear the smile in his voice, but couldn't take her eyes off the amazing transformation long enough to glance back to confirm it.

It only took a few strides to cross the reception area. She opened the black enamel door and was stunned for a second time that day.

"If it's not to your taste —" Hudson began, but she'd already spun around and wrapped her arms around his neck.

"You're giving her to me? Are you sure?"

"If I ever had a single doubt, and I didn't, the look on your face just now would have taken care of it. Every part of this was my pleasure."

"But . . . when did you decide — what if we didn't — you'd have given up —"

He stopped her rush of words with a kiss. Then another one. Then she turned to look at the stunning little law office Hudson had created for her, and turned right back and kissed him again.

The space was small, but the clever planning allowed room to fit everything necessary for her to launch her law business in style. "I can't believe you did all this." She took in the beautifully restored desk, with two small padded chairs sitting on the opposite side for her clients. There was a full wall of shelves behind the desk, and more filling the space on either side of the door. A neatly tucked away printer and fax machine sat on a small stand to the right. There was even a small coffeepot and microwave.

"I did close in the open back end of the caboose so you wouldn't have to go across the street to the library to use the bathroom. I know it changes the look from the outside, and it's tiny, but I think —"

"It's perfect," she said, her eyes glistening. "You're perfect."

"Well, I needed to make sure I was living up to our stage-three motto."

She laughed. "You've far surpassed that."

"Martin Collier, the woodcarver at the mill, will make you whatever shingle you want to hang out front. Tanzy will work with him to do up a wrought iron stand to hang it from."

"Hudson, I can't let you —"

"Well, it appears that Martin and Tanzy need help combining their two businesses together." He smiled. "Looks like we're not the only new couple in the Falls. I said you might be able to find the time to look over their paperwork and tell them what they need to do. They'll pay you, of course, if they need any actual legal work done, but —"

"Of course I will. I'll be more than happy to." She turned and looked around the place again. "I just . . . I can't believe it."

He turned her around, back into his arms. "There is one more thing. I planned to do this over dinner, after I'd lulled you into a food coma, lowered all your defenses."

"What more could you possibly do beyond — oh!" Her hand flew to cover her mouth when he slowly bent down on one knee. "Hudson, are you sure?"

He simply looked up at her and smiled, all the love, affection, and the amusement she seemed to effortlessly spark in him right there for her to see. "Are you?" he asked.

She nodded, and the tears that had threatened to flow upon seeing the overwhelming gift of her very own law office spilled over as she saw everything she'd banked her hopes and dreams on, everything both of them had worked so very hard to achieve, coming true for them.

"Moira Aileen Brogan," he began, "you

came into my life in a swirl of green silk and flying fists." He grinned. "And it only got more entertaining from there." He reached for her hands and covered them with his own. "I've watched you grapple with disappointment and fight like a warrior when your path finally became clear. You've made me realize that some things in life are worth making happen, and not just taking them as they come. Your spirit and fortitude, and your unwavering sense of humor throughout, have been a constant inspiration to me. You've been true to yourself, going back for that bar exam, making endless lists, charts, and grids mapping out every detail of your big transition to the East Coast, to join my world, to join me. And you've done the hardest thing, too, throwing caution to the wind to give a bloke like me a chance, and giving me your heart. Thank you for trusting me with it. I promise I won't ever forsake you."

Moira dabbed at her tears and sank to her own knees, holding their joined hands between them. "Hudson Laramie Walker," she said, noting his surprise that she'd learned his middle name. She wiggled her eyebrows, making him laugh. "I'm a very good researcher," she said by way of explanation; then she grew serious. "You've been . . . well, everything. My sounding board, my rational thinker, my biggest champion, my fiercest defender. You've become my very best friend, who turned out to also be my beautiful lover. You've housed me, fed me, and loved me like I never thought was possible. We truly are in this together. Partners, lovers, friends. If we're about to do what I think we are, I want us to do that together, too."

His eyes might have been a wee bit glassy, too, but they were both smiling now as he pulled her into his arms. "We haven't done any other part of this relationship thing the conventional way," he said, "so, I couldn't agree more."

He cupped her face in one palm and she did the same to him.

"Ready?" he asked.

She nodded, and they both said, "Will you marry me?" at the same time.

"Try and stop me," he said at the same time she said, "I thought you'd never ask."

They both laughed, then kissed, then laughed again as Hudson fell over backward and took her with him.

"I do have one request," he said, still sprawled on his back, with her on top of him.

"Name it."

"Well, we've a wedding to plan now. I think you'll agree, there's really only one choice for the perfect date for our wedding."

She looked confused for a moment. Then her mouth dropped open. "No. You can't honestly mean —"

"You have to admit, love, it's pretty much a must do."

"I . . . can't believe I'm saying this, but I think you're right," she said, shaking her head in disbelief.

"And unless you have your heart set on wearing white, you have this green silk number I'm a pretty big fan of. It doesn't have to be a big production —"

"You have met my family," she said dryly.

"Right. True."

"And I am the last Brogan to tie the knot, so hold on to your horses there. How about we make a deal. Christmas wedding, I wear white, we cut loose and throw a real shindig for the whole clan." She leaned down and kissed him. "Then we come back home, and I'll wear the green dress. A candlelit dinner for two, and a dance in front of the fireplace." She grinned. "I'll even sleep in it and leave my makeup on and you can fix me breakfast the next morning."

"Yeah," he said, and smiling, he rolled her to her back. "I don't think that's going to be possible, but I like the way you think."

"Why won't it be possible?"

"We won't be home the next morning."

"No? Where will we be?"

"On a plane to Australia?"

Her eyes widened in stunned pleasure. "Are you sure?"

"You've introduced me to your family, shown me your hometown. I want you to meet the people I consider to be my family, show you where I grew up."

"Yes," she said, and reached up to kiss him. "To all of it, yes."

Six months, one week, and two days later, they said their I do's at her brother's winery in front of a soaring Christmas tree. Moira surprised Hudson by wearing that green dress, all the way down the aisle and into his arms.

Christmas weddings. "Thank goodness no one passed that law," she whispered, as her brand-new husband finally kissed his bride.

■ ■ ■ ■

HOLIDAY
HOME RUN

PRISCILLA OLIVERAS

■ ■ ■ ■

CHAPTER ONE

"He's here! He's, like, *in the building*!!!"

Julia Fernandez winced at the squeal of hysteria that punctuated her coworker's announcement as the college coed pushed open the glass conference room door.

At the impressionable age of twenty, Carol Prescott practically vibrated with excitement, her gray eyes wide with elation. Her normally pale complexion was flushed from a combination of her race down the office hallway and the reality of finally meeting the "man of the hour."

At least, that's how many of the gala committee members often referred to Benjamin Thomas.

The former big league baseball player had agreed to serve as the Holiday Soiree's emcee for the third year in a row. Much to everyone else's relief.

While this was Julia's first year on the committee — the first of many, she hoped

— for years she'd seen Ben giving interviews on one sports TV channel or another. Over the past couple of months working with the committee, she'd heard rave reviews about Ben's ease in front of a live audience. Not to mention his charismatic, friendly personality and chiseled good looks that enticed donors to give a little more for a worthy cause like the Chicago Youth Association.

In fact, with him at the mic, the soiree had raised record amounts for area youth centers.

Julia might not have been living in Chicago during those events, but she'd done her homework. Had spent countless hours researching the organization and its past fund-raisers. In fact, she'd studied several other organizations along with multiple event-planning companies in the Chicago area in the last six months. All with an eye on making the move from Puerto Rico.

Of course, she'd kept this hidden from her parents and three brothers. No one knew about her ultimate goal.

No one except her cousin Lilí, here in Chicago. But that was only because Julia had to confess her plan to *someone*.

The guilt. The doubts. The excitement.

They all thrummed in her chest like a swarm of *picaflores* hovering. Tiny wings flapping at race speeds as the hummingbirds readied to dive-bomb into her belly when doubts sprouted.

She'd come to Chicago over Labor Day weekend on the guise of visiting her three *primas.* Two of her cousins were married now, popping out babies like all their *tías* expected them to do. Especially Julia's mami.

Lilí was the youngest of the three sisters. Since Julia was barely a year older than her, they'd always been pretty close. Or, as close as social media, WhatsApp, and occasional visits back and forth between Chicago and the Island facilitated.

Both were still single and approaching their midtwenties. Both working on finding their niche in their respective fields, Lilí as a victim's advocate and Julia as an event planner. Both ignoring the pressure from members of their *familia* to "find a good man and settle down already."

For Julia, those cries were tied to the never-ending questions about when she planned to take over the catering business her parents had started years ago. No one ever asked if that's what she wanted. Somewhere along the way it had simply become a given.

The expectation was that she'd find a nice

man on the Island. Marry. Start a family. Continue in her mother's footsteps. And eventually take over the family business.

The problem was . . . while she admired her mami's tenacity in building the catering company from a small venture, preparing food for neighborhood and church parties, to the well-recognized and respected business that handled large corporate affairs, Julia wanted something different.

Somewhere different.

Some place a little less suffocating.

Never mind that no one had ever assumed one of her brothers would step in. *Dios mío,* not when their whole lives revolved around baseball. A good chunk of her childhood had been spent on her way to a ballpark, at a ballpark, or leaving a ballpark, thanks to her three brothers.

In Puerto Rico, baseball was like a religion. One her parents and brothers faithfully worshipped. She'd been baptized in the sport's waters, raised on the catechism of Major League Baseball and Puerto Rico's winter ball. Knew all the stories of the greats, like Roberto Clemente and Orlando Cepeda and so many more.

Frankly, she was relieved to be missing the start of winter ball this year. If she did things right with this temporary assistant position she'd lucked into, thanks to Rosa's mother-in-law, Julia might be staying in Chicago for good.

She'd deal with how to deliver that news to her parents and brothers when the time came.

For now, she was focused on helping to plan the best-attended, highest-earning Holiday Soiree the Chicago Youth Association had ever held. If that meant dealing with yet another baseball player, one whose mere name caused grown women to swoon and whose career stats drove grown men to envy, she'd keep her personal qualms to herself and "just do it."

She'd dealt with big-name players in the past. Many whose big bank accounts and prowess both on and off the field created inflated egos that left much to be desired.

Down the hallway, the elevator doors dinged.

Carol visibly shivered with glee. The young intern patted her long blond hair, then ran a jittery hand down her wool skirt.

"How do I look?" she stage-whispered from her perch near the glass door.

Julia pushed back her rolling chair, rising to stand at her place at the long conference table. "You look fine. What's the big deal?"

"What's the big . . . ? Um, it's *Ben*

Thomas."

If Carol's bug-eyed expression didn't scream "What's wrong with you?" her outstretched hands certainly did. "Chicago's most eligible bachelor? Probably the best baseball player who's ever lived?"

"*Bueno,* I'd have to counter that last statement," Julia answered, holding up a hand to stall the girl's rant. "But no matter what, I'll tell you this —"

She broke off as Laura Taylor and several others came into view through the glass conference room walls. Standing a full head taller than everyone else was Ben Thomas.

Even though he was dressed in a navy, ribbed turtleneck sweater to ward off the mid-November chill, rather than a baseball uniform and cap, she immediately recognized his square jaw, straight nose, and piercing blue eyes.

Not because she was a groupie. *Por favor, no.*

More so because her youngest brother Martín had the guy's rookie season baseball card stuck on the wall over his bed. Martín's main goal in life was to pitch as well as Ben did. Or rather, as well as Ben had before injuries took him out of the game way too soon.

Ben had been a pitching phenom. One for

the record books. Every baseball executive had clamored to get his arm on their team. Players had raved about his leadership in the dugout and the locker room. His coaches and managers always wanted him in the game. That desire to have him deliver on the mound had led to him blowing out his arm. Needlessly, if you asked her.

However, pitching phenom or not, to her, Ben Thomas was simply the emcee of the Holiday Soiree that could be her ticket off the Island and a huge help to setting her on her way to starting her own independent life. Nothing more.

Admittedly he was definitely a *papi chulo,* as her cousin Lilí liked to say when describing a hot guy. But Julia wasn't in the market for a guy. Not right now anyway.

"Tell me what?" Carol prodded.

Straightening her shoulders, Julia looked her new friend in the eye, hoping to calm Carol's nerves. "Remember this, famous pitcher or not, Benjamin Thomas puts his pants on one leg at a time, just like the rest of us."

Carol's brows dipped together in a deep frown that matched her perplexed, "Huh?"

Julia laughed, the sound louder than she intended. It drew the attention of Laura Taylor, the five other committee members, and Ben Thomas as they entered the room.

Ben's gaze caught Julia's. A twinkle shone in the blue depths of his eyes, a sexy grin tugging up the corners of his full mouth.

She sucked in a quick breath, cutting off her laugh.

Ay Dios mío, that grin, in person, was far more enticing than when seen on the television screen or in the sports section of the newspaper.

As the other committee members found their seats, Ben strode forward to drape a light jacket over the back of a chair. Dark jeans hugged his strong legs. A pair of brown lace-up leather boots and the light scruff dusting his cheeks gave him a rugged look he wore far too well.

Laura began the introductions with Carol, who had remained near the door, her awe obvious in her stuttered greeting. The poor girl's cheeks flamed as she stumbled over her own name.

"Pleased to meet you," Ben said, inadvertently worsening the fan-worshipping Carol seemed unable to control.

"S-same to you," she murmured around the hint of a giggle.

"Carol's a student at DePaul," Laura said. "She's interning with us for the semester and is a marvelous addition to our team."

Julia admired how Laura, half of one of Chicago's most respected power couples, managed to maintain a regal, unflappable manner while making everyone around her feel comfortable and welcome. In the short amount of time Julia had been working with her, Laura had become a true mentor.

Laura gestured toward her. "Ben, I'd like you to meet Julia Fernandez, the brains and creativity behind this year's theme for the Humboldt Park Youth Center."

"Well, it's more of a group effort. That old sports cliché 'There's no *I* in team' comes to play here." Julia stepped to her right as she spoke, meeting Ben and Laura at the head of the conference table.

Someone else in the room chimed in to agree with Laura, adding their praise for Julia's entertainment idea, but Ben's large hand engulfed hers in a firm handshake and whatever else was being said faded.

A rough callous on his palm rubbed against her soft skin. The smile in his eyes turned the icy blue to a warm winter sky, the kind of blustery Chicago morning Lilí complained about but Julia actually enjoyed.

"I've heard rave reviews about your thoughts for the soiree," Ben said, a teasing note in his deep voice.

If he'd been clean shaven, she might have

seen the sexy dimple in his left cheek. The one female fans, and some male ones, too, sighed over. With the light scruff he now sported, the dimple was hidden from her view, though she found herself checking for it. Not that she was attracted by his sexy, rolled-out-of-bed appeal.

"I'm looking forward to working with you," Ben added.

"Likewise," Julia answered.

She took a deep breath, willing the *picaflores* flapping their little hummingbird wings in her belly to calm. Unfortunately, her deep breath brought her senses in close and personal contact with the hint of his woodsy cologne, its spicy undertones heightening her awareness of him.

All of a sudden she found herself needing to repeat the reminder she had shared with Carol earlier. This time, for her own good.

Ben Thomas was just like every other guy. No need to go all *boba* over him. She didn't *do* boy crazy. *Ever.*

It was simply a matter of remembering: Pants. One leg at a time.

Ben tried hard to keep his focus on the details Laura Taylor, Jeff Louis, and the rest of the committee discussed throughout the meeting. Hell, he was a master at focusing.

Ask any of his old teammates. Nothing got him out of the zone unless he wanted it to.

Problem was, right now his zone seemed to be honed in on one Julia Fernandez. It had been since he'd walked into the conference room barely thirty minutes ago.

Not only because her petite frame, delicate features, and wavy, long, black hair had made him take a second look, then a third, followed by a . . . hell he'd lost count.

While he hadn't been able to stop glancing at her, though, she never seemed to have trouble not looking his way. Barely making eye contact. A hair shy of aloof.

He wasn't used to women not being interested in him.

As soon as the thought flashed through his mind, he pulled up short.

It wasn't that he expected to be the center of attention. In fact, most of the time he worked hard to go incognito and avoid recognition.

With Julia, though, something made him want her to take notice.

Something more than her attractiveness.

It was the confidence she exuded as she brought the committee up to date on several tasks for the event.

It was the way she praised others, acknowledging their efforts.

It was the slight lilt to her words. The touch of her Spanish accent that reminded him of home and growing up surrounded by the Cuban influence in Miami.

His first real crush had been his buddy Octavio's older sister, Amada. A short-lived crush as she'd become more like a sister since Octavio's place had become Ben's second home, his teammate's family semi-adopting him once the two boys started playing select ball together and it became apparent that Ben's parents weren't around much.

Two professors, Ben's mom and dad had always been elbow-deep in their research. Oh, they'd been supportive, more or less encouraging him to pursue his goals. They simply hadn't truly connected with him in sharing his love for the sport.

His "family" dinner experiences had taken place around the Ramos's table. That's where his affinity for Latin food, Cuban food in particular, had been born.

Listening to Julia talk about her plans for the holiday fund-raiser, all with a Latino flair, heightened his melancholy for the loss of family and sense of home he'd been dealing with since his forced retirement from playing ball.

"Since the funds raised at this year's event

will benefit the Humboldt Park Youth Center, which serves a large Hispanic community, the entertainment will feature the kids giving a pseudo rendition of a *parranda* or a *posada*," Julia told him, her Spanish accent hugging the words.

"I hate to admit that I had never heard of a *parranda* before," Jeff Louis said. The middle-aged bank executive had removed his suit jacket and now leaned back in the black leather chair, his expression earnest. "Despite the number of Hispanic kids and families we serve. Makes me realize I have a lot more to learn."

That's what Ben liked about working with this committee and the Chicago Youth Association's auxiliary board in general. They were comprised of individuals who were committed to their mission statement and the children.

"Now a *posada*, yes," Jeff continued, smoothing a hand down his tie. "I'm familiar with that Mexican tradition. People caroling from house to house like a *parranda*, but with statues of Mary and Joseph. Like they're seeking shelter. I think introducing the cultural aspects, both the Puerto Rican caroling with the *parranda* and the Mexican *posada*, will enrich the event."

"Exactly." Laura Taylor gave a firm nod.

"Having the kids as the singers is a beautiful touch. We've never featured the youth in the past and they're the reason why we're here. Why we do what we do, right?"

Hands clasped on the slick black tabletop, the older woman looked around at each of the members present. Answering nods of agreement along with a murmured, "Damn straight," from Dan Roberts, a local builder, met her perusal.

With her blond hair smoothed back in a tight bun low on her head, Laura looked the epitome of the high society matron often featured in the local pages of the paper. Straight-laced, savvy, and dedicated to the charities she worked hard to assist.

Ben had met her during his rookie season with the Cubs when he'd volunteered for a youth baseball clinic. Now, eight years later, he was still involved with helping out Chicago youth.

Actually, thanks to Laura's uncanny ability to lure a person into her world of volunteerism and civic duty, he'd kept his head above water — barely — the past few years of injury, surgery, rehab, and ultimately, early retirement.

Between his work with the youth centers and his burgeoning sports-casting career, he was putting one foot in front of the other.

Not dwelling on the what ifs, should haves, and if onlys. Most days, anyway.

"When I first met Julia at a family gathering over Labor Day weekend and heard about her background in event planning in Puerto Rico, I mentioned the upcoming soiree," Laura said, drawing Ben's attention to the beautiful woman seated across from him.

The bright, mid-November, late afternoon sun shone through the picture windows behind Julia, creating a halo of light around her dark hair. In a short-sleeved ivory sweater dress, a delicate gold necklace with an intricate cross hanging to her midchest, she was almost like a holiday angel here to guide their efforts with her creativity and vision.

"By the end of the evening, I knew she'd be the perfect addition to our committee," Laura said. She reached out to place her hand over Julia's and gave her an endearing, almost maternal smile. "I think we all agree that's been the case."

Julia's tanned complexion darkened with the hint of a blush at Laura's praise and the answering "You got that right!" and "Most definitely!" heard around the table.

"Gracias," she murmured.

Ben liked that she accepted the praise

rather than brushing it off. She knew her worth and didn't shy away from accepting the compliment.

She mouthed a thank-you to several others in the group, but when her gaze fell on him he could have sworn the smile in her eyes dimmed. Before he could be sure, she moved on to wink at the young intern who'd yet to say a complete sentence to him. Poor kid.

During their short break earlier, he'd done his best to ease her sports star awe, asking about her major, classes, and expected graduation date. Typical icebreakers among college students. So far, no dice.

Give her another meeting or two, the run-through for the event at the very latest, and she'd see he was a regular guy. One who happened to throw a ball pretty fast, occasionally with a mean curve that brushed a batter back off home plate. At least, he used to, anyway.

"I'm heading to the youth center for a choir rehearsal tonight. It's only our third, but we've had a decent response to our call for participants." Julia ran her fingers through her hair as she spoke, combing it back off her shoulders.

"There's also a nice mix of ages. From as little as five . . . *ay,* Bernardo's a cute little guy without a shy bone in his body." Julia chuckled, a low husky sound that had others joining in and Ben wanting to do whatever he could to elicit that sound again. "To a handful of students in their high school choir. I asked if they might help recruit a few more for good measure."

"Let me know if you'd like some help drumming up singers," Ben said.

"Really?" Julia's brow furrowed, a mix of surprise and doubt clouding her features.

"Sure." Ben shrugged, wondering at her reaction to his offer. "I'm involved with the baseball camp the Humboldt Park Youth Center holds in the summer. I could probably round up a few of the athletes."

"Um, okay. Thanks. I'll see how it goes tonight and will ask Laura to get in touch with you if we need assistance."

There was definitely a strong note of hesitation in Julia's voice. Whether she doubted his sincerity or his ability to come through for her, Ben couldn't be sure. Neither reason was a good one as far as he was concerned.

For most of his life, few people had doubted his ability to accomplish anything. Some had even believed he'd beat the odds after his last surgery, eventually getting his pitching arm back to full strength.

However, while Julia's exuberance, striking good looks, and ease with the others on her team intrigued him, it was evident that when it came to him she had some reservations.

Why that would be, he had no idea.

Nor did he understand why that bugged the hell out of him.

"As I mentioned at our last meeting, if anyone would like to join me for a rehearsal, feel free," Julia said. "I'm having a great time working with the kids."

One by one the reasons for why a committee member couldn't make it to that night's rehearsal went around the table, ending with the college intern, who apparently had a date.

Looked like Julia was on her own.

At least, she had been.

"Actually, I'm free this evening. I'd love to come along with you," Ben said.

"That's a wonderful idea!" Laura clapped her hands together in front of her chest. "I had mentioned to Julia earlier that she might want to chat with you about the script for the event. Perhaps the two of you can put your heads together once we're done here."

Just like that, Laura Taylor unknowingly greased the wheels for him.

"Sounds like a plan. Why don't we chat over a quick dinner on our way to the Humboldt Park area?" Ben tilted his head in question at Julia.

Her hazel eyes narrowed the tiniest fraction, like a batter staring him down from home plate as Ben stood on the pitcher's mound preparing to throw his next pitch. Sizing him up.

He found the fact that she didn't jump at a chance to spend more time in his company when many scrambled to do so refreshing. Something told him that while Julia could be polite and professional when the situation warranted, she wasn't one to hold her tongue if pressed for the truth.

And he wanted to know the truth behind her reluctance where he was concerned.

More importantly, he hoped she'd give him a chance to change her mind.

CHAPTER TWO

"So tell me again, how did you find this restaurant?" Julia asked as she walked beside Ben along Division Street, the late fall sun slowly making its descent behind the businesses and apartments.

Once the meeting had wrapped up, they'd left the Chicago Youth Association's office building on Wabash Avenue together. Since she'd taken public transportation, they'd driven in his Range Rover over to the Paseo Boricua area of town.

The popular Puerto Rican section of Division was bookended by large steel replicas of the Island's flag, with red metal stripes, its blue triangle, and a cutout for the large white star seemingly waving in the wind. Along the street in between the flags, you were treated to several of the famous Humboldt Park intricate murals celebrating love of culture and their Island, along with a Walk of Fame recognizing those who had paved the way. Christmas wreaths with tiny Puerto Rican flags already hung on business doors and streetlights in preparation for the holidays. Evidence of how the buildings, shops, and citizens in this part of the city proudly wore and lived their Puerto Rican heritage.

It was Julia's favorite street to stroll down because she almost felt like she was back home. Without the ever-present pressure to fall in line with her parents' old-fashioned thinking weighing her down.

"My rookie season, the team was flying back from the West Coast. I started talking about how much I missed the Cuban food I'd grown up eating in Miami. On our next day off, one of the guys hustled me down to Gloria's for lunch," Ben said. "One taste of her *amarillos* . . . Mmm-mmm, that woman knows how to cook a sweet plantain, not to mention her rice and beans. And the *lechón asado*."

He rubbed his flat belly like it was already full. Or maybe in anticipation of it being filled with the foods of her own childhood.

"I'm telling you her roast pork is to die for," he went on. "Unless I'm on the road, it's kind of a weekly ritual for me to pop by Gloria's for a home-cooked meal."

"You should taste my mami's cooking. No

matter how hard I try, I'm not sure I'll ever be as good as she is."

A little pang of homesickness pricked at Julia's heart as she thought about her mother. The role model who'd taught her the value of working hard for your dreams. That's what fed Julia now, despite knowing her dreams would take her away from her Island home and family.

"I'd like that," Ben said.

"Hmm?"

Lost in thought about her family, it took Julia a moment to realize what Ben meant.

Diantre, she hadn't intended that as an invite. Wow indeed. There's no way her mami would ever meet Ben. Julia certainly didn't plan on sharing his involvement in the fund-raiser with her brothers. Martín would have a conniption fit.

Unsure how to smooth over the verbal gaffe, she opted to let it go.

A brisk breeze picked up and Julia huddled into her jacket. Head bowed against the cold she was still getting used to, she didn't realize Ben had removed his own jacket until he draped it across her shoulders.

"Oh!" she said on a gasp, touched by his gesture. "*Gracias.* I mean, thanks."

He squeezed her shoulders briefly before

he dug his hands into his front jeans pockets. Briefly, yet long enough to send shivers of awareness traveling down her arms, into her chest.

"De nada," he responded. *"¿Tienes frío?"*

His question about whether or not she was cold, spoken in Spanish with what was actually a really good accent, had her footsteps faltering in surprise. Then she remembered an interview she'd seen on a Spanish sports channel with him and one of his Latino teammates.

"You okay?" he asked, stopping to wait for her.

She nodded as she walked the few paces to catch up with him. "I forgot that you're fluent. Your question took me by surprise."

"Forgot? As in, you knew that about me already?"

One of his brows arched, giving him a rakish look that had far too much appeal.

No way would she clue him in that she knew far more about him than she should. Thanks to her baby brother's fascination with Ben's career. Plus her older two brothers who played and coached and could rattle off anyone's stats, background, and probably blood type if somehow that aided in a player's ability.

"I heard you give an interview a while

ago," she admitted. "You speak Spanish well."

"*Gracias.* I've worked at it. Learned on the field first as a kid, then around the dinner table with friends," Ben answered.

The wind ruffled his dark blond hair and brought a rosy tint to his cheeks under his scruff. She caught the way he shortened his strides to match hers, angling his body in her direction when they spoke, as if she had his undivided attention. His courteous manner was charming. Unexpected from a man who was typically the center of everyone else's attention.

"My brothers often interpret for some of their teammates who don't feel as comfortable with their English," Julia said, carefully stepping over a crack in the sidewalk to avoid scraping her boot heel. "I bet being able to speak with your catcher in his native language strengthened your connection when you played with the Cubs."

¡Ay que estúpida!

She gave herself a mental smack on the back of the head at her blunder. Reminding Ben that he was no longer in the game wasn't her smartest move. If he was like every other injured athlete she'd known, it was eating him up inside. He definitely wouldn't like being reminded.

"So you have brothers in baseball?" he asked.

Dios mío, forget worrying about his undoubtedly touchy subject. She wanted to talk about her family and personal life even less than his shortened career.

On the drive over, sitting snugly warm in Ben's classy Range Rover, the scent of leather from the plush seats mixing with his woodsy cologne, the sight of his strong hands gripping the steering wheel, and his camera-ready grin flashing her way, she'd caught herself relaxing with him. Enjoying his easy conversation as they'd made idle chatter about living in Chicago.

Then he'd asked what she liked to do in her free time.

A warning bell had gone off in her head and she'd reminded herself to stick to nonpersonal topics, preferably only the soiree.

This was a business dinner. Nothing more.

Yet, now she'd gone and opened the door leading him to poke around her personal life.

"¿Tienes hermanos en beisbol?" Ben repeated his question about her brothers in Spanish when she hadn't responded.

"Yeah," she answered.

"How many?"

"Three."

"Older? Younger?"

"One older."

Ben responded with a bark of laughter.

An older gentleman exiting a *farmacia* on the corner looked their way, his dark eyes widening with recognition when he saw Ben. Thankfully he only waved and welcomed them to his neighborhood rather than stopping them for an autograph.

Ben returned the man's greeting in Spanish. When he glanced down at her, the corners of his mouth pulled up in that playful smile that inevitably made her stomach flip-flop.

"What's so funny?" She tilted her head in question, eyeing him with uncertainty as she slowed her steps.

Once again Ben followed her lead, coming to a stop.

A woman pushing a baby stroller edged around them, her little one bundled up against the cold. Ben murmured *"buenas noches"* and received a mutual "good evening" in response.

Once the woman was several feet away, Ben turned his attention back to Julia.

The intensity of his clear blue eyes, focused entirely on her, had the world around them fading to nothing more than a blur. As if only the two of them existed.

"Back at the association's office," Ben answered, "when you talked about your ideas and the kids you've been working with, excitement dripped from your words. The way you described the decorations, adding the Three Kings to the mix out of respect for your Latino culture, I doubt anyone had trouble visualizing it all."

"And?" she asked when he trailed off.

"And now that I'm trying to get to know you, I can't seem to get more than a one- or two-word answer. How come?"

Had Ben's tone been pushy, or his body language hinted at any amount of wounded ego petulance, she would have easily given him a firm answer meant to ensure he understood she wasn't interested. She'd done it before with other guys who felt compelled to assert their misguided machismo.

But the honest inquiry in Ben's slightly furrowed brow and the sincerity evident on his handsome face indicated his genuine interest in her answer.

Maybe the good guy persona was more than a facade for the media and endorsements. Laura Taylor spoke very highly of him, and Julia valued the woman's opinion.

Suddenly the wind whipped down the street, sending stray leaves and a few empty cans rattling over the cement sidewalk. Julia grabbed the edges of the jacket Ben had draped around her, shivering with cold.

He immediately stepped closer, blocking her from the wind and gently grasping her upper arms. "Why don't we table the inquiry until we're seated inside? Gloria's place is on the next block. I'm thinking your Island blood isn't used to the Chicago weather yet."

Once again, his chivalrous nature thawed the chill she had been intent on keeping between them.

"Wait," she said, covering one of his hands with hers. "I don't . . . I don't mean to be rude."

"You haven't been. I mean, usually I get people who —"

"Fall over themselves, giddy with awe at spending time with an MLB All-Star, now the network's new voice, like Carol did?"

The words slipped out before she could stop them, goaded by the remnants of her anger over a local ballplayer from her hometown who had dated one of Julia's closest friends for years, only to toss her aside when he moved up to the big leagues. Apparently the groupies in every city held more appeal than the commitment he'd made before leaving the Island.

"Carol?" Confusion flit across Ben's face. It cleared moments before he said, "Oh, the intern."

Julia nodded, wondering how he'd react to her mini rant. That quick temper her mami always warned her about had chosen an inopportune time to flare.

The last thing she needed was to offend the soiree's prized emcee thanks to her own personal hang-ups.

"You play hardball, don't you?" Ben murmured.

His sheepish grin splashed cold water on her heated temper.

Julia closed her eyes on a sigh.

Ay, ay, ay. She'd never been this unprofessional in her life.

Why now? Why with this man?

Bueno, she knew why him. Because despite her promise to herself to never get involved with a ballplayer, this one seemed different. More approachable. Less ego-driven.

Yet, that had to be foolish thinking on her part. She'd seen too many girlfriends burned by a smooth-talking All-Star before. *Dios* only knew how many times a friend had cried on Julia's shoulder, brokenhearted over some guy.

"Me, play hardball?" she asked, trying to

come up with a way to smooth over her outburst. "Maybe."

That rakish brow of his arched again, calling her bluff.

"Fiiiine," Julia said, rolling her eyes on an exaggerated groan.

Ben's mouth quirked in a grin and she couldn't help but respond with one of her own.

"I guess you could say that," she continued. "But here's the thing."

She took a step back, making his hands slip from her arms to drop at his sides. So what if she missed his touch. At this point, she couldn't allow herself to.

Ignoring the chilly breeze that nipped at her, she squared her shoulders, determined to shove any personal feelings to the back, keeping things between them platonic and businesslike.

"Right now, all my energy and focus is on the Holiday Soiree. Ensuring its success. For me, it's like a one-game playoff. Win or go home. And going home, back to Puerto Rico and my suffocating though well-meaning family, isn't what I want." Brushing her windblown hair out of her face, she stared back at him, willing him to understand the utter importance of the situation for her. "I need to knock this out of the park, Ben. I promise, you, Laura Taylor, the association, and especially the kids can count on me to give my best."

Ben didn't say anything. His expression remained schooled in that serious game face the television networks had repeatedly zoomed in on when he'd stood on the mound.

She had no idea what he was thinking. Which, she understood, was the point of his game face. Leave the opponent wondering, unsure what to expect.

Dios la ayude if he thought of her as the opponent now. Only, she doubted even God would be able to help her if she'd shot off her mouth and offended the All-Star.

After several gut-clenched-with-worry seconds, Ben gave a quick jerking nod. "I definitely understand a must-win situation. And I've been known to hit a home run in my time."

Relief flooded through her at the olive branch he extended, especially since she should be the one doing so.

"The 2015 post season," she said. "Game two of the Division Series against the Cardinals. Your shot to the left field bleacher seats was a beauty."

"You saw that one, huh?"

The juxtaposition of Little Leaguer joy

461

brightening his eyes and the confident, all-male grin tugging his lips had a laugh bubbling up from her chest.

"Are you kidding me? The whole world saw that hit. I mean, even if they weren't watching the game live, there's no way anyone missed the highlight reels running on practically every media site."

Hands deep in his front pockets again, Ben let out a heavy breath. "Hitting that ball against our rivals did feel pretty great. Especially with the ups and downs of the next season, what with . . . well . . . never mind."

Belatedly, she realized 2016 had been his last full season. While it had been a banner year for the Cubs, Ben had struggled at times due to his injury.

"That was a good game. A good day," he murmured, head down, lost in his own memories. A dark cloud passed over his features, dampening the softness of his nostalgia. "Don't get many of those anymore."

A pang of regret for the shoulder injury that had sidelined him pierced her chest. She'd watched her older brother Alfredo deal with a similar situation after his car accident. The loss of the dream of making it to the big leagues still tore at Freddie, despite his move from player to coach.

"But you're doing good things," Julia told Ben. "You see that, right?"

Without realizing her intent, she moved closer, pressing a hand to his chest. Through the ribbed material of his turtleneck sweater his heart beat heavy against her palm. Strong. Slow. Steady.

"Different ones, sure," she continued. "Think of the lives you shape with the clinics you sponsor. The ones you help with the money you raise."

His confident grin had faded, replaced by a wistful smile. "Which brings us back to our mission here: grab a quick bite while we go over your thoughts on the script, then head to rehearsal at the youth center. Right?"

Subdued, his playful persona sadly missing in action, Ben turned to face the direction of the restaurant, poking out his elbow for her to hook her hand through his arm.

She got the message. The discussion about the new path his life had taken, post-baseball, wasn't a topic he cared to discuss.

Everyone had their own dragon to slay. Hers revolved around her bid to move out from under her family's thumb to forge her own path. Ben's was . . . actually, she didn't really know.

Frankly, she had no business asking him about it, even less business wondering or worrying.

CHAPTER THREE

"Okay, okay, *esperen un momento!*"

Sitting off to the side, Ben watched Julia calling for the kids to wait a moment.

Laughter lingered in her voice. It softened her face and danced in her hazel eyes at the antics that had ensued as soon as she brought up the idea of some of them performing a solo during the *bombazo* part of the program.

Little Bernardo, the five-year-old firecracker she'd mentioned during the meeting earlier today, had been the first to jump up out of his seat.

They had gathered in one of the larger classrooms at the Humboldt Park Youth Center about fifteen minutes ago. Desks had been cleared out to accommodate an electric keyboardist and a guitar player in one corner. Regulation plastic school chairs with metal frames were scattered about for the kids to sit on while they practiced. The center didn't own choir risers, but apparently Julia had rented a set for them to use for the soiree.

While two adult volunteers accompanied them on the keyboard and guitar, the group of teens who sang in their high school choir had taken charge of the various percussion instruments. Two girls with heavily lined eyes and pouty lips held a pair of maracas, one set more like little eggs that made a shushing sound when the girl moved her hands to the rhythm. A third girl with straight dark hair and a shy demeanor gripped the *pandereta,* as they called the instrument, its silver jingles sounding with each shake. A scrawny kid with a wide smile grasped the dried, hollowed-out gourd called a *güiro* in his left hand, creating a scraping sound as he dragged a wide metal comb up and down the ridges carved into one side of the instrument. Finally, an older teen named Rico, a husky guy with a football player's physique who seemed to be the leader of the group, held on to a *plenera,* keeping the beat by tapping a steady rhythm on the tight leather spread across the top of the tambourine-looking hand drum.

In the midst of the hoopla, young Bernardo stood center stage, shaking his hips in a solo dance, his chubby belly jiggling with his efforts.

Ben chuckled and Julia shot him a "you're-not-helping glare." He covered his grin with his fist. Message received: the rambunctious kid did not need any encouragement.

Hands raised to gain the group's attention, Julia joined Bernardo in the center of the room.

Rico laid off on the beat, earning Ben's respect when the rest of the group followed his lead. Including Bernardo, who slumped in a chair next to the older boy.

"*Bueno,* if we want to do a round of *bombas,*" Julia went on, "who here wants to take one of the shout-out verses in the middle of the song?"

About ten of the thirty-five or so kids raised their hands. Naturally, Bernardo raised both of his.

Julia reached over to ruffle the boy's hair playfully, slapping his raised palm in a high five. Her ease and comfort with the kids made Ben wish she felt the same camaraderie with him. But no, from the moment they'd walked into the youth center, she'd been all business.

Of course, it probably didn't help that it'd taken them an extra twenty minutes to work their way through the throng of kids who had rushed him near the entrance as soon as he'd been recognized.

Countless selfies, a few Snapchat and Insta story videos, even a call to a brother working his pizza delivery job but who supposedly was the world's biggest Cubs fan, and too many autographs for Ben to keep track of had transpired before they left the open lobby area to make their way down the right wing, which housed the larger classrooms for the arts programs.

"You're like the Pied Piper of Humboldt Park," Julia had murmured.

A quick glance behind them gave credence to her claim. Along with those returning for the second rehearsal, his arrival had picked up enough new choir members to fill a baseball team's starting lineup, and then some.

Unfortunately, the one person not responding to his Pied Piper call was the outgoing, confident, engaging woman standing before him.

He hoped to change that, if she gave him a chance.

So far, he was batting .000 when it came to learning more about her.

Their dinner conversation had remained solely on the event. Any time he'd tried to veer off topic, she expertly countered his

468

maneuver.

Once the rehearsal had started, it'd been all bets off as her attention had rightly remained on the kids.

"Will you be singing with us?" Bernardo pointed to Ben, seated in one of the black plastic chairs near the guitarist and keyboardist.

Julia spun around to face him, her long, black hair fanning out behind her before settling to drape across her shoulders. The dark tresses contrasted with the cream material of her sweater dress, a color that heightened her silky smooth tan skin.

Confusion swam in her hazel eyes, her mouth opening and closing as if she was unsure how to respond.

Ben stood up, grasped the back of his chair, then moved it closer to the little boy's. "I'll already be on stage as the emcee. If you don't mind, I'll gladly join the *parranda* party."

"*Oye,* he pro'bly don't know the *lenguaje,*" a teen from the back of the room called out. "But maybe the songs in English, no? That'd be pretty cool."

Swiveling in his chair, Ben scanned the group, searching for the kid who'd piped up. He spotted him when another boy reached out to give him a fist bump.

"Mira, no soy Latino, pero puedo hablar español. Mejor, puedo cantar," Ben answered.

Several jaws dropped.

A few fists covered mouths that howled a "No way!" exclamation at Ben's claim that while he might not be Latino, he could speak Spanish, and even better, sing.

But the shouted *"wepa!"* a cheer he'd heard many Puerto Rican teammates yell after a good play, made Ben grin.

The sound of Julia's spiky boot heels tap-tap-tapping on the linoleum floor had him looking to his right. She laid a hand on his shoulder, then gifted him with a sweet and genuine smile of thanks, her glance warm, maybe even inviting.

"Sí," she responded. "Ben can definitely speak our language. Now, whether or not he can sing might be another story."

She punctuated her teasing challenge with a wink and, hot damn if he didn't feel like he'd just won Pitcher of the Month.

Rico gave Ben a tough guy chin jut of approval that he acknowledged with a tilt of his head.

"Here." Julia handed him a packet of papers with the song lyrics. "Looks like you're going to need these."

"Yep, and I guess that means I'll also need to attend rehearsals with you."

Something flared in Julia's hazel eyes. Wariness or interest?

Before he could be sure, she blinked and it was gone. Replaced by the same cool confidence she'd shown at the meeting, then again later over dinner.

"Well then, you better get ready. I can be a hard taskmaster when the need arises."

"No worries about me slacking," he teased back. "I'm ready to hit this out of the park."

She huffed out a short laugh. It sparkled in her eyes, giving her face an appealing glow of joy that made him want to make her laugh again and again.

Back-peddling to the center of the room again, she extended her arms out to her sides, like she meant to gather the group around her.

"All right, everyone, let's start at the top of the song list and go through each one. For anyone who thinks they'd like to try a *bomba*" — she pointed at those who'd raised their hands earlier — "think about what you might say over the next week. Instead of having you make up your words on the fly like we normally do, for this occasion I'm going to need to give your verse the okay beforehand."

A few grumbled about the lack of spontaneity, but settled down once the keyboardist played a few bars of the first song.

Rico tapped out the beat on the *plenera* hand drum and they started with what Julia had told him was a classic, *"Ábreme la Puerta"* — a call from the carolers for the home owner to "open the door" for them.

Bernardo wiggled his chair closer to Ben's, leaning over to read the lyrics with him. The boy's easy acceptance, the kinship shared by all the students as they sang and smiled and moved in their seats to the Spanish rhythm, reminded Ben of the times he'd hung out with Octavio's family in Miami. The get-togethers he'd been invited to by other Latino players. They all thrummed with the same close-knit camaraderie experienced in a team's locker room and clubhouse.

Suddenly an undercurrent of longing grabbed a hold of him. So strong, so forceful, it threatened to drag Ben under. His chest tightened. His throat constricted and he struggled for breath.

All his life, any sense of belonging had come through sports. Through baseball. Without that connection, he'd been lost. Adrift for the past year and a half — since he'd left the game.

But spending time with these kids and watching the joy on Julia's face as she wove through the chairs, encouraging the shy singers, giving a youngster a friendly pat on the back, joining one of the teen girls in a shoulder shimmy duet. Her feet and hips moved naturally to the beat, her lilting voice joining in the melody.

For the first time since he'd announced his retirement, Ben felt a connection to something. To someone.

To her.

Maybe it was crazy. They'd only met today.

All he knew was, he didn't want today, with her, to end.

Now he simply had to figure out a way to keep the music playing, or at the very least, how to replay it again. Soon.

CHAPTER FOUR

Julia couldn't pinpoint exactly when, but somehow during the hour-long rehearsal, something in Ben had changed.

Sí, the playful glint in his icy blue eyes remained the same, but a strange sort of intensity crackled in the air whenever she caught him looking at her.

He'd laughed and joked with the kids, especially Bernardo, who'd moved his chair so close to Ben's, the five-year-old might as well have sat on Ben's lap.

Now, the ballplayer stood over near the far corner, talking with the cop who had agreed to play the guitar for them. The policeman taught guitar lessons at the center and had recruited a couple of his students to sing.

The older gentleman who'd volunteered as their pianist, a retired businessman who also regularly helped at the center, was busy packing up his keyboard and stand, though

Julia noticed him occasionally joining in their conversation.

With rehearsal at an end, she called out good-byes to some of the kids and answered a few questions from others. All the while, her gaze kept straying to Ben.

His relaxed, laid back manner made him seem more like the handsome boy next door rather than the face that had graced the cover of nearly every sports magazine on the shelves, and a few other nonsports related ones, too.

She allowed herself to admire his athletic build and chiseled profile for a few short minutes.

With the central heat on inside the center, Ben had pushed up the sleeves of his navy sweater. The muscles in his forearms flexed as he held the acoustic guitar, following the cop's instructions on where to place his fingers so he could strum out a chord.

The strength in Ben's large hands as he finessed the strings had her fantasizing about his fingers on her. Strong yet soft in a skin-tingling caress.

Her pulse sparked at her silly imaginings and she pulled her thoughts up short. *Estaba loca.*

Sí, she had to be crazy, allowing her mind to go down a path like that.

The last few stragglers finally drifted out of the room and Julia strode over to a nearby seat where she'd left her thin jacket along with Ben's. She'd really have to invest in a better coat with winter approaching.

As soon as she picked up Ben's, she caught the scent of his cologne lingering on the material. The hint of spice in the undertones piqued her senses, making her body warm in intimate places. Just in time, she stopped herself from bringing his coat up to her nose so she could take a deeper whiff.

Ay Dios mío, talk about groupie behavior.

Reminding herself about her priorities, which did not include going all *boba* over a ballplayer, she headed over to meet up with the musicians and Ben.

"*Muchísimas gracias,* I appreciate you playing for us. Tonight *and* the night of the benefit." Julia shrugged into her jacket as she thanked them.

"My pleasure," the cop answered.

"It's Diego, right?" she asked, waiting for his nod before she turned to the older gentleman. "And Señor Pérez?"

The keyboardist tipped his head in greeting. He made a few smart suggestions about the playlist order and Julia jotted down the notes. After reassuring her they'd return the following week, they exchanged farewells, then the two volunteers headed out with their instruments.

That left her and Ben alone in the empty classroom.

The sound of the musicians' footsteps faded, blending with the murmur of voices drifting down the hallway from the common area.

Hands in his pockets, Ben swiveled on the heels of his leather work boots to face her. He rocked forward on his toes, leaning closer. "Looks like it's just you and me now."

That intense scrutiny was back in his expression. Like a scientist studying an intriguing specimen, he honed in on her.

His interest was clear. No way was she misreading the gleam in his eyes.

The tilt of his body, the teasing quirk of his mouth . . . they were all signs she'd learned to read. Read and avoid. She didn't have time for relationships and the drama. Her sights were set on landing a permanent position here in Chicago.

"Um, yes, I guess it is." She shuffled a step to the side, moving in the direction of the door. "Thanks again for sitting in tonight. You were a hit with the kids." She combed her hair back, brushing it over her shoulders. "I should get going. Need to either call for an Uber or start the walk to the train station."

"Don't do that. I can drive you."

She waved off his offer. Mostly for her own sanity. "That's okay. My place is out of your way."

"How do you know that?" Ben drew back, his brows angling with confusion.

Julia gave a mental head shake at her slip of the tongue.

She knew because her fanatic younger brother had read, often out loud, every article he came across that mentioned Ben. Including the one about him and several other teammates who lived near Wrigley Field, where they enjoyed walking or biking to the ballpark.

Not that she'd admit to knowing that much about him. No need to sound like a stalker.

"Um . . ." *Ave María purísima,* how to explain this one. Hail Mary full of grace indeed.

Ben tilted his head in question, waiting.

"Umm, I just figured. Assumed, I guess?" Lame answer if she'd ever given one.

"I'm in the Wrigleyville area. The Southport Corridor neighborhood, actually," Ben said, lifting his left shoulder in a half shrug. "But I don't mind taking you wherever —"

"You see? I'm downtown, in the opposite direction. Thanks anyway." She flashed him a smile meant to cover her own uncharacteristic awkwardness.

"I was going to say, it doesn't matter. I can drive you. No need to wait for a car or take the L when I'm free, and willing, to give you a lift."

There was really no good reason for her to refuse his offer.

Bueno, other than her own sanity. But he didn't know that.

Unbelievably, Julia found herself drawn to an athlete. Despite her vows to never let that happen.

After living with three her entire life, you would think she'd had enough of their smelly uniforms stinking up the house. Their annoying habit of tossing baseballs back and forth or, God forbid, bouncing a rubber ball against the wall between their rooms. The superstitions, the confidence that often crept into cockiness and, even worse, the competitive drive that seeped into every single aspect of their lives.

Yet, she'd seen none of those last ones from Ben.

In fact, he'd been generous with his time and quick with his laughter, even poking fun at himself when he'd flubbed some of the Spanish lyrics that ran together like a tongue twister.

"So, what do you say? Shall I be your chauffeur home?"

Ben did that lean-in move again, an expectant, hopeful expression lighting his handsome face, and . . . a*y, Ave María purísima,* if she didn't want to meet him halfway. Erase the distance between them and steal a kiss.

The very idea had her drawing back with a jolt.

"A simple ride home among new friends," Ben said. "That's all."

As if he sensed her teetering on the edge between yes and no, but didn't want to push her, Ben scooped up the strap of the black shoulder bag with the small percussion instruments. She noticed he slung it over his left, noninjured shoulder and she wondered if his right one might be feeling sore.

"You sure you don't mind?" she asked.

Waiting outside for her car to arrive or, worse, standing on the cold L platform waiting for a train didn't sound nearly as comfortable as a ride in the warmth of his Range Rover, cradled in the plush leather seats.

That's the only reason she would say yes, she assured herself. Uh-huh.

"I wouldn't offer if I minded," Ben answered.

The genuine note in his deep voice persuaded her.

"Okay, then, thanks." She tucked her hair behind her ear in what she knew was a nervous gesture. "I appreciate it."

"Any time."

Ben flashed his heartthrob smile and her breath hitched.

Too late she realized that maybe a frigid wait for a train would have been smarter. It certainly would have helped to cool the heat simmering inside her whenever she was around him.

"Shall we go?" Ben gestured toward the door, waiting for her to lead the way.

She could change her mind. No harm, no foul. But when it came down to it, she didn't want to.

Fool that she might be, she bowed her head in a slight nod, then started toward the door.

One ride home . . . What could it possibly lead to?

CHAPTER FIVE

"Let me get this straight. Ben Thomas, THE Benjamin Thomas. As in, the Cubs pitching ace whose jersey hangs in my closet at the condo has been giving you a ride to *parranda* rehearsal the past two weeks and this is the first time you're telling me?!?"

Julia swiveled in the passenger seat of Lilí's Corolla to face her cousin, lifting a shoulder, then letting it fall in a blasé "and so?" shrug.

"No lo puedo creer," Lilí murmured.

"You can't believe what?" Julia asked.

Her right hand on the steering wheel, the other pressed to her forehead, Lilí gaped at her with a wide-eyed, slack-jawed expression.

Since starting her job as a victim's advocate out of college a few years ago, her cousin had decided to grow out the sassy pixie 'do she'd worn, choosing to go with a longer, more professional look. However, the style change had done nothing to tame her cheeky personality.

As close as Julia was to Lilí, she'd purposefully not told her about how Ben had taken to stopping by the association's main office the past two Tuesdays to go over sponsor updates and other details with her. How they'd fallen into the routine of meeting, then grabbing a bite to eat on their way to *parranda* rehearsal at the youth center.

They'd gone back to Gloria's once, then grabbed deep dish pizza last week.

Working dinners. Between friends.

That's the way Julia continued to think about the hours she spent with Ben.

Yet, she'd kept the information from Lilí because . . .

Because her cousin put the "die" in diehard Cubs fan. Her love for the sport rivaled that of Julia's brothers. As soon as Lilí had heard about Ben's involvement with the soiree, she had jumped at the chance to serve as an extra pair of volunteer hands the night of the event.

So, when Julia found herself spending more time with Ben, she hadn't said anything to avoid this exact reaction.

"I can't believe you held out on me like this," Lilí continued with her complaint. "*Chica,* you've been hanging with baseball royalty all this time. How cool is that?"

Lilí's gaze darted back and forth from the highway to Julia as they traveled from the cousins' family home in the nearby suburb of Oakton back into the city.

They'd spent Thanksgiving Day celebrating with Lilí's sisters and their *familias*. That's how Julia's not-so-secret secret had gotten out, thanks to Jeremy, Laura Taylor's son, who was married to Julia's cousin Rosa.

Right after his "please pass the *tostones,*" he'd casually said, "So my mom tells me you and Ben Thomas have been working closely together on the soiree."

Julia had been so shocked, she'd nearly dropped the tray of fried green plantains she held out to him.

Lilí had actually spit out her water, drawing a howl of laughter from her sisters' toddlers and a shoulder-shaking giggle from her nine-year-old niece, María. Naturally, Yazmine and Rosa had been none too pleased with Lilí's lack of table manners. Equally as naturally, Lilí had taken their older sister admonishments in stride, waving them off for more important matters. Like talk about Ben Thomas.

At first, Julia had tried skirting the topic at the dinner table. Every question Lilí tossed at her had been lobbed back with a noncommittal answer tied to the soiree. Julia had carefully kept her tone light, devoid of her conflicting feelings for the hunky ballplayer. As soon as she could, she'd changed the subject.

No way did she want to risk giving away any hint of her burgeoning attraction and have it inadvertently make its way back to her mami. And it would. With Rosa pregnant and due in early January, Julia's mom called to check on her fairly regularly.

Unfortunately, Lilí had remained undeterred, pushing for details. "All the good ones," as she'd put it, her eyebrows waggling playfully.

Thank goodness having little ones at the table kept their parents occupied, often missing part of the table conversation. So while Yazmine, Rosa, and their husbands tended to their kids, Julia had sent Lilí a narrow-eyed glower, mouthing "later" before taking a big gulp of wine.

Looked like "later" had become "now."

Night had fallen and they sped along I-90 toward the city, on their way to post-dinner cocktails and dessert at the Taylors' downtown penthouse.

The entire Fernandez family had been invited, but after the day's festivities, the little ones were overtired and Rosa's obstetrician had ordered her to get more rest over the school break.

That left Lilí and Julia to represent the family for an invite many A-listers in Chicago and its surrounding areas would clamor to receive.

"Quit holding out already," Lilí pressed. "What's the guy like? I mean, he seems like *buena gente* in his interviews. Is he really?"

Was he good people, like her cousin asked?

Julia didn't have to think twice about her answer.

"*Sí*," she replied. "He actually is."

And that was the problem.

Ben actually seemed too good to be true. Friendly, considerate, quick to laugh. Humble.

And yet, there was a sad undercurrent she often sensed when one of the kids, someone at the office, or a fan on the street asked about his playing days.

He didn't talk much about his wins or stats. Surprisingly, any talk about his playing days focused on the people and relationships he'd formed. In the locker room, while traveling, during practice, on their days off.

The times he asked about her family, the conversation steered more toward their traditions, whether she would miss being home for the holidays.

If you asked her, he seemed lonely. But how could a man everyone wanted to be friends with feel alone?

It didn't make sense.

Most of the time she wondered if she might be projecting the little homesickness she felt onto him.

"Has he shared any insider baseball stories with you? You know, the kind we don't hear on the news?" Lilí asked, intruding on Julia's musings.

"We actually don't discuss baseball all that much."

"Ha! It's crazy," Lilí said on a chuckle.

"What is?"

"Your situation. I mean, how often have you told me that you're tired of living and breathing baseball with your brothers? Then you come here and wind up working with one of the best this city's seen in ages."

Lights from the oncoming traffic shone through the windshield, illuminating Lilí. She shook her head, a corner of her mouth quirked in a satiric smirk.

"I guess that's good for the Youth Association and Mrs. Taylor." Lilí flipped her signal as she maneuvered her Corolla to exit I-90 onto West Congress. "No worries about you being star-crazy. If there's one type of guy you'd never fall for, it's an athlete."

"You got that right," Julia answered.

She turned away to stare out her passenger window at the blur of holiday lights decorating the downtown city streets.

"No chance of that happening," she murmured.

All she had to do was keep reminding herself of that.

Ben stood near one of the fire pits strategically placed around the expanse of Sherman and Laura Taylor's penthouse terrace. After the gourmet Thanksgiving meal shared at their Victorian-inspired dining room table, the group of fifteen or so had moved outside to enjoy the atypically mild late November weather.

The Taylors were known for hosting intimate gatherings like this, where important, oftentimes invaluable, personal and professional networking took place. Once, Ben spent an evening enjoying drinks and the picturesque Chicago sunset with several bank execs and their wives, discussing everything from fishing off the coast of Miami to investment opportunities. By the end of the night one of the men wound up donating a hefty sum to the youth baseball clinic program. Without any prodding or mention of the need for funds on Ben's part.

But tonight, while the prominent players in Chicago's business and legal professions seemed content to relax around the dancing flames with their bellies full, Ben strategically sat on one of the dark brown wicker ottomans facing the formal living room inside. From his vantage point he had a clear view of the archway that led into the foyer with the penthouse's private elevator doors.

The same doors Julia would enter through once she arrived.

That's the main reason he was still here, other than his manners reminding him of the rudeness of leaving so soon after dinner.

He'd thought about going to Miami for the weekend. Touching base with his parents, spending time with Octavio's family. Then Laura had issued her invite and mentioned the Fernandez sisters and Julia should be here.

The idea of spending more time with Julia and meeting the cousins she spoke about with love and laughter in her voice had him bagging his travel plans to stay in town.

Through the thick glass windows he spotted the housekeeper striding into the living room, heading toward the foyer. He couldn't see the gilded metal elevator doors, but he hoped the older woman was on her way to greet . . . his thought trailed off as Julia came into view.

She and another petite, dark-haired woman with a similar athletic build and golden tan skin strolled around the corner, stopping under the archway.

He watched as Julia unbuttoned her cream winter jacket, slipping it off her shoulders to reveal a dark green sweater over a black pencil skirt and black knee-high boots. His pulse sparked as she brushed her fingers through the length of her black, satiny hair. It was a habit of hers he'd noticed over the past couple of weeks.

A habit that made him want to run his own fingers through her tresses and feel the silky strands. Among other parts of her.

The housekeeper took Julia's jacket from her and, while Ben couldn't read Julia's lips as she said something, he caught her gentle smile of thanks.

The other young woman, probably Lilí, followed suit before the two cousins began making their way across the mottled white and cream tiled floor. They strode past the ornate antique hutches displaying priceless vases and sculptures, on their way toward the sliding glass doors leading to the expansive terrace. And while others may have

490

been drawn to the beautiful decorations and touches in the Taylors' artfully designed home, Ben only had eyes for Julia.

He rose from his seat, anxious to be with her again.

The past three Tuesdays hadn't been enough. Not for him.

Laura Taylor excused herself from a small group standing near the outdoor bar off to the right and she and Ben reached the doors at the same time as Julia and her cousin.

Politeness had him holding back, allowing the hostess to greet her guests. Warm hugs were exchanged, then Laura held out her arm, welcoming him into their close-knit circle.

"Lilí, I'm sure you know who this is, as I'm aware of your baseball knowledge. But Ben, I'd like you to meet the youngest of the Fernandez sisters, Lilí. She's a victim's advocate at a clinic that serves the Humboldt Park area."

He extended his hand to shake, but Lilí leaned in for a hug as was customary in her Latino culture.

"Hugging's in my DNA," she said with a laugh. "But even if it wasn't, I'm giving myself this one chance to fan-girl over you. Then I promise to be on my best behavior."

Ben chuckled at her cheeky grin. It turned

into a full out laugh when Julia rolled her eyes and murmured an *"Ay Dios mío."*

"What would you two like to drink?" Laura asked.

Julia declined, so Laura and Lilí headed toward the bar together. As they moved away, Julia turned toward him, that easy smile of hers curving her lips.

"Happy Thanksgiving," she said.

Stepping closer, she lightly grasped his upper arms and rose up on her toes to press her cheek against his in the not-quite-a-kiss gesture she'd greeted him with the other day. Instinctively he placed a hand on her waist, taking in a deep breath sweetened by her floral scent. The urge to wrap her in his arms, give her the kind of hello kiss that would knock her stiletto boots off, pounded in his veins.

But she'd given him no clear sign that she was interested in moving their relationship out of the friend zone into something more. Until he was sure, he'd play it casual. All while upping his game, determined to woo her.

"It's good to see you again," he said, pleased when she didn't move away after their brief hug. Instead she stayed close, keeping their conversation intimate. "When I heard you were having a family dinner in

Oakton, I wasn't sure if you'd make it."

"Lilí and I skipped dessert. Though I may or may not have snuck a sliver of Rosa's flan on the way out."

The teasing glint in Julia's hazel eyes easily drew an answering smile from him. He wanted to whisk her away to a quiet corner where he could have her to himself. Spend the evening enjoying the heat from the fire and sharing a bottle of wine while the lights from Navy Pier in the distance and the stars sprinkled across the sky sparkled around them.

"With that sweet tooth of yours, I'm sure Rosa expected you to sample," he told Julia, pleasure warming his chest when her smile broadened into a huge grin.

"Ah, you know me too well."

"Not yet."

Julia tilted her head, giving him a speculative look. Before she could respond to his not too subtle intent, Sherman Taylor approached, his hand outstretched in greeting.

The prominent lawyer ushered them over to chat with two middle-aged couples seated in a pair of dark brown wicker patio couches and matching ottomans. A brick and metal gas fire pit nestled in the center of the gathering space creating a warm, inviting ambiance.

Introductions were made for Julia, then Sherman drifted away to pour her a glass of pinot noir. One of the husbands, a salt-and-pepper-haired criminal defense lawyer, asked Ben how he enjoyed living near the ballpark in Wrigleyville. This led into a discussion of the relatively new area known as the town square, the Park at Wrigleyville.

"Have you been yet?" the lawyer's wife asked Julia.

"No, I haven't. Though I hope to get there to try a bit of ice skating," she answered. "That would be a first for me."

"You should go!" the woman encouraged. "I took our kids last weekend and they had a great time."

The conversation moved on to other topics, though Ben listened with only half an ear.

He was too busy concocting an idea. One he hoped he could entice Julia to say yes to. So far, any mention of sharing dinner or coffee outside their event planning had been politely declined. But this . . . it just might be the ticket.

A short while later, Lilí joined their group. He started to rise and offer her his seat on an ottoman, but Julia slid over on the deep red sofa cushion to make room for her cousin to sit in between her and one of the wives.

The move brought Julia closer to him, their knees brushing against one another's. Like a randy adolescent sitting next to his first crush, Ben felt his body hum at the innocent contact. Surreptitiously, he tugged on his dress pants leg, adjusting himself.

Though she didn't say anything, Ben noticed Lilí placed a cell phone on Julia's lap. She furtively tapped the screen to draw Julia's attention to something displayed there.

Julia ducked her head to read the message. Her mouth thinned the slightest bit and he caught her heavy sigh.

"Will you excuse me?" Julia said to the group. She pushed off the couch, bringing Ben to his feet alongside her. "I'll be right back."

Ben waited for her to pass by, then followed her inside the penthouse, concerned about the frown marring her normally smooth brow.

"Everything okay?" he asked, closing the door behind them and silencing the din of conversation.

Though they had gathered to celebrate Thanksgiving, Christmas music played softly on hidden speakers. Laura even had a stately Douglas fir, artfully decorated in red and gold ornaments and ribbons with tinkly white lights, holding court near the far bank of windows overlooking Navy Pier and Lake Michigan.

The tree lights glinted off Julia's gold crucifix necklace. The brightness clashed with the apprehension stamping her features.

"Yeah, it's fine," she said, belying her expression. "I've been avoiding a phone call, but apparently it can't be put off anymore."

She held Lilí's cell in a death grip, her fist jiggling the device back and forth at her side. Her gaze shot around the living room, into the formal dining room up three steps off to the right, then across to the sitting area on the left, as if searching for a place to make her call.

"You might want to try the library. You'll have more privacy there," he suggested.

"Thanks, I'll ask a staff member where I can find it."

"Here, I'll show you the way." With a hand on her lower back, Ben led her through the room, down the hall toward the office and library.

Tension vibrated in her stiff shoulders and shadowed her smooth features.

"This is my favorite piece in Sherman and

Laura's collection." As they neared it, Ben pointed at an oil painting of the Chicago skyline inspired by Van Gogh's *Starry Night.*

Julia briefly glanced at the gold-framed painting, her mind clinging to whatever had her anxious.

"Beautiful colors," she murmured.

"I actually bought another one in the collection after seeing this. Then I reached out to the artist about creating something similar with a Miami backdrop."

That got her attention.

She paused in front of the artwork, angling her neck to look up at him.

"Your two cities. Your homes."

"Well, that would be more like a ball field, but . . ."

He let his voice trail off, the ache of having lost the one place where he'd felt most at home, the most sense of family, clogging his throat.

As if she sensed his loss, Julia reached for his hand. She linked her fingers with his, surprising him.

"Sometimes, a move away from the place where we're the most comfortable allows for the best kind of growth."

Said the woman determined to leave her family and Island behind for a new life. It was the one thing about her he didn't understand. Mostly because he'd give anything to be back in the clubhouse with his "baseball family," ribbing the other guys, grabbing their gloves to run onto the field, knowing they had each other's back, win or lose.

While she, in a sense, was turning her back on her family's legacy.

Despite his inability to comprehend how someone with the type of family connection he'd always craved could just walk away from it, Ben had a hard time finding fault with her decision to pursue her own dreams. Not when following her own path had led her to cross his.

The cell phone vibrated in Julia's other hand signaling an incoming message.

"Ay," she said on a groan. "I better get this. My mami won't be deterred."

He started in surprise.

Her mom? That's whose call she'd been avoiding?

A slew of questions raced through his mind. But Julia had already started moving down the hall again.

"Here we go." Ben ushered her into the library.

Her light gasp told him this must be her first time in the space.

Eyes wide with appreciation, she took in

the intricately carved bookshelves covering an entire wall, the shelves filled with titles varying from classics to contemporaries and from easy reads to legal tomes. A window seat with views of Michigan Avenue took up the outer wall, while a fireplace dominated the third. A dark brown leather settee with two matching armchairs squared off in front of the inviting fire, providing comfy spots to curl up with a book.

"My cousin Rosa must love it here," she said.

"The librarian?"

"Mm — hmm. Laura's daughter-in-law," Julia answered. "I'm sure she's gotten lost in this room many times."

The loving note in her voice when she talked about her cousins, and usually her parents and siblings, too, brought a dull ache to his chest. He'd never had that type of relationship with his parents. He barely remembered his grandparents, who had all passed when he was a kid. As the only child of two parents who'd been only children themselves, he didn't have any family to rely on or turn to. No aunts, uncles, or cousins.

It wasn't until he found baseball and when the Ramos's had welcomed him into their home that he'd finally felt the true sense of *familia.*

"Well, I'll leave you to make your call," he said, backing away. "I'm going to make my way to the bathroom, then I'll wait for you out front."

"You don't have to," she said, waving him off. "Go back to the party."

It wasn't much of a party for him unless she was there, too.

Rather than admit that, he said, "No worries. It'll be nice to enjoy the soft music and quiet before joining the fray again."

"I . . . I shouldn't be long then."

"Take your time. I'll be here whenever you're ready."

Whether she understood his subtext — that he'd be there when she was ready for more than friendship — he had no idea.

Not wanting to scare her away, he gave a quick wink, then headed out.

CHAPTER SIX

"Ay, Mami, por favor, no seas así," Julia said, struggling to keep the whine and the frustration from her voice.

If not, her mother would ignore her plea to stop acting this way. Unfortunately, Paula Fernandez was the queen of passive aggressive behavior. Especially when she was on a roll.

Like she was now.

A heavy sigh blew through the cell speaker at Julia's ear and she rolled her eyes. Immediately giving thanks her mother couldn't see her.

"Am I not supposed to be hurt that my only daughter is not home for the holidays?" her mother steamrolled on. "That when I ask when she will return to celebrate *Las Navidades* with her papi, *hermanos,* and me, to help with the cooking and preparations, she will not answer me?"

Reproach dripped from Mami's words.

Each one a tiny pinprick of guilt to Julia's heart.

"Who will I rely on when the catering orders come in?"

"Allegra is there," Julia answered. "She does a better job at being your right hand than I do."

"Ha!" her mother scoffed. *"Esa nena no sabe."*

"Yes, she does know, Mami. More than you give her credit for."

In fact, her older cousin had been getting her hands messy in the kitchen several years before Julia had been allowed to even step inside.

"She's too much like her mother, and you know I can only take so much of your Tía Sonia. Why my brother had to marry that woman . . . *ay,* do not get me started."

Too late. The litany of woes had begun.

Complaints about her sister-in-law, a recent issue with bookkeeping for the business, a new recipe she wanted to try but hadn't found the time because she was short a helper . . .

Julia rubbed her temple, desperate to ease the pounding slowly increasing in her forehead.

"Mami, me tengo que ir," she interjected, when her mom finally stopped for a breath.

"What do you mean you have to go? We have barely talked."

Correction, Julia had barely talked. As for Mami, her guilt trip was flying first class.

"I told you, I'm at the Taylors' for a post-Thanksgiving dinner party. It's rude of me to have disappeared this long already."

"*Bueno,* you should not be disrespectful. I will let you go."

Julia let out a heavy sigh, quickly pulling the phone away from her face so her mother wouldn't hear. The woman had the ears of a bat, capable of picking up the slightest sound. Especially one you didn't want her to catch.

"*Gracias, Mami. Adio —*"

"Wait!" Her mother's cry stalled Julia's good-bye.

"*¿Sí?*" she asked, taken aback by the urgency in her mami's plea.

"When I called to check on Rosa, she mentioned your big fiesta to raise the money for the children is in two weeks. After that, your work there will be done, *no?*"

Julia's knees buckled under the weight of parental expectations and she sank onto one of the leather love seats. Elbow bent on the armrest, she cradled her forehead in her palm, Lili's cell phone pressed to her ear.

"*¿Hola, nena? ¿Estás allí?*"

503

"Yes, I'm here," Julia answered, like the obedient child she had always been. Until now.

Her heart pounding, she gazed into the fireplace. The flames danced and teased, suffocating the pieces of wood in the same way she felt her life being suffocated by the plans her mami and papi had mapped out for her.

"I'm — I'm not sure. There may be something more for me to do here."

Another heavy sigh came through the line. *"Bueno, cuídate nena. Te quiero."*

"You take care, too, Mami. And, you know I love you, too, right?"

"Sí. I do."

On her mami's melancholy words, the call disconnected.

Julia dropped her head into her hands, hunched over, engulfed by the guilt of keeping her true intentions from her mom. Yet, disappointed and keenly frustrated that those closest to her couldn't understand or see how her dreams differed from theirs.

Ben eased his way down the hallway leading to the library, straining to hear any hint of conversation. If Julia was still on the phone, he'd turn around and go back.

Twenty minutes had passed already and

his unease hadn't quieted. Not when he couldn't stop picturing the worry that had knit Julia's brow earlier.

Then again, a twenty-minute chat between Julia and her mom might be the norm. Simply because his parental phone calls were the epitome of a quick three-pitch strikeout didn't mean hers weren't more along the lines of a batter knocking off foul ball after foul ball, making you throw a slew of pitches to get the guy out.

Ben paused at the library door, unwilling to interrupt her. Silence greeted him.

Cautiously leaning against the wood frame, he peeked inside. As soon as he saw Julia, shoulders hunched, palms covering her face, he hurried over to her side.

The heels of his wing-tip shoes slapped the tile floor with each step. She didn't even seem to notice.

"Hey," he said softly, not wanting to startle her.

She glanced up, dejection blanketing her delicate features.

"Hey," she answered.

The edges of her wide mouth quivered, as if trying to smile, but finding the effort too difficult.

Ben sat down beside her, the need to comfort her driving him to wrap an arm around her delicate shoulders.

"You doing okay?" he asked, half expecting her to pull away.

Over the past few weeks she had started to relax in his company, greeting him with a brush of their cheeks rather than an impersonal handshake. But the demonstrative manner she shared with the kids during rehearsal — an encouraging hand on a shoulder, a playful hair fluff for Bernardo, warm hugs hello and good-bye for all — had not been extended to him.

Not until she had reached for his hand out in the hallway earlier. He hoped that was a sign of progress.

"I've been better," she answered.

"Care to talk about it?"

Her shoulders rose and fell with a sigh so heavy it seeped into him, forging his desire to soothe whatever pained her.

"It's not easy trying to figure out how to balance love and commitment to your family with your own goals and dreams. You know?" she said.

Actually, he didn't know. His parents had never held any strong expectations for him other than that he do well in school and find an area where he excelled. Sure, they'd probably thought it would be in academia, but they hadn't balked at his choices.

They'd been too wrapped up in their own research and studies.

But he'd spent enough time at Octavio's house to understand the pull a person's family could have on them. The compulsion to make them proud, to give them your best. To remain loyal.

It's what Ben had found with baseball and his teammates. It's what he missed.

"Well, I may not know your family, but in the time we've spent together, there's definitely one thing I know about you."

Julia slid sideways on the leather sofa cushion, angling to face him.

His arm slid off her shoulder, falling at her side to rest near her hip.

She stared up at him. A mix of doubt, sadness, and hope swam in the depths of her hazel eyes.

"You care about those around you," he continued. "And you give one hundred percent to your commitments. I bet your parents would be proud of the work you're doing here."

She ducked her chin, giving a slight shake of her head. "I don't know about that."

"I do. If they raised you, they're good people."

"Yeah, they are."

"That means even if they don't understand what you need to do for yourself right now, eventually they will. In the long run, I'm betting they only want you to be happy."

A beat of silence passed, then she covered his hand with hers on the sofa cushion. The warmth of her palm matched the warmth in the sweet smile she gifted him with when she gazed up at him.

"*Gracias,*" she murmured.

"For what?"

"For calming the crazy thoughts salsa dancing in my head." Her gentle laugh held a note of self-deprecation.

"Anytime," he answered, smiling back. "Though, you should know, I can also hold my own on the salsa dance floor. In case you were wondering."

Julia threw back her head and laughed. The rich sound tugged at his desire for her, enticing and strong.

"I'll have to verify that sometime," she teased.

He sure hoped so.

Her cheeks brightened with laughter, the gloomy melancholy that had weighed her down moments ago dissipated.

Ben grinned back at her, pleased to have helped lighten her mood.

"*Bueno,* I guess we should head outside,

huh?" Julia rose to stand next to the otto-man.

She surprised him once again by holding out her hand to him.

Not one to miss an opportunity, Ben placed his hand in hers. The smoothness of her palm pressed against his as she gently tightened her grasp.

When they reached the doorway, Ben drew to a halt.

Now or never. Once they returned to the group, who knew if he'd have a moment alone with her again.

"Before we go back to the party, I have a quick proposition for you," he said.

Julia glanced up at him, curiosity arching one of her brows. "Oh really? And what might that be?"

The soft sound of the holiday tune "Blue Christmas" drifted down the hallway from the living room. An appropriate song for how he'd feel should she continue to keep him at an arm's distance.

"I was thinking we could cross something off your bucket list this weekend. If you're up for it."

She angled her head in question, lips curved in a playful smirk as she gave him a narrow-eyed once-over. "That sounds more like a challenge if you ask me."

"If it were, would that encourage you to say yes?"

Her smirk blossomed on a husky chuckle that called out to the loneliness he kept hidden.

"In my house, with my three competitive brothers, you never back away from a challenge. So, what are you throwing down?" she asked.

The way she jutted her chin with confidence, her other hand balled in a fist on her slender hip, had his pulse quickening.

"I'm thinking you, me, a private ice-skating session after the rink closes to the public. What do you say? Are you up for it?"

Chapter Seven

This was not a date. Merely a fun evening with a friend.

Julia repeated the words to herself as her driver steered his car through the darkened streets of downtown Chicago Sunday evening, headed toward Ben's home in the Southport Corridor neighborhood near Wrigley Field.

The sounds of cars honking and snow crunching under the tires mixed with the voice of Michael Bublé crooning "I'll Be Home for Christmas" over the radio. Outside her window, holiday decorations and lights flashed by, illuminating the car's interior, casting shadows that matched the shadows of doubt she'd been battling all day.

Lilí had practically pushed her out the door with an exasperated, "*¿Nena, estás loca?* Why would you *not* go?"

Instead, Julia wondered if she was crazy

for coming.

Huddled in the backseat with the rush of the car's heated air warming her, thoughts of Christmases on the Island swarmed her. The fiestas with her *familia* and friends, the late night *parrandas* going from house to house singing and playing instruments. She missed the comfort of the *coquís* serenading her at night when she fell asleep with her window open. Like the Islanders themselves, the miniature tree frogs indigenous to Puerto Rico had survived the horrors of Hurricane María and the aftermath. Battered, but not beaten.

The strength to survive, something Mami and Papi had driven into her and her brothers, especially in those months after the storm, guided her now. It fed her determination to succeed here in Chicago.

Which is why she had no business allowing herself to be distracted by heart-flutter-inducing romance. With a ballplayer.

Ex-ballplayer, as Lilí had reminded her.

The driver turned down a quiet neighborhood street adorned with holiday flair. Lighted santas, reindeer, and nativity scenes glowed in the small, snow-covered front yards. Christmas trees brightened windows and colored lights outlined many of the homes.

They must be getting closer to Ben's place. Julia's shoulders shimmied with excited anticipation.

After making a left turn onto West Addison Street, the car slowed to a stop in front of a gorgeous, redbrick, two-story home with a dark, burnished metal fence that matched the window accents.

It was a large house, built to hold a growing family more so than a single guy who spent half of the baseball season on the road.

"Here we are." The gray-haired driver turned to look at her over his shoulder, his chin hidden by a thick green scarf wrapped around his neck.

"How much do I owe you?" she asked.

"It's already covered by the guy who booked the car. Have a nice evening, miss."

Julia thanked him and offered the same, then slid out of the vehicle.

Gingerly stepping over the snow plowed off to the side of the road, she made her way up the cobblestone path and several cement stairs to Ben's front door. The porch light welcomed her, though a strange lack of Christmas decorations left his place the odd one out compared to his neighbors. She peeked at the front windows, but couldn't spot a tree inside either.

For someone who seemed more like a

homebody than the partying bachelor most single, multimillion-dollar athletes were, Ben's lack of holiday spirit surprised her.

As she stood in front of his door, her gloved finger hovering over the black, rectangular doorbell, a mix of emotions assailed her.

Eagerness, at spending more time with him.

Fear, that she was coming to look forward to seeing him. Far more than a mere friend should.

Empathy, for a good man that life had thrown a major curve.

Ben might not have openly admitted it, but she'd caught the sadness in his eyes, the dejection in his slightly sagging shoulders when the topic of his playing days came up.

Just like with her brother, Alfredo.

Only, the pang she felt for Ben wasn't brotherly. Not in the least. And that's what worried her.

The wind kicked up, blowing a swirl of snow at her feet. A chill shuddered through her and she quickly pressed the bell.

Seconds later the door opened to reveal Ben, all six foot plus of hunky male in dark jeans and a light blue sweater that heightened the icy blue of his eyes. His dark blond hair was slightly mussed, like he'd recently run a hand through it.

His chiseled face brightened when he saw her. The grin he flashed made her heart flip-flop like a fish on the end of her papi's favorite fishing pole line.

"Hi," Ben said. "It's good to see you. Come in."

Moving aside, he gestured for her to enter.

Julia stomped the snow off her boots before stepping into the house, then paused inside the foyer, biting her lip to keep her jaw from dropping open.

While Laura and Sherman Taylor's home might be grand opulence at its finest, Ben's house was a veritable oasis. Intricate light and dark geometric patterns marked the inlaid wood floors while miniature palms rose up from the basement to tickle the first floor steps of a floating staircase connecting the home's three levels. Columns in the same dark wood separated the various rooms on the main floor, with a trail of little wooden orbs the size of ping-pong balls stained to match dotting the curved arch-ways of the cream-painted walls.

"Here, let me take your coat," Ben said. "Make yourself at home."

Eyeing the strong lines and intricate details in the design and structure, she slowly unwrapped her scarf. "This is absolutely beautiful, Ben."

"Thanks. It's a comfortable place to come to at the end of a long day or an even longer road trip."

"I'm sure." And yet, it lacked holiday spirit. She couldn't resist asking why. "No tree though? Aren't you expecting Santa to come down your chimney with gifts?"

Ben chuckled. "Probably not. My parents weren't really into the holidays. And these days I'm usually traveling or celebrating with others at their place."

The thought of a young Ben left to his own devices as a kid or now, alone in this sterile, albeit breathtaking, house devoid of revelry and tradition made Julia a little sad. Maybe because, for her, this time of year had always been filled with fiestas and customs shared with her *familia*.

Glancing at the living room that faced Addison Street, she easily pictured a stately fir holding center court in front of the middle window. A nativity scene at the tree's base, a few wrapped presents beside it. A trail of garland looping the staircase railing. Ooh, the possibilities here were endless.

Hands on her hips, she faced Ben again. "Well, I hate to tell you this, but from the outside, your house looks kind of Grinchy. We might have to do something about that."

"Oh really?" Ben hooked his thumbs in his front pockets, eyeing her with speculation.

"Uh-huh," she pressed, unable to resist the fun in teasing him a little.

"Hmmm." His brow furrowed, as if he was considering something. "And you think you can help me spruce up my Christmas image among my neighbors?"

"Oh, definitely."

"Okay, I'll take you up on that offer."

Too late she realized she'd practically invited herself to help decorate his house. The satisfied gleam in Ben's eyes told her he knew it, too. And he probably wouldn't let her off the hook.

Not that she really wanted off anyway.

"But first, we have some ice skating to tackle. Come on, I was about to start heating our hot chocolate on the stove. Unless you'd like a tour of the place." Ben had taken a few steps to his left, but then he turned so abruptly Julia ran into his chest.

"Oomph!" she grunted, her hands grabbing onto his biceps to steady herself.

Ben's arms came around her waist, snugly wrapping her in his embrace.

Julia gazed up at him, the light from the intricate wrought iron chandelier turning his hair a burnished gold.

All of a sudden time stood still.

She watched his gaze drop to her mouth before slowly moving back up to meet hers.

"You okay?" he asked, his voice a husky rasp that had intimate places on her body thrumming.

Ave María, she was nowhere near okay.

More like confused.

Certainly turned on.

Not trusting her voice, Julia nodded. She licked her lips nervously. Ben's gaze followed the motion, desire flaring in the depths of his eyes.

His head dipped. Paused. Waited for her reaction.

That pause, the gentlemanly action that told her he'd do nothing without her consent, pushed her over the edge of reason and into passion-fueled insanity.

Rising up on her booted toes, Julia slid one hand behind his neck. Her fingers dug into the cropped hair along his nape, urging him to continue.

Ben did her bidding with a muffled groan.

His lips covered hers in a heated kiss. His hands moved from her waist to her hips at the same time the tip of his tongue laved her lower lip. She opened for him, catching a faint taste of mint as he deepened the kiss.

His woodsy, earthy scent intoxicated her

brain and she pressed closer, until nothing separated them. Still, it wasn't enough.

Suddenly the kiss softened. Ben eased back, nipping at her mouth and jawline with tiny pecks and little bites, then moving to press a moist kiss against the column of her throat.

"I'm afraid if we don't stop, we might not get to your bucket list item," he whispered in her ear.

"You're doing a fabulous job at distracting me from your ice-skating challenge," she answered.

A chuckle rumbled through his chest and into hers, drawing an answering smile from her.

"So, about that tour?" Ben asked.

Linking her fingers with his, Julia leaned back and held their arms out at their sides. "I'm thinking that might not be a good idea. We may get distracted again and wind up swapping one adventure for another. One we're probably not ready for yet."

A playful grin curved the corners of his mouth as they eyed each other for several moments. Attraction crackled in the air between them. She was oh so tempted to throw caution to the wind. And yet . . .

Ben must have sensed her hesitation because he tossed her a quick wink before tugging her toward the left part of the first floor. "Come on. Our hot chocolate isn't going to heat itself. We have a mission to accomplish tonight."

As she followed him through his gorgeous home into a gourmet kitchen with marble and onyx counters and professional-quality appliances her mami would have loved to cook with, Julia couldn't help wondering when "make out with a Major League All-Star" had been added to her bucket list.

Because if you asked her right now, that wish had leapfrogged everything else to make it number one.

"Does that feel tight enough?" Ben adjusted the black buckle straps on Julia's rental hockey skates.

Kneeling down on the sidewalk in front of her, he spanned the ankle part of the blue skate with his hand, jiggling back and forth lightly to ensure a snug fit.

What he really wanted to do was glide his hand up the length of her trim leg, imagining the softness of her skin under her skinny jeans. Capture her mouth with his again. Start back up where they'd left off in his foyer earlier.

He pulled his thoughts up short before his body betrayed him by reacting to the heated memory of having her in his arms. Instead he grasped her other foot, checking the tightness of the straps.

"Uh, yeah, it feels good."

The hitch in Julia's voice had him glancing up at her. He squinted under the glare of the lights off a nearby Christmas tree. It was one of multiple trees lining the length of the left side of the ice rink, separating it from part of the Christkindlmarket at the Park at Wrigley.

Despite the entire area being closed for their private skate time, the market booths remained illuminated, their red and white striped roof material glowing. Strands of twinkling white Christmas lights criss-crossed the air above them, matching the large white snowflakes perched at the top of each metal light pole in the market square and the sidewalk along Clark Street.

Holiday music drifted softly through hidden speakers, and off in the far corner of the rink, a young teen wearing a heavy jacket bearing the park's logo leaned against the glass dasher boards wrapping the perimeter of the rectangular rink. Other than the teen and a night manager, Julia and Ben had the place to themselves.

Julia scanned the area, her expression filled with delight. Bundled up in a navy wool coat and leather gloves, a red knit beanie cap keeping her head and the top of her ears warm, she looked more like a cute snow bunny than an island girl.

"When you said 'private skate' I guess it didn't register that you'd rent the entire facility," she said.

Ben lifted a shoulder in a lazy shrug. "It's easier this way. Things can get a little precarious when you're swarmed with fans in the middle of the ice."

"Ahh, I see," she murmured. "Sometimes I catch myself forgetting who you are."

He tilted his head in confusion. "What do you mean?"

"You know. Cubs superstar and fan favorite. The MLB's golden child. New face of the network."

"You say all that like it's a curse."

"No, but it *is* a reality." Her forehead creased, her brows drawing together like she was struggling to make sense of something. "Yours anyway."

She shook her head as if to clear it, then turned to gaze out over the rink.

Ben rose from his haunches, his left knee cracking as he moved to sit next to her on the wood-slatted bench.

Something about the way Julia emphasized "yours," like she needed to differentiate her reality from his, bothered him.

As if his connection to the sport he loved was a negative in her mind.

The idea was preposterous.

Sure, he'd noticed her reticence to talk about her brothers' involvement with baseball, but he'd attributed it to her desire for privacy. Not any ill-will toward the game itself or the lifestyle being linked to it required.

Baseball had been his connection to every semblance of family he'd ever had. The only problem he saw with that was his inability to figure out how to replace it now that he'd been forced out.

But a negative? Never.

"So let me ask you this," he ventured, trying to wrap his head around the idea that for the first time in his adult life, his status as a big-time player could be a deterrent to something, someone, he wanted. "Is my baseball career or my ties to the game a problem for you?"

Julia's eyes fluttered closed as her chest rose and fell on a heavy sigh.

Ben's pulse blipped, skipping a couple beats. Her reaction did not bode well for him.

"Not a problem, so much as a . . . a deal breaker," she finally answered.

He sucked in a sharp breath like she'd drop-kicked him in the gut.

Several seconds of stunned silence passed while her words sunk in. His mind rolled over them, considering. "Wow, I wasn't, uh, wasn't expecting that."

She swiveled to face him, her gloved hand covering his on the bench between them. "It's not you. It's me."

"Ha!" The harsh laugh burst from his throat.

"It's true!"

"Come on," he said, torn between laughing at the irony or cursing at his rotten luck. "Why does this sound like a line from a bad Dear John letter?"

"Look, you're a great guy —"

"Aw, man!" Ben let his head fall back as he sent his plea to the heavens. "Not the dreaded 'nice guy' description? This just gets better and better!"

"Stooooop." Julia drew out the word, squeezing his hand to get his attention. "You know what I mean."

Sure he knew what she meant. He was getting the brush-off. Him. *People* magazine's sexiest MLB player of the year, not that he ever threw that designation around. The guys had had a field day with that one in the locker room. Jokes and pranks for weeks on end.

His teammates had known he could handle the ribbing. They also knew that when he had his sights set on accomplishing something, he gave everything he had to see it come to fruition. He studied film. Read scouting reports. Learned about the players on the opposing team. And when it was time to step onto the field, his entire focus honed in on that one person at the plate.

Over the past few weeks he'd been doing everything possible to get to know all he could about Julia. Only his efforts this time weren't about winning a game.

No, this time, the outcome felt bigger. More important.

Before he could figure out how to convince Julia to give him — give them — a chance, he had to know what stood in his way.

"Fine," he said on a huff of breath. "So, I'm a nice guy, but . . ."

He let his words trail off. Brows raised in question, he looked at Julia.

The streetlamps and string lights left her face in partial shadow, while they reflected in her dark eyes.

"But my life has been consumed with baseball for years. In my family, our schedules revolved around my brothers' practice, games, tournaments, team gatherings. Even my *quinceañera* party got pushed back a month because every weekend in July there was something baseball-related on the calendar."

He, on the other hand, had relished spending his August birthday with his teammates as summer league wound down before school started. It beat the low-key one candle stuck in a cupcake celebration with his parents. If one of them even remembered to stop by a bakery on their way home from their research labs on campus.

"For the first time in my life, I'm missing winter ball league in Puerto Rico," Julia went on, her voice raw with conviction. "And honestly, it's a relief. Most days anyway. Then one of my brothers, Ángel or Martín, sends a text with their game highlights and I feel bad that I wasn't there to cheer them on. But the thing is, I doubt they've ever wondered what I might want or need for them to cheer for me about. Coming here to Chicago, it's a risk. It's a big leap of faith in myself. For myself."

"I know. You've shared that with me," Ben said, wanting her to see that he understood her drive. Hell, he respected it. "I'll do whatever I can to help. This fund-raiser will be the best one yet. And you'll be turning down offers for you to plan other events around the city."

Julia's lips curved in a sad smile, a pained expression creasing her beautiful face.

"Gracias," she murmured. "You're confirming my 'great guy' opinion."

Ben scowled.

"The thing is," she said, "I've always stayed away from getting involved with a ballplayer . . . at first because my brothers would have beaten up anyone who even looked my way. Later, as I grew older, because I saw girlfriends hurt by guys who moved up the ranks. Wait, I know what you're going to say —"

She held up a hand to stall the argument he was primed to give. There was nothing he could do about how other men had treated her friends. He could only be responsible for his own actions.

"But mostly," Julia went on, "because I know how consuming the game can be. Honestly, I don't know if I want that to be a part of my life anymore. As much as I love the game, too."

Regret tightened Ben's chest. God, he'd do anything to get back in the game, and here she was shrugging off any attachment to it.

His only saving grace was the love she

readily admitted to having for the sport. It was something the two of them shared.

That affinity, plus the commitment to her loved ones, her dedication to the kids at the youth center, and her determination to succeed at her job were a large part of what attracted him to her.

He shared those same traits, giving them more in common than simply baseball. Or the mutual attraction he felt sparking between them.

Maybe he wasn't sure where things were headed with her, but he sure as hell wanted to find out.

As far as he was concerned, the only reality that mattered right now was one involving her and him. Enjoying themselves and getting to know each other better.

If she held any reservations about being with him, he aimed to dispel them, starting tonight.

Pushing himself to a wobbly stand in his skates, Ben flashed her his most convincing grin. "How about if we agree to concentrate on having some fun. No expectations. Just two people who enjoy hanging out."

Julia gazed up at him intently, as if gauging his veracity. Slowly the stressed expression on her face faded, replaced by a dawning ease.

"I'd like that," she answered.

A smile tugged up the corners of her full lips, loosening the knot of disappointment her earlier admission had gnarled in his chest.

"Good. You ready to wow me with your skating skills?" he asked, because as far as he was concerned, pretty much everything else about her wowed him already.

CHAPTER EIGHT

"Are we all ready?"

Ben's simple question coming from behind her startled Julia, heightening her nervous jitters. She tore her thumb from her gnawing teeth before she ruined another manicure. Her second this week thanks to the terrible nail-biting habit she couldn't kick in times of high stress.

And tonight was definitely a high stress moment.

Months of committee meetings, phone calls, and networking with local vendors and the event-planning company had coalesced into this moment: bringing her vision for the fund-raiser to life.

"It looks amazing," Ben said, awe tingeing his deep voice.

Pride swelled in Julia's chest.

"You've done an incredible job," he added.

"Everyone has. Tonight's a huge group effort."

Ben nudged her shoulder with his as he joined her at the gilded balcony railing overlooking the expansive Wintrust Grand Banking Hall. The scent of his earthy aftershave tinted her next breath, an intoxicating aphrodisiac.

Together they took in the view below where workers bustled about, finalizing last minute preparations to the open-aired space.

The well-known building's neoclassical and Gothic Revival architecture, often photographed and admired in magazines and Web sites, had been transformed into an island holiday celebration. Round tables with seats for eight were elegantly dressed in deep red, green, and gold linens. Several towering Christmas trees flanked the wide columns on either side of the space, each tree decorated with Puerto Rican-themed ornaments. Glittering balls with the country's red, white, and blue flag, miniature musical instruments commonly played during *parrandas,* beach-inspired baubles, and little doll-sized *pavas,* the traditional straw hats worn by many Islanders, hung from the branches. Potted palm trees interspersed among the traditional Christmas firs along the hall floor and across the back of the stage, their fronds glistening with tiny white lights that sparkled.

In a nod to the importance of the Three Kings in Latino cultural celebrations, life-sized carved and masterfully painted wooden statues of the three figures bearing their gifts stood at the entrance of the room, facing the stage erected at the far end. In the back left corner of the stage, on a thin bed of hay, nestled similarly crafted statues of Mary, Joseph, and baby Jesus in a manger.

A set of choral risers had been set up center and stage right, with Ben's emcee dais, a simple lectern in brushed black metal, placed down center stage. Lightweight, it could easily be lifted and placed out of the way on the floor level once the *parranda* started with the kids.

Above the stage, an illuminated Star of Bethlehem measuring three feet from tip to tip hung in the air. A guiding light for the *Tres Reyes* on their journey toward the baby.

In Julia's mind, and she hoped in the minds of the attendees as well, the children from the youth center signified the future. The money raised tonight, gifts from those more fortunate, would provide much needed funding for resources that would assist with better ensuring these inner city kids and others in similar situations had more opportunities to grow and flourish and achieve their goals.

"Team effort, huh?" Ben asked. "How did I know you'd forgo taking credit for envisioning the wonderland that awaits ticket holders tonight?"

Julia glanced at him on her left, her snappy comeback faltering in the face of his devastating handsomeness.

A dark navy tuxedo clung to his broad shoulders and muscular thighs as if it had been tailor made for him. The color heightened his icy blue eyes, the wool material stretching over his biceps and across the expanse of his wide chest. The silk trim at his lapel and pockets along with the silk stripe trailing down the outside seam of his pants, neatly complementing the navy silk bow tie, had her thinking of him as her very own Christmas present. One that, as time passed, she wanted more and more to unwrap and keep all to herself.

Edging a minuscule step closer, Ben placed a hand on the small of her back.

"I know I already said this, but it certainly needs repeating. . . . You look incredible." His deep voice caressed her fidgety nerves, calming her.

At the same time, the warmth of his palm

on her bare lower back sent waves of desire undulating through her.

She'd wondered what Ben would think of her dress when she'd slipped into it earlier. Seeing the flare of appreciation in his eyes made her happy she'd followed Lilí's fashion advice.

The wine-colored, slim-fitting, backless dress had been a last minute splurge. Earlier in the week, Lilí had balked at the plain, black, midcalf sheath dress Julia had planned to wear.

"*¿Pero, chica, qué es eso?*" Lilí had screeched.

"What do you mean, what's that? It's my outfit for the benefit," Julia answered, scowling at her meddling cousin.

"No way!" Lilí had gaped at her, scandalized. "I've been to a few of the Taylors' fund-raisers before. Listen, you're the mastermind of this one! You want to shine, but not look like you're trying too hard. And this" — Lilí pinched one of the long sleeves that flared to a bell shape at the wrists — "this is definitely *not* shine worthy."

A coffee-fueled run to Filene's Basement on Michigan Avenue Wednesday afternoon had resulted in the bargain-priced, floor-length gown. Sleeveless, it featured a cowl back that draped open nearly to her waistline. The red, stretch crepe material clung to her curves, flaring slightly in a trumpet silhouette that highlighted her slim figure and made her feel sexy, yet stylish.

Julia had swooped her long hair up in a loose, messy bun, then settled on natural makeup with red lips. Simple diamond studs and a cubic zirconia sterling silver tennis bracelet she'd borrowed from Lilí capped off her ensemble.

Ben's appreciative gaze made the extra expense and the frazzled shopping trip completely worth the effort.

Trailing a finger down his silky lapel, she glanced at him from under her lashes. "You don't look too bad yourself."

Understatement of the year.

The man was drop-dead gorgeous whether in a fancy tux like now or in jeans, boots, and a thick wool jacket with a knit cap tugged over his ears. The cap had helped him remain incognito last Wednesday when they'd spent the evening scavenger hunting for garden gnomes at the Lincoln Park Zoo Festival of Lights.

Under a blanket of clear night sky, surrounded by a winter wonderland, they had sipped mulled wine and admired the lights until the cold soaked into her bones and she'd cried uncle. Her Island blood was still getting used to the frigid Chicago winter.

Ben had dropped her off at Lilí's place with a gentlemanly kiss on the cheek. The soft brush of his lips on her skin had her toes curling in her boots. Her body had cried out for more, while her head cautioned her to keep things slow.

"How's your tree?" she asked, referring to the Douglas fir she and Lilí had brought over earlier this week. She and her cousin had descended on Ben's home with tinsel, ornaments, bows, and a tree fresh off the lot.

"I still can't believe you tricked me like that. Dropping off a script revision, yeah right." He tucked a loose curl behind her ear, his tender expression negating the hint of accusation in his voice. "You two were like a whirlwind of holiday hoopla."

"And you loved it!" Julia gave his chest a teasing push, her hand lingering to give him a gentle caress.

Ben captured her hand under his. "Yes. I did. Thank you."

She ducked her head, feeling the heat of a blush climbing into her cheeks.

The evening had been wonderful. Ben heating up hot chocolate. Cueing up *parranda* music on his home sound system. Laughing with Lilí and her as they sang along while decorating the tree together.

It was a night she'd never forget. Capped off by a soul-stirring kiss after Lilí had hurried down the front stairs to her car parked nearby, all in the guise of warming it up while Julia and Ben exchanged good-byes.

The past three weeks had flown by in a mix of rehearsals, last minute planning, and spending time with Ben.

"As much as I don't mind pulling out this monkey suit for a good cause," he whispered to her, "I'd much rather the two of us be somewhere a little more private."

So would she, though she wasn't quite ready to voice the thought.

Not yet, with so much up in the air in her life.

Laura Taylor had yet to sit down with her to discuss the potential for Julia staying on full-time as her assistant. Although, the owner of the event-planning company they were working with had mentioned to her that there might be a position opening up. If so, Julia hoped her work over the past few months and tonight's results would serve as a superb testament to her skills and suitability for his company.

If neither option panned out, she might be heading back to Puerto Rico after the New Year. Should that happen, starting a relationship with Ben would be futile.

"I'm not sure that's the best idea."

"I know," he said, gently brushing a knuckle along her jaw. "That's why I'm not pushing. But the offer stands, when or if you *are* sure."

Julia's heart melted a little more for him.

Ave María purísima, his willingness to give her the space she needed, when he'd made it clear he was more than ready to take their relationship from friends to . . . *bueno,* to more . . . didn't make her indecision any easier.

Her cell phone vibrated in the black wristlet wallet hanging from her left arm. Either a reminder alarm she'd set for herself or a call from someone.

Unzipping the pouch, she slid out her phone to see Lilí's image on the screen. Julia frowned. Her cousin should have been here by now.

"*¿Hola, donde estás?*" she asked.

"I'm still at the women's shelter," Lilí grumbled.

"Oh no! Are you going to make it here?"

Ben's brows rose in surprise at her alarmed tone.

"Is there something I can help with?" he whispered, while Lilí continued explaining about the client she'd been assisting since

538

late that afternoon.

Julia shook her head at him.

"I'm so sorry I can't be there for your big night, *prima,*" Lilí apologized. "But I can't leave until she and her kids are settled and I know they're okay."

"Of course. I understand." Julia knew her cousin's commitment to her clients came a close second to both of their commitments to their *familia.* When kids were involved in domestic violence cases like the ones Lilí worked with on a regular basis, it made her job as a victim's advocate even more invaluable.

"I hope to make it out to Oakton for the *parranda* with Yazmine, Rosa, and everyone else later tonight," Lilí said. "Maybe Ben can give you a ride if he's still going, and I'll meet you there."

Her cousin had invited Ben to their annual *parranda* a couple days ago when he'd stopped by the condo to drop off some sponsor information.

After their home-decorating affair at Ben's place her cousin had moved past the awed-fan phase where he was concerned. Now Lilí treated him like a family friend. Or, her cousin's *dreamy love interest,* as the cheeky girl liked to tease when it was just Lilí and Julia lounging on the leather sofa, talking

539

about their day before they turned in for the night.

Julia's phone buzzed against her cheek. She pulled it away to see a text from David, the assistant manager at the Humboldt Park Youth Center.

About to pull up in front of the building. Where should the kids and I meet you?

Julia quickly tapped out a response: I'll be waiting by the main doors. Use the valet.

"*Ay*, I have to go. The kids are about to arrive," she told Lilí. "Fingers crossed we'll see you afterward."

"That's the plan. Listen, you've worked hard for this. I hope you're happy with . . . well, with everything."

"Okay." Julia drew out the word, her cousin's hesitant tone catching her off guard.

"You better go," Lilí cautioned. *"Cuídate."*

"You take care, too."

"Hey, wait! Break a leg!" Lilí yelled.

"If you say so," Julia said around a grin.

Since Lilí's oldest sister, Yazmine, had been a Broadway dancer and she now worked as a local instructor, none of the three sisters had given her a "good luck" or *"buena suerte"* cheer today. Yaz and Rosa had sent "break a leg" text messages earlier. They were home with their little ones, preparing food and drinks for the *parranda* that would start at Rosa's house around ten p.m.

The last thing Julia heard as she disconnected the call was Lilí's throaty laughter.

"Everything all right?" Ben asked.

"Yeah, though Lilí's caught up at work. I'll need to find a ride out to Oakton afterward."

"You know I won't mind giving you a lift, if you'd like."

Dropping the phone back into her wristlet, Julia glanced up to find Ben leaning toward her, his head inches from hers. Her breath caught in her throat at the flash of desire darkening his eyes.

"I am *really* excited to meet everyone tonight," he said. "Thanks for the invite."

Technically, the invite had come from Lilí. Her cousin had run the idea by Julia first as they'd poured wine and gathered cheese and crackers in the kitchen the night Ben had come by and wound up staying for a visit.

Ben had said yes immediately.

Now Julia gulped, trying to push down her rising jitters.

This was a big step. Introducing him to

not only her family here, but their extended Latino community. People who were *familia* in every sense of the word except by blood.

"A *parranda* is always a ton of fun. I think you're going to love it. But first, time to concentrate on making sure tonight is a success." She glanced at her watch. "Laura should be arriving shortly. She texted a little while ago to say she had to make a quick stop somewhere first."

Ben's lips spread in a broad smile, his face lighting up like her baby cousin's on the morning the Three Kings left their gifts.

"Yes, she did," he said. Pulling out his cell from his tuxedo jacket inside pocket, he read something on the screen, before sliding the device back into place. "And it looks like Laura will be arriving around the same time as the kids. I know you'll need to get them settled in the rehearsal room before the Happy Hour begins, but I think you'll be thrilled to find out why Laura took that detour."

Excitement radiated off him as he guided her away from the railing, toward the stairs leading to the hall floor.

Intrigued, if slightly wary, Julia fell into step beside him. Tonight was far too big of a night for her to deal with surprises.

At the bottom of the stairs, Ben led her

around a group of volunteers who were putting the finishing touches on a tree. She paused to thank them, but after a few minutes he placed his hand on the small of her back, the gentle pressure urging her to wrap up her conversation.

"What's going on?" she asked under her breath once they had moved away. Her wariness grew as he hastened his pace.

"You'll see."

When they reached the building's entry, Ben drew to a stop.

"I wanted to make sure you were here for . . . this." He gestured toward the main doors.

Julia gasped. Her stomach free-falled as she watched the doorman usher two women inside the Wintrust Bank Building, then quickly tug the door closed to keep out the frigid early December weather.

Dios mío, it couldn't be.

Her heart pounding in her chest, Julia gaped in disbelief. "Mami, what are you doing here?"

CHAPTER NINE

The strange mix of surprise and shocked dismay on Julia's face was not what Ben had anticipated when he first spoke with Laura about potentially bringing Paula Fernandez to Chicago for the fund-raiser.

Surprise, yes.

Dismay, not even on his radar of the emotions he'd anticipated from Julia.

Through the glass doors, Ben noticed three super-sized white vans with the youth center organization's logo pulling up to the curb. Any minute now the thirty-five kids would come spilling out, demanding Julia's attention.

"I mean, *que sorpresa!*" she amended, opening her arms to envelop her mother in a hug.

"A good surprise, *verdad?*" her mami asked.

"Definitely." Julia leaned back, grasping her mother's elbows to stare down at her.

The older woman's chin-length, wavy, dark hair, olive-toned skin, and delicate features resembled her daughter's. Paula's figure was rounder with maturity, but seeing the two of them together, Ben had a good idea what Julia would look like later in life. More and more he realized that was something he hoped she'd want him around to watch.

Catching the sheen of tears in Julia's eyes now, Ben wondered if he'd misread her initial reaction.

"Welcome, Señora Fernandez." He stepped forward, reaching out a hand to shake.

Paula Fernandez gave a double take, her mouth opening and closing before she shot a wide-eyed, questioning look at Julia.

She nodded at her mom. "*Sí,* it's him. And yes, I know Martín will flip when he finds out I've been working with Ben. That's partly why I haven't said anything. I haven't had time for the twenty questions I know he'd be texting me daily."

Her mom clasped his hand with both of hers. The coldness of her touch reminded him that coming from the Caribbean, Paula might not own proper Chicago-winter attire. He'd check with Julia and purchase whatever her mom might need while visiting.

"Paula Fernandez," the older woman introduced herself.

"*Encantado de conocerla,*" Ben responded.

Paula's smile brightened at his Spanish. "It is a pleasure to meet you, too, Benjamin. My son Martín, Julia's youngest brother, is a big *fanático* of yours."

"Then I look forward to meeting him."

"*Ay, mi hijo* would love to —"

"Hey, Julia!"

"Wow!"

"Check this joint out!"

The chorus of greetings and exclamations of awe as the kids pushed through the glass doors interrupted whatever Julia's mom had been about to say. The kids poured into the building on a rush of energy.

"Paula, why don't we check our coats and move into the VIP area." Laura Taylor, classically fashionable as always in a dark green, floor length gown with long sleeves and a short turtleneck, signaled for the attendant to approach. "I'm sure Julia and Ben have last minute preparations before happy hour begins in thirty minutes. My husband Sherman should be joining us shortly."

"Can I help you with something, *nena?*" Paula unbuttoned a hugely oversized coat that swamped her body.

"No, it's okay, Mami. Go enjoy yourself, we'll talk later. It's . . ." Julia's voice trailed off as the kids swarmed around her, the younger ones clamoring for her attention. "It's good to see you."

She hugged her mom one more time, then turned to quiet the group.

While Julia was peppered with questions, Ben caught Laura's eye. The prominent socialite flashed him a sly thumbs-up.

Last week, when he and Julia had attended an exhibition at the National Museum of Puerto Rican Arts and Culture, the nostalgia in her voice when she talked about her family back home had planted the seed of an idea in Ben's head.

Later, over coffee and dessert at one of his favorite restaurants, she'd mentioned her desire for her parents to see how she'd taken the lessons learned working with her family's catering business and applied those skills to her work on the fund-raiser.

The seed of the idea to fly Paula Fernandez in for tonight's event had blossomed. Ben privately mentioned it to Laura, more to bounce the idea off her than intending for her to take the ball and run with it.

But run she did.

After checking with her daughter-in-law

Rosa for help reaching Julia's mother, Laura had overseen all the flight reservations and logistics. The only snag in the plan had been Lilí not being able to pick up Paula at the airport.

Unflappable as always, Laura had called an audible and opted to pick up Paula herself.

The two older women moved deeper into the hall, so Ben followed Julia and the kids to the private room that had been prepared for them to warm up. Diego, the Chicago policeman who would accompany them on the guitar, and Señor Pérez, the keyboardist, were already there having arrived earlier to help with the sound check.

As he reached the group, Ben noticed the worried glance Julia sent her mother's way. Her lower lip caught between her teeth.

Unease marched like angry army ants across the back of his neck. Maybe he hadn't been mistaken earlier.

For some reason, Julia didn't appear exactly thrilled by Paula's appearance. If so, no telling what she'd say when she found out the visit had been his idea.

Before Ben's dread about his surprise potentially blowing up in his face could morph into something bigger, Bernardo sidled up to him.

The boy's crooked smile, the delighted way he smoothed down the front of his dress shirt and tie, lightened Ben's mood. Reminding him of the reason they were all here tonight. Another common goal he and Julia shared: helping these kids.

"This place is pretty *padre,* huh?" Bernardo craned his neck, gawking at the intricate scrollwork carved into the tall ceiling, then gazing out at the ornate decorations blanketing the hall.

Ben grinned back at him. "Yeah, it does look pretty cool. Julia and the team have done an incredible job. And having you kids performing is going to make it that much cooler."

Bernardo beamed with excitement.

"Okay, everyone, *silencio, por favor!*" Julia called out when everyone was seated in the rehearsal room. She waited until the chatter had quieted before continuing. "I know we went over this earlier this week, but I'd like to review the program. Make sure everyone remembers when they should join in the singing from their table, then start slowly making their way to the stage."

Ben stayed off to the side, quietly admiring her ease with the large group of visibly anxious students. Even Rico, their fearless leader, thrummed his fingers on his knee, his expression serious, nodding in agreement as Julia went through their plan.

During the happy hour, the kids would wait here, warming up with the musicians. About forty-five minutes in, they would head to assigned dinner tables where they'd join attendees for the meal and dessert. The idea was for donors to get a chance to meet and interact with some of the kids. See firsthand the individuals they were helping.

After dinner, Ben would head back to the stage, only to be "interrupted" by Rico tapping out a beat on the *plenera* stashed under his chair. At a nearby table another student would break out a *güiro,* heightening Héctor's hand drum beat. At that same table, a girl would join in with a set of *palitos,* adding further to the beat by knocking the two wooden rhythm sticks together.

A nod from Rico was the signal for the musicians to start the first verse of the carol and move toward two other tables nearby. The students seated there would rise, join the carolers, and continue heading toward the stage, picking up the others as they passed each table.

It wasn't quite a true *parranda,* where carolers went from house to house, stopping to sing and eat, before heading on to the next house. Traditionally the revelry would continue through the night going from one house to another, the group growing in size until the sun came up.

Tonight, the kids would wind up on the stage where they'd sing a set of songs in English and Spanish. For the finale, attendees would be encouraged to join in a bilingual version of "Silent Night" with the help of lyrics printed on the back of each program to facilitate participation.

"Does anyone have any questions before I head out to check on a few items with the caterers?" Julia looked around the room. When no one raised a hand or voiced a concern, she clapped her hands together and grinned.

"Okay then, you've got" — she twisted her wrist to check her watch — "about an hour to relax, go over the songs, and get ready to wow this crowd. I'm going to run, but I'll swing by in a bit to check on you."

She wiggled her fingers in a good-bye wave, then swung toward the door. Only then, with her back to the kids, did a tiny V of concern crease between her brows. Without even glancing at him, she hurried by.

Ben turned to follow, hoping it was nothing more than typical pre-event stress rather than her mother's appearance that had Julia troubled.

"Once again, we appreciate your attendance tonight," Ben told the audience, scanning the hall and making eye contact with donors throughout the dining area. "Now, we hope you enjoy the savory meal Chef Salcedo has whipped up to give us a taste of Puerto Rico's delicious cuisine. Afterward, we have a special performance in store for you. But first, *buen provecho!*"

On his "enjoy" cue, a trail of servers in white dress shirts with black pants and ties marched into the hall carrying trays of roast pork, fried plantains, and pigeon pea rice. Between the table chatter and the tinkling of forks and knives on china plates, the din in the room increased.

Ben left the stage to rejoin Sherman and Laura Taylor, Julia, her mother, and several donors at their table.

Julia sat beside him on his left, and while for all intents and purposes she appeared her usually poised, confident self, her right leg jiggled nonstop with what seemed to Ben like nervous energy. Occasionally her knee knocked his, then she'd wince, sit still for a few seconds, only to start jittering again in seconds.

He wanted to place his hand on her thigh,

intending to offer calm or comfort. But even with the cover provided by the table linens, he kept his hands to himself, unsure how she would react to such an intimate touch. Especially with her mom next to her.

Midway through the meal, the discussion took a natural turn to the Chicago Youth Organization and the Humboldt Park Center's mission. Eventually it circled back to Julia's involvement in the fund-raiser.

"So have you fallen in love with our city and decided to move here yet?" Sherman asked her.

"Um, well, it's been busy, but I've certainly enjoyed my time in Chicago." Julia's gaze cut to her mother before she flashed a wobbly smile.

"And she's doing amazing work, as you can see." Laura raised her hand, palm up, indicating their surroundings. "I have been waiting for the perfect moment to sit down with her so we can discuss making her stay here permanent."

Both Julia and her mother gasped at Laura's comment.

Paula glanced back and forth between her daughter and Laura, a question flashing in her dark brown eyes.

"Mami, no he decidido nada," Julia rushed to assure her mom.

Ben blinked in surprise. He would have said the opposite, that her decision *had* already been made. She'd told him from the beginning that her goal was to land a job here so she could stay.

What he hadn't known was that, apparently, her family still remained in the dark.

"I know this would be a big change. For Julia and for you, Paula," Laura continued. "While I believe Julia is interested, when Ben first proposed the idea of inviting you to Chicago, my hope was that by meeting me and witnessing the fabulous opportunities here for your daughter, you would feel reassured about my offer."

"Gracias, I am thankful to be here. We are very proud of our *nena."* Paula patted Julia's hand on the table. "But her place is at home. On the Island. Right, Julia?"

Like a thief caught in the glaring lights from a cop car, Julia froze. Pained indecision stamped her features. Then she turned her gaze on him.

Ben sucked in a swift breath at the accusation burning in her hazel eyes.

Suddenly, his earlier dread rose up to grab a choke hold on him. Somehow he had miscalculated.

"Do you know what? I realized that we never went over that last minute script

554

change for the second part of the evening." Pushing back his chair, Ben tipped his head to the others at their table. "If you'll excuse us. I need to make sure I have the correct sponsor information from Julia."

Without waiting for anyone else's response, Ben set his napkin on the table and gently grasped Julia's elbow. "We should talk, right?"

Her lips pressed in a thin, angry line, Julia nodded. Stony-faced, she rose from her seat.

CHAPTER TEN

"How could you?" The words burst from Julia, threatening to drag the tears clogging her throat along with them.

Agitated, she pressed a hand to her forehead and paced the length of the room. *Dios mío,* she'd made a complete fool of herself in front of the whole table.

"Julia, I had no idea your mother was unaware of your plans."

"Well, she knows now after *that* debacle." Julia flung out her arm in the direction of the hall in frustration — with herself for her inability to level with her parents and with Ben for initiating her arrival at this crossroads.

"Is that a bad thing? That she knows?" Ben asked.

His question had Julia spinning around to glare at him. He stood near the closed door, hands deep in his pants pockets, his handsome face scrunched in a frown.

"Are you kidding me?" she cried. "This is terrible!"

"Why?"

"Why?" she mimicked, her frustration rising. "It's bad that you forced my hand. That by . . . by interfering with my family life, I feel like you've forced me into a corner. Tonight of all nights!"

He took a step toward her, right hand outstretched in supplication. "You have to believe that wasn't my intent."

"*Sí,* I'm sure it wasn't, but that does no good now. You promised not to push for more from me."

Ben reared back as if she had slapped him. "I'm not. This . . . bringing your mom here, that was all for you. Because you've worked so damn hard and, you're so close with your family, I thought you might want to share this with her."

"You should have asked me."

His mouth twisted in self-reproach, Ben bobbed his head in the tiniest of nods. "I see that now."

Heaving a sigh filled with resignation and regret, Julia sank down into one of the padded folding chairs. This mess was on her really. She should have leveled with her parents sooner.

Instead, she'd put it off. Figuring, if she

didn't get a job, she'd go home and none of this would matter. But it did. Because if she went back to Puerto Rico, she wouldn't be happy.

Ave María purísima, she'd made a mess of things now.

Dejected, Julia picked at the polish on her thumbnail, marred from her nervous nail biting. Out of the corner of her eye she watched Ben dragging a chair closer to sit by her.

"What can I do to help?" he asked.

"Nothing."

"Come on, if I started this snowball rolling . . ." He nudged her knee with the back of his hand playfully.

"Stop being so nice, maybe?"

"Excuse me?"

His voice pitched higher on the last word and Julia's lips tugged up at his obvious confusion.

"I want to be mad at you, but you're making it very difficult," she complained, tilting her head to look up at him under her lashes.

Ben flashed his sexy grin. The one that never failed to make her insides heat.

"Stop that." She swatted at his leg, but Ben captured her hand with his.

His expression sobered. "In all seriousness, I don't want to mess this up."

The sincerity in his blue eyes sucked the air from her lungs.

"I admit this is fast," Ben rushed on, "and you have a lot up in the air. But you should know, this isn't a game to me. Whether you're here in Chicago or back in Puerto Rico, I want to keep spending time with you. See if this goes . . . where I'm hoping it does."

Julia stared back at Ben, rocked by his heartfelt admission.

"You should talk things over with your mom. Be honest with her." He rubbed his thumb gently across the back of her hand, evoking tiny tingles of desire that sparked through her. "Whatever happens, I'm on Team Julia."

He pressed a kiss on her knuckles, then stood, drawing her up alongside him.

"Come on, we have a show to put on. I'm betting your vision and those kids' charm is going to fill the youth center's coffers."

Still grappling with his words, on top of her concern over finally admitting her plan to Mami and her elation over Laura's potential job offer, Julia made herself take a deep breath and straighten her shoulders.

The kids were counting on her. No way would she let them down. Even when her entire professional and personal life hung in limbo.

Bernardo beamed at her from his spot on the first choral riser and Julia gave him two thumbs up. The audience clapped wildly in a standing ovation as the *bomba* portion of the performance drew to a close.

Everything had gone according to plan, with the crowd's reaction even better than Julia could have imagined.

On the stage, Ben tucked the cordless mic under his arm to join in the clapping. The kids grinned and hugged each other. Rico high-fived their guitarist, Diego, before stepping over to share a fist bump with Señor Pérez.

Eventually the clapping subsided and Ben reached for his microphone. "I think you'll all agree that these kids definitely have talent and personality."

Laughter and chuckles tittered through the crowd.

"We'd like to thank each of you for your generosity this evening, but before we close the show with our final carol, the organizing committee and I wanted to bring up one special person."

Julia turned to Laura, thinking perhaps her mentor, as the committee chair, had asked Ben for a few minutes at the mic.

Laura gave her a smile of encouragement, but didn't make a move toward the stage.

"Julia Fernandez is the visionary who brought the rest of us along for this culturally rich and magnificent ride. Thanks to her creativity, enthusiasm, and expertise, we've enjoyed what I think you'd agree has been an amazing evening."

Once again applause thundered through the room.

"So, Julia, the kids and I are hoping you'll come up here with us as we wrap things up with 'Silent Night, *Noche de Paz.*' Everyone, please join in. Lyrics are on the back of your program."

"*¡Vete, nena!*" Mami elbowed her as she encouraged Julia to go.

Bernardo hopped off the riser and hurried to the stairs on the right side of the stage. He held out a hand, his chubby cheeks rounding bigger with his wide grin.

Moments later, as she stood in the midst of all the kids, Ben at her side, with the cacophony of voices both on stage and off singing the well-known Christmas carol, Julia's heart swelled with joy.

Mami sat at their table in the front row, eyes glistening with tears, hands clasped in prayer at her chest as she sang.

They had a frank conversation ahead of

them. One Julia had been dreading. No matter what though, Julia knew she'd remember this moment.

Remember and cherish it for years to come.

Chapter Eleven

"How come you never told me, *nena?*"

Julia's shoulders sagged at her mami's simple question.

They sat in the backseat of a private limo Ben had ordered for them after everything had finally wound down and Rico, Bernardo, and the rest of the kids had piled back into their vans.

Once the kids had left, Laura had shooed her off, telling her the event planner could handle the post-event wrap-up. "Your mother mentioned how anxious she is to see Rosa and the rest of the family. Don't worry about a thing here. You and I can chat in the next couple of days about where you'd like to go from here."

Moments later, Julia and Ben had stood in the shadow of a large Christmas fir in the grand hall, partially hidden from others bustling about in cleanup mode. "Let me order a car for you and your mom. You two need some quiet time together, before the hoopla of the *parranda* when you get to Rosa's."

"Are you still planning to come?" Julia had asked.

"Is the invitation still open?"

That he cared enough to ask, to not push like she'd accused him of earlier, made her even more hopeful that they might have something worth pursuing.

"Of course," she had answered, brushing his cheek with a kiss.

Then she and Mami had left, with Ben promising to follow shortly.

"I was worried about disappointing you and Papi," she admitted now as the limo sped down the highway. "*El negocio* means so much to you."

"*Sí,* but it is just that, a business, and we are *familia,*" Mami answered matter-of-factly.

Julia stared at the blurry city lights in the distance, wondering if somehow she'd lost clarity. Or if Mami simply didn't recognize the pressure she'd put on Julia.

Ben had been right. She owed it to herself and her *familia* to be honest with them. If not, nothing would change.

Scooting sideways on the leather seat, Julia faced her mother. "You've been groom-

564

ing me to take over for years. Earning my business degree 'would benefit us,' you said, remember? And yes, the knowledge will help me run the company, but not once did you ask if that is what I wanted."

"And why would you not want to own your own business? To have a successful company handed down to you?" Mami scowled at her, the same disapproving look she'd given all her kids when she was unhappy with their behavior.

"Because catering isn't all I want to do," Julia answered.

"The company I have built up is not enough for you? Is that it?"

The hurt lacing her mami's voice pierced Julia's heart. "Mami, I am so proud of you. What you have accomplished, going after your own dream, it fuels me."

Mami huffed with displeasure, but in the wavering light from the passing streetlamps Julia thought she caught Mami's mouth curving above the edge of her scarf.

"The boys are going after their dreams," Julia went on. "Maybe Alfredo's has changed, coaching and managing now instead of playing ball, but we have always championed them. I'm sorry for keeping this from you. I just . . . I only hope, some day, you can be as proud of me as I am of you."

Her throat thick with tears, Julia wiped the moisture under her eyes with her gloved finger.

"*Ay nena,* I'm already proud of you. I have been since the day you were born."

Mami opened her arms for a hug and Julia fell into the embrace.

Relief flooded through her, releasing the tears she had struggled to keep at bay.

They held on to each other tightly. Julia breathed in her mother's floral scent, the same one she'd worn for as long as Julia could remember. It conjured memories of similar hugs, shared love, and the security of *familia.*

"Tonight was *increíble,*" Mami said when they had finally pulled apart and she dug in her purse for tissues.

Julia blew her nose as she nodded. "Yes, it was definitely incredible. Especially the amount of donations! Ben and the kids did a fabulous job encouraging people to give more."

"Mm-hmm, and speaking of Mr. Benjamin Thomas . . ." Mami arched a brow, a knowing smirk on her gently lined mouth. "He seems *muy interesado* in you. Is there something I should know about?"

Excitement swirled with longing in Julia's chest. *Ay,* how she hoped Mami was right and Ben truly was *very interested* in her. "I'm not sure. I mean he says . . . but it's too early to tell."

"*Bueno,* I knew your papi was the one the first time we met. The night he tagged along with his brother when Reynaldo's *trío* played at my cousin's birthday. All the girls were crazy for the musicians. Not me."

This story had been told and retold countless times, yet Julia never tired of hearing it. Or seeing the wistful look of young love blanketing Mami's face.

"*Sí,* but with Ben and me, the situation is different," Julia said. "You know I've stayed away from dating athletes. And even though he's no longer playing, broadcasting will keep him on the road. If he decides to move into coaching, baseball will dominate his life. I'm not sure I'd want that."

"*Ay nena,* with the right person, someone who looks at you the way I saw Ben looking at you . . . The way your papi looks at me . . ." Mami raised a finger, emphasizing her point. "You are happy no matter what the situation is. As long as you have each other."

CHAPTER TWELVE

Ben headed up the darkened stairs at the Fernandez sisters' childhood home, pausing to glance back down at Julia's mom and her cousin Rosa.

Both women stood at the bottom, shooing him up with encouraging hand waves.

He could have changed out of his tuxedo at the Wintrust Bank Building, but his clothes had been in his car and he hadn't wanted to waste any time getting out to Oakton. Anxious to see Julia, hoping things had gone well with Paula on their drive to the suburbs.

At the top of the stairs he waited for his eyes to adjust to the dim lighting, then he turned right on the landing. The bathroom should be the second door on the right, according to Rosa's instructions.

Halfway down the hall, a door on the left opened.

Julia jumped, giving a startled *"Ay Dios*

mío" when she spotted him.

Light from the bedroom streamed into the hallway, leaving her face in shadows while outlining her trim figure in a golden aura.

"Sorry, I didn't mean to frighten you," he said. "Your mom sent me upstairs when I asked for a place to switch out of this monkey suit."

Julia pressed a hand to her chest. "No, that's okay. I just wasn't expecting anyone else up here."

Leaving the door open, she moved into the hallway. Dressed casually in slim-fitting jeans, a shapely black sweater, and ankle-high, thick-heeled boots, her long hair now loose around her shoulders, she looked beautiful.

Heart pounding, Ben waited for her to approach. Pleased to have this moment alone with her before they met up with everyone else downstairs.

"I'm glad you came." She stopped several feet away, her expression, if he read it correctly in the half shadows, a sweet mix of hopeful pleasure.

"I wouldn't have missed this for anything," he said.

There was no missing the flash of her smile at his response.

"I've been thinking about what you said

to me before the fund-raiser tonight." She edged closer.

Every cell in his body screamed for him to meet her halfway, swoop her into his arms, and kiss her till neither one of them could think straight.

But he owed it to her. Hell, he owed it to himself, to give her the time and space she had asked for. No pressure.

No matter how hard it was for him to keep his feet rooted to their spot. Allowing her to take the lead here.

"And what have you been thinking?" he asked.

In the living room, someone turned on some music. The *merengue* beat of a *parranda* tune carried up the stairs to them, a sound Ben would forever equate with the amazing woman in front of him.

"That, despite my not-so-secret secret desire to stay here and the fact that I've missed my *familia* in Puerto Rico, even though I have Yazmine, Rosa, and Lilí here, there's been someone else lately who's helped me forget about that spurt of home-sickness I've been trying to squelch. Some-one who makes me want to stay in Chicago even more."

Forget waiting for her to reach him.

Dropping his duffel on the floor at his

feet, Ben closed the distance between them. Sliding his hands along her hips, he dipped his head to press his forehead against hers. "Please tell me I'm the someone you're talking about."

Julia gazed up at him, her minty breath warming the little space separating his mouth from hers.

"Yes," she whispered.

That's all he needed to hear.

Capturing her lips with his, Ben kissed her the way he'd been longing to do from the moment he'd watched her slip her wool coat off her shoulders revealing the amazing red dress she'd worn to the fund-raiser.

Julia's arms looped around his shoulders, her fingers digging into the short hair at his nape. She moaned with pleasure, opening her mouth for him.

Wanting more, he deepened the kiss. His body tightened with need.

Downstairs laughter rang out. The raucous interruption reminded Ben that her family waited for them to join the party.

Reluctantly he broke their kiss, trailing soft nips along her jaw before finally forcing himself to pull back. Gently he tucked Julia's hair behind her ear, then dropped a kiss on her smooth forehead.

"I'm not sure what lies ahead either," she

said. "But if you're on Team Julia, I wanna be on Team Ben."

He chuckled, recalling his cringe-worthy admission earlier.

"I've been a little lost since I had to retire. But being around the kids the past few weeks, being around you" — he cupped her jaw, warmth and something he felt sure was love blossoming in his soul — "you've given me a sense of *familia* I'd only found in baseball. As far as I'm concerned, I want there to be a Team Us."

A huge smile curved Julia's sweet mouth. It shone in the depths of her hazel eyes.

She brushed her lips gently against his, then rose up on her toes, her arms squeezing him in a tight hug.

"Team Us," she whispered in his ear. "Knocking it out of the park together."

Feliz Navidad — Merry Christmas Wishes to You!

Christmas is my absolute favorite holiday, so I jumped at the opportunity to be part of this anthology. I adore the idea of sharing a romance that blooms during this heart-warming time of year, when *familia* and friends gather together.

Holiday Home Run gave me a chance to introduce readers to one of my beloved Fernandez sisters' favorite cousins — Julia, named for my *abuela*. Julia's a confident, creative woman with a strong devotion to her *familia* and her career — and who, like my *abuela,* also happens to possess an insane amount of baseball savvy. Then there's Ben, an ex-MLB player my *abuela* would have loved to watch on the pitcher's mound. As a fan of telenovelas, I think she would approve of this baseball- and Christmas-inspired romance.

I had such fun writing about Julia and Ben! From losing myself in childhood memories of caroling late into the night at *parrandas,* to creating holiday outings for Ben and Julia in one of my favorite cities, to introducing readers to aspects of my Latinx culture that are as much a part of me as the "rr" that easily rolls off my tongue when I speak Spanish.

I sincerely hope you enjoy this little peek into my Latinx culture and find yourself falling in love with the Fernandez *familia* as much as I have. May the music, revelry, and joy of the holiday season bring you and yours much peace, love, and happiness. And maybe a little salsa dancing, too!

From *mi casa* to your house, I wish you a *Feliz Navidad*!

Abrazos / Hugs,
Priscilla Oliveras

ABOUT THE AUTHORS

Fern Michaels is the *USA Today* and *New York Times* bestselling author of the Sisterhood, Men of the Sisterhood, and Godmothers series, as well as dozens of other novels and novellas. There are more than ninety-five million copies of her books in print. Fern Michaels has built and funded several large day-care centers in her hometown, and is a passionate animal lover who has outfitted police dogs across the country with special bulletproof vests. She shares her home in South Carolina with her four dogs and a resident ghost named Mary Margaret. Visit her website at fernmichaels .com.

USA Today bestselling author **Donna Kauffman** is a RITA finalist who has seen her books reviewed in venues ranging from *Kirkus Reviews* and *Library Journal to Entertainment Weekly and Cosmopolitan.* The author of more than 50 books, she is also a regular contributor to *USA Today*'s Happy Ever After blog. She has won the National Readers Choice award, a PRISM award as well as numerous awards from *Romantic Times*. She lives in the lovely Virginia countryside. Please visit her online at DonnaKauffman.com.

New York Times and *USA Today* bestselling author **Kate Pearce** was born in England in the middle of a large family of girls and quickly found that her imagination was far more interesting than real life. After acquiring a degree in history and barely escaping from the British Civil Service alive, she moved to California and then to Hawaii with her kids and her husband and set about reinventing herself as a romance writer. She writes for Kensington, Penguin Random House UK Rouge Romance, Carina and Cleis Press and is known for both her unconventional heroes and her joy at subverting romance clichés. In her spare time she self publishes science fiction, erotic romance, historical romance, and whatever else she can imagine. You can find Kate at her website at katepearce.com, on Facebook as Kate Pearce, and on Twitter @Kate4 queen.

Priscilla Oliveras is a four-time Golden Heart® finalist who writes contemporary romance with a Latino flavor. Proud of her Puerto Rican-Mexican heritage, she strives to bring authenticity to her novels by sharing her Latino culture with her readers. Since earning an MFA in Writing Popular Fiction from Seton Hill University, Priscilla serves as adjunct English faculty at her local college and also teaches an on-line course titled "Romance Writing" for ed2go. Priscilla is a sports fan, a beach lover, a half-marathon runner and a consummate traveler who often practices the art of napping in her backyard hammock. To follow along on her fun-filled and hectic life, visit her on the web at prisoliveras.com, on Facebook at facebook.com/prisoliveras or on Twitter via @prisoliveras.

The employees of Thorndike Press hope you have enjoyed this Large Print book. All our Thorndike, Wheeler, and Kennebec Large Print titles are designed for easy reading, and all our books are made to last. Other Thorndike Press Large Print books are available at your library, through selected bookstores, or directly from us.

For information about titles, please call:
(800) 223-1244

or visit our website at:
gale.com/thorndike

To share your comments, please write:
Publisher
Thorndike Press
10 Water St., Suite 310
Waterville, ME 04901